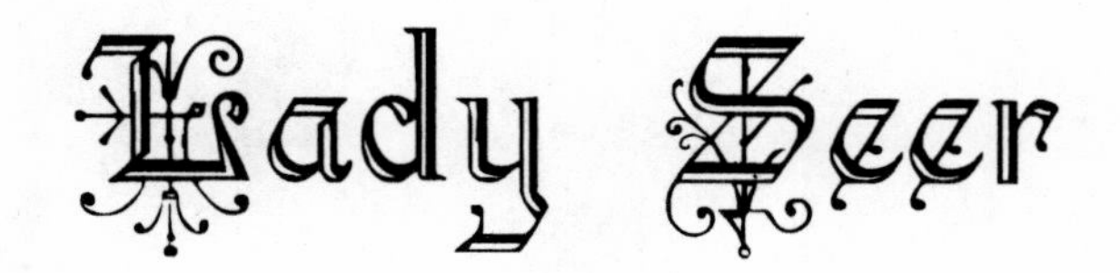

Lady Seer

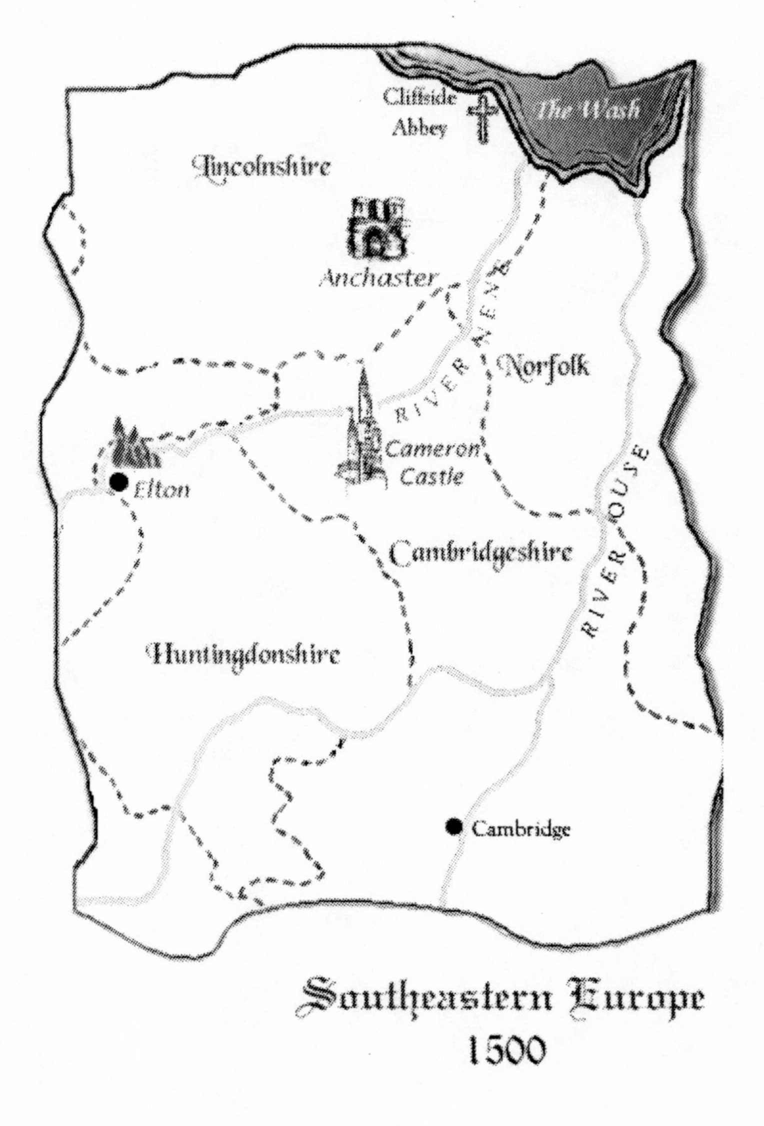

Southeastern Europe
1500

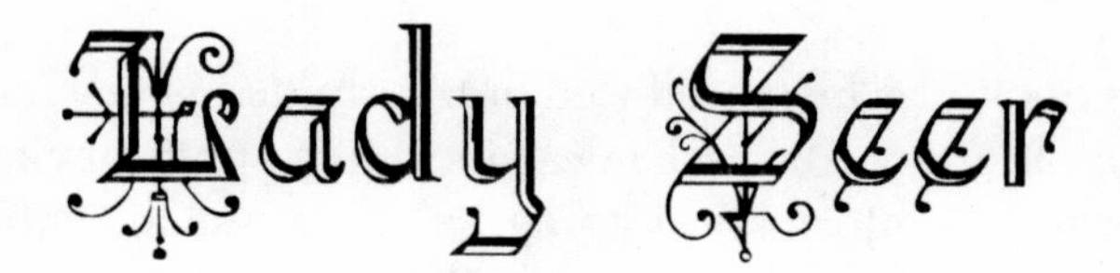

Lady Seer

Book Two of

The Lady Trilogy

Evangelynn Stratton

Writers Club Press
San Jose New York Lincoln Shanghai

Lady Seer
Book Two of The Lady Trilogy

Writers Club Press
an imprint of iUniverse.com, Inc.

For information address:
iUniverse.com, Inc.
5220 S 16th, Ste. 200
Lincoln, NE 68512
www.iuniverse.com

ISBN: 0-595-14859-X

Printed in the United States of America

This book is dedicated to the more than 100,000 people, mostly women, who were prosecuted throughout Europe on charges of witchcraft. May their souls rest in peace.

Rejoice, and be exceeding glad: for great is your reward in heaven: for so persecuted they the prophets which were before you.

Matthew 5:12

Acknowledgments

I would like to thank my family for supporting me through my vast research and rewrites:

My husband for remaining civil while I hogged the computer; my daughter Felicity for being my sounding board;

My son Paul for listening to me even when he had no idea what I was talking about;

And especially my daughter Melanie for her inspiration, her encouragement, and for designing both the front and back cover art.

Some Terminology used

Avener: A servant who oversaw the stable.

Anon: At once or soon.

Barbican: The outer defense area of a castle that visitors entered before reaching the main gate.

Demesne: Land held directly by the lord.

Destrier: "Great horse" mostly used for jousting.

Great Sword: Two-handed sword, also known as the broad sword.

Manor: Estate consisting of lord's demesne and tenant's holdings.

Oblate: Someone who entered the church at an early age.

Palfrey: A well-bred, easy paced mount used for travel.

Prioress: A nun at the head of a priory or nunnery.

Solar: Noble's bedchamber.

Steward: Chief official of an estate.

Sumpter horse: Horses that carried baggage for travel.

Villein: English term for serf.

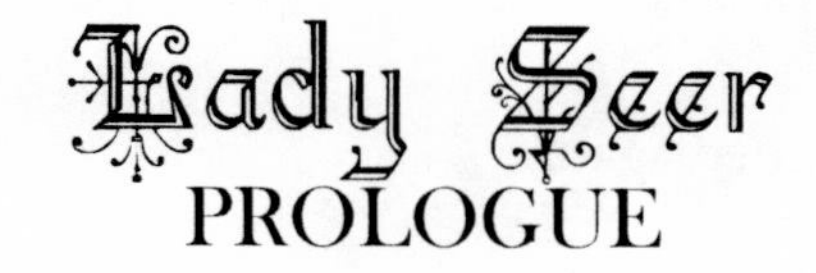

PROLOGUE

Frantic screaming awakens the little girl. Billows of gray smoke rise all around, attacking her lungs and distorting her perception. She calls out repeatedly in terror, but no one answers. Flames flicker from under the door, and the child runs up to the polished-horn window. Her little fists bang on the panes as the screaming outside the door grows louder and the flames become more intense. The girl stares at the panes, willing them to open in a silent plea to save her life. As if to obey her command, the panes suddenly burst outward, allowing in precious air and also giving her a means of escape. She climbs up on a chair and peers outside to the ground, two stories below. In her innocence, she closes her eyes and imagines herself flying like a bird safely to the ground. Suddenly a red angel appears from behind, and wraps its wings around her—large, cool wings that block the smoke. They fly to the ground together. As she hits, the impact jars her very being, but she is safe from the fire. The angel carries her away, and tells her she is safe. Before she lapses into unconsciousness, she sees a man outside the house laughing with glee. She squints to make out his face, and then darkness envelops her.

Elanna sat up sharply with her hand to her chest, gasping from the imagined pain in her lungs. This time the dream was so vivid, so clear—she almost felt the hot flames and smelled the smoke. She got out of her small bed and took a few deep breaths, as if to assure herself the air was clear. She quietly left her room, walked down the long, barren hallway, and finally stopped at a door. Pausing for just a few seconds, she raised her hand and gently rapped.

"Who is it?"

"Prioress? It happened again."

"The red angel?"

"Aye."

The door opened, and the nun stared sadly at the beautiful girl before her. Elanna looked back with eyes so transparently blue that they depicted fine stained glass. The old nun smiled through crinkled eyes. An oblate, arriving at the convent at age five, Elanna both warmed her heart and saddened her soul.

"Come in, child, we shall pray." Elanna nodded, entered the small room, and instantly knelt on the hard floor, her palms together with head bowed in reverence. Her white-blond hair flowed in waves onto the floor and around her ivory gown, depicting a kneeling angel in prayer. The prioress bowed beside her and began praying, like so many times before when Elanna came to her with disturbing visions.

They prayed for over an hour, asking God to lift the burden from Elanna's soul. The Prioress was confident that everything was in control, when Elanna suddenly snapped her head up. Her eyes stared forward in a daze.

"What is it, child?"

"He is coming for me. He will be here anon, in the deepest of the night."

"Is he alone?"

"No—there are men with him."

The nun lovingly stroked Elanna's fine, soft hair, and pursed her lips. "Is there a chance you could be wrong?"

Elanna shook her head. "I am to marry."

The prioress frowned, her eyes intense, serious. "That is impossible."

"Yet, 'tis true. He will take me away, and force me to marry." She turned and frantically searched the old nun's eyes for answers. "What am I to do?"

The Prioress lowered her head, as tears welled in her eyes. "You have no option. You know what you must do." She stood up, and offered the stricken girl her hand.

Midnight came, and true to Elanna's word, he arrived demanding entrance. The Prioress was ready. When the dark, baneful man strutted into her office, she frowned at him in condemnation. If she ever came close to sinfully hating someone, it was Giles Dayen. She had come to believe he was the devil incarnate.

"I should have suspected you would do this! She sensed your coming; your hate is so strong. Your ruse of using the darkness did not help your filthy scheme."

Giles Dayen removed his gloves and long, black cape, and then sat down with a cocky jeer on his deceptively handsome face. He made no attempt to hide his arrogance and malevolence. "I am pleased to see you also, Prioress. And, I have no doubt she sensed me. Where is she?"

An angry scowl came over the nun's face. "With her creator, I would suppose. She chose death to your evil scheme."

He jumped to his feet in rage. "She would not dare! I have plans for her."

"Sometimes plans can go awry."

"Impossible!" He stopped short and took a composing breath. "The king has demanded her to marry and obtain a lord for her lands, and I must comply. Since I am her legal guardian, she shall marry the man I have chosen. Then she will be returned to you within a short time, unharmed and untouched."

"Not if she is dead."

He drew a breath, and then smiled diabolically. "Then show me her body."

"'Tis hard to believe you are her uncle; you hate her so."

"She should have died with the rest of her wretched family, then the lands would be mine."

"How can you say that? 'Tis your brother you speak of!"

"Aye, my weak and kind brother. Kind and stupid." He stood and grabbed his cape. "Then again, if she has chosen suicide, I get Ancaster anyway, as last remaining heir. Again I ask, show me her body! I shall return it for burial with the rest of her worthless kin."

The Prioress hid a bitter smile. "Very well, follow me."

Hundreds of candles lit the small sanctuary where Elanna knelt before the altar, a dagger firmly grasped in her hands. As tears ran down her face, she raised it and pointed it to her heart. She had been praying for the strength to carry out her only escape from her fate. Suicide was an immoral sin, one for which you could never be forgiven. But her soul was already condemned. Her death would be a relief.

"Forgive me, Lord." As she took a last breath to make ready the plunge into her chest, a vision suddenly came to her. A young man on horseback, handsome and kind, stared at her and smiled. His eyes lit up her heart, and new hope sprang within her. She lowered the dagger.

When the prioress and Giles reached the sanctuary, they found her waiting for them. She stood peacefully in front of the altar, the candles lighting her from behind as if she were a vision in white sent to haunt them. The prioress let out a gasp. Giles turned to the nun and laughed.

"Dead, huh?"

The prioress ran to her, and pulled the child she loved so dearly into her arms. "What have you done, child? Now you must go with him."

"It shall be fine," Elanna whispered in the nun's ear. "I had a vision; a man shall rescue me."

Giles motioned to his men, and they entered the room, holding ropes and a black hood. As they carefully approached Elanna, she calmly held her hands together out in front of her. The wary men tightly bound her hands, and placed the hood over her head. Giles had been careful to remain at the door, and the prioress noted his distance with satisfaction. Elanna depicted all of what Giles feared. Power with discipline. Innocence without fear.

"Still afraid of her?"

"Not afraid, simply cautious."

"Why do you treat her so? She is just a child!"

He turned his wrath to the nun. "She is a witch! If not for me, she would have been burned years ago. At least this way, she lives."

"Some life! Hooded like a falcon because of your fear!"

"Spare me your rhetoric, Sister. She shall be returned when Ancaster is mine. You shall have your precious little seer back, believe me, I am not anxious to keep her around."

The prioress gazed steadily into his black eyes. "Do you really expect me to believe that you will let her come back?"

"Believe what you want." He turned to his men. "Take her to the carriage, and lock her in!" He strode away, his long cape flowing behind him as he followed his men leading the small figure in white.

The prioress crossed her heart, and bowed her head. "May God have mercy on her."

Chapter One

England, January 2,1500

Luke urged his weary horse on down a thoroughfare of birch trees, in dappled sunlight that would soon turn to crimson.

"Come on, boy, just a little further." He had been riding for three days in cold, dreary weather to reach Ancaster castle in Lincolnshire, to meet a woman the king had asked him to consider for marriage. He had rebuffed a Sumpter horse to make for a speedier trip, choosing to carry only what his horse could bear. Twenty-four years old and the second son of the powerful Cameron family, he was considered a prime catch for any noble woman. The fair-haired Luke was shy around women, who always found his boyish good looks, dancing blue eyes and muscular body an overpowering combination. His charm matched his wit, as well as his uncanny ability to make money. It was simply a fluke that some enterprising matchmaker or young maiden had not snared him before now. Some had tried, but their actions weren't recognized as flirting and he didn't reciprocate. In many ways, his indifference rendered him more innocent than some of the maidens pursuing him.

He knew nothing about this possible match, except that her name was Elanna Dayen, and she was the remaining heir to Ancaster manor. Having now reached marriageable age, King Henry demanded she take a lord for her extensive lands, and suggested Luke as a possible suitor. Since Luke's father and Henry were longtime friends, he couldn't turn down the request. He hated to leave so abruptly. His brother Matthew and his warrior wife Pet had just finally reconciled their differences and he would have enjoyed their company a while longer. He hadn't even taken the time for a haircut. The wind whipped his long hair about his face, and he had an unsightly growth of beard. He was still a bit hung-over from the huge New Year's party he spent in a tavern, celebrating not just a new year but also a new century. He celebrated a little too hard. He was almost thankful there was no mirror to reflect his blood-shot eyes. This poor woman would probably take one look at him and scream. No matter—he was fairly positive she would meet him and turn him down regardless, as he always got tongue-tied around the gentle sex and ended up embarrassed. Joking was usually his way out of an uncomfortable situation; he didn't know the flowery words of a lover. He hadn't had a serious relationship, and very few non-serious, which was fine with him. He preferred the company of a fine horse. He didn't feel big and dumb around them.

Ancaster loomed before him, a beautiful old castle with well-kept fields and surrounding pasturelands. As he passed through the barbican he could not help but consider the possibilities. The lord's demesne seemed far-reaching. Cherry trees, grand in summer, now bore naked limbs along the avenue leading to the manor. Several villeins raked fallow fields as they watched him go by. His mind instantly began figuring yields and active estate management. One field could be planted with alternating crops, and the pastureland would be wonderful to raise horses, his passion. By the time he reached the main gates he had already increased the coffers of the estate by half.

His arrival was announced, and a servant led him across an elegant, rather ornate hallway and into a lavishly furnished room. Masculine, hide-covered chairs made a circle in the center for easy conversation, and relics of all sorts embellished the walls. Displayed suits of armor—each with lance and shield—stood in the corners, as if to guard the room from trespassers. The castle was indeed impressive; this Dayen woman could prove to be a profitable merger when his own large inheritance was considered. He strolled around the room, passing the time by looking at lavish paintings and an array of display weapons, when the double doors opened and a man that could only be described as ominous appeared. Luke disliked him immediately. The room seemed to grow cold simply by his presence. He was tall, almost as tall as Luke's six feet four inches, with expertly styled black hair and well-trimmed beard and mustache. His clothes reflected prosperity, and his hands displayed several flamboyant rings. His eyes were cold and dangerous, even when he smiled and extended his hand to Luke.

"Lord Cameron…'twas good of you to make this trip, although I regret to inform you 'twas for naught." His voice was smooth and controlled.

"For naught?" Luke repeated with a frown. "By what do you speak? Who are you?"

The man raised a hand to his forehead and let out a short, loud breath. "Forgive me, where are my manners?" He smiled charmingly. "My name is Giles Dayen, uncle and guardian to the love-struck child you were haplessly sent to meet."

Luke made no attempt to hide his irritation. He did not like this man. There was no particular reason, but he didn't. "What do you mean, love-struck?"

"I fear she has already chosen her mate. She already had a young suitor whom I fear none knew about. Contacting you was impossible; all we could do was simply await your arrival."

Luke instantly felt relieved, then felt guilty for feeling so. "'Tis fine, I understand. There is no telling what will attract a woman's heart."

"Exactly." He laughed smoothly. "The wedding shall be next month. I am so sorry for your inconvenience."

"Think naught of it, Lord Dayen. If you do not mind, I would like to pay the young lady my respects and take my leave."

Dayen's face grew a little paler, and Luke detected a tinge of apprehension. His eyes darted around the room in an attempt to avoid eye contact. "Ah, well…I fear that may be difficult at this time. She is…at the dressmakers being fitted for her wedding gown. You understand."

Dayen's mannerism made Luke pause. He had an overwhelming instinct not to trust him. Be that as it may, this was not his problem. He was off the marriage hook, and could leisurely travel home. He bowed to Dayen, and took his leave.

He exited the castle gates and made his way to the town he had passed on his way in. If memory served him, an inn was nearby where he could rest his weary body, drink excessive amounts of ale, and forget this whole trip. He could reach the inn by nightfall. A bath sounded good, too. A bath, a shave—the more he thought about it, this worked out fine; he still had his freedom and the lady was marrying the lover of her choice. Pity about Ancaster, though. He could have done so much with those fields.

The road narrowed through a dark wooded area, and Luke kicked his horse into a canter on the soft dirt road. Suddenly, a white figure darted out in front of him, forcing his horse to rear up as he quickly reined it in. The figure stumbled in the road, then got up and fell again. Luke leapt off his startled horse, and ran to the small white heap in the road. When he got up close, it appeared to be nothing but a mass of blond-white hair. He gently turned the girl over, and gazed into the face of an angel. A dirty angel, as she had managed to fall in slimy mud, but an angel nevertheless. Her small perfect features—high arched brows, small nose, and heart-shaped lips—complimented flawless, albeit mud-caked, skin. Her thin white gown was torn, wet, and soiled, and she wore no coat or cloak. Being the middle of winter, it was a miracle the girl hadn't died from exposure to the elements. Her body shivered uncontrollably, and he quickly took off his jacket and threw it over her.

"Are you all right?" he frantically asked. As he impulsively touched her chilled face, her eyes flew open.

He took in a breath at the sight of her eyes. They were the palest blue imaginable yet still be human, and seemed to advance inside his very soul. She reached out and touched his warm face with an icy hand. Even with her chill, her touch could not have affected him more than if someone had put a hot brand to his skin.

"Luke, please help me."

He searched her face, grasping for recognition. "Do I know you?"

Her tormented eyes beseeched him, pleaded with him, and his heart melted into a helpless puddle.

With his coat carefully wrapped around her, he carried her effortlessly to his horse. She encircled her arms around his neck, and laid her head on his shoulder. Luke could not explain the fierce sense of protection he suddenly felt for this stranger. He placed her on the front of his saddle, and then mounted the horse, careful to not let her fall. Her frailty was compounded by the cold.

"T-they are after me," she stammered through her shivers. "Please, do not let them take me."

"No one is going to harm you, you are with me." He kicked his horse into a gallop and headed for the town, holding her with one hand, and controlling the horse with the other. She was so small, so helpless—he couldn't imagine anyone wanting to hurt her. What threat could this small whit of a girl be to anyone?

Galloping down the muddy, rutted road, Luke prayed the horse had enough energy left to reach his destination. He promised it an extra bucket of oats for not dropping dead from exertion. Not really a fitting reward, but it was all he had.

When they reached the inn, he tossed his reins to the stable boy and carefully carried her inside. Slamming his fists on the counter, he practically demanded a room. The innkeeper, a man small in stature, was not going to argue with the massive Luke. After ordering a bath, Luke carried the girl past the downstairs tavern, which was not yet rowdy with patrons, and up to the room. He gently laid her on the bed.

"I shall be right back. Rest, you are safe here."

The girl closed her eyes and nodded.

Luke bounded down the stairs and went directly back to the innkeeper. "I need a woman," he ordered.

The innkeeper looked Luke over warily, and narrowed his eyebrows in suspicion. "Did you not bring one in with you?"

"What?" Suddenly aware of the implication, Luke flushed, and shook his head. "Nay, nay, I mean, I need a woman to give a bath to…my, uh, *niece*. She is dirty and cold, and I also need a dry gown. Quick, man! There is extra coin in it for you!" The innkeeper nodded enthusiastically while Luke leapt back up the stairs to the room. The girl slept peacefully, much to his relief. He sat down on a stool and rested his elbows on his knees, staring at the vision in front of him. What the hell was he going to do with her? He didn't know her name, or even who she was, and he already felt as if she were part of him. Was he letting his emotions cloud his judgement? Is this what his brother Matthew had described when he first met Pet? His heart beat faster with the thought.

The door opened, and two servants carried in a wooden tub. Several servants followed, each carrying a bucket of hot water, and dumped them into the tub. A woman servant remained when all others left.

"Milord, you requested help with a bath?"

"Aye, my…niece took a walk and…became lost, I fear. She is quite cold, and I understandably cannot give her a bath myself." He winced; he was a horrible liar.

"Very well, Milord. What is her name?"

Luke blanched white. "Uh…her name? Er, well…"

The girl slowly opened her eyes and gazed at him. "Elanna."

He quickly looked at her, and smiled with relief. "Ah, aye, Elanna. Her gown will need to be cleaned, also. I shall wait downstairs." He cast Elanna one last look, and smiled. She smiled back, and he felt weak in the knees. What was wrong with him?

After checking on his horse, he waited in the tavern, downing tankards of ale as if none would ever be made again. Why was he so nervous? She was just a small bit of a girl; she could be just a child, for all he knew. Nay, the way the wet gown clung to her when he first saw her belayed that notion—no child could have breasts like that. He shook his head in bewilderment; what was he thinking? This was not like him, to fantasize over a woman, of all things. A fine horse, perhaps, but never a woman. Had she totally bewitched his mind?

After a horribly long wait, the maid tapped him on the shoulder. "She is done, Milord, I apologize for the length of time—her hair was quite a chore." She held out her hand in expectation of a large tip, which he gladly forfeited.

"Is she, uh, dressed?"

The maid nodded. "Aye, we are laundering and mending her gown, and she is using a loaned dress until 'tis ready. It should be ready by your departure tomorrow." She gave a knowing smile. "I must say, Milord, your…*niece* is very comely."

Luke cleared his throat, and stood up. "Aye, she is." He left the maid as fast as his muscular legs would carry him.

When he entered the room, Elanna was sitting on the bed combing out her masses of hair with a small comb. The dismal, brown, common dress she wore could not diminish her radiant beauty. She raised her head to look up at him, and smiled shyly. He pulled up a stool and sat down, facing her while he studied her fresh-scrubbed, pink face.

"I knew a pretty girl was underneath all that dirt."

"Thank you for the bath." She lowered her gaze, displaying long, sweeping eyelashes that framed her fascinating, transparently blue eyes.

"You are most welcome. They are also cleaning and repairing your white gown. 'Twill be returned shortly." He paused, unsure of what to say next. "Er…are you hungry?"

She shook her head.

"Can I get you anything?"

Another shake.

There could be no more stalling. He attempted a stern expression, and cleared his throat. "Very well, young lady, I believe you have some explaining to do."

"You want to know what I was doing outside alone in the cold without a cloak, and how I know your name."

He sat up straight, his face displaying surprise. "Well, that will do for a start."

"You also want to know who I am, and who is after a little thing like me."

He folded his arms and frowned. "Well, actually, aye. I do."

"You also want to know…"

"All right, that is quite enough of what I want to know, why do you not just tell me?"

Her lower lip trembled, and she looked down at her lap. "I am sorry…I did not mean to invoke your anger."

He reached out and lifted her chin, then smiled assuredly. "I am not angry. I am simply concerned."

She looked into his eyes, and smiled back. "I know."

"Therefore, why do you not start by answering all those questions that I did not get to ask?"

"My name is Elanna Dayen."

"Dayen? You are the woman I was to meet!"

"I know nothing of that, only that I escaped from a dreadful fate, and now you have rescued me. I knew you would."

"Dreadful fate?" He stroked his chin in thought. "I believe your uncle told me you were to be married. To most young ladies, that prospect is not so dreadful."

Her eyes flashed in desperation. "To a man of his choosing, that he paid. 'Twas all a ruse to get Ancaster. He was going to kill the poor unwitting villager after he married me, and keep me locked up in the cellar for a reasonable amount of time to make it appear the marriage was a success. Then he was going to send me away. Ancaster would be lost to me forever."

"He told you all this?"

She lowered her gaze. "Not exactly."

"Then, how do you know this?"

"The guard that locked me up…"

"Oh, then *he* told you this."

"Not exactly."

He gave her a confused scowl. "Well then, *exactly* just how do you know?"

She pursed her lips and fell silent.

"All right, then. By God's bones, why would someone lock you up in a cellar?"

Her voice lowered to a soft, whispering tone, as if she were talking to herself. "To keep me in darkness."

He leaned back, raising his eyebrows in contemplation as he processed all this confusing information. "Perhaps you should start at the beginning."

"I cannot."

"And why not?"

Her eyes flickered from fatigue, and Luke instantly felt like a great fool.

"Of course, you are tired. I shall let you rest." He stroked his scrubby beard. "I could do with a bath and a shave, myself."

She nodded, and lay down.

Luckily, Luke was able to secure another room right next to Elanna's. The hot bath also brought out his weariness, and he closed his eyes while soaking—for just a few seconds, he told himself—while the strange, yet fascinating girl slept. He awoke a while later in a cold tub. Shivering and feeling like an idiot, he climbed out of the tub and dried himself off. The tavern down below him was full and rowdy, by the sounds of it. He immediately felt compelled to check on Elanna.

He quietly opened the door—as if it would be heard above the noise emanating from downstairs—and peeked in. The white gown had been returned, and was lying across the chest at the foot of the bed. She was peacefully asleep. Good. Whatever her plight, it would appear better in the morning after a restful night. He closed the door and went back to his room. In a few minutes he was fast asleep.

Miles away, Giles Dayen was red with rage. He paced the study, stopping only to glower at his accomplice and step-nephew, Patrick, who stood unwaveringly before him.

"How did she escape? I thought you had a man posted outside her door?"

"We did. He took a small break to relieve himself, and she seized the opportunity to flee."

"How did she get out of her ropes?"

"How do you think?"

"This is what I get for being generous. I should have locked her in the cellar straight off."

"Generous? You abduct her in the middle of the night, bound and hooded, and then keep her confined to a small room in the tower? Well, I guess in your eyes that is generous."

Giles banged his fists on his desk, causing several items to bounce and relocate in disarray. "That little witch! She should have burned with the rest of her wretched family, then Ancaster would be truly mine."

Patrick flinched at the display of total hatred. "How unfortunate that she escaped the fire."

"The miserable guttersnipe! Her fate would not have been life if I had found her first, I can assure you!"

"Quite true; I have no doubt you would not have hesitated choking the life from a five-year-old."

Giles snorted. "Do not be so melodramatic. My worthless brother's entire family had to die in order for me to gain Ancaster, you know that. Her living was not in my plans. And now, thanks to that stupid, meddling King Henry, she must marry to obtain a lord for her lands. If she were not a witch, I would marry her myself; I would like to have that little body of hers in bed. Unfortunately, I cannot get that close to her."

"Aye, she would finally know who killed her family."

"Is that a judgmental tone I hear? Come now, Patrick, let us not forget your little part in all this."

"I did not set the fire!"

"But you barricaded them all in. You sealed their fate as much as I."

"You did not tell me you planned to burn the inn to the ground. You said you simply wanted to frighten them." His hands clenched with the foul memory.

"And I am quite sure they were most frightened before they all burned to ashes."

So why do you not just kill her, and get it over with?"

"Only because her death at this time would look suspicious, and we cannot have the king poking his nose around here, now can we? Nay, 'twill look better if she marries and turns her land over to her new husband. Then I can send her back to the convent where she can live out her miserable life as a nun."

Patrick frowned with disapproval. "How generous of you to let her live."

"May I remind you that if our smuggling ring is revealed, we shall hang for sure? Piracy might be rewarding, but it has its risks. Do not worry, if it becomes necessary I am not beyond still killing her, believe me."

"I have no doubt."

Giles smirked, then his voice rose again in frustration. "But first we must find her! Get your men back out there; she cannot have gone far with no food or coat."

"But 'tis dark. We are not likely to find her tonight. We have already searched the woods."

"Then go to neighboring villages; see if someone found her. With her fetching looks, she might have someone helping her."

"Very well. Do not worry, we shall find her—dead or alive." He reached up and grabbed a faded red cloak from a hook by the door. It was well worn, patched in several sections, the hem line long ago fallen to a jagged edge.

"Are you still wearing that horrid thing? You look like a peasant in that rag; for appearance sake you should buy a new one."

Patrick ignored him as he fastened the clasp. "You know I like this cape. It was the last thing my brother gave me."

"Oh, yes—I forgot it has sentimental value." He smirked and reached inside his coat. "But in case you change your mind, here!" He tossed Patrick a gold coin high over his right side.

Patrick reached out, but was not able to catch it. It clinked to the floor as Giles began laughing in a mocking tone.

"Still not able to use your right arm very well?"

"You know I cannot." He picked up the coin with his left hand and tossed it back. "But then, I would rather use my mind. I leave the brutality to you."

As Patrick left, Giles slumped in a chair and nervously tapped his fingers on his leg. The girl had to be found; all his plans hinged on it.

Chapter Two

"uke, wake up!"

Luke opened his eyes and tried to focus in on whoever dared awaken him in the middle of the night. The only light was from a single candle burning in the corner. His muddled mind finally identified Elanna's voice.

He sat up and rubbed his eyes. "Wha—what is wrong, Elanna?"

"They are coming."

"Who is coming?"

"Dayen's men."

Even though he couldn't clearly see her face, he heard the urgency in her voice. "How do you know that?"

"Luke, please trust me. They will be here anon; we must flee."

"Now, wait a minute, 'tis dark and cold out, and this bed is very warm. Go back to bed; you probably just had a bad dream." He lay back down and plopped his head on the pillow.

"Luke, please! They will be here, and you will not be able to fight them off."

He opened one eye. "Would you care to tell me how you know all of this?"

"Aye, later…right now we must run!"

He let out a weary sigh. "Very well. Go get dressed."

"I already am."

"Oh. Well, then leave the room so I can get dressed."

"I do not want to be alone. Besides, I cannot see you, anyway."

"Very well. Help me find my boots." He patted the end of the bed for his pants and struggled putting them on in the darkness. "Very well, I am now decent—you may bring that candle closer."

Upon returning to the bed she tripped over something. "I found your boots."

"Fine, just drop them."

She did—right on his foot. He yelped and let out a curse.

"Sorry," said Elanna. She didn't put the candle down, preferring instead to hold it close to her, as if the light somehow strengthened her. "Hurry! They are near!"

He didn't know why he believed her, except his instincts overruled his reason and he did. He had just managed to put on his shirt when Elanna gasped in fear. "They are outside!"

"Did you hear them?" He got one boot on, and hopped in a circle while he put on the other.

"Um, in a way. Hurry!"

"All right, done. To the stairs!" He grabbed his pack and they scrambled to the top of the staircase, where down below several late-staying patrons still sat in a stupor. Luke and Elanna could hear voices, and bits of conversations.

Elanna put her hand up to stop Luke. "Wait."

The front door suddenly banged open, and several men entered the tavern. They began questioning the customers. Some words stood out clearly in the din from below.

"*Escaped.*"

"*Might have help.*"

"*Long blond hair.*"

Elanna dropped to her knees and put her face in her hands. "Oh no, we are too late."

"Not if I can help it." Luke pulled her to her feet, and rushed her down the hall to the back of the inn.

"But," she protested, "there is no back way out!"

Luke looked at an open-shuttered window with a lattice frame covered in resin and tallow-soaked linen. It faced the back overlooking the roof of a small outbuilding. In one powerful motion, he smashed his fist through the window. "There is now," he replied. "After you."

Elanna looked out the hole he had made, her eyes wide in astonishment. "Y-you expect me to jump?"

"'Tis only a few feet, then we can climb down the roof to the stables. We can grab my horse and be out of here. Here, put on this coat."

Elanna's face turned as white as her dress. "B-but I cannot..."

"Would you rather face those men downstairs?"

"Nay. All right, I will do it." She took the coat and put it on, then nodded that she was ready.

"Good girl. Here, I shall boost you up." He gingerly put his hands around her small waist, and lifted her up to the window. She bravely climbed to the sill and suddenly froze.

"Jump," urged Luke.

"I-I cannot."

Luke rolled his eyes, and lifted himself up. "Here, grab hold of me, and I will jump." When he received no response, he looked into her eyes. "Elanna? Did you hear me?" She appeared stunned and did not seem to recognize him.

He heard a commotion down the hall, and men clambering up stairs. He had no choice but to throw Elanna over his shoulder and jump the small distance to the other building. Once there, he maneuvered to the edge and lowered Elanna safely down. Then he jumped down himself.

Elanna seemed to have returned to normal. "I am sorry," she uttered when he joined her on the ground. "I am afraid of high places."

"Fine time to let me know." He grabbed her arm and began taking large strides to the stable, causing her to run along side him. Once in the stable, he quickly found his horse and did the fastest saddling job he had ever done. The stable boy was awakened, and staggered out to see who would be getting their horse this late at night.

"Here, what's goin' on?"

"Nothing," Luke replied. "We are just leaving. Tell you what—I will give you some coins if you tell anyone who asks that we headed west."

The boy's eyes lit up and he nodded enthusiastically. "Aye, milord—west 'tis!"

Luke plopped some coins in the boy's outstretched hand and lifted Elanna on the horse. He then mounted, and very quietly walked the horse away from the stables.

"Should we not be going faster?" Elanna whispered close to his ear.

"It would be stupid to gallop away, and alert everyone inside to our direction. Now hush."

He felt her sigh against his back, and couldn't help but grimace. What was he doing, busting holes in windows, leaping over roofs, and sneaking away in the middle of the night? Was he mad? This was something his knightly, daring brother Matthew would do. Or maybe Paul, his younger brother. His thoughts wandered to Paul, who had left to find his fortune on one of his father's ships. He frowned at his attempt to fool himself; Paul left because he disowned Matthew. Being the middle brother was never easy. No matter whom he sided with, the other would be hurt.

A thought suddenly came to him. He could take Elanna to Elton, where Matthew and Pet should have returned by now. No one could get past Matthew and England's only lady knight.

When he was a fair distance away, Luke kicked the horse into a gallop and headed south. If memory served, another town was about an hour ride away. They would be safe if the stable boy did as he was told and detoured the men the other direction.

He ran the poor horse hard, but Luke knew the animal's limits and would never exert it beyond its capability. Luke had purposely chosen a young horse that could easily make the long trip. He had almost brought his favorite horse, a gray palfrey he named Annabelle after a young maiden that once caught his eye. Funny, at that moment he couldn't remember what that girl looked like.

They didn't talk until they reached the town, where Luke was only able to secure one room from the grumpy innkeeper, who had to be awakened. Luke made sure his horse was properly taken care of, and then joined Elanna in the room. He came in, threw his pack on the single bed, and gave Elanna an exasperated look.

"Well, that was fun! I vandalized an inn, sneaked out without paying my bill, and probably have the law after me by now. I think you owe me an explanation."

"You are right. I am sorry to have gotten you involved. I had no right."

His mood instantly softened, and again he felt like the helpless fool he always became around women. "I did not have to get involved; I chose to. I just need to know the truth. Why are you running? What is really going on, here?"

She took a deep breath. "I have been raised in a nunnery all my life. I was sent there after my family all perished in a fire. I was only five. My uncle was made my guardian, but could not deal with me, and relinquished my care to the prioress. He took over the running of Ancaster."

"Deal with you? He could not deal with a small child?"

She stared at him in silence for a few seconds, then a look of extreme sadness washed over her. "I was the only one of my family who survived the fire, but I have little memory of it, or of any time before. Soon after, I am told, is when it all began."

"What began?"

She gave him a look of anxiety that came from deep pain buried within her. "If I tell you, are you going to turn me in?"

He chuckled. "Turn you into what?" Her stricken look made him quickly sober his face. "I am sorry…I sometimes tend to make light of things. Now, to whom do you think I would turn you in?"

She rose from the bed, and walked to the window. The shutters were slightly open, letting in a gentle breeze that caught small stands of her hair and floated them around her face. Luke was not sure she was going to answer him as she stared out into nothingness.

Finally she spoke. "Luke, I am a witch."

At first he displayed no reaction, then a smile spanned his face that quickly materialized into a snicker. Finally he just laughed out loud. "A witch, you say? Perhaps 'tis you who shall be turning *me* into something!"

"'Tis not funny, Luke!"

He walked over to her, completely amused at this small girl with her overactive imagination. "Elanna, you are no more a witch than…my big toe! Now, why do you not just tell me the truth? Did you fight with your betrothed? Did you have a change of mind?"

"You do not believe me?"

"You are the witch…you tell me." He chortled some more.

"All right. I learned a lot in the ride over here. You are the second of three brothers. Your mother and father are both still living. I believe your older brother just became married. Your mother's name is…Ellen. Your older brother is Matthew, and your younger brother is Paul."

He stared at her for a spell, and then slowly smiled. "Ah, you could have learned all of that from your uncle. King Henry no doubt sent some information about me when he asked for the meeting. Everything you just said is common knowledge."

"But he told me nothing!" Pinkness developed in her face, a reflection of frustration in his disbelief and her unwillingness to fully expose her powers. "Hence you want uncommon knowledge? Very well." She reached out and took his hand, then closed her eyes and remained quiet for a short time. Her small hand was dwarfed by his, and he rather liked the way she felt holding him, even if she was a bit peculiar.

"There has been a recent family upset, and you are worried about your younger brother, who has left from anger at…Matthew, that is it; he is angry with Matthew. As for you, you are kind, shy, and love horses.

You are rather fond of a gray palfrey named Annabelle that you could not bring because she suffered a stone bruise that has not yet healed. You just purchased a whole herd of ponies for a large number of children, and you worry that one of the children might fall off and 'twill be your fault. You plan to take me to Matthew's, because you are at a loss to what else to do with me."

"That is enough!" He jerked his hand away, and she opened her eyes.

"I could go on."

"I have no doubt." He drew back in disbelief, and then softened when he saw her devastated expression. Taking her small hands in his, he rubbed them softly in hopes of regaining her trust after his rudeness.

"All right, you are an incredible guesser. That does not make you a witch."

"You think I *guessed* all that? Are you blind to the truth?"

His next words had to be carefully chosen. He could go along with this frightened, strange girl, help her perhaps, or alienate her. Something deep inside him didn't want to alienate her, not even a little. "Elanna, if you have certain powers—and I am not saying you do—that does not make you a witch. I have read about people like you. They are called seers. 'Tis a gift, not a curse."

"Tell that to my uncle. He fears me so much that he hid my face in a black hood and tied my hands when he removed me from the nunnery. He knows I cannot see thoughts when I am in total darkness."

"Yet you say you sensed his men back there at that inn?"

"Aye. I kept a candle burning by my bedside. I was able to feel their eminent arrival. If my uncle himself had come, I would not have needed it. For some reason, I have always been able to detect his presence. 'Tis like a rush of evil, a coldness overcoming me."

He snorted. "Well, I felt the same way around him, and I am not a witch."

That got a small smile from her, so he pressed on for more information. "Why would he fear you so?"

"Are you saying you do not?"

He chortled again, and shook his head. "Of a small girl? Why should I fear you?"

"Because I can tell your thoughts."

"That causes me no fear…my thoughts are not that special. Now, if you could change me into a toad, or a bat…"

"You are not taking this seriously!"

"Sorry—this is all a little hard to take. I keep expecting you to disappear in a puff of smoke."

She almost smiled at that. "I am, as you say, a seer, not a magician. When I first started exhibiting my 'gift', as you call it, my uncle became panicked, and ordered me to stay away from him. It soon became that the servants would not come near me. It got worse; I began having visions of things that had not yet happened. He told me I should burn as a witch, but he would spare my life and send me to a holy place, where the devil could not enter, and perhaps my soul would be saved. I was sent away, to return when I was an adult. He visited me yearly, always keeping a good distance from me, as it became known that I could only see thoughts from within a close range. I was always reminded that if anyone found out about me, I would be burned as a witch. Two days ago he came and got me, saying I was to marry. My new 'husband' would then control Ancaster, and then I would be returned to the nunnery forever. I heard them say if I refused, they would expose me as a heretic. I managed to escape the tower the first night, and I ran until I met you. They look for me even now."

Luke put an assuring hand on her small shoulder. "They shall not find you. I am taking you…"

"To your brother's place, I know."

He frowned, and then let out a small grunt. "'Twould be nice if I could complete a sentence."

"Sorry." She pursed her lips and looked at the floor.

"Hence, you have lived your whole life, believing you would burn if you exercised your rights to your family fortune. Your uncle is quite clever. I am afraid 'tis King Henry who messed up his well-planned scheme. He is the one who demanded you marry and find a lord for your manor."

"Luke, he will not stop until he finds me. What am I to do?"

"Right now, get some sleep. I shall sleep in the stable with my horse, and…"

"Nay! I—I do not want to be alone. Please stay with me?"

He folded his arms and tried to look stern. "That would not be proper. I shall not jeopardize your reputation."

"Luke, I live in daily fear of being burned at the stake, and you think I am worried about my reputation?"

"When you put it that way, I suppose not."

"Then you will stay?"

He gazed about the room with great unease. "I guess I could send for a pallet. You may take the bed."

"Nay, I shall take the pallet."

"I think not, Elanna. I shall not stand by and let you sleep on a hard pallet."

"But, I have ne'er had such a bed. I fear 'twould be too soft."

Luke frowned. "You have ne'er slept in a soft bed?"

"Nay—'tis a sin to award oneself with too many comforts."

"That is a nun talking."

"I wanted to become a nun."

"You?" He let out a throaty snicker. "Now, that is an image I find hard to fathom."

"'Tis true. I wished for nothing else since age five."

He cocked his head in curiosity. "How…?"

"I am eighteen."

"You could have let me finish the question."

She sighed. "Sorry."

"Most nuns take their vows before your age. Why have you waited?"

"The prioress could not get the church's permission for me to take my vows. I am not worthy. Lately I changed my plans and planned to reclaim Ancaster, sell it, and give the money to the church. I hoped then that I would be allowed."

"If you are not worthy, then heaven help us. And 'tis obvious your uncle would not let you sell Ancaster. He has run it for too long, and has no plans of giving it up. But I digress. You are sleeping on the bed, and that is final." He stomped to the bed, and drew back the covers. "Get in!"

She cringed at his tone, but didn't argue as she slowly crawled into the small bed, which was nothing more than a mattress stuffed with straw. To her it felt like heaven. He tucked her in, and stepped back with satisfaction as she closed her exhausted eyes and fell promptly to sleep. As he watched her, a strange feeling overtook him, the knowledge that his life would never be the same again. She lay on her back with masses of curls flowing all about her as she slept. He had the sudden urge to lean down and kiss her on the forehead, which he did.

"Sleep well, little seer." He quietly backed away and left the room to seek a pallet.

He came back in a few moments, his mission successful. He lay the pallet down beside the bed, rolled out the thin bedroll, plopped down the straw-filled pillow, and then spent the most miserable ten minutes of his life attempting to get comfortable. It was a total lost cause; his feet stuck out the bottom and the pallet was so damned hard he felt like he might as well be sleeping on the ground. As he pondered his dilemma, he heard whimpering sounds coming from the bed. The whimpering turned to cries, and he quickly rose from the floor and looked over at the tossing, frightened Elanna. Her face was contorted into a mask of terror, as she grasped the air for an unseen object. She was deeply involved in a nightmare, or so he assumed, as he sat on the edge of the bed and put a hand on her shoulder to rouse her.

She suddenly sat up, her eyes wide with terror, and put a hand to her chest. Her breathing came in jagged gasps as she struggled with the image she had just suffered.

"Elanna, I am here."

She turned and looked at him with fright piercing her wide, water-blue eyes. "Luke?" Without thinking, she threw her arms around him and began to sob uncontrollably.

Being at a loss, and inexperienced with crying women, Luke simply followed his instincts and held her, stroking her hair gently to calm the distressed girl.

"Would you like to tell me about it?"

When she was finally able to speak, she drew back to look into his concerned face. "I began having a dream about a year ago. The prioress thinks 'tis a memory that has just now surfaced, but I am not sure."

"What is the dream about?"

"A fire. I have been terrified of fires as long as I can remember. In the dream, a small girl leaps from a window to escape a burning building. She is rescued by a red angel."

"A red angel? I thought angels were white."

"Not this one. And there is a man—he is laughing—and it does not make any sense. Oh Luke, I fear I am losing my mind!"

"Nay, you are just frightened."

"Luke? Please lay with me—just for a while?"

He swallowed hard, not knowing what to do. This tiny girl needed him desperately. She was alone, terrified, and an innocent. All at once he decided protocol be damned…he would do whatever it took to soothe her.

"Very well, Elanna, lay down." She instantly complied, and he carefully crawled into bed with her. Her small body curled up next to his, and she rested her head on his shoulder as he wrapped a large arm around her. She promptly fell asleep. He lay there wide-awake, holding the sleeping girl, liking the way she felt next to him. He drew her closer, and leaned his head on hers. He suddenly felt the need to pray for restraint as his mind wandered into forbidden thoughts; this girl was not to be abused, especially by him. His thoughts bothered him. He had never felt this way about a woman. But she was so small, so helpless; he had to protect her. Soon his own eyelids grew heavy, and he fell into a restful sleep, interrupted briefly by dreams of turning into a bat and disappearing in a puff of smoke.

Chapter Three

When he awoke the next morning, Elanna was still cuddled in his arms, sleeping as soundly as a babe. Luke had to admit he slept rather well himself. Elanna cried out a few times in the night, but she quieted down after he tightened his hold and talked softly to her. Luke had never felt like this toward a woman; he couldn't quite explain it. What the hell was Matthew going to say when he showed up with her?

He slowly removed his arm and rose without awakening her. Some bodily functions were summoning him, and he was famished. He assumed she must be also, and quietly exited to purchase some breakfast.

When he returned carrying a tray of food, she was on her knees beside the carefully made-up bed, deep in prayer. His heart leapt to his throat when he thought of the life she had led. This girl had known no joy, laughter, or friendship, just terror of her only relative and praying to cleanse her supposed condemned soul. Even with her awesome cognizant ability, Luke could not imagine anyone being afraid of her. He wondered if she could ever lead a normal life.

Her eyes fluttered opened as he gazed on her, and she peacefully looked up at him. He smiled nonchalantly and put the tray of food on the bed.

"I thought you might be hungry."

"Thank you, I am." She slowly rose, and for the first time he noticed the cross hanging from a long gold chain around her neck. It was about an inch long, with a green gem in the center. It looked extremely old.

"That is an unusual cross," he said.

"It was my mothers. It is the only thing I have left of her. She gave it to me when I was just a baby. I remember her telling me that some day it would save my life."

"Save your life? How is that possible?"

"I know not. Although…" she stopped and touched the cross.

"Although what?"

"I know this might seem silly, but sometimes I feel a tingle from the stone. As if it harbors some sort of power."

Not sure how to respond to that, he just narrowed his eyebrows and stared at her.

"You think me mad." She tucked the cross under the dress and hungrily looked down at the food.

"I do not. I think you might have an over-active imagination."

"Forget I mentioned it." She continued to look at the food.

"Well, go ahead—eat!"

"The food must be blessed first."

"Then for heaven's sake, bless it, and eat!"

She gazed at him in despondency, and then lowered her gaze to the floor. "I cannot. My soul is too impure. I always had to have my food blessed by another."

Luke felt the heat of anger rise to his face as he reached a hand out to cup her chin and lift her head. "That is nonsense! Your soul is most likely the purest I have ever seen. You have been fed with lies your whole life because of people's ignorance. Very well, here—I shall bless the blasted food." He uttered a quick dinner prayer he learned as a child, and then handed her a piece of bread and cheese. "Here, now eat."

She gingerly took the food and began eating while Luke sat on the stool and watched her, making sure she was getting some nourishment into that small body of hers. He could only think of how beautiful she was. She raised her head and smiled timidly.

"Thank you."

He sat up with the realization she had seen into his thoughts. "You are most welcome, I think."

A wounded deer could not have looked more pitiful. "I have displeased you again."

"Nay—you have not. I must remember to control my thoughts around you, that is all."

"Only when you are close. I cannot see thoughts from a distance."

"But you knew about those men…back at the other inn."

"Yea, but that is a different type of feeling." She took a bite of cheese and chewed between sentences. "I am able to just know sometimes what is about to happen. Or sometimes, I have visions. But thoughts are only heard within a short distance."

"How short a distance?"

"About a room's length."

"Rooms are different sizes, Elanna. How big a room?"

"About…from this bed to the door."

He calculated the distance. "Hmmm, about fifteen feet. I can live with that. We shall simply wave at each other a lot." His smile relieved her tension.

"I knew you were good and kind when I had a vision of you."

"You had a vision of *me*?"

She shrugged and took another bite. "Aye, right before I was about to plunge a dagger into my heart, and end my life."

Luke's mouth went dry with the image of her lying dead in a pool of blood. "I am glad 'tis my face that stopped you. Why would you do that?"

"To keep from being forced to marry. I must not ever, you see."

"And why would that be?"

"I must ne'er bear a child—'twould be the devil's spawn, as I am."

Her opinion of herself broke his heart. His anger sparked, but he retained his composure with the aplomb worthy of a nobleman. "Elanna, you are *not* the devil's spawn."

"Aye, I am."

"Nay, you are not. The devil could not spawn one as beautiful as you. Besides, you said your uncle was to kill this 'groom' and you were to be returned."

"I did not know that at the time. I could only sense that I was to marry, but I failed to detect the whole devious plan. I learned this all from the guard stationed outside my door. My uncle does not get close enough for me to totally see his thoughts. He is afraid of me."

"And I still say there is reason for that fear, something no one knows and he does not want known."

"He fears me simply because I am a witch."

His voice rose in anger. "I shall have no more such talk around me, understand?"

She lowered her head in submission, and he felt like a fool when tears ran down her cheeks. "Very well, I will not speak of such around you, but it shall not stop me from thinking it."

"Elanna…" He could not help himself from taking her into his arms. Her head barely reached his chest, and she softly cried into it as he stroked her hair. "I did not mean to sound so gruff. I am not experienced with women. Please, Elanna, do not cry, it breaks my heart to hear it."

She stepped back and bravely smiled. "I shall try."

"Good. Now, I shall send up some warm water in order for you to refresh thyself, while I attend to the matter of a cloak. You cannot travel with me without warm clothing." He reluctantly left her and went downstairs.

He paid for the room, again apologizing for their late arrival, and asked the innkeeper about the purchase of a cloak. The innkeeper's face lit up.

"My wife's wealthy sister visited lately, and accidentally left behind this." He went into his office and returned holding a blood red, hooded cloak lined with fur. "'Tis most warm, and will look dazzling against your lady's light hair. I only ask a fair price for it."

The 'fair price' turned out to be a king's ransom, and he left with the cloak and the revelation that he had made the first bad deal of his life. No matter—Elanna would now be warm. He was distressed with the notion that all reasoning left him when it came to this girl.

He returned to the room and showed Elanna her new piece of clothing, holding it up proudly with a smile. Her face, however, fell into dismay.

"'Tis so bright! I have ne'er worn bright colors."

"Why is that?"

"I was only allowed to wear white, in hopes of purifying the evil within me. Bright colors bring the devil."

"Oh, the devil's arse! What nonsense!"

"Luke, do not speak so! What if the devil hears you?"

"He has heard much worse from me, I can assure you. Now, get ready. We have a long trip ahead of us."

He waited downstairs until she appeared on the stairs, which made him draw in his breath in awe. Her platinum hair cascading over the red cloak made a striking contrast that even a king's court could not ignore; her beauty would pale a room full of noble women. He held out his hand to her, and she willingly took it as he smiled adoringly at her. Suddenly he wanted to give her everything she never had, including love.

Outside, he mounted his horse and without effort pulled her up behind him. She held on, putting her arms around as much of his girth as she was able, and they rode off. He tried to find out all he could about her as they traveled.

"Elanna, tell me about your typical day at the convent."

"I rose at dawn, made my bed neatly, and performed my morning prayers. I was allowed a morning meal when I was a child; later that was relinquished as a punishment for my sins."

"What sins?"

"We all have sins, Luke."

"I suppose, some more than others. Look at me, my sin is gluttony. I was punished by growing to the size of an ox, as my younger brother is only too glad to remind me."

"Oh, no—your size is wonderful! I would love to be as large as you."

He chuckled. "I have a problem visualizing that. But we have wandered off the subject again. Then what did you do?"

"After prayers, I worked in the hospital until my evening meal."

"And what was that? Cold gruel to cleanse your soul some more?"

"Not quite. There was usually porridge, honey, bread, cheese, and fruits and vegetables in season. I helped serve the meal, and I ate alone in the kitchen."

"Alone? Why?"

"The other nuns did not want their thoughts heard while they ate, or any other time for that matter. I was alone always, except for my studies with the prioress."

"So you had no friends?"

"Very few. Occasionally a visitor would happen by. I was allowed to meet very few, especially the men."

"I can understand that. A beautiful creation such as yourself can cause a man to have unwholesome thoughts."

"Not from you. Your thoughts are only for my well being."

He took a deep breath, and wondered if she knew how he liked the feeling of her pressed up against his back. He immediately tried to change the subject.

"Are you warm enough?"

"Aye, I am. And shame on you."

He let out a throaty laugh. "You are a fascinating woman, no doubt. I feel our relationship shall be most interesting."

After a few hours they needed to rest. He chose a grove of oak trees by a small lake. The sun sparkled off the water while several ducks bobbed for fish, their tails making comical little spikes piercing the surface. He lifted Elanna off the horse, whereupon she grimaced as her stiff legs responded to the unfamiliar exercise.

"How do men do this, ride a horse all day? I am so sore I can barely walk!"

"It shall get better with time." He absent-mindedly picked up a flat stone and skipped it across the lake, sending several ducks noisily fleeing from the rude intrusion. "Ah! Four times, a good skip."

She giggled like a small child. "How did you do that? You made the rock fly on the water like magic!"

He relished in her youthful innocence. "Here—let me show you." He found a good, flat rock, and put it in her hand. "Now, the secret is to throw it sideways. Nay here, like this. There, now toss it!" She threw the rock, and it landed in the water with a plunk.

"Alas, I fear I do not share your talent at flying rocks."

"Here, let me show you again." He skipped another rock; this one skipped five times before falling into the lake. "Aha! A new record. They should erect a plaque proclaiming my skills!"

She let out a lilting, musical laugh, and then quickly straightened her face.

"Your laugh is delightful, why did you stop?"

"Such an outburst is improper."

"Oh, balderdash! The world has been deprived of your laughter for too long. I am just going to have to make up for that." He wiggled his eyebrows and began tickling her ribs. She jumped backwards in surprise.

"What are you doing? Oh, stop that!" She began laughing uncontrollably as he gently tickled her, causing him to laugh along with her as she feebly fought him off.

"'Tis called a tickle, and I am most profuse at it. I have won awards for this, also."

She giggled again and tried to run away, but he grabbed her towards him until she fell to the ground, helpless with laughter. He dropped to his knees as he continued tickling her.

"You are without honor!" She was giggling so hard her sides hurt. "You would ne'er make a knight!"

"Nor would you. You would most likely end up being used as a practice dummy, you are so small and scrawny." He rolled her over on top of him, and she feigned a fight as he mercilessly attacked her ribs. Suddenly their eyes locked. The giggling and tickling stopped abruptly as he gazed into her mesmerizing eyes that fascinated him so. Her face was so close he could feel her breath, soft and warm. The urge to kiss her was overwhelming. Again she picked up on the one thought he wished she hadn't.

"I have ne'er been kissed." Her heart began thumping so fast she feared it jumping out of her chest.

"Would you like to be?"

"I think so."

He brought his hands up to her face and cupped it; they practically covered her whole head. Gently, slowly, he brought her mouth down to his and kissed her lightly. She closed her eyes and reveled in the moment of her first kiss. He observed her frail, trusting face with a tinge of puzzlement, as he ended the kiss and drew away. His thoughts again betrayed him, as she opened her eyes and smiled down at him.

"Of course I liked it, how could I not? 'Twas my first kiss."

He rolled her off him, and got on his side, facing her. The gentle kiss had stirred him more than he wanted to admit. He instantly made a compulsive decision. "Elanna, you are ne'er going back to the nunnery. I am going to get Ancaster back for you."

Her smile faded. "How?"

"My father is a friend of the king. Henry shall help you."

Her face immediately fell into a panic. "Nay! They will burn me at the stake! My uncle has told me so."

"Your uncle is a liar. His only goal is to obtain Ancaster as his own, legally or not. I disliked the man at once; he reminded me of a rat. He needs you alive, now that the king has ordered you to take a husband."

She cocked her head and stared at him, then her eyes widened with revelation. "*You* were to be that husband?"

"Only if you would have me."

A sad sigh escaped her, and she stood up, her long cape dragging the ground as she walked away. He rose and followed her as she strolled to the water's edge and gazed solemnly across the lake.

"I would have you without hesitation if I were an ordinary girl, but I am not, and I cannot pretend to be. You deserve a normal girl, with normal dreams and wants, not a freak like me."

He turned her around by her shoulders, perhaps a bit too rough, and gave her a gentle shake. "You are not a freak!"

Tears ran down her face, and she blinked to stop them. "I am! He shall expose me, and I shall burn!"

"Nay, Elanna, I have a feeling your uncle has a reason for his extreme fear of you. We will figure a way out of this mess, I assure you."

"We?"

"Aye, we."

"Luke, this is not your problem."

He put a hand to her cheek to calm her. "It just became so." He smiled, pleasantly taken aback with the discovery that this girl had completely stolen his heart.

"We had better get moving. It looks as if it might snow." He took her arm and they went back to the horse.

Ancaster was awash in activity as Giles Dayen sent every available man out to search for Elanna. When once again Patrick returned empty-handed, he suffered an onslaught of Dayen's anger.

"Three days! She has been missing three days, and still you cannot find her! Are you all idiots?"

"We tracked her to the town, and was told a woman answering her description left with a man headed west. My men searched all night, with no food or rest, and found nothing. Apparently the information given us was incorrect."

"Or perhaps you are all feather-brained morons!"

"That is not fair, Giles...she can sense our presence, and can hide easily. We could search forever and not find her."

Giles narrowed his eyebrows in contemplation. "A man, you say? Any idea who he is?"

"None. We did not stay long for questioning, in hopes of catching up with her."

"Probably some traveler she begged for help. No telling what she told him. No matter—if he is still with her when you find them, you will simply have to dispose of him."

Patrick drew a breath to protest, then reconsidered. "If he is found with her, he will be questioned. If he knows too much, then I will deal with him."

"Then get the hell back out there! I want her found!" He lowered his voice and moved in closer to Patrick. "May I remind you what could happen if she knows about our smuggling ring?"

"There is no way she could know about that," Patrick snapped.

"Oh, no? And would you stake your life on that?"

Patrick gave that some thought, and then shook his head.

"No? Well, neither will I. Now go find her! She cannot evade you forever."

Patrick frowned, gave a short nod, and briskly left.

Chapter Four

Luke and Elanna rode the rest of the day, and finally stopped at an inn when it became too dark to travel. After handing the reins to a stable boy, Luke turned to Elanna and flung the hood over her head. "Elanna, keep the hood on, and your face down. Those men are still out there."

She nodded, and the hood flopped down over her face. She frowned. "I feel like a monk."

"You may feel like one all you wish, as long as you do not look like one. Now, stay close, and I shall book us some rooms."

She took his arm, but stopped just short of the door. "Luke? I—I do not want to be alone. Please stay with me."

He smiled, and brushed an untidy wisp of hair from her face. His protective instinct took over against his better judgement. She had every reason to be afraid, and her innocence compounded her fear. "Very well, I shall only book one room. Now hush, and follow me."

This inn was a bit nicer and bigger than the others. Their room proved to be quiet, for which Luke was thankful, as the day had taken its toll and he was tired. Elanna had never once complained. He marveled at her endurance since she was such a little thing; she should have dropped from exhaustion long ago.

He brought his pack in from the horse, and took out a white shirt.

"Here, Elanna, wear this tonight to sleep in. It should be more comfortable than your gown."

She held the shirt up to her; it fell down below her knees. "Is it not a wee bit big?"

"Maybe just a bit." He smiled at her cuteness. "I shall go fetch some food, you prepare for bed. He left her inspecting the shirt with consternation.

When he returned, she was sitting cross-legged on the bed wearing the shirt. Her hair fell like great waterfalls around her as she smiled up at him. He fought not to stare at her delightful bare legs and feet. Everything on her was so small, so perfect. She looked like a child waiting to be tucked in by her mother.

He put the tray of bread and meats down on the bed, pulled off his boots, and joined her, sitting cross-legged across on the other side of the bed. She didn't wait for the food to be blessed this time, and attacked it with zeal. In a moment she let out a pleasant laugh that warmed his heart.

"What is so funny?"

"What you were just thinking."

He narrowed his eyebrows as he recalled his thoughts. "That we are having a picnic on the bed?"

She laughed again. "Better than outside in the cold."

"I have ne'er had a picnic on a bed before. I am glad 'tis with you."

"Will there be more?"

He chewed a piece of pheasant. "Picnics? Only if you wish there to be."

"I do."

"Then consider it done." He watched her a while, then it suddenly occurred to him that he would like to watch her for the rest of his life. He had never had such feelings about a woman. She had so much to offer a man, would she ever consider marriage to someone like him?

She raised her head and her smile faded. "Do not think such things, Luke."

He felt like kicking himself in the head for thinking. "Forgive me…I forgot you…"

"…were a witch?"

"Damn it, Elanna! You are not a witch."

Her smile returned. "You are sweet, Luke, to try to spare my feelings. Let me tell you what I learned today from you. The brother you worry so about, Paul, is gone on a voyage. You are upset that you left your favorite pair of riding boots at home, but your mother demanded you wear new ones to impress your future bride. Your right boot has caused a blister on your big toe. You are concerned what Matthew is going to think of me. You are very fond of his pet."

Luke snickered with an unconcerned face. "You were doing well until the pet. She is his wife, and she is not a pet, her name is Pet."

"It does not bother you that I know these things, even though we did not discuss them?"

"Elanna, 'twould only bother me if I had something to hide. Actually, 'tis very convenient. It cuts down on useless conversation, and leaves time for other things, such as picnics."

She looked surprised, then giggled. "I really do not bother you?"

"Oh, on the contrary, you bother me a great deal, with your bare legs and pretty feet and all that hair. You drive me to distraction."

She glanced down at her legs, then grabbed a corner of the blanket and covered herself up. "There. Now I no longer bother you."

"Nay, now you shall still have to put a sack over your head."

"I shall not!"

"Then I am still bothered."

"You are not being fair."

"I ne'er said I was fair."

"You are impossible!"

"To that I agree." He laughed deeply, and soon she was giggling with him.

All too soon their meal was done, and bedtime loomed. He turned down the sheets, and motioned her in. As she snuggled into the sheets, he felt a forbidden heat rise within him and he took a step backwards. "Elanna, I cannot sleep next to you."

She gave him a blank, innocent look. "Was I bothering you again?"

"You have no idea." He noticed the opening at the bottom of the bed. "This bed has a trundle. I shall sleep there." He pulled out the trundle, and lay down on the straw mattress. In a few minutes he heard her even, quiet breathing, and knew she had fallen asleep. The question remained whether he could fall asleep with her so close by.

When he awoke the next morning, Elanna was snuggled next to him. He had no idea when she got there, as he slept rather soundly once he fell asleep. A smile crossed his face as he watched her, resembling an angel in heavenly repose. What did fate have in store for this innocent, childlike girl? Whatever, he was determined to be there for her; he had to be. Did she not have a vision of him?

She slowly stirred, and opened her eyes. When she saw his bemused smile, she gave him a sheepish grin. "I got cold."

He brought his face down to hers and kissed her on the nose. "You are a delight, my little angel, but you sorely test my restraint."

Her eyes widened innocently. "Restraint?"

"Aye…when a man is around a beautiful woman, 'tis difficult not to want to,…ne'er mind." He crawled out of the low trundle bed and stood up.

"Not to what?"

He tried to get across the room in hopes of putting sufficient distance between them before his thoughts betrayed him. Too late, she playfully threw a pillow, hitting him in the buttocks. He whipped around in surprise as she burst out laughing.

"That is for thinking wicked thoughts!"

He picked up the pillow, which was nothing more than a linen case stuffed with straw, and raised an eyebrow. "Wicked thoughts, huh? Hence, tell me my little seer, what am I thinking now?"

She let out a small gasp. "You would not dare!"

"Oh, would I not?" He lifted the pillow and tossed it at her. It missed her by inches as she jumped up on the large bed, and grabbed another pillow. She feebly tossed it at him as he moved toward her. He caught it with one hand.

"Ah, 'tis a fight you are wanting!" He threw the pillow, hitting her square across the body, knocking her down on the bed. She giggled when the straw fell out, making a big mess all over the bed and spilling over to the floor.

"Now see what you did! The poor pillow has lost its stuffing!"

"But this one has not!" He picked up the other pillow, and she squealed as it came flying at her. "Stay still! How can I pummel you when you dart around like a rabbit?"

She jumped off the bed holding the pillow and he chased after her, the both of them laughing hysterically. She bopped him across the chest; in response he grabbed her around the waist and lifted her up. She snickered with delight.

"'Tis no fair picking up your opponent! 'Tis most un-sportsmanlike!"

"I am not a sportsman." He tossed her on the bed and dove in after her, only to have her roll out of his grasp, giggling the whole time. She mock-protested in laughter as he snagged her foot, and pulled her back.

"Aha! Now I have you!"

She wriggled and squirmed as he began to tickle her. "No fair!" she shrieked.

"'Tis so fair. You attacked me first. As the wronged party, I demand satisfaction."

"And what must I do to right my terrible wrong?"

He pulled her up to her knees. "I think perhaps a kiss shall do nicely."

Her laughter quieted to a shy smile. "Very well, you may kiss me."

"Nay, you must kiss me. I am the wronged party."

"But, I do not know how! I have only tried one!"

"'Tis not so hard. Well? I am waiting." He closed his eyes and puckered his lips in a playful pose.

She brought both hands up and cupped his face, then tilted her head and brought her lips up to his. His eyes flung open when she began kissing him; it certainly wasn't the little peck he had expected. She deepened the kiss with closed eyes, running her hands through his hair with unexpected passion. He responded in like, grasping her shoulders as he drew her near. Within a few seconds, they were lying on the bed, holding each other with a desperate need.

He finally drew away, leaving her gasping as he was. She looked at him with wide-eyed innocence.

"Was my kiss not good?"

"Good?" He shook his head. "Nay, 'twas not good. You simply turned me inside out, and I believe all the hair on my chest has fallen off."

She smiled. "Does that mean you liked it?"

"Elanna, if I liked it any more, you would now be in a very compromising position. Now, get dressed...we have a long way yet to go." He rose from the bed and began to pull on his boots.

Confused by his sudden gruffness, she stared at him and searched inside his mind. The mixed emotions she received confused her even more.

"Why do your thoughts not match your actions?"

He turned and looked at her. "How do you mean?"

"You are acting angry, but your thoughts are soft and loving."

"Elanna..." He came back and sat down. "You are so innocent, you have no idea what you do to me. I am simply frustrated, for I want you."

"You...want me?"

"Aye, damn it. Very badly. Hell, I am not a saint! I know you think I am your savior, but I am just a man."

"I am sorry." She lowered her head and the spanked puppy look came back on her face.

"Elanna, 'tis not your fault I want you. If anything, you should feel honored; I do not want many women." His attempt at levity didn't work, and large tears began to run down her face. "Come hither." He took her into his arms, and she began crying softly into his chest. "Oh, please, do not cry. It kills me when you cry."

"I have behaved most badly. I should be whipped for my actions."

"Oh nonsense. You have done nothing wrong, under the circumstances."

"I have tempted you like...like a trollop."

"Elanna, stop!" Even as he spoke, he felt as low as the smallest insect. "'Tis my actions that make you feel so. How could you possibly think 'tis your fault?"

She drew away from him as a frightened look engulfed her. "I—I am sorry. I have enjoyed your company so, I forgot who—and what—I am. You are the kindest person I have ever known; you make me laugh and forget my plight." Turning away, she fought for control of her tears.

He reached out and lightly touched her on her back, and she instantly stiffened. His heart quickly sank, as a reality struck him like a bolt of lighting. "Elanna, show me your back."

She frantically shook her head.

"I shall not take no as an answer." He parted her hair and carefully lowered the huge shirt off her shoulders, then clenched his jaw at the sight of the welts that streaked across her thin back. "Oh, my God, you really have been beaten." Tears stung his own eyes, and he raised the shirt back onto her shoulders. "By all that is holy, who did this to you?"

She turned around, her huge eyes sad beyond his reasoning. "The convent was visited regularly by certain Benedictine monks. One in particular took an interest in me, and when I refused him, he said my beauty was a sin and that I tempted him. Every month he visited, and every month I resisted. He ordered me whipped. His thoughts were full of sinful practices, not like yours."

"Why did the prioress allow this?"

"The prioress could do nothing to stop it—his rank was higher."

"Life has been cruel, you did nothing to deserve this." He held her close, and gently stroked her back. "Elanna, no one shall ever hurt you again. I promise."

"Do not make promises you cannot keep."

"Is that what you think I do?"

"I do not think you mean to, but making promises to me is futile. My fate lies elsewhere."

"But…you said you had a vision of me."

"Yes—of helping me get away. I must go far away, Luke. So far my uncle cannot find me."

"Elanna," he began, then stopped when he wasn't sure how to word his next sentence.

She drew away and turned her back to him. "No, Luke, that is not an option."

"But if you married me, I could help you get Ancaster back. My father is a powerful man, and personal friends with the king."

"No, Luke. Do not even think it."

Closing his eyes, he fought disappointment, anger, frustration, and a gamut of other emotions that all sprung up at once. He had expected rejection from the start of this misadventure, but did not anticipate the hurt of receiving it. "All right, Elanna. I shall accept that for now. But I shall be attempting to change your mind."

She turned and looked at him, and their eyes locked in a timeless moment of penetrating awareness. Their souls seemed to touch, as Luke reluctantly broke the mood.

"Come, we must prepare to leave. We shall reach Elton tonight if all goes well."

Chapter Five

The riders thundered up the road to Ancaster, their horses hot and foaming from exertion. Patrick was the first to dismount and confront the anxious Giles, who was waiting in the courtyard, an angry scowl on his face.

"Do not tell me she eludes you still!"

Patrick removed his riding gloves and gave his step-uncle a smirking smile. "Aye, but we have a lead. A girl matching her description stayed at a close by inn two nights ago." He paused and raised an eyebrow. "She was still with a man."

"Indeed?" Giles paced and rubbed his chin as he thought of this latest development. "Did you get a description of this man?"

"Just that he was big, a noble, and also purchased a cloak."

"Big? I wonder if it could be that Cameron fellow? He was quite large, if memory serves." He narrowed his eyebrows in contemplation. "But why would he be helping her?" He sneered in answer to his own question. "Aye, why indeed—she has bewitched him with her beauty and that lithe body of hers. Which way did they head?"

"Southwest."

"Southwest? If I recall, Cameron is from Cambridgeshire. Why isn't he just heading south?" He waved a hand nonchalantly. "No matter—send men both directions. He will have to cross the Nene River at some point, and she will be hard to hide. Seek out every village and manor, have our men take jobs if necessary to glean information. She must be found!"

"If she is with this Cameron, how do you purpose to get her back?"

"We shall solve that problem when it presents itself. Now gather fresh horses and men; they already have a two day lead on us!" He snarled, and entered the castle, leaving the weary Patrick to his unpleasant duty.

Luke and Elanna rode all day, stopping only when necessary for rest and food, and reached Elton late afternoon. Again, Elanna did not complain once. They engaged in light conversation, carefully avoiding all mention of marriage. Luke couldn't wait to talk with Matthew—he was more experienced with women, and should be able to tell him how to win this little seer forever.

Matthew was in the courtyard checking a scratch on his magnificent horse, Excaliber, when he saw them ride up. Luke he recognized immediately, but who was that behind him, a vision in a red cape and light blond hair so long it seemed to encompass her? Had he really done it, taken a bride so fast? Matthew didn't think he'd ever see the day.

Luke dismounted, and helped Elanna off the tired horse. William, Matthew's twelve-year-old adopted son, instantly appeared and greeted Luke, chattering happily, assuring Luke that he would take care of his horse. Luke gladly relinquished the reins to the horse-crazy boy, and turned to his brother, who was standing with his arms crossed and an amused expression.

"Matthew, 'tis good to see you! What is new?"

"I believe that is my question, my towering hulk of a brother…I see you brought a beautiful nymph to grace our presence."

Luke laughed heartily. "Matthew, meet Elanna. Elanna, this is my knightly brother Matthew."

Matthew took her hand and gave it a gentleman's kiss, as he bowed with a great, over-exaggerated flourish. "The pleasure is all mine, Milady…'tis not often I am visited by an angel made flesh with beauty that rivals the stars."

As Elanna giggled, Luke broke the handhold, while frowning at his flowery brother who always seemed to have the right words. "All right, that is quite enough. We come seeking assistance, brother."

Matthew's demeanor changed immediately. "Assistance? Are you in trouble?"

"Er…not we, Elanna is in a sort of predicament…'tis a long story, and this courtyard is cold. Are you not going to invite us in?"

"Of course, my weary brother. A warm fire awaits us." He hollered into the barn at the boy removing the horse's saddle. "William! See to Excaliber for me!" He held out his arm gallantly. "May I have the pleasure of escorting the young lady?" Luke frowned as Elanna delicately took his arm, and now knew how Matthew felt when another man dared look at Pet.

As Matthew took a step, he winced in pain. His brother could not help but notice.

"What is it, Matt?"

"Oh, this damn leg always becomes sore whene're the weather turns cold. 'Tis most annoying."

Elanna reached out and touched Matthew's leg. A strange expression engulfed her face as she closed her eyes. "'Tis from the break you suffered when you fell out of a tree at age twelve. The leg did not heal straight." As she rubbed her hand over the affected limb, Matthew felt warmth, then a subsiding of pain. She withdrew her hand, and then wavered a bit off balance before both men reached out to steady her. Matthew gave Luke a wary look.

"Is there something you are not telling me, brother?"

Luke seemed as befuddled as Matthew. "I am not sure…I have ne'er seen her do that before."

They watched as Elanna took a few deep breaths, as if cleansing her system of some unseen substance, then return to normal. Only then was she aware both men held her by her arms, aghast looks on their faces.

"I am fine, you may let go."

Matthew relinquished her arm, giving her a troubled look that matched his thoughts. Elanna instantly recoiled back from him, and pressed next to Luke in fear.

"I—I am sorry. I did not mean to upset you."

Matthew instantly saw her terror, and smiled in spite of being overwhelmed by what had just happened. "On the contrary, I am most pleased. Luke, who do you bring whose very touch soothes my suffering?"

Luke turned the cowering girl toward him, and attempted to keep his voice calm. "Elanna? Would you like to explain thyself?" It came out more abrupt than he intended.

Her face fell in despair, her eyes misting over as she gazed up at him. "I have displeased you again."

"Nay, you have not. Here…let us go inside. I am cold, as I know you are."

The three entered the manor and proceeded to the great hall, where a roaring fire warmed the room and their spirits. The evening meal had concluded, and servants were stacking the tables against the walls for the nightly cleaning. Matthew was most aware of how dependent the small girl seemed to be of Luke, and wondered what exactly was going on between the two.

Luke knew he had to talk to Matthew alone; although he did not show it Matthew was disconcerted by the show of Elanna's power.

"Elanna? You must be tired. Would you like to rest or…uh, freshen up a bit? Matt, where is Pet? Perhaps she could see to Elanna's needs?"

Elanna backed away from Luke, her sad eyes focused on the floor. "Luke, if you wish to speak to your brother without my presence, 'tis fine. I am used to being sent away."

"Sent away?" Matthew furled his eyebrows in curiosity. "Why would you want to send her away?"

Elanna turned to Matthew. "So I cannot…"

"Elanna, please let me converse with my brother alone. Go warm thyself by the fire." Luke was frantic to the point of being rude.

Matthew was totally confused by his brother's actions. "Her presence does not concern me, Luke. Why do you want to…?"

"Trust me brother." He took Matthew by the arm and forcefully led him to the other side of the room. Matthew could not help stare at the sad girl as she walked to the fireplace and took off her cape. Her rare beauty stunned even him. Luke finally stopped and frowned in thought as he considered the distance.

"This should be far enough."

"Far enough for what? Good heavens, Luke! You practically ordered the poor girl away! What has come over you?"

"Matthew,"

"'Tis not like you to treat a girl so! And such a beauty! Is she your wife?"

"Nay, I…"

"Your betrothed, then?"

"Well, nay, not exac…"

"If she is not your betrothed, then why do you bring her hither and send her from your sight? This is most confusing, Luke!"

Luke exhaled a sigh of resignation. "Believe me, it does not get better."

"How do you mean?"

"Matt, will you cease blathering long enough for me to explain?"

He folded his arms and gave Luke a condescending look. "Very well…I am waiting."

Taking a deep breath, Luke cast Elanna a concerned glance then turned his gaze back to his waiting brother. "Matt, I…"

He suddenly changed the subject. "Where is Pet?"

"She is gone, but shall be back shortly. I am waiting, Luke."

"Matt, Elanna…"

He paused, wondering how to not sound totally mad.

"Aye?"

"Elanna is a Seer." He let out a relieved breath, glad to have it finally out in the open. Matthew, however, expressed no reaction, except maybe a tinge of amusement. "A

Seer?"

"Aye, and apparently she also has healing abilities."

"Apparently."

"I was not aware of that aspect of her personality until today."

"And what else? Can she fly?"

"Of course not!"

"Or, mayhap she can turn rocks into gold? That would be convenient."

"Matthew, I am being serious!"

"Oh, come now, Luke!" He unfolded his arms, and gave Luke a small punch to the belly. "I know your humor. This is but just another of your jests! A seer, indeed!"

"Matt!" Luke paced in exasperation while Matthew looked on, quite amused at the discomfort his younger brother was exhibiting. "I am telling you she can see your thoughts from a close distance. That is how she knew about your leg; I ne'er told her. She has been confined to a convent where she has been starved, whipped, and made to feel she is the devil's spawn. I have rescued her from her uncle, who plans to use her to take over her inheritance. She feels she is evil, and shall not marry me, and I brought her here because I know not what else to do!"

The smile disappeared from Matthew's face. "Good Lord, you are serious?" His eyes darted warily to Elanna, who was talking with a servant girl who had brought her tea. "She is so small and captivating—why would anyone want to harm her?"

"Because they think her to be a witch. Matthew, I love her, and I want nothing more than to make her my wife. But she must be made to believe she is wanted, and loved. I am not good at that sort of thing."

"Aye, I know…you were not here five minutes and already had the poor girl in tears."

"She thinks all she does is displease me, and is frightened of people. Please treat her kindly. She needs friends."

The smile on Matthew began slowly, then widened until it took over his face. "Hence, a woman has finally stirred your blood."

"Stirred? She has sent it to frothing like the finest ale. I have ne'er felt like this."

"Luke, you have not...compromised this girl, have you?"

"Nay, not yet, but it has not been easy. She is so willing to love, starved so to speak, and even more willing to accept it. It has been all I can do to contain myself."

"Sounds like you are ready for the altar."

"Oh, very ready...but she is not. Matt, I need your help. I cannot say the right things."

Matthew nodded knowingly. "Just do not make the same mistake I did with Pet. Tell her you love her, now."

"I have already done so."

"And that did not sway her?"

Luke sighed. "'Tis complicated. She feels she is unworthy of me, and cannot risk marriage in fear of passing on her...*affliction* to offspring."

Matthew slapped his lovelorn brother on the back. "Enough talk. Let us go speak to this little seer of yours."

The men strolled back to Elanna, who was sipping her tea and patiently waiting. Her face lit up when her eyes met Luke's; Matthew had no doubt where her feelings lie. Luke took her hands as she stood up, and gave her an assuring smile.

"'Tis all right, Elanna. I explained everything to Matt, and he shall be your friend."

"No harm shall come to a single hair on your head, Milady, and that is no small promise." Matthew bowed with a large smile.

"Now," Luke began. "I am curious as to how you cured Matt's leg. This seems to be a small detail you withheld from me."

The men waited as she seemed to gather her thoughts. "'Tis something I have always been able to do. I take the pain onto myself, and my body sheds it away. But 'tis not healing, only a saint or Jesus could truly heal. I simply remove the pain. I am sorry, Luke. I have displeased you again."

"Nay, you have not. By the saints, Elanna, quit apologizing! We were simply curious."

Her gaze flew to Matthew. "You do not believe me."

He shuffled in unease, not sure how to answer her. "Let us say I am…skeptical."

Luke jabbed him in the ribs. "Matthew!"

"'Tis all right," Elanna interrupted. "He simply is concerned for you, Luke. He is worried that my beauty has captured your heart, but left you blind to what I truly am."

Matthew's eyes widened, and he stepped backward a few feet. "I did not say that!"

"But apparently you thought it!" Luke's voice rose in anger.

Elanna smiled. "And nay, I cannot fly."

The three exchanged glances, emotions ranging from anger, disbelief, and finally amusement. Matthew burst out laughing, and was closely followed by Luke. Finally Elanna joined them, and a bond of friendship was melded between the three. Suddenly a voice called out behind them.

"What is so funny?"

Matthew instantly stopped laughing, and his face paled in horror. "Oh my God—Pet!" He whirled around to his wife, who had just entered the hall and was taking fast steps toward them. Luke grinned enthusiastically and went to greet her, while Matthew quickly addressed Elanna.

"Elanna, my wife is a very…private person. She takes great pride in her mind control, and shall not see kindly to someone…"

"Well, who is this?"

He whipped around to find Pet standing two feet from them, waiting for an introduction. He attempted a wide smile that came out more like a pained grimace. "Pet, sweetheart! Luke is here!"

She raised an eyebrow, and looked at him as if all his senses had left him. "I am aware of that, Matthew—he is standing right in front of me."

Luke stepped in for the introduction, seeing how Matthew had just turned into a mass of spineless jelly. "Pet, this is Elanna—the woman the king sent me to meet."

Pet turned to size up this newcomer. She was a pretty little thing, but not at all what she thought Luke would end up with. She had enough hair for five people, very interesting eyes, and was staring at her with an odd look on her face.

Elanna looked at the striking raven-haired warrior with the almond brown eyes and was immediately taken back by her. She dressed in men's clothing, all black, and sheathed a sword by her side. She looked every bit the warrior Luke had said, but her appearance was secondary—something else was missing. Elanna narrowed her eyes to search Pet's mind...and found nothing. She stammered for something to say.

"You...you are very beautiful, like Luke told me."

Luke and Matthew held their breath as Elanna circled Pet slowly, while Pet just followed with her eyes.

"That is odd...I was just thinking the same of you."

Elanna stepped closer and stared at Pet with a peculiar look, as if something was terribly wrong. "Were you?"

Desperately trying to intervene, Matthew attempted to have Pet leave for any reason. "Pet, dear, I believe some tea for everyone..."

He was ignored completely. "Aye, you are very beautiful. Luke is very fortunate. Are you two married yet?"

Elanna just stared at her oddly, causing Pet to feel like a hunk of meat being inspected for a roast. Finally Elanna backed up, an amazed look commanding her face.

"This has ne'er happened before. Luke, I cannot sense her!"

Matthew winced.

Pet frowned. "*Sense* me?"

Luke cleared his throat. "Elanna has a strange, ah, talent."

"Aye, I am a seer. I can read people's thoughts. But I cannot sense you." Her face suddenly exploded in a wide smile. "Do you know what this means? I can carry on a normal conversation with you!"

Wide-eyed, Pet backed up until she bumped into Matthew, and turned to whisper in his ear. "Is this girl all right?"

"She is fine. But you seem to have unnerved her."

Elanna was ecstatic. "This is wonderful! I can actually talk to you, and you can talk back, and I won't know what you are going to say! Oh, I know I sound totally insane, but I assure you I am not. Luke, did you know of this? Is this why you brought me here?"

Luke took Elanna's arm and shuffled her away from the befuddled Pet, who was exhibiting a priceless expression that in a different circumstance would have had him chuckling. He spoke in low tones so Pet couldn't hear, which was doubtful anyway because she was having her own 'discussion' with Matthew.

"Elanna, you just cannot blurt out something like that! Pet knows nothing about you."

Large tears flowed down her face and he again felt the fool for talking so harshly. He drew her into his arms and held her tightly. "'Tis all right, I am sorry for being so bad tempered."

Pet walked up at that point, having gotten the particulars from Matthew, and tapped Luke on the arm. "Luke, I would like to talk to Elanna—alone."

"But…"

"Now."

Not one to argue with Pet when she was determined, Luke let go of Elanna and stepped back to join Matthew, who apparently also had been told to keep his distance. Both men stared helplessly at the women,

Matthew not having the faintest idea what Pet was going to do, and Luke just hoping she didn't hurt Elanna's feelings any further.

Pet stared at the small girl with tears still wet on her cheeks, and had to remind herself that this actually was a full-grown woman. "Elanna, Matthew told me about you. It sounds as if you have not had an easy life so far, and I would like to make it better. Would you care to stay here, in Elton, with us?"

Elanna expressed shock, then relief. "You…you would welcome me here? Even though I am a…"

"…beautiful young woman who is to become Luke's wife, so I am told. That makes you family."

"But I have not accepted Luke's hand. I cannot, for I am a witch."

Pet grunted a low chuckle, expressing exactly what she thought of Elanna's statement. "Nay, you simply have a wonderful ability—except where it concerns me, I gather. Which makes you perfectly normal to me, and that is all that counts."

"Oh, Pet! Will you be my friend? I have ne'er had a female friend, or any friend for that matter. And to have one whose mind is not open to me! Just like right now—you have no expression, and I do not know what you are thinking! Is this not exciting?"

Pet stroked her chin in contemplation as she observed the child-like girl before her; she found the whole situation humorous. "Very well, Elanna, I shall be your friend—on one condition."

Elanna was a bit taken back, and then laughed in glee. "A condition! All right, but you are going to have to tell me what 'tis, for I cannot sense it. Is this not fun?"

"Perhaps you may not consider it so much fun when I tell you my condition. I want you to consider Luke's hand in marriage."

Elanna's smile faded, and she stepped back, her face falling into anguish at Pet's request. "You shall not be my friend if I do not marry Luke?"

"Nay, I did not say that. I said you shall simply have to consider it. Very seriously."

Elanna had the feeling that considering it and doing it were very closely related. "You want me to condemn Luke to life with a freak? To someone who knows his words before he says them?"

"You are not a freak. And, it does not seem to matter to him."

"But it shall. He is such a wonderful man; he makes me laugh and he kisses me so well, although I have naught to compare it with, as I have ne'er kissed a man before. I do love him so, that is why I cannot marry him. I am evil, Pet, and shall end up being burned unless I return to the convent."

"Where you shall be starved and beaten? I think not. Married or not, you are staying here with us. I would rather it be married."

Elanna lowered her head and nodded. "Very well, I shall consider it."

"Very seriously?"

"Aye."

"All right…regard thyself as my friend. Now, should we join the men?"

Elanna nodded, then touched Pet's arm and smiled warmly. "Could we spend some time together tomorrow? Just you and me? You could tell me everything about thyself and Matthew, and oh, all about Luke, too. Please? 'Twould mean so much."

Pet could barely keep from laughing out loud at Elanna's innocent enthusiasm; she was almost like one of Pet's adopted daughters. The girl was delightful. No wonder Luke was so taken with her.

"Very well, Elanna. I shall make sure of it. Now, the men look nervous, so we should join them."

Elanna giggled. "They are more than nervous, they are almost in a state of panic. They thought you were going to…" She stopped, not sure if she should divulge any further information.

"Going to *what*?"

"Oh, nothing bad. They thought you might hurt my feelings by insisting I keep my distance from you."

"Oh, did they?" Her eyes now flashed anger. "As if I would treat Luke's future wife as such!"

"I am not Luke's future wife," Elanna said absent-mindedly. Then, remembering her bargain with Pet, quickly added, "but I am seriously considering it."

Pet stormed up to the wary men and firmly gripped Matthew's arm. "We need to talk, *dear*." She sweetly smiled at Luke, and motioned to Elanna. "Ask her to marry you again. I feel she may be more receptive." With that she cast Matthew a sour look and marched him from the room.

Suddenly Luke was alone with Elanna, with not even a busy servant to distract them. He glanced around the room and sighed, then back at the arched doorway where Pet could be heard admonishing Matthew for his low opinion of her.

"She is very angry."

"Nay, she loves him very much. The only thing I can sense is her love for Matthew."

Luke looked down at Elanna, and gave a closed-mouth nervous smile. "Hence, you have met Pet…what do you think of her?"

"She is wonderful. I can see why she has captured your family's hearts."

"You shall also, Elanna. Have you…thought about my offer of marriage?"

Elanna swallowed hard, her face growing grim with indecision. She couldn't find a voice to immediately answer him, but finally, in a small soft tone, found words to reply. "Aye, I have thought more, and I am reconsidering it."

Luke beamed from ear to ear, and took her little hands in his. "You are? Oh Elanna, that is all I ask. I know I am not the best…"

"Luke, do not think that! You are all that any woman…a normal woman…could want. I would take you as my husband this moment if I were normal, but alas, I am not."

"Elanna, with me as your husband, I would become lord of your lands, and your uncle could lay no claim. I would waste no time in ordering him away, and your lovely Ancaster would be yours."

"And what comes then? Do you harbor hopes of living happily ever after like a fairy tale? Nay, do not answer, simply listen. Luke, I remember little about my childhood before I was sent to the nunnery, but the one thing I do remember is the fear. Every servant—every maid, cook, and groom—feared me and shunned me, except for one cook who was kind. At least at the convent I knew what to expect. Nay, Luke, you are thinking people change, but they do not when it comes to their fears. And do not think my uncle shall simply hand Ancaster over with a smile and ride away happy. He is determined to keep it under his control."

Luke realized he could simply stand there and think his reply to her, but was damned if he would be deprived of talking just yet. "Elanna, let me speak, even though I have no doubt you know what I am going to say. I have the resources of the king himself at my bidding. I guarantee your uncle would be forced away. And let me take a hazard at your thoughts; you are wondering if he would try to declare you a witch and have you condemned in order to gain your lands. Nay, not with me as your husband. The king would not hear of it. Elanna, 'tis the only way you can win this fight with your uncle."

She blinked back tears as she sought his mind, knowing his words were real. "Oh, Luke, I do not know. I need to think. Give me time, that is all I ask."

"Very well, Elanna. You have all the time you need." He leaned down to gently kiss her cheek. She turned her head, and he found her lips touching his, and with a groan he took her into his arms as he desperately solicited her mouth. A clearing of the throat brought them to their senses, and they both broke away to see Pet and Matthew staring at them with amused smiles. Matthew appeared sufficiently castigated, and Pet asked the first question.

"Hence, has the date been set?"

Luke sheepishly grinned at his brother and sister-in-law, then down at Elanna, who harbored the exact same expression. "Not exactly. She is considering it."

Pet raised an eyebrow. "That is good to hear." She cast a knowing look at Elanna.

Matthew clasped his hands together and put on a chipper smile in an attempt to break the uncomfortable mood. "Well! You two must be tired; let us make arrangements for your rooms. Are you hungry? We can have the cooks bring bread, meat…"

"Nay, thank you," Elanna answered. "We ate but just a while ago. Luke is thirsty, howbeit."

"I can speak for myself, thank you. Er, some ale would taste enjoyable right now, brother."

They all burst out laughing.

Rooms were made up for their guests. Pet purposely put Luke and Elanna's room next to each other, not that she was encouraging any premarital activity between the two, but because she had a feeling Elanna needed to know Luke was close by. Her dependency was strong, and he seemed to relish, indeed need, her reliance on him. Luke was almost not the same person.

Later that night, after Pet and Matthew had enjoyed slow, lingering lovemaking, they lay in each other's arms as they did every night since they had returned to Elton. Matthew twirled a lock of her hair around a finger, as she rubbed a leg over his thighs in playful affection.

"Those two are in love," Matthew stated. "They remind me of us, after we finally admitted we loved each other."

"Let us hope it does not take them four months, as it did us."

"Luke is not as bone-headed as I. He has already declared his love, now 'tis up to her."

Pet lay quiet, and Matthew sensed her change of mood. "What are you thinking?"

"I wonder why she cannot see into my mind."

"That is easy. You have the most incredible mind control I have ever witnessed. It has always been a marvel to me."

"Indeed?"

He sat up suddenly with an enlightened look. "Pet, do you think you could teach Luke your mind control?"

She glowered as she pondered this question. "I know not. I have ne'er thought about how I do it, just that I do it."

"If you teach him—and I have no doubt you could—Elanna would have one less excuse of why not to marry him. 'Tis at least worth a try, do you not think?"

"Very well, I shall talk to him tomorrow. Right now I want less talking, and more cuddling."

He chuckled and drew her close. "Aye, my love."

Chapter Six

Luke, an early riser, was surprised to see Pet the next morning sitting in the lessor hall, nursing a cup of tea while she waited for him. Taking the seat across from her, he grabbed a piece of bread, gnawed on the chewy crust, then washed it down with a gulp of hot, strong tea while keenly aware that she was studying his every move.

"All right," he cautiously asked, "what is wrong?"

"Nothing."

"Pet, 'tis true I do not know you as well as I should, but I know you enough to tell the word 'nothing' does not match your face."

"Very well. Matthew and I had a talk last night—about you."

"You do not appear pleased with the outcome."

"I am not sure. He says I should talk to you about mind control."

He chuckled deeply, his shoulders heaving with merriment. "Me? I am not sure I have enough mind to control."

She shrugged, relief showing in her otherwise emotionless face. "Fine, forget the whole thing." As she began to rise, he reached a long arm across the table and lightly grabbed her wrist.

"Not so fast. What kind of mind control, and why does Matt think I need it?"

"To block Elanna from your mind, as I apparently do." She sat back down.

"Hmmm." He furled his eyebrows as he became deep in thought. "That would please her, I am sure, as well as me. It has been very hard not to think, er, manly thoughts. She drives me mad with all that hair and her wide-eyed innocence." He gave a determined look and nodded. "Very well, I am willing. What do I do?"

"I am not sure." She leaned back, a pensive and troubled look crossing her face as she observed his hopeful one. "My need for control came about in order to repress an event in my childhood. I began by counting backwards from one hundred in my mind."

He wrinkled his nose as he pondered this revelation. "Why backwards?"

"Because you have to concentrate harder. 'Tis simply a means to focus your mind. Gradually I changed to an image; I concentrate on it and bury my real thoughts somewhere else."

Luke shook his head. "I do not believe I could ever do that."

"Luke, Elanna thinks I am the most wonderful person in England because she cannot see my thoughts. Would not you rather she thought this of you?"

"Well, when you phrase it that way…"

"Then you must try. The next time there is a thought you do not want her to know, start counting. All she will 'see' is numbers."

"All right, Pet," he sighed with lack of enthusiasm. "'Tis worth a try."

Pet narrowed her eyes at his exuberance. "Luke, it took me years to achieve what I have now. This shall not happen overnight."

"I am not stupid, Pet. Give me some credit."

"Very well." Her gaze lifted upward as she peered over his shoulder. "Here is your first test. Elanna is coming."

Luke suddenly felt as tense as a cornered fox. "I am not ready for this."

"You shall ne'er be ready; you have to start sometime."

He swallowed nervously as Elanna approached, counting in his mind to quell the thought of how eager he was looking to their marriage when he would have her alone in bed. She got within ten feet before her smile faded and she stopped, looking at him in bewilderment. Her face contorted into a sour grimace, and she took a few steps backwards.

"Why are you counting?"

Pet suppressed a grin, and Luke simply stared at her, continuing to count. Elanna put a hand to her head, her eyes growing narrow as if she was in pain. "Stop, please! I hate numbers!"

Pet leaned into Luke. "Do not stop; 'tis working."

Luke was finding this experiment extremely interesting. The thoughts of how beautiful he thought she was, how beguiling she became every waking moment and others more lustful were still in his head, but the counting was covering them up. Elanna was effectively stumped.

Elanna backed up until she was out of range. "Numbers! I hate numbers, why were you thinking them? Are you trying to torment me?"

Luke stood up, and went to her, not wanting her to think he was purposely being mean. "Of course not, I simply wanted to know if I could block you from seeing into my mind. Apparently I can."

Elanna glowered at Pet, and put her hands on her hips. "You put him up to this!"

Pet smiled and shrugged. "Guilty."

"Numbers! They are my downfall. I cannot add two and two together and get the correct answer; I am simply terrible." She pushed through Luke and sat down at the table with Pet, lamenting this new turn of events as she leaned forward on her elbows. "I learned four languages, can write beautifully, read quickly and fluently, but cannot cipher numbers. The nuns tried everything. I was forced to add the same numbers over and over for hours until I could get it right, and the next day I would forget everything." She cast a mournful glance at Pet. "Why did you have to tell him to think *numbers*?"

"It worked, did it not? You cannot see into his mind."

Luke joined them, a wide, boyish grin on his amused face. "Do not fret, my little angel. Now that I have an effective weapon, so to speak, against you, I shall only use it when my thoughts prove to be embarrassing." Her eyes beckoned him; they were dreamy, almost mesmerizing, like right before she kissed him that night at the inn. "Like now." He started counting.

Elanna jumped to her feet and put her hands on her head. "Augh! Stop! This is no fair, Pet, I shall get even with you!"

Pet was suppressing laughter at this point; this being the funniest thing she had seen in a great long time. "I am sorry, Elanna." She let go with a snicker, effectively countering the apology.

Luke stopped counting, and Elanna let out a large sigh of relief. He put his arms around her as he let out a great belly laugh, and pulled her close. "Pet was only trying to help me. Do not be angry with her."

A pout crossed Elanna's face, which changed slowly into a crooked smile. "I am not. Pet would ne'er hurt me on purpose, that much I can sense. I fear I am rather a big baby when it comes to numbers."

Just then Luke saw Matthew enter, and let Elanna go. "I have plans today with my brother, and I believe you two ladies are going to spend some time together." He gave her a small kiss on the forehead. "Do not let Pet torment you further." He winked at Pet, and went to join his brother.

Elanna gave a chastising look at Pet, who was still trying not to laugh. "You think this is all very funny, do you not?"

"Actually, I do. Having you around is going to be interesting, to say the least. Now, I have children to rouse, breakfast to supervise, and you are going to help me. Do you like children?"

Elanna's face brightened. "Oh, aye! I find them refreshing; their thoughts are so open and innocent. However, I was not given much of a chance to be with many young. Luke told me how you and Matthew took on the care of nine serf children after a terrible raid left them orphans. You are good to do so."

"You might not think so after you meet them. I fear they are a bit wild."

"I cannot wait."

"Then let us go?"

The two women left the lessor hall, passing the men in the passageway on their way to the children. Matthew grabbed Pet as she went by, pulling her into a lavish kiss that made Elanna's face grow red. She faced away, only to find Luke giving her a suspicious grin.

"Someday we shall be like them; not able to get enough of each other."

Elanna's blush grew even deeper, waiting until Pet was able to push her over-zealous husband away, but not before he whispered just exactly what he would be thinking of all day. Elanna thought her face would burn off.

When the men finally walked away, Pet resumed her course to the children. Elanna felt her face return to its normal temperature, and smiled at the passion she sensed in Matthew.

"I cannot express how much he loves you."

Pet simply smiled. "You do not have to. I know."

"He harbors much guilt. He feels he has hurt you terribly in the past."

Pet stopped and looked back at the men, now just leaving through the front door to their self-appointed tasks. "Still? I thought we were past that."

"Oh, nay. He anguishes inside for the pain he has caused you."

Pet lowered her head and stared at the floor as she thought about the turbulent last four months the two of them had gone through. "I hurt him, also. He must forgive himself, as I have."

"Maybe you two need to talk."

"We have—that is about all we did the entire trip back from his parent's home in Cambridgeshire. He opened his heart to me, and I mine." She looked at Elanna with a steady and calm face. "Men—who shall ever figure them out?"

At that, Elanna laughed.

Giles Dayen was sitting at his desk when Patrick entered. His full eyebrows arched high, he rose quickly to greet him, his voice gruff and impatient.

"Well? Any news?"

Patrick crossed his arms and gave a satisfied smirk. "We have a lead. They were overheard at another inn saying they were going to a place called Elton. 'Tis west of Peterborough, on the Nene River."

"Aye, aye…I know of it." His face drew into contemplation. "I believe that is the township that was just granted 1000 acres by the Ramsey Abbey. Aye, I am positive, I was present at the castle myself. Some warrior woman saved the queen from Gideon, the blasted fool. The king knighted her on the spot, and whisked her away to get married. What was the name of that chap?" He paced in front of the complacent Patrick, who couldn't understand what this all had to do with their problem. "Of course, Sir Matthew Cameron. Damn!"

"I bring you news of her whereabouts, and you curse?"

"Do you not see? Luke Cameron must be this Sir Cameron's brother. It might be harder than I thought to retrieve her; the Camerons are personal friends of Henry. I do wish Gideon had succeeded in his mission; imagine, letting yourself get cut down by a woman. Bah!"

"I am surprised you ever got him to work for you."

"He thought I was carrying on the work of Lambert Simnel. He was too stupid to know what he had actually been hired for."

"Killing women and children to cover your pirating operation."

"Oh, please, are you turning soft on me again? Really, Patrick, you must contain this part of your personality. There is no room for empathy in our line of business."

Patrick felt his face grow warm, and fought to remain calm. "Henceforth, what now?"

"Elanna must be hiding her affliction, pretending to be lost or some other such thing. No one would knowingly harbor a witch, who knows what elaborate story she has made up? All right, here is the plan…send some men to Elton, then have them seek jobs in the manor."

Patrick sneered with satisfaction. "I have already done so. I fear this time I am way ahead of you."

"About time, I grow weary of always having to be the brains. Did you take care to warn them not to get close to her?"

"Absolutely. They are to observe her from a distance only. I have also set up a communication rally. Four men are positioned a half-day's ride from each other. When news of importance happens, one man will leave Elton and ride non-stop to the first relief man, who will take up the message in the same manner. We should receive messages quite quickly."

Giles looked Patrick over with consternation. "Well, it appears you have matters under control, for once. I want her every move observed. I shall either have her returned to me, or she shall burn for her disobedience, which is something I am highly looking forward to seeing." He let out an evil laugh. "She would look good in flames, do you not think?"

Patrick pursed his lips and remained quiet.

Matthew and Luke cantered their horses through the forest trail until they reached the first trap. They retrieved the dead animal, and Matthew threw it in a bag, and then remounted.

"Pet refuses to do this; apparently this is where she was when the outlaw gang attacked Elton and killed her brother." His voice grew low and remorseful. "Damn, I wish I had been there, I might have been able to save him."

"Now, Matt, we both know your fighting skills were not what they are now. You would most likely be dead if you had been there." His eyes turned soft. "Brother, if everything did not happen just as they did, you would not be where you are now. Do not mourn the past, live for today."

Matthew's somber mood turned brighter, and he smiled. "Of course, you are right. I just wish Pet did not have to experience so much pain, especially the multitudes that I caused."

"She appears to have forgiven you, why not forgive thyself?"

"Never, I do not deserve to be forgiven. She still hides much grief, even though I was finally able to jar some much-needed tears from her. I sincerely hope you and Elanna do not have to go through a painful episode like we did."

"Elanna also has much suffering in her short life, but I aim to soothe it with our marriage. I am determined no one shall ever hurt her again."

"What of this uncle of hers? Do you expect him to relent so easily?"

"He shall have no choice. Once we are married, I become Lord of Ancaster. Wait until you see it, Matt! 'Tis a lovely place, although they have not made the best use of their fields. I believe I shall be able to increase production by…"

He was interrupted by Matthew's laughter. "Now, there is the brother I know! A woman has not taken you completely away!"

Luke laughed with him. "Almost, Matt, almost. I have ne'er felt like this. She is truly special, and I mean to have her. We shall be quite happy, I know it."

"So do I, Luke. Call it a feeling." He laughed, and they rode to the next trap.

The room was filled with what seemed like hundreds of children, bouncing and running so fast that Elanna's head was spinning. She was suppose to be helping a little girl put on a dress. The child turned her back so Elanna could fasten the ties, wiggling the whole time. Elanna giggled and finished her task, then turned the child to observe her.

"Well, Constance, you are finally dressed, but I must say 'twould be easier to dress a squirming piglet!" Another girl hopped up and jumped up and down excitedly.

"Me next!"

"All right, turn around, and do try to hold still!" The child obliged, except for the part about holding still. Elanna let out a sigh of exasperation. "Quit moving, Rosie."

"How did you know my name?"

Elanna paused. "Your mother told me. There, you are done." She glanced around the room; children jumped, squealed, and played everywhere as clothes were being tossed all over. She cast a weary look at Pet, who was just finishing lacing up Julie.

"Howe'er do you find the energy to do this every day?"

Pet smiled sheepishly. "I do not. My servants usually do this, but I take o'er every once in a while, just to remind myself I have children." A child ran by and Pet reached out and grabbed her, then proceeded to tickle her unmercifully. She finally let the giggling, wriggling child go, and turned back to Elanna. "They are going to their morning lessons, and we are going into town. You are going to have to wear something besides a dress in order to ride a horse. I do not have a side-saddle."

Elanna turned white. "But, I have ne'er ridden a horse alone! I know not how! I will fall for sure, then Luke shall become most displeased with me, and then…"

"Elanna! Calm down! 'Tis not difficult to ride a horse; I shall teach you."

"All right." She still harbored a worried look, and Pet just dismissed the worry with a wave of her hand.

"Really, Elanna…'tis hard to believe you have ne'er ridden a horse by thyself. We need to find you some suitable riding clothes. Hmmm." She became deep in thought as she stared at the petite girl, which caused great anxiety in Elanna.

"It kills me that I do not know what you are thinking!"

"I thought you liked that."

"Not when you have that expression."

Pet chuckled, and motioned to the door. "I was simply trying to think of a lad from whom I could steal clothes. I think I know of someone. Follow me." She exited the room, with Elanna following close behind.

The hapless lad—Pet's nephew, William—was found, and he gladly turned over a pair of hose and a doublet in Elanna's size. She wore her own soft leather shoes, as her small feet did not fit any boots Pet found. The weather was chilly, but dry, ideal for Elanna's first riding lesson. William, who spent most his time in the stable, saddled a horse and led it out to the waiting Pet.

"All right, get on." Pet gestured to the horse.

Elanna looked at the horse in dismay, then back at Pet. "How?"

"Put your foot in the stirrup, and lift thyself up. Nay, Elanna, you always mount from the left side. Try the left foot this time, if you use your right you shall be sitting backwards. There! You are on."

Elanna looked down at Pet, her eyes wide with fright, then suddenly turned to the smirking William. "You would look funny too if you had ne'er ridden a horse before!"

William wiped the smile from his face. "I did not say anything!"

Pet quickly stepped in, saving her nephew from further embarrassment. "That is quite all right, William, you may go."

"Aye, Aunt Pet." He backed up, cast a curious glance at Elanna, and went back into the barn.

Pet put a hand on her hip and cast a disconcerting gaze at Elanna. "Honestly, you cannot just go snapping at people when they have not spoken!"

"I am sorry, his thoughts were most vivid."

"Well, try to be more understanding. You were about to mount the horse backwards; of course he was amused. Now, take these." She handed Elanna the reins. "These control the horse, at least that is the idea. Some horses have a mind of their own. This one, howbeit, is most gentle. The children have ridden her."

"Fine, I am holding these long things. Now what do I do?"

"This horse neck-reins quite nicely. You lay the rein on the left side of her neck to turn right, and on the right side to turn left."

"Well, that certainly is confusing. What else?"

"You pull back to stop, or back up."

"How do I make it go?"

"You give her a little kick, but we will do that after…Elanna!" Pet watched with alarm as the horse bolted forward from the swift kick that Elanna had just executed. Elanna screeched and instantly dropped the reins, stopping the well-trained animal immediately. Pet ran up and grabbed the reins, and gave Elanna a stern look.

"Elanna, ne'er drop the reins!"

"But…but it moved!"

"You kicked her, of course she moved!

"This is not going to work, I want off."

"Nonsense, you must learn to ride, especially if you are to become Luke's wife."

"Everyone seems so certain I am to marry him! I have only said I would think about it."

"I suggest you think harder, or I might just leave you up there on that horse."

Elanna gasped. "You…you would not!"

"Nay, most likely not, but your stubbornness is annoying. You are almost as bad as I am. I fought Matthew with all I had, even though I fell in love with him the first day we met." She handed her the reins. "You and Luke are in love, 'tis obvious. You should be married."

"Pet, you do not understand." Elanna looked down with sad, imploring eyes that wrenched Pet's heart. "'Tis not that I do not want to marry him, indeed the prospect is most pleasant to think about. I am thinking of him. 'Tis not fair that such a wonderful person be married to me."

"Why do you not let him worry about that?" Pet went to her own horse, and mounted in one graceful move. "Now, hold on, and follow me. And do try not to fall off." She rode past the gentle horse she had put Elanna on, knowing it would follow hers, and together they left the courtyard.

After a few minutes Elanna started to relax. "This is kind of fun! I have not fallen off yet, at least. Where are we going?"

Pet kept a straight face; they had only just entered Elton. "We are going to visit the baker's wife, she is heavy with her first child and has been ill."

"Do you always visit your townsfolk?"

"Aye, every day I see someone. Matthew feels I am most mad, but 'tis important to me."

"Matthew does not think you mad. You can do no wrong in his eyes."

Pet scoffed a small grunt. "Oh, you think so? Just let me do something to provoke his anger, and you shall see different."

"He has been angry with you? I find that hard to believe."

"Do you jest? It used to be all we did was fight. He was always angry with me, in between trying to seduce me." She sighed. "He is such a difficult man."

"And yet you love him."

"With all my heart; I would die for him. Ah, here we are. Bring your horse right over hither." She pulled up and dismounted as Elanna watched.

"You make it seem so easy."

"'Tis—just put your foot in the stirrup and swing your leg over."

"Nay, I did not mean that. You make loving him seem so easy."

"Love is easy, if you allow thyself to do it. Now, get off your horse."

Pet smiled inwardly as she watched Elanna swing her leg over, catching it on the saddle's cantle, effectively throwing her off balance. She fell over the side, her left foot caught in the stirrup, but didn't hit the ground thanks to Pet's strong arms. She finally managed to get her foot uncaught, then stood up tall and brushed herself off.

"Well! That was not so bad!"

Pet laughed out loud. Suddenly the baker rushed out of his shop, almost knocking them over. When he saw Pet, his deeply etched, tanned face expressed great relief as he grabbed her arm and begged her to come with him.

"'Tis time, the babe comes! She screams with pain, and the midwife has not arrived! Please help!"

Turning white, Pet attempted to swallow, as her mouth just went completely dry. "I do not know how to deliver a babe."

Elanna sprang to life, taking control as she took the man's arm to assure him. "'Tis all right, I have delivered lots of babies, take me to your wife."

"This way! He led her into the bakery shop, and up the stairs to his wife, who was lying on the small bed, sweat rolling off her face as she struggled alone with childbirth. Elanna instantly knew something was wrong. Feeling helpless, Pet watched as Elanna knelt beside the young wife and put her hand on her huge belly.

"'Tis fine, breathe deep, that is it, real deep breaths." The woman let out another scream as a hard contraction racked her body, then her face went calm and her breathing slowed as Elanna closed her eyes and absorbed the pain with her empathic abilities. The young woman dozed off for a few minutes as the pain subsided. Opening her eyes, Elanna quickly stood up and motioned Pet off to a corner, a grim look encompassing her face.

"The baby is coming out backwards."

"How do you know...ne'er mind, what can we do?"

"I am going to have to turn her, or she will die, and the mother, too."

"You know the babe is a girl, just by a touch?"

"Of course, now listen. Get rid of the husband, he shall simply be in the way. Then I need your help."

Pet prayed for her blessed control to get her through this. "All right...what do you want me to do?"

When Matthew and Luke returned to the manor late that afternoon, they walked in to a curious sight. Pet and Elanna sat at the table, drinking tea, laughing as if they had known each other all their lives. They made quite a contrasted pair; Pet, tall, muscular, with shoulder-length black hair, and Elanna, small, fragile with cascading long blond hair. The men watched as the women they loved giggled and congratulated themselves, for what, the men didn't know. Luke cast Matthew a confused look, and Matthew returned it, twice-fold. The women ignored them and continued to discuss whatever was making them so happy.

"Did you see the look on his face when I showed her to him! What a beauty!"

Pet nodded. "And such a nice name, do not you think?"

"Aye, I rather like the sound of *Elanna Rose*."

"And the look on the midwife's face when she finally made her appearance, only to discover you had delivered the babe already! I thought she was going to turn red with jealously!"

"Her thoughts were not pleasant…she wanted to strangle me! That is what she gets for being late!"

Loud clearings of two throats interrupted them. They turned casually and smiled at their men.

"Hello, Matthew! How was your day?"

Matthew raised a single eyebrow at his wife's chipper mood. He crossed his arms and gave a stern look. "Have you two been nipping at the wine?"

Elanna giggled, then sat up straight and sobered her face. "And how many lives did *you* two save today?"

Luke finally found his tongue. "Would you two like to tell us what the hell you are talking about?"

Pet opened her mouth, but Elanna put her hand up and stopped her. "Let me tell them! You two better sit; this may take some time."

Obedient, the men sat across from the women.

"First I leaned to ride, by myself mind you, and only fell when I attempted to get off, which does not count, Pet said. Then when we got to the baker's, his wife was having her baby, and Pet and I delivered it."

"You delivered it, I simply stood by feeling dumb."

"Nonsense, you did wonderful. The babe had to be turned, which I was able to do."

"Expertly, I may add…"

"Why, thank you, and they named the babe after us since we saved the birth. After that, we visited the miller, to pick up flour for the baker, who said he would bake up something special for saving his wife and then we dropped off the flour, then we came back and of course we were all bloody from the birth, so we had to wash up, then we felt like some tea, and we made some and here we are!" She took a breath and blew it out, having finished her rendition of the day's events.

The men glanced at each other, then back to the women. Finally Matthew smiled.

"You helped deliver a babe? You, Pet? That is amazing!"

She nodded in enthusiastic agreement. "What is even more amazing is that I lived through it."

Luke reached across the table and took Elanna's hands in his as he explored her eyes with pride. "You helped the pain, did you not? Like you did with Matt's leg?"

"Aye, she was in great pain…at times 'twas more than I could bear."

All eyes suddenly were on her, with Luke conveying a look of absolute horror.

"You are saying you just do not take away the pain, you actually feel it?"

Elanna shrugged nonchalantly. "Only for a few seconds. 'Tis nothing."

Pet's mood was also less jovial. "Elanna, what would happen if someone were dying, or in such pain you could not handle it? Would there be a danger to you?"

"I do not know, that has ne'er happened. Anyway, 'twould not be important."

Luke grabbed her shoulders and gently shook her. "Your life is not important?"

"Not when it could save another."

Luke jumped up, rage rolling through him like a clap of thunder. "Your life is important to me! Do I mean nothing? Apparently not!" He strode from the room, leaving them all stunned. Matthew was more bewildered; he had never seen Luke display such a temper.

Tears ran down Elanna's face, and she lowered her head in shame. "I have angered him again."

Pet put a comforting hand on her shoulder. "Nay, you have frightened him, can you not sense it?"

"He left so fast I did not have time to sense anything. Except anger." She left Pet and Matthew, who watched her walk forlornly through the archway. Pet started to rise to go after her, but Matthew pulled her back.

"Luke will seek her, let her go." Pet reluctantly agreed.

After his unexpected outburst, Luke went outside to cool off, feeling ever much the fool. The thought of her taking on someone else's pain was too much for him to bear, but that gave him no reason to yell at her. He must be in love; he had never lost his temper like that with any other woman. When he came back in, he saw Elanna climbing the stairs. Taking long strides to the staircase, he bounded up the steps until he reached her. He grabbed her arm, and spun her around.

"Elanna, I am sorry. Please forgive me, I am an utter fool."

She hesitated, then fell into his arms and broke out into sobs. He held her, feeling worse every passing second for making her cry. Could he do nothing right?"

"I promise ne'er to be angry with you again. Please stop crying, Elanna."

The sobs softened into sniffles, and soon she bravely smiled up at him. "You do not understand, Luke…all my life I have been taught that my life was worthless, and I should be willing to forfeit it for the life of another."

"Your life is more precious than any other I know. You are loved now, Elanna, ne'er forget that."

"I shall try."

Although she stood one step higher, her head still was not even with his. He had to lean down to give her forehead a little kiss, and then took her hand.

"'Tis almost time for dinner. Let us go back and join Matt and Pet."

Upon hearing their names, Matthew and Pet—who were standing in the doorway watching this tender scene—quickly went back into the lessor hall to sit down and pretend they knew nothing. When the two lovers entered, they looked up casually, hiding smiles behind stone faces.

"Have you two decided to join us for dinner?" Matthew asked.

"Aye, I am starved, and I assume Elanna is also after her exciting day."

Elanna nodded in agreement.

Suddenly the room exploded with children. Two weary servant girls followed close behind the ecstatic, yelling mob, as they all tried to get Pet and Matthew's attention at once. Pet rounded them up and got them settled at a low table, then came back to the lord's table to join the others.

"Whew! I wish I had half their energy."

"You do, my dear, and then some." Matthew gave her a light kiss on the cheek, and whispered something in her ear.

Elanna felt her face turn red again, and turned to Luke, her eyes wide in wonder. "Is that all that man thinks of?"

Luke just chuckled.

Dinner was pleasant, with no more outbursts or excessive show of emotions. Pet observed Elanna carefully, noticing how she was slowly beginning to adapt to a normal setting; not once did she tell Matthew or Luke their thoughts. She had been so brave that day, saving the lives of the mother and child. The women had bonded in friendship delivering the baby, and Pet was glad to have a woman friend with which to share. She had no way of knowing how grateful Elanna was to have a friend at all.

As Matthew and Pet lay in bed that night, he cuddled up and began enticing her by nibbling on her neck. She bore this disreputable behavior for a while, and then forced herself to pull away and give him a serious look.

"Matthew, we need to talk."

He groaned and flopped on his back, visions of lovemaking fleeing his mind. "What did I do now?"

"Nothing, actually, 'tis what you did *not* do."

He rolled over to face her and leaned up on one elbow. "What have I not done?"

"You have not forgiven thyself."

He instantly knew what she meant, and his face sobered into a solemn gaze. "I cannot, Pet. I shall ne'er be able to erase the hurt I caused you."

She brought a hand up and touched his cheek; he closed his eyes at her touch. "Matthew, I love you, and I have forgiven you totally. 'Twas not all your fault, I caused us both pain by ordering you away. We both share blame."

He pulled her to him, embracing her as if she might disappear any second. "I was such a fool."

"We both were. Now, 'tis time to forgive each other, and ourselves."

He pulled away and faced her. "Very well, 'tis done. We shall ne'er mention it again. Now come hither, wife." His eyes sparkled playfully. "Because of our stupidity, we are still making up for lost time."

Pet sighed, and brought her hands up to his chest, running them over the firm muscles, relishing in his manliness. "Aye, I know."

He brought his lips down on hers, and they became lost in consuming passion.

Chapter Seven

That night the temperature plunged, and everyone awoke to a fresh blanket of snow. Luke insisted that Elanna spend the day with him. He felt he had to make up for his outburst the day before; he could barely sleep that night for dwelling on it. What a fool he had been, yelling at Elanna as if she had committed a crime. It was important to him that she felt he was not always an ill-tempered idiot.

The children, of course, were anxious to play in the snow, and jumped about excitingly during breakfast. It took all of Pet and Matthew's patience to control them through the meal. As the servants rushed the wild bunch off to get dressed for playtime in the snow, Luke noticed Elanna peering longingly out a window. He wondered if she, too, would like to 'play', and before he could ask her face lit up and she nodded enthusiastically.

"Oh, aye!" she gushed. "I have ne'er played in snow, although I have always wanted to. The nuns considered playing a sin."

Luke shook his head. Her child-like lust for life was refreshing, and it broke his heart to know her life until now had been so dreadful. "Then I shall take you." He gazed on her flimsy white dress, knowing she would freeze in the snow, even with the red cape.

This time Pet seemed to read his mind. "Well, she cannot go out in those clothes," she chimed in. "She can use the riding clothes she wore yesterday, but I need to find her a warm jacket and some boots. Also, some gloves." Her face fell into contemplation. "Hmmm. Let me think."

While Pet thought, Elanna continued. "I have always wondered what 'twould feel like to run in the snow and dive right into it, and how the cold would feel against my face. Or to make a giant snow castle and kick it—for no reason—just kick it!"

"My brothers and I used to make a snow castle, complete with a moat. We would spend hours making at least a hundred snowballs. Then we would sit in the center and plaster anyone who ventured close." Luke chuckled from the memory. "We made father so angry he threatened to tan our bottoms. Instead, he started throwing snowballs back at us. That was the most fun we had in weeks."

"I remember that," Matthew added. "I also seem to remember Paul and I catching you unaware once. You destroyed the whole snow castle getting back at us. Most unfair."

"Well, you ne'er ambushed me again!"

"Nay, we did not. You outweighed both of us, you big ox."

"I could not help it if you two stopped growing—especially Paul."

"True, but what he lacks in size he makes up for in his analytical skills." Matthew chortled. "Remember when he was determined to solve our mysterious thefts?"

"Ah, the disappearing items! Small things, but most annoying. Mother was sure we had a spirit whisking things away from right under our noses, from locked rooms even. Paul was the only one who figured it out."

"Aye," Matthew agreed. "'Tis all he thought about. Of course, if I had really wanted to, I could have solved it." He sniffed in false indignity.

Luke grunted, his eyes lit with amusement. "Oh, certainly you could. Actually, I wish you had; he was most self-satisfied when he announced that a rat was taking things and storing them in his burrow."

"A pack rat, he called it."

"He even built a little cage and caught the blasted thing!"

"He was so smug, we could not live with him for a week."

"Ha! Those were good times."

Matthew lost his smile as he nodded. "Aye, they were." He paused morosely, and then added, "I wonder where he is right now."

"On a ship, having the time of his life. You know how much he always wanted to sail. He has probably already forgotten he is angry, and is off solving another mystery. When he returns home, everything shall be fine."

"I pray you are right."

A short pause followed until Pet blurted, "I have it!"

All eyes turned to look at her.

"You have what?" Matthew asked with a puzzled face.

"The solution to Elanna's clothing problem. Some of my old clothes are stored in a trunk upstairs. I believe there is a coat she can wear. Come on, Elanna. Let us go see." She hurried for the door with Elanna, who hopped almost as excitingly as one of the children behind her.

With the women gone, the brothers could talk with more candor. "She is very special, that lady knight of yours," Luke said. "Can you blame Paul for loving her?"

"Nay, damn it, that is what makes this so hard. He was taken with her the first time he met her, as I was. How can I fault him for that?"

"You cannot. He is young and impulsive; he will get over her."

Matthew lowered his gaze to the floor. "Perhaps, if he ever comes back."

"Father is convinced a year at sea will do a lot for him, including make him homesick. He will return, do not worry." Luke put a consoling hand on his brother's shoulder. "He is your brother—he shall forgive you."

"That is easy for you to say. You are not the one he hates."

Upstairs in a storage room the women rummaged through a huge trunk. Pet pulled out clothes she had long ago forgotten. "Look at this," she exclaimed as she held up a red tunic. "I wore this when I was ten.

Oh, and this! This was the first outfit Robert and I had made when we began our training." Her smile faded. "That seems so long ago."

"Robert—he was your brother?" Elanna asked.

"Aye."

"I am able to detect great sadness. Your emotion for him is very strong."

Pet nodded. "He was my twin." She put the outfit back, and quickly changed the subject. "Here—this is the coat. See if it fits."

Elanna accepted the coat and tried it on. As she laced the fasteners, she didn't need her cognizant abilities to sense Pet's mood. "Tell me about him," she asked innocently.

"Robert?" Pet shrugged. "There is not much to tell."

"That cannot be true."

Pet hesitated. "Elanna…" she began.

"Please, Pet. I sense your pain, but I do not know why. Please tell me."

"All right." She bit her lower lip as she paused, holding back tears she had denied herself for so long. One slipped through, and made its way down her cheek. "Robert was my life. We were ne'er apart, not one day." She closed her eyes as memories surfaced. "He was always there for me, helping through all my insecurities, and made me strong. He even made me face my worst fear."

"Fear? You? That is hard to believe."

The corners of her mouth turned up ever so slightly. "Believe me, I have one fear, and no one knows about it—not even Matthew."

"Oh, a secret! Tell me, please! It will be a pact between us, like sisters."

Pet cleared her throat, trying to hold back her disgust for herself. "'Tis rather foolish, really. I am afraid of heights."

Elanna's face fell in disappointment. "That is it? You fear high places? But that is a common fear. I also am afraid of heights."

Pet shook her head. "Nay, I mean I *really* fear high places. My head gets all dizzy and I cannot breathe. Robert made me climb a big tree, then he climbed up with me. We sat in it all afternoon. I cried and blubbered like a big baby, but he made me stay. We were still quite young, but he taught me to face my fears. Even so, to this day, I hate that tree. I prefer to avoid situations that will require me to go up high."

"That is most likely wise. What happened to him?"

"He was killed in a renegade attack. He died in my arms." She paused while she gathered her composure. Unbeknownst to her, the raw emotion was allowing Elanna a small insight into Pet's mind. The grief was overwhelming. For the first time Elanna understood the amazing control Pet kept over her emotions.

"Soon after that I met Matthew. He was insufferable, overbearing…"

"And you fell in love with him."

Pet smiled and let out a short chortle. "Aye, I did. He gave me no choice."

"As did Luke to me. It must be a Cameron trait."

Pet laughed out loud at that. "Aye, it must. Well, the coat fits…now let us find you some gloves, and soon you will be playing in the snow."

As Elanna stepped outside, bundled up, booted and gloved, the glaring sun reflecting off the snow temporarily blinded her. She put a hand over her eyes and squinted. "'Tis so bright!" she cried out to Luke. "How does one get used to it?"

Luke, who had been outside for several minutes before her, picked up a handful of snow and formed it into a ball. "By running from an attack!" He held up the snowball and smiled widely.

"Augh!" She quickly began running in the other direction. The snowball hit her in the middle of the back with a thump, and she began laughing. "Now 'tis your turn!" She scooped up some snow and began forming a ball.

He beat her to it. She dodged this throw, and tossed her ball. It missed by a considerable distance.

"You are going to have to do better than that," he chortled. She shrieked as he began running toward her, a snowball raised high in his hand. This play-fighting continued for several minutes as the children began emerging from the house one by one, all bundled up, the smaller ones barely able to move for all the clothes they wore. Pet was taking no chances on winter sniffs and sneezes. The girls all joined Elanna in her conquest against Luke. The boys, of course, sided together against the girls, who outnumbered them. William was commandeered from the stable to help balance the male forces. Snowballs flew everywhere; no one escaped getting hit at least once.

Pet and Matthew watched safely from the doorway, not wanting to intervene on anyone's fun. Pet winced every time one of the children got hit; Matthew just laughed and encouraged harder throws. Soon the girls tired of the boys' superior throwing abilities, and grabbed Elanna to find some undisturbed snow to make snow angels. The four boys ran off together, chattering about forts and burrows.

Luke followed Elanna and the girls. Julie, who seemed to have taken a particular liking to Elanna, motioned to a nice area of flat ground.

"Here, Elanna! Watch me make a snow angel!"

"All right, I am watching."

Julie flopped on the ground and began moving her arms and legs up and down, back and forth. Finally satisfied her angel was complete, she carefully got up and stood back, admiring her snow art.

"Wonderful!" Elanna exclaimed.

"Watch me, watch me!" the other girls burst in unison. Each one took to the ground to prove she could make the best angel.

"Mine is best," Constance insisted.

"Nay, Mine is!" Rosie countered.

"Is not!"

"Is too!"

Elanna put up her hands to stop the arguing. "They are all pretty!"

"Now 'tis your turn," Luke said with a smile. "You are bound to make the prettiest angel of all."

"Aye," Anna agreed. "Over here, Elanna! This is a good spot!"

The cheering group grabbed Elanna's hands and pulled her to the spot Anna was pointing at. They laughed and giggled when she lay down and began to move her arms and legs.

"This is fun," Elanna said with a large smile.

"Make the wings bigger," Cassandra suggested.

"I get to make one next to hers!"

"Nay, I do!"

"Do not!"

"Do too!"

Luke happily watched Elanna engage in the child's game, thinking to himself that he would deny her nothing. A childhood so bleak to have never even made a snow angel was hard for him to fathom. He suddenly realized she had stopped moving, but continued to lie there in the snow, staring straight up at the sky. Her face had gone blank. The children noticed it, too, and stopped laughing and arguing.

Luke dropped to his knees and looked in Elanna's eyes. She stared right through him; indeed, he doubted if she even saw him. He gave her a little shake.

"Elanna! Are you all right?"

She instantly sat up in one swift movement and looked at him. "Something is wrong," she said in a soft, yet firm voice.

"Wrong? What do you mean?"

"We must find him—quickly." She rose to her feet, with Luke and the children looking on with alarm.

"Who? What?" Luke followed her as she walked across the courtyard. The girls followed behind him, knowing only that the mood had been broken and they were no longer having fun.

This scene didn't go unnoticed by Pet and Matthew. They abandoned their roles of passive by-standers and came to walk beside Luke.

"What is happening?" Pet asked, more with alarm than curiosity.

Luke shrugged. "I am not sure. One minute she was smiling and happy, then the next minute she is saying something is wrong."

Elanna stopped and closed her eyes. "He is very cold."

Matthew, not dressed for the outdoors, hugged himself and rubbed his arms. "Could she narrow that down a bit? Hell, I am cold. We all are!"

Pet jabbed him hard in the ribs, and he shut his mouth.

"Who, Elanna?" Pet asked. "Who is cold?"

"Cold and wet," Elanna answered, seemingly talking to herself. "He is not breathing—we must find him!" She took off running in the direction the boys had all gone just minutes before.

Pet brought a hand up to her mouth. "Oh my God, the boys!" She began running after Elanna and all the rest followed close behind, confused and becoming increasingly frightened.

Elanna swiftly ran across the north meadow, so fast the others couldn't keep up with her. Even Pet, who was undoubtedly the most athletic of them all, couldn't catch her. Elanna seemed to have taken on supernatural strength. Soon they all heard the screams and shouts of the boys, all gathered around a small lake looking helpless and scared. William was running across the meadow to get help when he met Elanna half way.

"Yon! Hurry!" Elanna ran past him, not stopping for even a second to ask who or where. He scurried to the following throng, who was several seconds behind her. Pet reached him first.

"What is it, William? What has happened?"

William, out of breath and crying, tried to relay the news through heaving gasps. "I am sorry, Pet! We were all sliding on the lake, and he went out too far! The ice broke, and he fell in! I tried to reach him, but I cannot swim."

Pet put her hands on the boy's shoulders and tried to calm him down. "Who, William?

"Georgie," he gasped.

Pet felt her heart sink to her feet. Georgie, who just had turned five, was the adventurous one. He seemed to fear nothing, which got him into the most trouble. "Show me," she ordered.

The rest had caught up and heard enough to know a grave situation was at hand. The girls began crying as they all continued to run toward the shouting boys.

When they all arrived, Elanna was already in the middle of the small, frozen lake. She had discarded her coat on the shore. Even though she easily outweighed any of the children, the lake accepted her weight as she walked carefully, haltingly. Pet started to bolt after her, but Matthew pulled her back. "Nay, Pet—your weight would only break the ice further."

"But I cannot just stand here and do nothing!"

Luke stepped a short distance out and they heard the ice crack beneath him. "You, too, Luke," Matthew barked. "We can be of no good if we all fall into the freezing water." He loudly ordered the children to stay away from the lake. He needn't have bothered; none were anxious to suffer Georgie's fate.

Luke watched as Elanna reached the small hole where Georgie had plunged. "I guess we all have to trust Elanna." He grimaced when she jumped without hesitation into the freezing water.

Everyone stood by helplessly as Elanna disappeared beneath the ice, surfaced, and went under again. The second time she came up holding a still little body. Pet closed her eyes and buried her head in Matthew's shoulder, hiding her face and the ravages of grief. He pulled her close as stinging tears attacked his eyes.

Only sobs from the children were heard as Elanna carefully carried the limp boy to the edge, where Luke was able to take him and lay him on the ground. The sight of Georgie lying white and lifeless produced a morbid silence, edged with disbelief and anguish. Elanna shivered uncontrollably. Luke drew her close to him and engulfed her with his massive size. Pet flew from Matthew's grasp and threw herself across the small boy's body.

"Oh, please, God, No! Do not take him!"

Matthew gently pried his grieving wife away and took her into his arms. No words came to mind to console her. A torturous memory stirred in Matthew's mind, to months before when the death of an orphaned baby girl had sent Pet into a numbing depression. He silently prayed to God to spare Pet this pain—not accepting that he hurt almost as badly—as he turned away from the tragic scene.

Then a strange thing happened. Elanna pulled away from Luke and knelt by the still boy. Luke was the only one who observed as she brought her lips down to the child, then in an unusual and curious move began to blow her own breath into the boy's mouth. Of course, Luke knew the effort was futile; once a body was dead only God could breathe life into it. At least that's what he thought until he heard the boy cough, sputter, and gasp as precious air was again drawn into his lungs.

"What the…?" He knelt by Elanna in disbelief. "This cannot be so!"

Pet and Matthew turned around, at first startled by Luke's voice, then their faces evolved into relieved joy. "He is alive!" Pet yelled, and jerked away from Matthew, who was staring with a gaping mouth.

"How can this be?" He joined Pet beside Georgie, who by now was sitting up and crying that he was cold. Matthew swept the boy into his arms, and quickly began carrying him back to the manor. The children all cheered in joyous delight and followed him, leaving only the freezing, dripping Elanna, Luke, and Pet.

Tears ran down Pet's cheeks as she took Elanna in her arms. "I do not know what you did, but thank you." She pulled away and ran after Matthew and her children.

Until this time Elanna had not spoken. Luke was lost for words. His emotions ran the gamut, a mixture of astonishment, skepticism and jubilance. As usual, he didn't have to voice his feelings.

"Nay, Luke—I did not raise him from the dead. Only our Lord and savior could do that."

"But—I watched you!"

"He was ne'er dead. He simply needed to began breathing again."

"But…"

He stopped when he happened to glance at her neck. In all the activity the necklace that she kept so carefully tucked in her dress had come loose. The emerald in the cross necklace was brighter, in fact glowing. Was it just the reflection of the bright snow?

She caught the look on his face and a hand rose to cover the cross. Her body began to shudder from the cold, and Luke once more felt like a great idiot. He instantly forgot about the necklace.

"Good heavens, let us go inside. You are freezing." He grabbed her coat and draped it around her, then in one swift movement picked her up and began trudging back across the meadow, taking long steps through the crunchy snow.

"Put me down, I can walk!" she protested.

"Sorry, I cannot hear you."

"What do you mean, you cannot hear me?"

"The cold must be affecting my ears."

"Luke! I am not a sack of potatoes!"

"Ummm, that sounds good—I must request potatoes tonight for supper."

"Luke!"

By the time he reached the courtyard, Pet had already ordered quilts brought out and draped around Elanna. Georgie was taken upstairs to get dry and warm. A flurry of activity kept everyone busy until the children were whisked off, assured that Georgie was all right. Pet grabbed Elanna and led her to privacy, where dry clothes were handed to her.

"These were Robert's," Pet said, "but right now we cannot be too choosy. Get dressed and come out to the fireplace."

When Elanna appeared, she presented a strange sight dressed in baggy black clothes. Pet, Matthew and Luke were waiting by the fireplace, each lost in private thoughts as they tried to interpret what they had just witnessed. Luke immediately put his arm around her and drew her close.

"Are you all right?"

She nodded. "Aye, I am fine. How is the boy?"

"He is fine, thanks to you."

Matthew, as usual the one willing to voice what everyone else was thinking, paced in front of the fireplace as he nervously raked his hand through his hair. "Excuse me! Am I the only one who thinks this is a little bizarre?"

Pet gave him a disapproving look. "Matthew!"

He brushed her off. "I am sorry, but what I saw could not be possible!"

"Perhaps," Luke said in a calmer tone, "we did not see what we thought we saw."

"I know what I saw!" Matthew yelled.

"Please, can we all calm down!" Pet insisted, giving her excited husband an even stronger look.

"He is right," Elanna interjected. "You all have questions that need to be addressed."

Luke gazed lovingly into her face, not willing to believe anything supernatural had taken place. "Can you tell us what happened out there, Elanna?"

Her face took on a sad resignation. "You are all frightened, and I suppose rightfully so. But I assure you, I did nothing that any of you could not have done."

"Elanna," Luke started, "I doubt if any of us could breathe life into a child."

"But you do not understand! I sensed he was still alive, but just not breathing." Her voice lowered to almost a whisper. "A doctor from France visited our hospital ward often. He had developed many controversial techniques, some he would not even talk about for fear of being branded a heretic. He confided in me, as he accidentally learned of my strange affliction and felt a kinship. I watched him breathe life into a drowned woman as you saw me do. His theory was that life sometimes did not end when a person stopped breathing. He felt if it had only been a short time, you could help the person begin breathing again. He taught me the technique."

"That is ridiculous," Matthew spewed.

"Perhaps not," Luke said. "Father told me about a man who believes the world is round. He even got the queen of Spain to finance a fleet to sail around the world."

"A round world?" Pet snickered. "Like a ball? Now, that is bizarre."

"Maybe not," Luke replied. "Are we so conceited that we think we know everything? There are some who believe that the sun is the center of the universe, and that the planets revolve around it."

Matthew snorted. "Well, that is crazy—everyone knows the heavenly bodies move around earth."

"Do we really know?" Luke reasoned. "Is any of that as strange as Elanna helping someone to breathe?"

Matthew paused, his expression changing from indignation to confusion. "Well, I suppose not. But, that does not explain why the ice did not break beneath Elanna. Reason that away, brother."

Luke fell silent. "I—I cannot." He turned to Elanna with a desperate look. "Elanna?"

She appeared as lost as Luke. "I do not know. I guess I simply willed it not to break."

"*Willed* it?" Matthew's voice rose again. "Now she controls the elements?"

Elanna quickly shook her head. "Nay—I meant, I *hoped* 'twould not break! I was very careful, and stepped in the right places. I just got lucky."

That answer seemed to placate Matthew, and Luke took the opportunity to get Elanna away from the interrogation.

"I believe Elanna needs to rest. Would you mind if I helped her to her room?"

Pet and Matthew both expressed agreement, and Luke took Elanna's hand. Together they walked up the stairs, silently, hand in hand. Once inside her room, Luke felt he could speak, knowing she would tell him what she feared to tell his agitated brother.

"All right, Elanna, tell me the truth. Tell me everything."

Elanna sat on the edge of her bed, lowered her head, and pursed her lips.

"Please, Elanna—I want to understand you."

"That is impossible; I do not even understand myself."

"Elanna, how *did* you walk on the lake without breaking the ice?"

She raised her head and looked at him with sad, tormented eyes. "I meant it when I said I must have willed the ice not to break. It happens sometimes."

"What does?"

"I seem to be able to stop things from happening, or to make things happen, depending on the situation. I cannot control it; it just happens. I remember thinking the ice could not break if I were to save the boy."

He sat down beside her and became quiet. "'Tis no wonder your uncle fears you so. Your abilities are remarkable—and a bit frightening."

"Please Luke, do not fear me also."

He gave her an incredulous look. "I do not fear you. You must know this to be true." He squeezed her hand in a playful manner. "You rest. Do not worry about the others; they shall calm down. Matthew is just a bit hot-headed, that is all."

"He is frightened of me, like all the rest."

"Nay, Matthew is different. Trust me, I know my brother."

"Do you? The doctor I spoke of, would you like to know what happened to him? He saved a child, much like I just did, and for his reward he was declared a heretic. He was whipped and sent back to France—with his right hand cut off."

Luke sucked in a deep breath, and took both of her hands in his. "I swear, Elanna, on everything that is holy, I will die before anything happens to you. So would Matthew and Pet. You must learn to trust someone."

"I trust you."

His heart swelled to twice its size. "That is good to hear. Now, you sleep."

"All right." She lay down and he gave her a tender kiss on the forehead. As he turned to leave, she called out.

"Luke? Do not tell Matthew and Pet the truth about the lake. Promise?"

Luke nodded. "All right, I promise."

She gave him a grateful smile, and closed her eyes.

During the few hours she slept, Luke had a chance to convince Pet and Matthew that they had nothing to fear from her. As promised, he didn't divulge Elanna's full abilities. By the time she awoke in the afternoon, they all had agreed to put the incident behind them. The rest of the day was spent indoors, talking, laughing, and simply enjoying each other's company.

Chapter Eight

Elanna's screams woke up the entire second floor. Luke was the first to reach her room; he burst the door open wearing only a nightshirt to find her standing in the middle of the room in a trance-like state. A single candle burned in the corner, casting a distorted eerie shadow against the wall. Her nightgown flowed over her small body and spilled onto the floor, making her a footless entity in the dim setting.

"Elanna! What is wrong?" He took her tightly into his arms, but she remained still, almost lifeless, as if she were not aware of her surroundings."

He drew back to look at her expressionless face. "Elanna! Wake up!" Just as he gave her a little shake, Pet and Matthew arrived at the door. They had both thrown on tunics. Pet reached them first.

"Is she all right, Luke?" Her voice was almost frantic, something not often heard from Pet.

"I am unsure. I do not think she knows I am here."

"Is she asleep and standing at the same time?" Matthew asked.

Pet wrinkled her nose in question. "I do not think that is possible...although we *are* talking about Elanna. She might be capable of that."

Luke nodded in agreement. "I agree—I think she is capable of anything." He turned back to Elanna, and gave her another gentle shake. "Elanna! 'Tis me, Luke. Wake up!"

Elanna blinked slowly, then focused on Luke's concerned face. When she opened her mouth to speak, only two words came out.

"The window."

Everyone took a glance at the window, which was shuttered closed at the moment, then back at Elanna. She remained still, not acknowledging anyone's presence.

"Elanna! Talk to me!" Luke became desperate, and shook her harder. This time she responded, and her eyes blinked several times as she recognized the people gathered around her.

"W—what is wrong? Why are you all here?" She was confused and frightened.

Luke laughed with relief, while Pet and Matthew let out large sighs. "That is our question," Luke answered. "Do you know you screamed?"

"Screamed? Nay…I remember nothing except…" Her gaze fell to the window, and she slowly moved toward it, taking hesitant steps as she reached out her hand to touch it. She traced its entire outline, then turned back to the three concerned people looking at her in mild alarm.

"The window…it disappeared."

The three cast blank looks at each other, then back at her. Luke put a protective arm around her.

"Elanna, I am older than you, and feel I can speak with some authority in this matter. Windows do not disappear."

"Nay, I do not mean disappear, as in magic…in my dream, I could not get out, and the window was there, and then gone. Oh, I know it sounds foolish."

Luke gave her a reassuring hug. "At least you have come to grips that the child in your dream is you."

Matthew folded his arms and frowned, not believing they had thought her in dire trouble. "You mean to say, this is all about a *dream*?" Pet elbowed him, effectively telling him to hush.

Elanna seemed not to hear, instead concentrating on Luke's comment. "What do you mean, the child is me?"

"You said, 'I could not get out,' indicating the child was you. The prioress was correct, you are having a repressed memory surface and revealing itself in a dream."

Elanna could not answer; large tears ran down her cheeks as she withdrew from her painful reality.

Pet finally decided to add her comments, having had just stood there feeling rather helpless up to this point. "I do not think Elanna should be alone tonight. I shall stay with her."

Matthew's face fell.

Luke bravely volunteered to save from separating the newlyweds. "I quite agree she should not be alone, and I shall stay with her." He caught Pet's hesitating glance. "Do not worry, Pet. I have no intentions of disgracing my lady's virtue."

Pet and Matthew left after being assured that everything was under control.

Once alone, Luke pointed to the bed and motioned Elanna over to it.

She hesitated. "Luke, there is more. I fear you will think me crazy."

"I doubt that. You already think you are a witch and that windows disappear. I do not think you are crazy yet."

That produced a small, brave smile. "Very well. I keep having images of an angel. A red angel."

He raised one eyebrow, but otherwise remained expressionless. "A red angel."

"It wraps its wings around me and flies me to the ground."

"Uh-huh."

"I told you that you would think I was crazy."

"I think you are mistaking something else for what you think you saw."

"But I remember the coolness as it wrapped its wings around me. The memory is very vivid."

"I think you are suffering from lack of sleep. Get in bed, Elanna. I shall lie with you until you are asleep."

Her eyes widened, a panicked look engulfing her petite features. "Nay, do not leave me Luke…ever."

"Ever?" He slowly smiled as the implication of her words sank into his sleepy brain. "Does that mean you will marry me?"

She took a deep breath, closed her eyes, and nodded.

"Oh, Elanna! You shall not be sorry!" He took her into his arms and held her, with joy springing through his heart.

"Nay, but you shall." Sadness and regret clouded her voice.

"Never—I loved you the moment I first laid eyes on you. Now lay down." He helped her into the bed and tucked her in, then lay on top of the covers, putting an arm around her. She snuggled into him, drinking in his closeness, feeling his warmth.

"Luke…we cannot have children." Her voice was soft and filled with remorse.

He wasn't going to let anything destroy his mood of ecstasy, and simply kissed her on the nose. "We shall discuss that later, right now we need to sleep."

"Shall you not get cold on top of the covers?"

"Trust me, you are safer with me up here. Now shush, and close your eyes."

"I love you, Luke."

His heart overflowed with love and joy. "I love you, my little lady seer." In seconds she was asleep.

He lay awake for several minutes as he watched her. A red angel. Preposterous.

The rest of the night went without incident. Elanna slept soundly in his arms, and even though he did get slightly cold, the warmth in his heart overcame the chill of his body. In the morning he quietly left her, and went back to his own room to dress.

Elanna awoke moments later with a strong feeling of foreboding. She searched her mind for a vision to substantiate her uneasiness, but found none. Fear crept up her spine, ending in a violent shudder on her shoulders. She was suddenly clear on what to do.

Downstairs Pet and Matthew were already eating when Luke walked in, a spring in his step and a gleam in his eyes.

Matthew winked at Pet, and grinned at his brother. "Henceforth, is there a reason for your unusual benevolent mood this morning, Luke?"

Luke took a seat, and poured himself some tea. "You might say that. My little seer has agreed to accept my hand."

"Well, finally," Pet said, a hint of sarcasm in her tone.

Matthew slapped his brother on the back with a sudden bark of laughter. "I always knew you would be joining me in wedded bliss! When is the date set?"

"Ah…we ne'er quite got around to discussing that, but anon."

Pet sipped her tea and gave a knowing smile. She would never tell the men the deal she had made with Elanna.

"We should send notice of our betrothal immediately to Henry. I have a feeling we shall need help with the uncle. I do not trust him."

"Nor I," Matthew agreed. "I shall send the messenger today."

Just then a large shadow was cast over the table, effectively blocking whatever sunlight shone through the polished horn windows. Without looking up, Pet motioned the perpetrator to a seat.

"Raymond, you block the light. I shall not be able to see what I am eating."

The giant man she spoke to let out a hearty chuckle, and sat beside Luke, who greeted him enthusiastically.

"Hence, where have you been hiding thyself, Raymond?"

"I have been searching for men to replace the ones we lost." The huge, red-bearded manor steward and Pet's mentor had become close friends with Luke months before, when Luke had helped rebuild the town after the terrible raid.

"And were you successful?" Pet asked.

"Aye, that I was. Came across two right on the road that needed jobs, and I hired them on the spot. They are in the courtyard now, waiting thy approval."

Pet stood up and looked down at Matthew. "Shall you accompany me?"

He shook his head. "Nay, I said I would not interrupt in the running of your manor, and I meant it. Besides, I trust your judgment...after all, you did marry me."

She cast him a mocking, cold glare, and he burst out laughing. She left as the men chortled over his little joke.

The two men, one tall, one medium height, stood nervously in the courtyard, their eyes darting all around as they waited for the lady knight they had heard so much about. When Patrick ordered them to come to Elton and seek jobs, they had no idea they would be working for a living legend. Word of Pet's heroics in London, where she saved the queen and was immediately knighted by Henry himself, had spread all over England, the tale growing more exaggerated the further north it got. The giant they met on the road brought them there, then told them they would be in the employ of the only lady knight in England. They were starting to have second thoughts.

"I hear she is huge, and outweighs most men," the shorter man offered.

"Aye, and ugly, too."

"Oh, very, with stringy hair and warts on her chin."

"I pity the poor soul that was forced to marry her."

"'Tis rumored she has been married five times, and killed all her husbands by slitting their throats while they slept."

The taller man looked aghast. "I had not heard that. Perhaps 'tis not too late to..."

"Quiet, someone comes."

They both watched as the figure approached, and gave a short sigh of relief.

"'Tis only a lad, it appears."

"Aye. I say we leave now, and tell Patrick they would not hire us."

"Silence, you idiot, he is coming right at us."

Pet walked up and looked the men over. One was no larger than her; the other was about the size of Matthew. She determined they would be trainable "Hello, I am Pet Cameron, Lady of this manor. My steward tells me you are looking for work?"

Both men's jaws dropped in astonishment at the realization that this lad was a woman, and not only that, *the* Lady Knight. The taller man swallowed openly, knowing this beautiful girl was as deadly as any five men, from what he'd heard.

"Er, ah, we—I mean, that is, I believe so, I think."

Pet frowned in confusion. "Does that mean aye?"

The shorter man found his tongue and offered a better answer. "We are fighting men in need of a manor to defend. Your steward told us you could use us, for fighting…or something."

Pet smiled inwardly at the obvious nervousness of the men. "Aye, we lost most of our defenders to the renegades."

The tall man smiled excitingly at the mention of the renegades. "You killed them all, did you not? All by thyself, one by one!"

Pet raised one eyebrow and smirked, having until that moment been unaware they knew who she was. "Not exactly. My husband helped, although he was not my husband yet. I fear the stories you hear are not all true."

The man's face fell with disappointment. "I suppose you have not been married five times, either."

That got a snicker. "I fear I would not have survived that many husbands; I am barely surviving this one. Come, I shall show you the servant quarters. You start training tomorrow."

As she turned her back, the short man drew his pointer finger across his neck in a cutthroat maneuver. The tall man elbowed him in the ribs, and with much trepidation they followed Pet to their lodgings.

When Pet returned to the manor, Matthew, Luke and Raymond were all in a rather jovial mood. Listening at the entrance for a while, she shook her head at the things men bragged about, and decided to leave them to their boasting. She rolled her eyes as they burst out in laughter at a joke Luke just told, and turned to head down the corridor to the kitchen. She saw Elanna descending the stairway at that moment.

Wearing the white gown she arrived in, her expression was somber, almost hopelessly so. Pet knew instantly something was terribly amiss, and waited at the bottom of the stairs until Elanna reached her. Elanna simply looked through her, blinking back tears as she focused on nothing.

"Elanna? What is wrong?"

The petite girl lowered her stare to the floor. "I must leave here, Pet. I cannot marry Luke."

Her eyes widening with apprehension, Pet took Elanna's hand and led her to the lessor hall, where the men still chortled and roared in camaraderie. Luke happened to look upward, and upon seeing Elanna his smile faded and he slowly stood.

"Elanna? What is wrong?"

Raymond saw the mood had suddenly changed, and not wanting to be involved in what appeared to be a lover's spat, quickly took his leave.

Matthew and Luke watched as Pet brought her in, Elanna's eyes cast downward in despondency.

Luke took her hands in his, and tried to catch her gaze. "Elanna? Are you all right?"

She slowly raised her head and stared at him. "I—I am sorry, Luke. I was wrong to say I would marry you." She pulled her hands away, feeling Luke's anguish.

"What? You have changed your mind overnight?"

"Please do not be angry. This is not easy for me to say. I must return to the convent."

Pet put a hand on Elanna's shoulder. "Did you have a vision?"

Elanna shook her head. "Nay."

"A dream, then?" Luke asked, fear creeping into his voice.

"Nay."

"Then why, Elanna? Last night you said..."

"Last night I was scared."

Pet noticed Elanna's trembling hands. "I would say you still are."

Elanna turned to Pet, her sad eyes beseeching her for understanding. "In a way, you are right. Last night I was scared for myself, a truly selfish emotion. Today I fear for you...all of you. I cannot explain it, 'tis just a feeling I woke up with that something terrible shall happen if I stay. I cannot be the cause of your destruction. I must leave, and ne'er come back." She turned to Luke, and upon seeing his stricken face quickly faced away as a single tear ran down her cheek. "I am sorry, Luke. I told you from the moment we met I could not marry. My destiny lies elsewhere."

"Nay."

The single word was spoken with such intensity that all eyes darted to Luke. Until that moment Matthew thought he knew his brother well, but the look Luke now displayed was like none he had ever seen—determined, resolute, uncompromising.

"I have already decided, Luke."

"I said, nay."

"But..."

"Elanna, I have ne'er loved a woman. You fell in my path, seemingly coming from nowhere, stole my heart, and I will be damned before I let you simply walk away."

"I did not mean for you to love me!" Her voice rose in desperation, and she backed away from him. "I cannot stay, if I do something is going to happen, something dreadful!" Before he could respond, her voice softened as she gazed tenderly at him. "I have ne'er loved before either, Luke. I could not bear it if I caused your death."

"I am not going to die, and neither are you. The only thing that is going to happen is you are going to marry me. Pet! Summon your priest! A wedding is about to take place."

Pet grinned, glad that Luke was not going to let Elanna slip from his grasp. "Come, Matthew…Father Samson must be notified." The pair took one last look at Luke, who was taking determined steps toward the still backing-away girl, and left to the chapel which was just next door outside the manor gates.

Elanna watched in wariness as Luke came closer to her. "Nay, Luke! Do not do this!"

"Shut up, Elanna!" He picked her up, threw her over his shoulder like a sack of flour and marched outside, with her kicking and shrieking. Everyone within earshot—every servant, groom, maid, and cook—came outside to watch. The two new men also saw the large man brandishing the squirming, protesting girl down the road and through the gates to the chapel."

The shorter one shook his head. "Dayen is not going to like this. We better send word."

Elanna couldn't believe this was happening to her. "Luke, put me down! I am not a wounded lamb you must carry!"

"Nay, you are a most reluctant bride." He entered the chapel to find Pet talking to Father Samson, who was smiling and nodding in agreement. A marriage for nobles was not performed every day.

Luke marched straight to the altar, and deposited Elanna at the priest's feet.

"Marry us! And make it fast!"

Matthew somehow contained his laughter; he never in his widest dreams imagined his calm, rational, joking, sensible brother in such a state.

The fat little priest instantly complied, and began rattling off the marriage ceremony. Luke shook his head impatiently. "Just get to the 'I do' part.

Father Samson nodded. "Have you the ring?"

All eyes turned to Luke, as he turned pale. "I—that is, 'twas all so fast, I forgot all about a ring."

Elanna was finally able to get a word in. "There, you see! Admit it, Luke—'twas not meant to be. Let us quit this nonsense, and…"

"Wait." They all looked at Pet. "Your pinkie ring, Luke. Use your pinkie ring." She gazed down at her finger; Matthew's childhood family crest ring was her wedding ring also. All the brothers had one, given to them by their mother when they were children, and replaced with larger ones once they reached adulthood. The childhood ring was demoted to the pinkie. She was finding this whole situation extremely entertaining.

Elanna blanched white. "Pet! You are supposed to be on my side!"

Pet shrugged. "I am."

Luke struggled with the ring, tugging and pulling to no avail. "The damned thing will not come off! I have not been able to get it off for years."

Father Samson puckered his face as he thought, then produced an inspired smile. "Perhaps some baptismal oil shall help?" He went behind the altar and came back with a small flask, then poured a few precious drops on Luke's finger.

Elanna was shocked. "Father! Baptismal oil on a finger?"

"'Tis for a good cause," the little priest rationalized. "Now, pull and pray!"

Luke pulled some more, and his face brightened. "I think it slipped!"

"Here, let me help," Matthew offered. Together the brothers pulled as the women looked on, Pet in amusement, Elanna in dismay.

"'Tis coming!" They tugged one more time, and the ring slipped off, throwing Luke off balance and causing him to fall backwards on the floor. He quickly got up and brushed himself off.

"All right, now we have a blasted ring! Let us get on with it!"

The jolly priest chuckled; never had he had so much fun at a wedding. "Put the ring on her finger, and I will ask the vow."

Luke turned to Elanna and forcefully grabbed her left hand, pushing the ring on her third finger. It was too big, but he figured he could get it sized later.

"Do you, Luke," began the priest.

"Aye, aye…I take her through sickness, crop failure, bad dreams, evil uncles, and whatever else life throws at us. Get on with it!"

The priest suppressed a giggle, and turned to Elanna. "Do you, Elanna,"

"She does, also! Now just pronounce us man and wife!"

"She has to say it."

Luke turned a stern gaze to Elanna, who was harboring emotions somewhere between fright and elation. The only empathy she sensed from Luke was confident expectation.

"Say 'I do', Elanna." His face was sober and grim.

Matthew and Pet held their breath as they watched Elanna purse her lips, her chin trembling in indecision.

"Elanna!" Luke's patience was wearing thin.

She looked down at the ring, then up at him. "Oh, Luke…are you sure?"

"I have ne'er been so sure of anything in my life! Now damn it, say 'I do.'"

"You curse at me to say my wedding vows?"

His voice fell lower, and his eyes softened. "I am sorry. Elanna, marry me, please. I love you, and I want to be with you for the rest of your life. Did you not once say you feel the same about me?"

She nodded. "You know I do."

"Aha! She said 'I do'! Pronounce us man and wife!"

Elanna turned pale. "But…"

"I now pronounce you man and wife let no man toss aside what God has joined you may now kiss the bride amen!" Father Samson got it out in one breath, and gave a satisfied smile.

Luke planted his mouth on the still sputtering bride, who somehow just managed to get married without her consent. She relaxed as the kiss deepened, and forgot her surroundings as he did his usual magic on her. When he finally yielded her lips, she was gasping for breath.

Pet and Matthew started clapping, and the two lovers suddenly remembered they were not alone. Luke harbored a sheepish grin as he turned to his brother.

"Well, 'tis done! A party is in order!"

Matthew grinned at his fellow bridegroom. "Two weddings within half a year! Mother is going to faint!"

Luke's face fell. "Oh, Lord…mother! She shall kill me, this makes two weddings she has missed!"

"We shall cross that bridge later, right now there is a celebration to hold!" Matthew motioned Pet over to him. "Invite all the townsfolk, and neighboring lords and…oh hell, invite everybody!"

Pet smiled, and nodded. "I shall order a grand feast. The townsfolk need something like this to lift their spirits after the raid." She left quickly to ready things at the manor.

Luke all of a sudden had a flash of guilt, and looked down at his bewildered little bride. "You did the right thing, Elanna. Now I shall get Ancaster back for you."

A look of unease furled her brow. "But at what price? How many shall have to die?"

"No one is going to die. I am sending an announcement to King Henry, and asking for a regiment of knights to come help us. Your uncle will not disobey a direct order from the king."

"You are wrong. Giles will do whatever it takes to keep Ancaster."

Father Samson, who had left temporarily to draw up the wedding certificate, interrupted them. "Well, here we go! You just have to sign it to make it official." He grinned at the couple, who were obviously in love, despite the abruptness of the ceremony.

A smile eased Elanna's look of trepidation. "Are you saying that our marriage is not completed until I sign this?"

"Elanna!" Luke swung her around, accompanied by a desperate widening of his eyes. "You have come too far to back out. We are married, and that is that!"

Her smile deepened. "All right, Luke…I shall sign it. I suppose I have no choice but to willingly accept my fate."

"Nay, you have no choice at all. You are my wife." The reality hit him suddenly that he was a married man, with a wedding night to look forward to. Elanna quickly sensed his thought.

"Luke, I meant it when I said we could not have children."

His face saddened at the idea of never totally fulfilling his love with her. "I cannot accept that. I am your husband, of course we shall have children."

"Nay! My affliction shall pass down to my offspring."

"The only 'affliction' you have is your stubbornness. I can live with everything else. Now, no more talk of this. A celebration awaits! Do I have to carry you back the same way you came?"

"You would not dare!"

"Oh, would I not?"

She read his thoughts, and quickly nodded. "All right, I shall walk."

"You shall do more than walk. You shall leave the chapel with a smile on your face, holding my hand with a look of bliss. Understand?"

"Aye, my husband. Are you always going to be so demanding?"

"I am just getting started with my demands." He smiled devilishly, and held out his hand. "If I know Pet, the streets outside are lined with well-wishers. We should not keep them waiting any longer."

Luke was right. As they exited the chapel, a throng of people began cheering, wishing the couple long lives and many children. Everyone followed them back to the manor, where music could already be heard playing in the great hall. Pet had sent out word for every man, woman and child to join the celebration, and by the looks of it, everyone was complying. People crowded the streets, the courtyard, and the hall, eagerly looking forward to a feast and party.

The celebration was soon in full force. Much ale was consumed, as well as three courses of cooked meats and fish, roasts of swan and peacocks, followed by numerous sweets and spicy dishes. At one point during the busy day, Matthew drew Luke aside, and showed him the announcement he was sending to the king.

"I have Raymond searching for a courier, one that is not drunk on ale, that is. I have hopes that someone has not imbibed profusely."

"Thank you, Matt. From now on, Elanna's life shall be nothing but bliss and happiness. I shall get Ancaster back, where we shall live out our remaining years."

Matthew nodded, and slapped his brother on the back. "You still have tonight to contend with. Let us hope your wedding night has a better ending than mine did."

Luke chuckled, having been told of Pet talking a chambermaid into taking her place without Matthew's knowledge. Matthew threw her out, and searched the rest of the night for his missing wife in a drunken rage.

"I do not think Elanna could do that. She needs me, Matthew. I just hope…"

"Lord Matthew?" They turned to Raymond, standing at the door with a much shorter man, which was a given for most anyone who stood beside him. "I have found a volunteer for the journey to London."

Matthew grinned widely, pleased that Raymond had completed his task so quickly. "Excellent! Come forth."

The man, whom Matthew had no way of knowing was one of the new men Pet had just hired that morning, stepped forward and gave a short, respectful bow.

"Thank you, milord, for trusting me with such an important venture. In my last post I delivered many messages for my lord, until his untimely death last year."

"Very good." Matthew handed him the letter, which he had sealed with wax, and gave instructions. "Tell a king's page you bring word from Sir Cameron and his Lady Knight. Henry shall see you immediately. Oh, there is extra coin for a speedy trip."

The man smiled and nodded. There would indeed be a fat purse in it for him—when he handed the message over to Giles Dayen.

Chapter Nine

As the celebration lasted well into the night, Matthew and Pet prepared the wedding suite. Pet ordered numerous pillows, fur-lined quilts, and fresh linen sheets, while Matthew took care of other niceties. He pulled the finest manor wine from the cellar, and brought two goblets to the room. When they were satisfied the huge four-poster bed was prepared properly, they slipped back downstairs to the party.

The attention and all the people overwhelmed Elanna. Her former life of solitude had not prepared her for such a cacophony of well-wishers. Luke, on the other hand, was having the time of his life, his shyness disappearing in direct proportion to the amount of ale he drank. Pet was finally able to draw him away, leaving Elanna with three giggling women extolling the virtues of the wedding night.

Pet motioned Luke into her study and shut the door, away from the loud din and merriment.

"Make this fast, Pet! My bride awaits!"

"I know." Her face grew serious. "Luke, right now I can empathize with Elanna's feelings. She is frightened, overwhelmed, even a bit angry."

Luke's mood instantly sobered. "How would you know that?"

"Because I was. In case you forgot, Matthew and I were also married rather abruptly."

"I did not forget, what do you think gave me the idea? It worked for him, did it not?"

She pursed her lips and glowered through him, causing his mind to clear rather quickly.

"What I mean to say is, look how happy you two are!" He smiled innocently, hoping he had made his way back into her good graces.

"Luke, I know you love Elanna, and I certainly feel she loves you, but all I am trying to say is." She stopped and frowned.

"What?"

She cleared her throat and licked her lips. "Ah, what I mean, is, Luke…tonight might be a little…er…"

"I get the meaning, you do not have to hit me on the head. She has already warned me that there can be no children between us, which would seem a wedding night is out of the question…or any night, for that matter." He sighed deeply. "I shall just have to talk her out of that notion."

"Well, I wanted you to know, if things do not go as anticipated, I have a separate bed ready for you…just in case."

"Thank you, I think."

Matthew popped his head in at that moment, and narrowed his eyes at the sight of his wife with his brother. "Here, flirting with my wife so soon after your wedding?"

Pet rolled her eyes. "Oh, for heavens sakes, I was just…"

"She was being the good little mother and lecturing me about my wedding night."

Matthew drew back and appeared dubious, then smiled crookedly. "You are jesting."

"I wouldn't call it *lecturing*, exactly," Pet reasoned.

Luke folded his arms, clearly in a huff. "Apparently your wife does not have a high opinion of my manly abilities."

Matthew let out a hearty chuckle, and put his arms around his wife. "Why do you not help Elanna? I feel she might need more help than my hulk of a brother. Besides, I can answer any questions he has."

Luke immediately became indignant. "I have no questions! She dragged me in here!"

By now Matthew was shaking with laughter so much his sides ached. "Oh, what a pair you two shall make, especially if Pet extols her wisdom to Elanna."

Pet drew herself up tall, and sniffed. "Well, I can certainly see my help is not needed. Perhaps I can assist Elanna in finding a willing chambermaid to take her place?"

Matthew stopped laughing. "Now, Pet!"

A devilish smile swept her face. "Excuse me…I have a bride to find." She turned on her heels and left.

Both men somberly watched her go.

"She was just trying to help, Matt. You did not have to be so rough on her."

"I tend to agree this time, brother. I have a feeling I might be sleeping with the horses tonight."

After leaving the room, Pet did indeed seek out Elanna, but not for the purpose she had told the men. Pet rightfully figured the bewildered girl needed to be taken away from the celebrating throng of villagers. When she finally had the blushing bride alone in a quiet room, Pet gave her a friendly hug, and Elanna returned the affection.

"This makes us sisters," Elanna bubbled. "I have ne'er had a sister!"

"Nor have I…Luke is a good man, I am so happy for you."

Elanna nodded. "He is more than I have ever hoped for, actually I ne'er thought it possible a man like him would want me."

A grim look crossed Pet's face. "About wanting you…do you know that Luke is feeling much apprehension about tonight?"

"I know. We have not had much time to talk."

Pet was not sure how to address the next subject, so decided a plain direct approach would have to suffice.

"Elanna, Luke very much wants to exercise his marriage rights."

The small girl looked surprised. "Of course he does…so do I."

Pet stopped cold, as a confused look engulfed her. "But…he said you told him there could be no children."

"That is true."

Now Pet was even more confused. "But if you…I mean, what if you, um…that is…"

Elanna suddenly realized what Pet was stammering about. "OH! You think…oh, nay! Pet, I am able to tell when my body shall conceive a child. We shall simply avoid those times. Tonight we are safe." She studied Pet's reaction with interest. "Do you mean to say all women cannot tell when they shall conceive?"

A feather could have knocked Pet over as she stared at Elanna's sincere expression. "I fear not. Does Luke know this?"

"Alas, nay. It was not a subject we spoke on. She lifted her hand to her head in alarm. "Does he think…?"

"I fear so. Tonight may come as a bit of a surprise."

Elanna giggled. "Perhaps I shall keep him thinking that."

Pet joined her with a snicker. "You have been around me too long."

They broke out in laughter, and left to join the party.

The celebrating died down, and it grew dark. People slept everywhere in the great hall, mostly where they passed out from the ale. The time finally came for Luke and Elanna to retire. He took her hand, and they walked up the staircase together, neither talking until they reached the door. He opened it, and they peered inside, observing the softly glowing candle, overstuffed bed, and multitudes of pillows. Luke was afraid to move, feeling much like a ten-year-old with his first crush.

"Would you like to be carried inside?"

"Nay, I shall walk, thank you. I have been carried quite enough for one day."

They stepped inside and Luke shut the door, and then nervously shifted his feet as he looked at Elanna. "Well, here we are."

She sat on the edge of the bed and tried to act natural, as if one got carried off and forced to marry every day. "Aye, here we are."

A long, uncomfortable silence filled the room. Both avoided eye contact as Luke remembered the other room Pet had offered him. She instantly stood up and looked frantic.

"Nay, I want you to stay."

"I did not say anything." He started counting backwards from one hundred in his mind.

"Stop counting!"

"Nay."

"Luke, do not close thyself to me."

He just stared at her and concentrated. *95, 94, 93, 92…*

"You are being difficult!"

91, 90, 89, 88…

"What are you trying to hide?"

He stopped counting. "I do not want you to know my passionate thoughts."

"I already know."

87, 86, 85, 84,

"I mean, 'tis our wedding night…"

83, 82, 81…

Luke, please stop!" She held out her hands to him, and he stepped forward to take them. She smiled as she looked at the boyishly handsome, powerful man she had just married, and could no longer keep him in agony. "'Tis all right, Luke. I also wish to consummate our marriage."

His palms turned sweaty and his heart felt like it just stopped beating. "But you said…"

"The act of consummation shall not conceive a child at this time."

Luke felt a tinge of disappointment, and at the same time extreme anticipation. "How do you know that?"

"I just know."

He nodded, not for the briefest second doubting her. "Hence, you are saying we, er, that is to say, we can…?"

She nodded.

"Very well." He was suddenly more nervous than he thought imaginable. This changed everything.

With that business over, she motioned to the bed and they sat on the edge together, side by side. Neither looked at each other nor spoke. Elanna finally broke the silence.

"I suppose we should undress."

"That would most likely help."

Neither moved a muscle. Luke finally cast her a sideways glance.

"You are not undressing."

"Nor are you."

He stood up quickly and began to pace. "This is ridiculous! Why are we so nervous? We were more comfortable with each other before we were married!"

"Perhaps if we did something to relax us—a game of chess, or cards?"

A look of incredulity spanned his face, changing to amusement.

"You want to play cards on our wedding night?"

She shrugged. "'Twas just a thought."

"A very bad one."

She jutted her lower lip out and frowned. "Fine."

"Besides, playing cards with you would be pointless. You would always know my hand."

"True."

"Then I suppose we are back to the matter of undressing."

"I suppose." Again neither moved.

"This is stupid! We have to do something!"

"You did not like my suggestions."

"Can you not come up with any other ideas?"

She stood up beside him. "'Tis all right…I shall start." She gingerly began unlacing her dress. Her hands shook with nervousness and she found the task difficult.

Luke noticed her dilemma. "Here, let me help." He began to loosen the laces, but in a few seconds frowned. "My hands are too large for such delicate work. Perhaps you should continue."

"Fine." She took over the chore while he began to unbutton his doublet. They both completed removing their one item of clothing at the same time. He was bare-chested; she still remained in underclothes.

She gazed upon his massive, wonderfully muscled chest and arms in awe; she had no idea his body was so magnificent. He looked as if he could conquer all of England single-handed. An unfelt-before longing drew her to his manliness. "You are so large," she uttered.

"And you are so small." He feared the act of lovemaking would hurt her.

She smiled. "Only compared to you. Do not worry, you shall not hurt me."

"If you do not cease invading my thoughts I shall begin counting again."

"NAY! I shall be good. Please, no counting."

"Very well, but speak my mind again and you shall suffer the longest counting spell in history."

"All right…I promise." With that matter taken care of, they again stared at each other in discomfort. "I suppose the rest of our clothes must come off?"

"I believe that might be necessary."

Her face suddenly brightened. "Perhaps if I blew out the candle?"

Luke shook his head. "I enjoy looking upon you. Unless…" His face grew serious. "Does looking at me frighten you?"

"Oh, nay." They stood in silence a while longer. "Luke, I truly need you to take the lead in this matter. I do not know what to do."

He swallowed in an attempt to find moisture in his dry mouth. "I am not that experienced myself."

"More so than I."

"True." He glanced at the bed that Pet had prepared for them, heaped with covers and pillows, and looking inviting. "Perhaps if we lay down?"

"Very well."

He went to one side, and she the other. They lay down carefully on their backs, each on their own side, not touching. Elanna turned and looked at him.

"Now what?"

He rolled to his side to face her. "'Twould help if we were closer."

She scooted over an inch.

"Nay, closer than that…oh, this is foolish! Come hither, Elanna!" He reached out and pulled her close to him. He gazed into her watery eyes and felt as if his whole body had turned to mush. "May I kiss you?"

She felt helpless being held in his massive arms. "Aye, I would like that."

He brought one hand behind her head, and the other cupped her chin. The mane of hair beckoned him, and he ran his fingers through it as he brought his mouth down to hers.

Suddenly she squealed. "Ow! You pulled my hair!"

"That is not hard to do; there is so much of it." He began to lift his hand from her head, and she yelped again. "Alas, I fear my ring is caught in your hair."

"Well, get it out!"

"I am trying!" The ring was hopelessly tangled, and to complicate matters he could not see very well in the dim light.

"Ow! Careful!"

"Sorry! Elanna, turn your head…nay, the other way…there, I think I can see it. Aha!"

He finally untangled the ring, and taking no more chances, took it off and placed it on the small nightstand beside the bed.

The humor of the situation was all at once too much for her, and she began snickering. "If we were any more clumsy we would fall over ourselves."

He chuckled, also. "I am sorry…I have ne'er been married before."

"Nor have I."

His eyes fell on the wine carafe and two large goblets sitting on the table in the corner. Good ol' Matthew; he thought of everything.

"Mayhap some wine would relax us?"

She sat up as he rose and poured two full goblets, then returned to the bed and handed her one. "Here, try this." As he brought his goblet to his lips, he glanced to see her gulping the wine down like water. He quickly grabbed her goblet, but it was too late—it was empty.

"Elanna! You are not supposed to guzzle it!"

She let out a little hiccup and giggled. "More?"

He gazed on her in consternation. "Elanna, are you accustomed to drinking—wine, I mean?"

"Of a surety! We had it during communion every Sabbath." She sat up tall and looked insulted.

"I am meaning more than a dip on a piece of bread. Have you drunk spirits before?"

Her eyes grew dreamy as she smiled crookedly. "Before what?"

"Elanna, I would like to complete our wedding night, but I would much prefer it if you were conscious while doing so. No more wine for you."

She frowned with disappointment. "You are no fun." Her eyes rolled a little and she touched a hand to her face. "Is it not overly warm in here? My lips feel fuzzy."

Luke stared at her in wonder, and then gulped down his own wine. A glassful would not make him tipsy; his little wife was another matter.

"Lay down, Elanna…I fear you are drunk."

"I am not! I am simply…relaxed."

"If you were any more relaxed, you would be dead. Now lay down."

"All right." She lay down and stretched her arms over her head, snuggling herself in the pillows. "Ummm, this feels good. Shall you join me, Luke?"

He frowned in uneasiness, and then slowly lay down, facing her. He couldn't believe she was actually his wife, even though he didn't give her much choice. Never once did he think that fortunes would smile so widely on him. She was so angelic, even when inebriated. He wanted to protect her; to keep her from any harm. Her uncle must first be dealt with, then they could lead a normal…whatever that was…life. As all these thoughts ran rampant through his mind, he suddenly realized he was allowing himself to think and she was showing no reaction whatsoever. He cocked his head in curiosity.

"Elanna? What am I thinking?"

She rolled to face him and blinked, trying to focus on him. "I know not…what *are* you thinking?" She let out another little hiccup.

He narrowed his eyebrows and stroked his chin as he gazed on her calm, smiling, highly seductive face. "You cannot tell?"

"Uh-uh."

For the first time since he had met her, he felt like a normal man. His thoughts were his own, and he didn't have to count to obtain this privilege.

"Come here, my little wife." He pulled her into him and brought his lips down on hers. She hungrily kissed him back. Lost in the passion, he rolled over on top of her, then instantly remembered his massive weight. He rolled over again to bring her on the top, the whole time engaged in the kiss. Elanna, liking the feeling of his weight on her, yanked him over back on top of her. Luke, caught off guard, again rolled off of her to bring her back on top. Unfortunately, he overestimated how much bed was left, and when bringing her over on top she lost her balance and found herself suspended in mid-air. She let out a squeal as she grasped Luke and the covers to prevent herself from falling. Luke, not braced for this turn of events, could not prevent them from crashing onto the floor, catching the nightstand along the way, which toppled over with a clatter that shook the walls. Luke's head hit the floor with a dull thud, and then he let out a choked cough when Elanna plopped on top of him. They stared at each other in surprise, then instantly started laughing.

A rap on the door interrupted them, and Pet's voice rang into the room. "Are you two all right?"

"Aye," Luke answered, still laughing. "We will try to be less noisy."

Matthew could be heard from down the hall yelling to Pet to leave them alone, and her footsteps were heard leaving the door.

Elanna scrambled to her feet and went straight to the wine carafe. "I need more wine," she said with a giggle.

"Elanna, nay!" By the time Luke got himself off the floor and to her side, she had gulped down another entire goblet full. He grabbed the goblet and led her back to the bed.

"Let us try that again." He motioned for her to lie down, and she plopped on the bed with a silly smile. As he lay down next to her, she stared at the ceiling with a changed expression.

"Is the ceiling supposed to move like that?"

Luke looked up at the perfectly still ceiling, and back down at her with a frown. "I fear you are a bit dizzy. You should not have drunk that wine."

"Oh posh, I feel fine." She closed her eyes and snuggled into him.

"Elanna," he began with a slight hesitation, "I have been thinking. I want our marriage to be wonderful. We have not had much of a chance to get to know each other. I did not mean to force you to marry me; I just could not let you go. Do you understand?"

She wiggled in his arms and murmured something incomprehensible.

"I have also been thinking," he continued, "perhaps it might be best if we did not—I mean, it might be better if we lived together, got to know each other before we actually…uh, well, you know what I am saying?"

"Ummm."

"Exactly. You need to discover more of life before you experience the marriage bed. Not that I do not want to make love to you—oh Lord, how I want to—but it must be the right time. We have all the time in the world, the rest of our lives. No one has to know. When we feel more comfortable with each other, then 'twill be your choice. Elanna, are you listening?"

Before his words were all spoken, she had fallen asleep in his arms. She was so still, so beautiful. The cross around her neck had fallen out, and he gingerly fingered it. The gem seemed perfectly normal. Just a stone. Could he have been mistaken the day she saved Georgie? With a smile, he brought his lips down to her forehead, and kissed her gently. "I love you, my little angel. Sleep well." Then he closed his eyes, drew her close, and slept also.

Chapter Ten

As would be expected, Luke and Elanna slept in rather late. Pet felt she terribly overslept, and left Matthew gently snoring as she went downstairs to rouse the multitudes of sleeping guests from the manor. Servants milled around, cleaning up dirty crockery, spilled food, and other assorted garbage left from the all-day party. Pet had managed a small dent in the mess when Matthew finally made his appearance, thankful that she had not sent him to the barn when he eventually came to bed and passed out. He harbored a headache and a sour stomach, not surprising for the amount of wine and food he had imbibed in. The great hall was too occupied for his liking, so he made his way over slumbering people to the lessor hall and plopped down in the nearest chair. Moments later Pet entered with two cups of tea, and handed one to him as she stared with her usual droll smile.

"You look terrible."

He looked up with bleary eyes. "I feel terrible. I woke up and you were gone."

"Sorry—I did not drink as much as you." She sat down and sipped her tea.

"That is not saying much—no one drank as much as me." He winced and put a hand to his head. "Except maybe Luke. Where is the happy groom?"

"Still sleeping, I would suppose."

"We shall have to send a message to mother immediately. After she gets over the shock of missing another wedding, she shall be ecstatic that Luke has married."

"Only one to go."

"Ah, aye, my fleeting baby brother, who hates the sight of me. I am surprised he was not the first to marry, considering his attitude toward women." He became quiet and lost in thought.

"He shall forgive you, Matthew. He does not know we are together."

"'Twould not matter. He feels I hurt you, and he is right."

"You said that subject was closed forever."

"I did, you are right." He tried to move, and flinched. "Augh, my head…why did you let me drink so much?"

"You are a grown man. You control your own actions."

"I am a married man. I need you to tell me when I am being stupid."

"If I did that, 'twould monopolize all my time."

"Thank you so much for your encouragement, wife."

"You are most welcome."

They smiled at each other; their playful banter not disguising the total love and devotion they held for one another.

As if on cue, Luke walked in, holding the hand of his lovely, radiant wife. Unlike Matthew, Luke looked wonderful and well rested. Of course, Matthew had no way of knowing that Luke spent his wedding night merely sleeping.

"Good morning, brother!" Luke boomed as he approached the couple. Matthew put a hand up and grimaced.

"Not so loudly."

"Oho! Harboring a headache, are we? Mayhap the ale has crept up on you?" The newlyweds sat down by Pet, Elanna in the middle, and smiled at Matthew's pained expression.

"It has not only crept up, it has stabbed me in the back. I am certainly glad a brother does not get married every day; I would not survive."

A servant appeared with a teapot and a tray of food and set it down in front of them. Matthew instantly reached for a piece of bread, and chewed profusely, hoping to calm his raging stomach.

Pet observed the quiet Elanna, who seemed content with just holding Luke's hand.

"And how is our little bride this morning?"

Elanna's smile deepened. "She is fine, thank you." Actually she remembered little after she drank the wine. She awoke in Luke's arms, and that was good enough for her.

Pet let it go at that. "Luke, 'twould appear that married life is agreeing with you."

"That is an understatement, little sister." He gave his bride's hand a gentle squeeze.

Matthew suddenly sprang to life. "Oh, I almost forgot!" They all watched as he rose from the table and made his way across the room. He picked up a large framed canvas in the corner, and brought it back, handing it to Luke.

"Here—a wedding present."

Luke turned the frame around to reveal a marvelous painting: a ship entering a harbor against a magnificent sunset. The ocean looked so real you could almost hear the water lapping against the shore, and the ship's sails straining as they billowed with the wind.

"This is beautiful, Matt! Where did you get it?"

"At a fair in London, during the time that Pet and I were estranged. A lad had a booth, and was selling them for his master. A king's aide even bought one, and Henry hung it in his solar."

"I shall treasure it forever. It shall look fine o'er a fireplace mantle at Ancaster."

As he talked, Elanna reached out and touched the painting, running her hand gingerly over the delicate brush strokes. No one paid her any mind as they carried on their conversation.

"They are simply known as The Blue Paintings, because the artist signs them 'W. Blue,' Matthew explained. "No one knows who he is, but he is becoming quite in demand among nobles."

Pet nodded in appreciation. "I can see why. This truly is fabulous, Matthew. Did you perhaps buy one for us, also?"

"Aye, my Pet. I bought several, and had them delivered at Cambridgeshire. When we left, I had them put on our carriage. I just have not had time to hang them yet."

Luke shook his head, smiling as he gazed at the painting. "I feel as if life could not get any better. Soon the king's men shall arrive, and Elanna and I shall claim Ancaster. I want to pinch myself to assure this is all real."

"I know how you feel, brother. I do not know how life could further smile on us. We are both married to beautiful women, who love us in return."

As Pet listened to the men extol their good fortunes, she couldn't help notice how quiet Elanna had become. The men seemed oblivious as Elanna blankly stared at the painting, her eyes seemingly looking past the picture into another realm.

Pet became mildly alarmed, and softly shook Elanna's shoulder. She displayed no response.

"Elanna?" Pet shook her again, with still no reaction. She raised her voice as she called her name again. The men finally stopped conversing when they noticed Pet's concern.

"What is wrong, Pet?" Luke asked.

"'Tis Elanna. She seems to be in some kind of trance."

Luke shook his wife, at first gently, then with added force. "Elanna?"

She stared with empty, unblinking eyes, into a space only she could envision.

"Oh, no," Luke practically whispered, "This is not good…she is having a vision."

"Are you sure?" Pet asked. "How do we make her quit?"

"I...I do not know." He hoped the others didn't notice the emerald glowing on her cross necklace. It was the brightest he had seen it so far.

Suddenly Elanna's eyes rolled upward and she slumped over, stopping only because of Luke's fast reflexes. He picked the limp girl up and gently placed her on the floor. Pet quickly ordered a pillow from a servant, and they all kneeled helplessly beside the unconscious girl.

"Luke," Pet pleaded. "She is your wife...what do we do?"

"I know not...I have only been married to her one day. I am hardly an expert."

"Well, we have to do something. We cannot just..."

"Quiet!" Matthew suddenly ordered. "She is waking!"

They watched anxiously as Elanna blinked, then looked up at the three concerned faces staring at her. She sat up slowly, as Luke kept his arm protectively around her, fearing she might collapse again.

"I am sorry. The painting...it almost seemed to draw me inside of it. I had a very strong vision."

"Can you tell us about it?" Pet asked.

"I do not think I want to." She appeared devastated, almost overcome with grief as she looked at Luke, then Matthew. "It concerns your brother, Paul."

Matthew froze in fear; Luke felt his hands start to shake.

"Paul?" they said in unison.

"Aye. Help me up, Luke, I fear I am weakened."

Luke practically jerked her to her feet, and Pet poured her a cup of tea after they all sat back down at the table. Elanna grasped the cup with trembling hands and gratefully sipped the hot, sweet tea, not realizing all eyes were on her waiting for further elaboration. Luke finally broke the apprehensive silence.

"Elanna, we are waiting." Again his voice was gruffer than he intended.

"Sorry." She took a few cleansing breaths. "The vision was most strong. Your brother's ship has foundered off the coast of France."

"What!" Matthew leapt to his feet, momentarily forgetting about his hangover. "That is impossible! Are you sure?"

Pet put a calming hand on her overwrought husband's shoulder. "Let her finish, Matthew. Sit." Her tone left no room to argue.

Luke had reacted to the news by burying his head in his hands.

"Is he…?"

"I sense he is alive," she answered to the unfinished question. "And, he is not alone." She turned her head to the painting. "Somehow this picture formed a link to him. I know not why. I have ne'er sensed someone this far away before."

"Perhaps," Pet suggested, "because Paul is on a ship, and this is a picture of a ship."

"Nay. There is something else…something strong." She closed her eyes and fell back with weakness; again Luke caught her.

"She needs to lie down, Luke. Take her to your room. Matthew and I shall wait hither for you."

Luke picked Elanna up and held her close. "Come, angel, you need to rest." Torn between his love for his wife and concern for his brother, he carried her from the room, his eyes stinging with tears.

As soon as they were out of earshot, Matthew exploded with his usual over-reactive temper. "I do not believe it! She cannot possibly tell what has happened hundreds of miles away!"

"Matthew, you are being emotional again. You need to calm down so we can think."

"I am not being emotional!"

She glared at him and he closed his mouth with a frown.

"That is better. I think you know that Elanna is correct. We have seen too much to start doubting her. Now, I believe we both know what must be done."

"Aye, and I am sorry, Pet."

She held out her arms to him and he fell into them, fighting back tears. "I have to go, Pet. He is my brother."

"I know." They held each other for a long while, neither having to speak their thoughts.

Luke came back into the room, avoiding their gaze as he slumped into a chair. "She is asleep. The vision has sapped her strength."

Matthew drew a deep breath. "Luke, we must…"

"I know, Matt. We have no choice."

The men's mood was so grim; Pet felt she had to make at least an attempt to shine a better light on the situation.

"Honestly, 'tis not as bad as you two make it. Elanna claims he is alive. 'Tis possible another ship picked him up."

Matthew showed a tinge of hope at her words. "Pet is right. By the time we get to Hunstanton, he could be waiting for us at the port."

"I hate to leave Elanna. We have only had one night together as man and wife. I feel I am abandoning her."

"We shall be fine," Pet insisted. "Your absence shall make us love you even more upon your return." She smiled bravely at Matthew, who knew her courageous words hid a doubtful spirit.

Luke stood up and cast them a somber look. "I will ready the horses. We should leave as soon as possible."

Matthew nodded as he continued staring at Pet. Lord, he hated leaving her. "I should help him. Would you pack us some food? There is no reason we should have to starve."

"Aye, go help Luke. I shall rouse the children so you can say good-bye."

"It seems circumstances keep forcing us apart. I am sorry, Pet."

"'Tis not your fault. I care about Paul, also. 'Tis only for a short while, the sooner you leave, the sooner you shall return."

"I love you, Pet."

"I know." He left to catch up with Luke.

Pet blinked back tears as she made her way to the children's rooms. Servants were already dressing them, so as Pet helped she explained that Matthew had to leave for about a month. They all took the news well, except Julie.

"He shall miss my birthday! He promised a special party."

Pet hugged the crying girl, stroking her fine, blond hair for comfort. "We shall just have to postpone the party until his return."

She left the servants with instructions to bring the children all down to the great hall as soon as possible. As she rounded the corner, she found Elanna standing at the top of the stairs, having apparently recovered from her vision. She stared back at Pet with sad, despondent eyes, and Pet knew immediately that Elanna had sensed the men were leaving.

"I am sorry, Elanna." It was all she could think to say.

Elanna just nodded. "The men feel much guilt at leaving us. We must make them feel more at ease. I shall try to put on a brave face." She fabricated a closed-mouthed, non-convincing smile that made Pet smile back, if only for the tremendous effort she was exhibiting.

"I agree. Are you feeling better?"

"Aye, thank you. I have ne'er had a vision quite like that. 'Twas most intense."

"Do not worry, Elanna, it shall be fine. The children will keep us busy. I can also give you more riding lessons, and perhaps we shall deliver some more babes."

Her attempt at humor made Elanna's forced smile develop into a more genuine one.

Outside, the tall man watched keenly as the lord of the manor and his brother saddled their horses. It did not appear this was just a short ride in the country; he overheard them say they would be gone at least a month. He was certain Giles would like to know this information. His comrade was almost guaranteed a fat reward upon delivering the intercepted letter to Giles. Maybe this latest bit of news would get him a reward, also.

When Luke and Matthew were done preparing the horses and stalling as long as possible, they went back inside to find their wives waiting. The children were all sitting patiently, with sad looks on their little faces. Matthew stopped in front of them, kneeled, and held out his hands. They all bombarded him at once, crying and whimpering.

Pet blinked back tears as Matthew hugged them all. "I shall be back anon, and will bring you all presents from the seashore. You must be brave for Pet; she will need your help."

Andrew sniffed and shook his head. "Pet is already brave. She does not need our help."

Julie tugged on Matthew's shirt. "You shall miss my birthday!"

"I know, Julie, and I am sorry. I shall be thinking of you all the time, and will bring you back something special."

"I do not want something special. I want you."

He gave her an extra squeeze, and fought the tears welling up most unmanly-like in the corners of his eyes. "I am so sorry, Julie."

The girl's eyes brightened and she suddenly drew back. "Oh! I almost forgot!" She bolted across the room and came back with a small box. "Here. I was saving it for a present, but I want you to have it now."

Choked with emotion, Matthew opened the box. Inside was a green felt hat, Robin Hood style, with a large red feather. He couldn't stop the single tear that streamed down his cheek.

"I heard you saying you wanted a hat like this. I bought it from a villager, and I found the feather myself. 'Tis a duck feather that I dipped in berry juice to make red."

He proudly put it on his head. It was too small, and threatened to instantly fall off. "I shall miss you all so much. Now I need to say goodbye to Pet." He rose to his feet and approached his wife, who had somehow kept her eyes dry during his farewells to the children. Now she was not so fortunate. Matthew pulled her to him, and held her as she cried softly against his shoulder.

"I am gladdened you have learned to cry, but now your tears bite through my heart."

She drew back and smiled bravely. "When you return I shall cry from happiness."

Luke had taken Elanna away to a quiet corner during all this, completely lost for words and not having to speak any, for Elanna reached inside his mind and grabbed his every thought.

"Elanna, I wish this did not have to happen. I…"

"I know, Luke. Just hold me, and tell me you love me."

He held her close, and let his tears flow. "You know I love you. But he is my brother, I have to go, you understand, do you not? Please do not hate me for leaving you."

"Luke, I am no more capable of hating you than I am of flying."

That produced a small smile. "Pet shall protect you. She is an able fighter with the skill of five men. Now, my little wife, promise me you shall not leave the manor without Pet."

"I promise."

"Good, that is one less thing I shall have to worry about." He drew back and looked deep into her eyes. "Elanna, yesterday you became my wife. I shall hold that close to my heart until my return."

"As shall I."

They embraced again, feeling each other's dread and pain.

The departure couldn't be delayed any longer. The sky was gray and cloudy, the air brisk with the threat of more snow. The men mounted their horses after tearful kisses and good-byes. Luke took one last longing gaze at his beautiful bride, and then turned to Pet.

"Take care of her Pet. I leave her in your care."

Matthew looked admiringly at Pet. "She could not be in better hands."

Pet almost blushed from all the compliments. "Do not worry, Luke, she shall be fine."

Matthew motioned to Pet, and when she drew close he leaned down in the saddle and gave her one last kiss. "I shall think of you with every breath I take." He sat back up, smiling down at the brave warrior he cherished beyond words.

She pursed her lips and stepped back, determined not to cry. "Farewell Matthew. Please hurry back, and bring good news."

"I shall. Come Luke, if we tarry longer it shall be midnight before we depart."

They kicked their horses and trotted down the courtyard through the manor gates. The children all waved and yelled various forms of good-byes, while Pet and Elanna stood in silence. When the men were out of sight, Pet turned to Elanna and attempted a carefree smile.

"Well, now that we are free of those messy, domineering men, what would you like to do?"

Elanna's tears turned to giggles. "Perhaps another riding lesson?"

No one noticed or questioned the tall man leaving the manor minutes later. No one saw him get off his horse down the road and pick up a green hat with a large red feather, blown off by a gust of wind.

Giles Dayen sat at his massive desk, reading the letter with great interest. "So, the little tramp has taken a husband who in turn is asking the king for help to reclaim Ancaster." He looked with unfeeling eyes to the man who rode two days straight to bring him the intercepted message.

"You did well. You shall receive extra coin for your efforts." He dismissed him with a wave, and the man bowed and left.

Giles turned his black glare up to Patrick, who was standing next to the desk, looking extremely concerned. "For God's sake, Patrick, sit down. You make me nervous hovering around like a falcon about to strike."

"What are you going to do?"

Giles put a hand up in exasperation and pointed to a chair. "Would you *sit*?"

Patrick reluctantly sprawled in the chair, not liking this latest piece of news at all. "I asked what you are going to do."

"I am not yet sure. Come Patrick, you seem to be the man with all the ideas lately, what do you propose?"

Patrick squirmed. "I think we should get the hell out of Ancaster."

Giles slammed a fist on the desk, causing Patrick to flinch. "Give up? I think not. We have a sweet deal here, Patrick. Using Ancaster as a smuggling base for our piracy has been quite profitable, or do you forget where those fine jewels you wear came from?"

"I have not forgotten, I simply do not feel like taking on the king."

Giles cast an evil smile and waved the letter. "We shan't. The king knows nothing, remember? We just need to use this little piece of knowledge to our advantage. So come, Patrick, I need ideas, not cowardice."

Patrick frowned, and then sat forward in the chair. "The situation hasn't changed, we still need to get the girl and bring her back. Once hither we can somehow get her to sign away her rights in Ancaster, giving it to us."

"Us?"

"Sorry, *you*. There is still the small matter of getting her here."

"Aye, that does seem to present a problem, does it not? I do not think we can simply ride in there and take her by force, not with that damned manor crawling with knights."

"Nay, she must come to us."

"And just how do you suggest we do that?"

"I shall have to think on it."

Dayen's black eyes turned even blacker and cold. "See to it you do not think too long; I want this matter settled and that little witch captured."

At that moment a young, nervous girl appeared at the door. Giles looked up and gave her a leering smile.

"Come in, child."

The girl, who couldn't have been more than fifteen, entered the study slowly, stopping several feet in front of the desk.

"I was told you wished to see me, Milord?"

Giles leaned back and folded his hands, looking the girl over with lustful arrogance. "Aye, I hear you support your widowed mother and younger brother?"

The girl lowered her head and nodded.

Giles stood up and circled the desk, stopping in front of the girl, towering over her small body. He cupped her chin with his hand and raised her head, forcing her to look at him.

"You are a comely lass. How would you like to make extra money for your family?"

The girl showed surprise, and then nodded with a smile, not realizing the implication of his words.

"Very well. Go to my solar and wait for me. I shall be up shortly and we shall talk." He produced a smug smile.

The young girl nodded, curtseyed, and left.

Patrick shook his head in disgust. "Talk, my arse. You plan to rape her."

Giles sneered, unapologetic, and leaned back against his desk with folded arms. "Of course I do, what else are supple young maidens for?"

"But, to turn her into a whore?"

Giles waved his hand casually and shook his head. "It remains to be seen if she shall become a whore. I am in the mood to inflict pain; there might not be enough left of her for that worthy profession."

Patrick jumped to his feet. "Mother of God, Giles! She is but a child!"

"Just the way I like them…virginal and terrified. They scream more that way." He stood back up. "If we have completed our business, I shall be going. I believe you have some thinking to do." He sauntered out, leaving Patrick feeling enraged and sickened. He had seen several young girls after Giles got through with them. He closed his eyes and brought a hand over his face.

"Swine," he muttered under his breath.

Chapter Eleven

Pet and Elanna spent the next couple of days keeping themselves frightfully busy. It was Pet's plan to wear themselves out to the point they would instantly fall asleep at night from sheer exhaustion, not giving them a chance to miss their husbands. It seemed to be working. The best part was the children were just as worn out as they were. By the third day after the departure, a breakneck pace was no longer needed. The women were becoming close friends, something both had needed and never had. They were determined not to sit around and pine away for their husbands. The king's men would soon be there. Then it was just a matter of waiting for Matthew and Luke to return. Neither gave any thought to Elanna's uncle miles away in Ancaster.

The tall man, smiling with the expectation of a monetary reward, stood before Giles and Patrick. Patrick showed no reaction. Giles was pleased with the news he brought.

"Hence, both the lord of the manor and our little Elanna's husband have seen fit to leave the women alone. Interesting. Very interesting." Giles thumped his fingers in the desk. "Well, Patrick, 'twould seem our luck has improved." He dismissed the messenger with a motion to the door.

"How so?"

"Patrick, I am disappointed you have not thought of a way to use this piece of news. However, I have. A very clever way."

Patrick frowned, doubtful that Giles would come up with anything clever. Brute force and cruelty were more his mode of operation.

"Very well, Giles, let us hear this clever plan."

Giles paused, looking up to the ceiling as he forced his brain to concentrate. "You said we needed to have the girl come to us on her own accord. I think I can arrange that."

"Oh? Pray tell, how?"

"By convincing her we have captured her husband."

Patrick stared at him with an amused look, then let out a small chuckle. "Once again you have demonstrated why you are not the brains between us. Elanna would know instantly that a person relaying that message was lying."

"Ah, but what if the person telling her believed it to be true?"

Patrick lost his smug smile and considered that for a few seconds. "That might work; she would have no way of knowing the informant was incorrect. But who can we get to do it?"

"Come, come, Patrick, I came up with the idea, 'tis up to you to find a way to implement it."

A pondering look washed over Patrick as his mind reeled with possibilities. "Is there anyone still working at Ancaster that called your brother master? Someone that might have known Elanna as a child?"

"Hmmm, let me think." Patrick waited patiently while Giles attempted to access his memory. "There are not many; most chose to leave when I took over…wait! If I recall, there is a married couple who had nowhere to go, cooks I believe. I let them stay purely out of generosity."

Patrick sneered; all the other cooks probably quit. "Very well, what are their names?"

"Oh, good heavens, Patrick! You cannot expect me to remember that. You are just going to have to ask around."

Patrick rolled his eyes; the man had no memory, whereas Patrick never forgot a name or face. That was why he had most of the ideas in their established smuggling ring.

"Very well. I shall also need a description of this husband."

"Ah, that I can give you myself. Large, fair, light eyes, fine clothes."

"That shall have to do. Is there anyone here that can impersonate him, someone involved in our…*business*?"

Again Giles had to strain to think. "The blacksmith, perhaps. He is large and loyal to me."

I do not believe I have met the fellow, but I shall take you for your word. One of our men brought back a personal item that might prove useful." He stroked his chin as he thought. "All right, I have a plan."

"I thought maybe you would."

The gray-haired cook was mildly alarmed when the stranger approached her. Judging by his clothes, he was obviously a noble, most likely one of Dayen's cohorts. He stopped in front of her, just as she was preparing to clean some onions for the afternoon stew.

"Elizabeth?"

The woman scowled, suspicious of this unfamiliar man who was invading her kitchen. "Aye, I am Elizabeth."

Patrick clasped his hands together and nodded. "Ah, good…I was told you have worked here for many years?"

"Twenty-five, next spring."

"Good, good." He noted the woman's dislike for him; that would help his plan very nicely. "Elizabeth, I come to you because I need someone I can trust. I work for Giles Dayen."

The woman frowned. "Aye, I figured as much."

"Elizabeth, we have the unfortunate circumstance of finding ourselves with a prisoner."

Elizabeth drew herself up tall and wiped a bead of sweat from her brow. "Prisoner?"

"Aye, some poor fellow Giles has captured. Apparently he is destined for execution, but until then we have to feed the poor chap, aye?"

"I suppose."

"Ah...yea, that is where you come in. I have been assigned to find someone to feed him, and I choose you."

Elizabeth shook her head. "I don't wanta feed no prisoner."

"But, you are the only one we can trust. He is down in the dungeon, I shall show you where. Come." He stood firm, not giving her a choice.

"Didn't know we had a dungeon."

"Well, actually 'tis an old wine cellar with a good, strong door. It serves the purpose."

She unwillingly followed him to an unfamiliar stairway, leading down to a dark, dank corridor. Patrick hoped the blacksmith had memorized all the material he and Giles gave him. He was most cooperative when he was promised a bigger share of the next pirated shipment.

He led Elizabeth to a wooden door with a small barred window. There was a narrow slot near the bottom. "Here the fellow is." He banged on the door. "How are we doing in there?"

A loud voice bellowed from inside. "Let me out! The king shall have your head for this!"

"Do not listen to him," Patrick warned. "He is likely to tell you anything."

Elizabeth peered cautiously through the slot, but couldn't see more than an outline of a very large man.

"Who is he? What did he do?"

"You ne'er mind that, just make sure you bring him a meal tonight and slide it through this slot. Lord Dayen said you shall be well compensated for your help." He hoped he was a good enough actor, and she was accepting all of it.

"Well, all right. Could I get back to my onions now?"

"Of course, you may go."

Elizabeth gave the prisoner one last glance, and hurried from the basement room as fast as she could. As soon as she was gone Patrick opened the jail door, and the blacksmith—a large man with black hair and massive arms—stepped out.

"How'd I do?"

"Great…now remember everything we told you when she comes back. You must be totally convincing."

"Oh, I will be…Dayen's payment for my bit of actin' is most generous. "I'll lay it on thick tonight."

"Not too thick…we do not want her to become suspicious."

"Don't worry…I guarantee she'll go runnin' fast as she can to the girl."

"Just ne'er let her see your face; keep in the shadows. The lord you are impersonating is blond. And speak formal English!"

The blacksmith nodded, smiling through yellow decayed teeth. "All right, do not worry. Giles will have Ancaster in the palm of his hand."

Elizabeth hurried back to the kitchen, and exited out the back door to find her husband, who was chopping wood for the stoves and ovens.

"Samuel! There is a prisoner!"

Her husband stopped his chore, and wiped his forehead. "Prisoner? Who?"

"I know not, only that he is someone Dayen has captured."

"If he is an enemy of Giles Dayen, then he is a friend to us."

She frowned, then nodded, knowing full well that her husband could not stand idly by while some innocent person suffered at the hands of Dayen. "I'm supposed to feed 'im."

"You go to the kitchen and act normally. I'll go talk to the prisoner. Is he being guarded?"

"I didn't see anybody."

"All right. Mention this to no one." He put down his ax.

The blacksmith sat in the corner of his cell, eating some venison and bread that Patrick had sent him. He also had blankets, a pillow, and other niceties that a real prisoner wouldn't have. Any minute he would go into his act. He rehearsed the story in his head over and over and thought he had it down, but was thrown off balance when he heard a man's voice outside the door instead of the cook Elizabeth.

"Pssst! You in there!"

"Who is it?" The blacksmith spoke in his best formal English, something he had to concentrate very hard to do.

"My name is Samuel. Who are you?"

"I am Luke Cameron, the proper Lord of Ancaster."

"What? How can that be?"

"Elanna Dayen is my wife."

Samuel had to pause a moment to comprehend that. "Little Elanna? She is married?"

"Aye, to me. Giles Dayen has given me one week to sign Ancaster over to him, or he is going to kill me. I will not do it."

"Is this place worth your life?"

"'Tis to Elanna. She has nothing else except Ancaster. She has special talents, you know."

Samuel nodded as distant memories surfaced. "Aye, I remember. Giles Dayen had her taken away when she was just a child. None of us knew what happened to her."

"Samuel, she can help me. Do you know someone who can take a message to her?"

"Where is she?"

"About two day's ride south, at a township called Elton. She does not know I have been captured."

"How do I know you are who you say?"

The blacksmith paused while he remembered his part. He was told he might have to prove his words. "Tell her they killed my brother Matthew. Give her this." He poked the hat through the bars.

Samuel looked at the green felt hat with the now tattered feather still attached. "Why did they do that?"

"We were traveling together. He was not needed."

"I'm sorry."

"Now I will die unless Elanna comes to help me."

Samuel looked at the thick chains and massive locks on the door; he now knew why a guard was not posted. "Maybe I can set you free."

"I think not…Dayen has the only keys to the locks, and as you can see, those chains are not easily broken." Patrick had purposely made releasing him look hopeless.

"I think you're right, very well, I will go to Elanna myself. Give me directions."

Later in the study, Giles listened to the plan that had been set in motion. Patrick himself kept a watchful eye while the cook's husband casually slipped away that afternoon, on his way to Elton. Giles was enthusiastically delighted.

"Well done! Set the blacksmith free, and tell the cook the prisoner has been moved and she need no longer worry about meals."

"'Tis already done."

Giles frowned; Patrick was always one step ahead of him. "Now we wait. Elanna shall certainly believe the man."

"Most likely."

"The poor sap," Giles said in a gloating tone. "If he had just thought for a moment, he would have realized that no man would put his wife in danger to rescue him."

"I counted on his low intelligence." Patrick lost his self-satisfied smile for a moment. "Giles, you do not intend to harm the girl, do you?"

"Never fear, my soft-hearted nephew. Once she signs Ancaster over to me, I shall set her free to go live with Brother Joseph at his monastery. No one will ever find her there."

"But what about her husband? When he returns, he might…"

"You worry too much, Patrick. I am assembling a small army even as we speak. In a few weeks I shall have more than enough men to defend Ancaster against an attack." He jeered as he leaned back in his chair and put his hands behind his head. "If that Cameron fool attacks, I shall have to strike them all down. I will be well within my rights."

"I fear you underestimate them."

"Oh pshaw. Besides, if we simply state we have not seen her, what can they do? Did you send for Brother Joseph?"

"Aye, he should be here shortly after Elanna arrives. Was it really necessary to involve him in all this?"

"He became involved when he agreed to obtain pirated wine and oil from me in exchange for his services. He has come in most handy."

"I hope this works."

"It shall. Ancaster is as good as mine."

Elanna smiled as the children held hands and moved round in a circle, singing ring-around-the-rosie, and falling down with hilarious laughter. Pet had given her the 'job' of watching the children that day while she attended to business. It had been a week since the men had left, a long week that felt like years to Elanna. Pet seemed to be holding up much better, and Elanna envied her for that. She missed Luke terribly. Of course, she had no way of knowing how truly devastated Pet actually was.

It had snowed the day before, and the children were all eager to play in it, but Pet wanted to have new warmer coats and boots made for all of them before they went out in the cold. The children all loved Elanna, who knew wonderful games and songs to teach them. Just as she was starting to gather them all up for another adventure, Pet came in from inspecting the cattle. The children all ran up to her in glee as she stomped the snow off her boots and coat.

"Pet! Come play with us!"

"Aye, do!"

They all began begging her, as she made a tired face and plopped in a chair. "Not now, I am worn out from the cold. Maybe later."

Elanna gazed suspiciously at Pet, who indeed looked fatigued, and got the children off to another room to draw pictures. Then she ordered some tea brought to Pet, and joined her in the lessor hall. As Pet sipped the hot liquid, she shook her head in dismay.

"I just do not understand it, I am not doing any more than I usually do, but I feel so tired lately."

Elanna put her hand on Pet's forehead, and looked pensive. Then she passed her hand closely over Pet's whole body, and finally stopped, displaying a small smile. Pet gave her a startled look.

"What? Am I ill?"

"Nay, you are not." Elanna's smile made Pet uncomfortable.

"Then, what?"

Elanna's smile got wider. "You truly do not know?"

"Know what?"

"Pet, you are with child."

"What?" Her shocked expression was priceless, Elanna wished Matthew was there to see it. "Are you sure?" Her expression changed to acceptance. "Although, I should not be surprised, with a husband like Matthew."

Elanna giggled. "Aye, his thoughts are most interesting when he is around you."

"I can imagine. The thought of becoming a real mother gradually hit her, as her hand automatically went over her belly. A smile slowly lit her face as she anticipated telling Matthew. Suddenly she missed him more than ever. Rare tears began to form as she thought about Matthew, where he was, how long he would be gone, and how happy he would be when he knew about the baby. She willed the tears back into her eyes, as she was too overjoyed to cry and certainly didn't want to waste perfectly good tears on happy news. She looked over at Elanna, not for a second doubting her word.

"How long? I mean, until the baby is born?"

"You are just barely pregnant, your belly will not even expand for quite a few more months."

Pet frowned. "Will Matthew still love me when I am fat?"

"Your Matthew would love you no matter what you looked like, and you will not be fat—you are carrying his child."

"Hence, now 'tis your turn."

The smile faded from Elanna's face. "What do you mean?"

"You know perfectly well what I mean." Pet's face was lit with a smile of condescension. "You and Luke will be starting your family."

Elanna fell silent, looking at Pet through solemn eyes that hid deep, unsurfaced pain. "Luke and I will not have a family."

"Do not be silly, of course you will. Although, 'twould help if he were here."

"No, I do not think you understand," Elanna continued. "I must not bear children."

"Are you still convinced that your—how did you say it—*affliction* will carry on to your children? Elanna, that is just foolish. You have no proof of that."

"And I have no proof that 'twill not." She let out a sigh. "Besides, at this time 'tis a moot point."

"How do you mean?"

Elanna did not meet her eyes, instead choosing to turn away to hide the tinge of pink on her cheeks. "W-we have not yet…"

Pet crossed her arms and raised one eyebrow. "You are joking."

She swung her head around to face Pet, causing her mass of hair to sway around her shoulders and cover half her face. "I meant to, really I did. We tried…I mean, he tried, but then I drank some wine, and the room got hot, and we fell off the bed, and I do not remember much after that." Her face got redder with each word.

Pet simply gave her a droll smile. "I see."

"And then the vision about the ship happened, and well, here we are."

Pet was trying hard to hold her laughter, not wanting to embarrass Elanna any more than she already was. "Well, these things happen. I am sure the…er…situation will be remedied upon Luke's return."

"I certainly hope so."

"Oh, I am positive of that. If Luke is a normal Cameron, you have nothing to worry about."

"As for now, let us celebrate your good fortune with a cup of hot tea."

"Aye, let's." She raised her cup to her lips as a thousand thoughts ran through her head, all centered on a new life growing within her and her marriage with Matthew.

Little did she know the threat to that idealistic life that awaited her in Ancaster.

Chapter Twelve

Matthew and Luke rode hard, sleeping and eating only when it was necessary, and reached the port town of Hunstanton where Paul had embarked on what was to be his great adventure. After finding a suitable stable for their tired mounts, they headed straight to the harbor. Their mood was somber, anxious and absorbed, as they lost no time in locating the harbormaster. The two exhausted men, unshaven and in wrinkled week-old clothes, blended in with the typical dockworker. People milled about, either preparing to embark or simply to wish departing relatives and friends goodbye. Every smiling face grated on their mood. Matthew was already in a foul state from losing Julie's hat. They were determined to not accept anything but a satisfactory outcome to their quest. They would know Paul's fate—and they would do whatever it took to find out.

Luke had wanted to stop in Cambridgeshire to inform their parents of Paul's dilemma, but Matthew, doubting mind prevailing, convinced him to wait on the off chance that Elanna was wrong. No sense in upsetting his father, and especially his mother. In his mind's dark recesses, he harbored hope Elanna was mistaken about Paul. But his grasp of reality told him the chance of that was slim.

The harbormaster looked surprised when he recognized the two sons of Baron Cameron. They looked horrible, with sunken cheeks and hollow eyes, as if they had ridden six days straight with no rest. Luke lost no time in getting right to the point.

"My father's ship—it departed soon after the New Year—have you heard word of it?"

The harbormaster gave them a scowl in reply. He was a proud man, who fancied himself an expert in just about everything. "The *Sea Dancer* is not due back for several months."

"Aye, we know, but…"

"I would be the first to know if anything was amiss. There is a pirate operating in the strait, but he has not struck for several weeks."

"A pirate? What do you know about him?"

Another man entered at that moment behind Luke and Matthew, and the harbormaster looked past the brothers with extreme impatience. "I have no time for this; I am terribly busy. I have a harbor to run." He brushed them aside and approached the other man.

Matthew, his hot temper flaring, pushed his younger brother aside. "Let me handle this." He stepped in front of the short, older man and puffed out his chest. "Look, we have reason to understand there might have been an incident. Tell us what you know."

"An incident? I know nothing of any incident! Now, move out of my way."

Matthew grabbed the man by the scuff of his neck and practically lifted the man off the floor with one hand. "I said, tell us what you know, or I will rearrange your face!" He dropped the harbormaster down with a thud.

Now intimidated by the larger Matthew, the harbormaster took a backward step as his face turned ashen. "I know nothing! Honest!"

The other customer turned to the two, alarm evident in his face. "What do you mean by an incident? Do you have news of the pirate?"

"There has been no news," the harbormaster insisted.

"See here," the man said, "what are you trying to cover up? I have merchandise coming in on a ship out there!"

"Nothing! Honest!"

Matthew and Luke exchanged looks. "Er," Luke began, "perhaps 'twould be better if we asked around the docked ships."

The harbormaster, greatly relieved the two troublemakers were leaving, nodded enthusiastically. "Go ahead, but it won't help—the *Sea Dancer* is most likely in France by now."

"But..." Matthew began.

"Come on, Matt, let us go," Luke said dryly. "He knows nothing." He grabbed Matthew by the arm and pulled him out the door.

They spent several hours walking the docks, asking any sailor who would talk to them about any news of the *Sea Dancer*. No one seemed to know anything. They mostly received odd looks when asked about an incident that might or might not have happened. After a while Matthew lost all patience.

"This is ridiculous! Everyone thinks we are crazy! I am dirty and tired, need a hot bath and fresh clothes, and here we are making total fools of ourselves!"

"Aye, I believe my mind is more fatigued than my body."

"I agree," Matthew said. "Perhaps a few hours in a soft bed would sharpen our minds."

"I do not know about my mind, but my backside could certainly use something soft. I have ridden so much lately I fear my bottom has molded to the shape of my saddle."

Matthew could not help laughing. "Very well, my soft-bottomed brother, let us find an inn and get some rest. Perhaps tomorrow will bring some news."

"I hope so. I want to get home to my wife."

"As do I," Matthew said with a grim nod. "As do I."

Back in Elton the women were faring no better, at least emotionally. They both missed the men, but were determined to make the best of it. After all, many women endured long absences from their husbands, why should they be special? Of course, many women also cherished those absences, as they had married for convenience and not for love.

Several servants had taken ill, and it appeared that a couple of new guards that Raymond had recruited had left without warning. Unthankful ingrates, Pet called them. This left Pet and Elanna having to do more work. Pet reluctantly had to leave Elanna for hours every day, so Elanna had to find ways to amuse herself. She loved the children, although their boundless energy wore her out, and she took every opportunity to get a moment's peace for reflection and prayers. One such afternoon she was walking outside enjoying the brisk air and bright sunshine, when she sensed a presence nearby. It was a presence she didn't fear; a familiar one that she couldn't immediately place. When an old man stepped out from behind some trees, she stood waiting for him.

"I know you," she said, as she cocked her head in curiosity.

"Aye, my name is…"

"Samuel. I was very young, but I do remember. You used to work for my father."

"I must speak to you." His voice was strained; his eyes weary. "'Tis about your husband."

Elanna eyed him suspiciously. "Come closer."

He stepped up to her. She studied him carefully, wordlessly. "You believe Luke is in danger."

"Aye—he has been captured by Dayen."

Elanna instantly felt a wash of horror flow through her. "Giles! I should have known he would try something like this!" She stopped suddenly and stared at the ground, deep in thought. "Why did I not sense this happening? Something is wrong here." Again she searched Samuel's mind, hoping to find deception, but finding only sincerity.

Samuel lowered his voice to a soft, sad tone. "I spoke to him myself. He is being held in the cellar. He-he told me his brother Matthew was…"

"Killed?" Elanna shook her head. "Nay, I do not sense this." She began to pace as she sorted out her feelings. "What is wrong with me? Am I losing my ability?"

"I know not. I only know what I heard and saw. He asked you to help him, and gave me this." He handed her the green felt hat.

As Elanna held the hat, a rush of adrenaline rushed through her. She remembered Julie presenting that very hat to Matthew. It was his; she could feel his essence. "Then I have no choice; I must go to him. Samuel, do you think you can sneak me into Ancaster unseen?"

"Oh, aye, milady…ol' Samuel got the slip on all of them. No one knows I have come for you. I can get you back in."

She nodded. "You are telling the truth. Come, let us go to the manor and get supplies for the trip back. You can tell me all the details on the way." She paused. "Speak to no one. I will do all the talking, do you understand?"

He nodded again.

Elanna forced a smile, which instantly faded. She had foreseen a catastrophe. Now, according to this man from her past, a good man whom she could trust, Luke was being held captive and Matthew was dead. Pet would be devastated. In a flash she thought about asking for Pet's help, but changed her mind. Pet was now with child, the only thing she had left of her beloved Matthew. She didn't need someone else's problems to battle.

It was clearly up to Elanna to save Luke. She had no choice.

When Pet came back that evening, exhausted from helping mend a broken fence, she was surprised not to find Elanna waiting for her in the kitchen dining room with a cup of hot tea. She shouted up the stairs, but received no answer. Still not terribly alarmed, she entered the children's wing and found them all playing quietly. No one had seen Elanna for quite a while. A few servants saw her earlier talking to an old man, but then she seemingly just disappeared.

Now feeling something was terribly amiss, Pet ran outside to the stable. William was just leaving, and Pet almost knocked him over as she plowed into him.

"William! Have you seen Elanna?"

"Not since she left for a ride. I was just coming in to tell yo..."

"A ride? That is ridiculous; she would not just go for a ride, not with more snow threatening." She glanced up at the crescent moon, which cast a frosty glow on the ground. Other than that, the shrouded sky was starless, perfectly black. Snow flurries danced on a unpredictable wind. "William, why did you let her go? What were you thinking?" Pet's voice rose only slightly, but her anger bled through her words.

"S-she said she would only be gone a short while. A man was with her."

Her eyes narrowed in contemplation. "A man? An *old* man?"

"Aye. She said he was an old friend, and she was just going to show him around Elton." He lowered his head and stared at the ground. "She asked me not to tell you, but I was getting worried. I-I am sorry, Pet." A tear ran down one cheek as his lower lip trembled.

Pet put her hand on the boy's shoulder. "'Tis all right, William, you did not have any reason to think anything was wrong. I am sorry I snapped at you."

"Perhaps she is lost," William offered.

"I doubt that." She rubbed her eyes with one hand and felt a flow of dread crawl through her like thick mud after a flood. William watched as she fought to keep her tense face composed. "This is all my fault. Luke asked me not to leave her alone, and it was my duty to protect her. I have let both Matthew and Luke down, not to mention Elanna."

"I think you are being too hard on yourself," William said with a frown. "Even you cannot be in two places at once."

She again looked up at the evening sky. "Well, at least there is some moonlight. It should not be too difficult to track her. Prepare Goliath."

William was temporarily stunned into silence as he watched her amble back to the manor. He finally found himself able to form words. “You are not going out *tonight* are you?”

She stopped and turned around. “Do I have much choice? She must be found.”

“But ’tis dark, and cold. And, like you said, it might snow.”

“All the reason to follow her now. In the morning her tracks might be gone.” She turned again, not willing to argue the point any further.

William watched with trepidation as the person he loved most in the whole world prepared to leave. What could he do? Raymond was gone for a few days, in his never-ending quest to recruit men to replace all the ones lost in the raids. He would be able to stop her; with his size he would be able to stop most anyone. But he was not there. With a sigh, William walked back into the barn and began to saddle Pet’s giant warhorse, Goliath. He knew it was useless to argue; Pet was too stubborn to listen to him. He was just a boy, not yet matured into manhood. Suddenly a smile formed as an idea popped into his head. Perhaps he couldn’t stop her, but that didn’t mean he couldn’t help her.

Luke opened one eye and tried to focus on the sound that so rudely awakened him. He glanced down at Matthew, who—despite the disturbance—was sleeping soundly on the cot beside the bed. The inn only had one room for rent, and after a brotherly discussion on who got the soft bed and who got the hard cot they settled the matter with a friendly game of arm wrestling. Hence, Luke got the bed while Matthew went to sleep muttering platitudes about being the oldest and therefore should be granted certain privileges.

“Matt, wake up,” he said in a deep, hoarse morning voice. “Someone is pounding on the door.”

Matthew rolled over and put his pillow over his head.

Seeing the task of answering the door was left to him, Luke maneuvered out of the bed and around the cot, then danced on the cold floor with his bare feet. Whoever was at the door had better well have a damn good reason for awakening him.

When he finally opened the door, he was surprised to see one of his father's business partners, Lord Bluthe. Luke remembered hearing his father say that he was offering Lord Bluthe half shares in the *Sea Dancer* cargo. The poor man seemed frantic, and pushed his way into the room.

"Thank God I finally found you! The harbormaster told me you two were asking questions yesterday about the *Sea Dancer*. Do you know how many inns there are in this town? I have been searching for you for hours!"

Luke shut the door. "Forgive me, but is it not a bit early for visiting?" He was unable to stop a long yawn, and even forgot to put the obligatory hand over his mouth.

"Early? 'Tis nearly noon. I fear I have grave news."

Matthew let out a snort, and Lord Bluthe glanced down at him. "Perhaps you should awaken your brother? This concerns him, also."

"I will be the judge of that," Luke answered, almost rudely. The man probably just wanted them to pass a message on to their father. These shipping tycoons were always worried by some thing or another.

"Very well. I was at port this morning when a British frigate came in. I heard the men talking about a ship they found in the English Channel. After a bit of prodding I discovered it was the *Sea Dancer*."

Luke's eyes grew wide as fear drained his face of color. "Matthew! Wake up!"

Matthew rolled over and looked up through bleary vision at the two blobs standing over him. "Wha…?"

"I said, get up. Lord Bluthe has heard news of the *Sea Dancer*."

Matthew sprang up from the cot, suddenly wide-awake. "Well, speak, man! What did you hear?"

Lord Bluthe began pacing the small room, then stopped and looked at the brothers through teary eyes. "The ship was abandoned, foundered to one side. It looked as if it might have been rammed. They said it was just a matter of hours before she sank completely."

Matthew cleared his throat in the vain attempt to cover up his emotions. "Were-were there any…bodies?"

"None that could be found. Funny thing, it appeared all supplies were missing, and they found no manifest, no sign of struggle, and no blood. The lifeboats seemed intact, also."

"Pirates?" Luke suggested, his voice grim.

"Perhaps." Lord Bluthe lowered his head and covered his eyes with a hand. He seemed too upset for a man who had simply lost an empty ship. Luke and Matthew knew their father always insured his investments, so monetary loss was not involved.

Matthew began throwing on his clothes. "We need to go talk to the sailors. We may be able to lease a ship, go out there and find out something."

Luke shook his head at that suggestion. "Nay, Matt, we are not sea men. Besides, if it were pirates, we would most likely suffer the same fate as the *Sea Dancer*."

"Well, we have to do something!" Matthew thrust his fingers through his long, tangled crop of hair.

"I agree," said Lord Bluthe. "Whatever it takes."

"We must remain sensible," Luke begged the others. "We must try to keep our emotions in check."

Matthew's voice rose louder as his face became angry and frantic. "Luke, for God's sake! That is our brother out there!"

"I know that, but remember what Elanna said…she sensed he was alive, and not alone."

"Who is Elanna?" asked Lord Bluthe.

Luke waved him off. "'Tis a long story. Let us just say we have reason to believe our brother is alive."

"And the others? What of the others?" Lord Bluthe's face became as frantic as Matthew's.

Losing patience, Matthew turned coldly to the older man. "Look, I am sorry about your stupid ship and crew, but we have family to be concerned about. We have lost our brother."

"And I have lost my daughter."

Luke and Matthew stopped dead, scarcely able to consider that someone else could be feeling the pain they felt. "You-your daughter?" Luke managed to stammer out.

Lord Bluthe went to the bed, and sat down laboriously, as if every bone in his body hurt. He reached into his coat and pulled out a piece of paper. "My daughter, Willow, is gone. I received this right after the ship sailed. 'Tis from your brother."

Matthew took the note and Luke looked over his shoulder while he read it.

My Dear Lord Bluthe;

Although I would like to think I am always in control of my situation, I find myself in an awkward position. It seems Willow has taken it upon herself to flee the country. I was not able to thwart this action, but I did manage to steer her aboard my ship so I can keep an eye on her. I will try to send her back after we dock in France on the first ship embarking for England. I do not know if that action will be successful, as she seems most determined, and we both know how stubborn she can be. Meanwhile, do not despair, I shall guard her with my life.

Your servant and friend,

Paul Cameron"

"Hence you see," Lord Bluthe said in a weary voice, "I have as much at stake as you do."

Luke put a comforting hand on his shoulder. "Perhaps even more. I apologize for my rudeness."

"As do I," said Matthew. "We did not know."

"So this Elanna you spoke of…she has information of some sort?"

"Well, not exactly," answered Luke. How could he explain about Elanna? He glanced at Matthew, but he looked just as helpless. Luke sighed. Sometimes the only thing to do was just tell the truth, however bizarre it might seem.

"You see," he began, then stopped. After a long pause, perhaps too long, he tried to continue. "Elanna is my wife. She...er...sees things, like in dreams. Some might call them visions."

"Visions? As like a prophet?" Lord Bluthe's eyebrows narrowed in skepticism.

"Well, sort of. She had a vision, way last week, of the ship sinking. But she also said she felt our brother was alive, and he was not alone. I have my own feeling that he is with your daughter."

Lord Bluthe blinked once, then again. "You are asking me to trust a vision?"

"Excuse me," Matthew butted in with his usual manner, "but it seems that is all we have. Elanna was right about the ship; I, for one, would like to believe she is right about Paul."

"Absolutely." Luke agreed in a reassuring tone, trying to convince himself more than anyone. "We are just going to have to trust her. However, I would like to talk to the sailors who found the ship myself. Perhaps there are some details missing."

"I agree," Lord Bluthe said. "I shall accompany you."

Further questioning produced no new details. It was as Lord Bluthe had said, the ship was found listing to one side, supplies gone and no bodies found on deck or in the water, with no blood or signs of struggle. Although the news wasn't exactly what the brothers had hoped for, at least a glimmer of hope strengthened them. Perhaps it wasn't pirates at all. Maybe the crew was rescued by another ship.

They could only wait. They stayed for three more days as Lord Bluthe's guests, then finally left for Elton with the promise that they would be contacted immediately if any new news was heard.

Chapter Thirteen

Elanna stopped her horse and looked back to see how far back Samuel was. His horse was slow and of poor breeding, which caused many delays and was fast becoming an irritant to her. Her thoughts were only on Luke, imprisoned at Ancaster awaiting her help. Fear and confusion were also building within her, as she still couldn't sense the danger to him. It was as if her powers were no longer functioning. But then, why was it that she could still sense Samuel's thoughts? Perhaps it was only her long-range powers that had disappeared. Could it be that her love for Luke had somehow canceled out her power when it concerned him? Then, following this reasoning, would this also happen with anyone she became close to?

Samuel's horse rounded the trail's corner and Elanna again kicked her mount to resume. They had kept to seldom-used trails, avoiding the main road. They would reach Ancaster that evening, if all went well. She rounded another turn and suddenly got a chilling, disturbing feeling. Samuel came up beside her.

"What is it?"

She shook her head. "I am not sure. I felt a presence, but 'tis not threatening. At least not now."

The old man took out a cloth and wiped his brow. "Should we turn back, or go on?"

"We go on." Elanna set her jaw in determination. "My husband needs me."

She almost expected her uncle's men to jump out from the woods at any moment and drag her away. Little did she know that she had only detected her uncle's outposts, hired to assure her arrival.

Patrick approached Giles, who was standing in the courtyard observing a new stallion he had acquired. The excited, black animal pranced defiantly as the trainer lunged him in a circle. Patrick stood watching silently for a few seconds, then addressed Giles.

"He has much spirit."

Giles nodded. "That he does. It will be a pleasure to break him."

Patrick frowned, and realized he was gritting his teeth. "Someday you might find an animal you cannot break."

"Never. A spirit can always be broken, be it animal or man." He took a deep breath. "In fact, man is the easiest. If he cannot be broken, he can be bought. But then, I of all people should not have to remind *you* of that."

Patrick, hot-faced and raging, turned briefly to hide his anger from Giles. He immediately changed the subject. "You might want to know that Elanna and Samuel are almost here. My outposts have reported them half a day's ride away."

Giles raised an eyebrow, but otherwise showed no emotion. "Excellent. Has she sensed your men?"

"It does not appear so."

"Good. Be sure no one pays them any mind. I want them to simply walk in with no resistance."

"Very well, then what?"

"As soon as she is in the castle we will seize her, then eliminate the old man."

Patrick frowned and his face puckered with concern. "Eliminate? You mean, murder?"

Giles turned to give Patrick a bored, condescending look. “Getting rid of a disloyal servant is not exactly *murder*. I am entitled to punish a traitor.”

“But you counted on his disloyalty to bring about the result you desired. And now you plan to reward him with death, and leave his wife a widow?”

Giles pondered this for a few seconds, and finally nodded. “Perhaps you are right.” Just when Patrick thought that Giles had actually grown a heart, he added, “Kill them both.”

“What?”

“Kill both the old man and his wretched wife. They were traitors together, they can die together.”

The bile began to rise in Patrick’s throat, and his hands clenched in tight fists. “But they are old. They will not live much longer anyway.”

“All the more reason to kill them now. They have outlived their usefulness.”

Patrick quickly left without comment, holding his tongue for the time being. When he was out of sight, he stopped and leaned against a wall in an attempt to control his rising temper.

“No,” he muttered with conviction. “I will not do it.”

Pet reined in her horse and listened intently; there it was again. She was unsure before, but now no question remained—she was being followed. Her stalker was sly, keeping just far enough away to remain almost undetected—almost. Fortunately, Pet’s warrior instincts told her something was amiss. She dismounted and waited in the brush for her elusive pursuer. Whoever he was, he would meet her sword. Not many lived past that introduction.

She waited silently as a horse approached her hiding spot. Then, as the rider was almost upon her, she leapt out and knocked the rider off the horse. It almost took no effort at all; the rider was small and weighed little. She quickly wrestled the small figure to the ground and brought a dagger to his throat. When recognition set in, she took an alarmed breath and jumped to her feet, pulling the boy up with her.

"William? What are you doing here?"

The lad raised a hand to his throat, realizing how fortunate he was that Pet was not the kind to slash now and ask questions later.

"I-I thought I could help you."

Pet folded her arms and gave her nephew a stern look. "Help me?"

"Uh-huh."

"*You* thought you could help *me*?"

William squirmed with the sudden insight that he might have stretched his luck too far this time. "You needed help." He batted his eyes innocently. "Did you not?"

Pet closed her eyes as she pondered this new development. She had been tracking Elanna for days through seldom-used trails, and was too far away to take William home. She would just have to take him with her, and pray he didn't get hurt.

"Very well, William, you may come with me, but you are to do exactly what I say, do you understand? Exactly."

"I understand."

"Fine, get back on your horse. Elanna is with another rider, and they are not far ahead of us. I must say, having you with me is not going to help me sneak up on her."

"Sneak? Why are you going to sneak up on her?"

"To bring her to her senses. She must think she is being honorable, or brave, or something. I know not why she fled Elton, only that I must bring her back. She cannot perceive me, but she will most likely sense you."

William immediately saw his mistake, and lowered his gaze to the ground. "I-I am sorry. I have really messed things up."

Pet softened, and ruffled his hair in a playful manner. "Actually, 'tis nice to have some company. You tracked me very well. Howe'er did you learn that?"

"Robert taught me."

Pet drew back as the forbidden name hit her heart. "Robert?" She had tried desperately to not think about her beloved twin brother. Now his name haunted her like his existence had been a mirage.

"Aye. He taught me how to track, and survive. I can build a fire and hunt for food." His voice lowered to a soft, sad tone. "I miss him."

Pet swallowed the lump that formed in her throat, and turned her face to hide her anguish. "So do I. Come, we must go, or she will get too far ahead."

The sign announcing Elton only two miles away spurred the two exhausted travelers onward. Matthew felt as if he had been gone a year. Luke threatened never to leave again. The trip was made a little longer while they stopped in Cambridgeshire to tell their mother and father about the *Sea Dancer*, also giving Luke the chance to pick up Annabelle, his favorite gray palfrey. Even though their mission was a disappointment, they couldn't claim it was a failure—Elanna had been correct. Now the only thing they wanted was to hug their wives, eat a warm meal, and crawl into a soft bed. Then, after a good night's sleep, the brothers would plan a strategy to get Ancaster back from Elanna's uncle. Life would return to bearable until they heard further word about Paul.

It was nearly nightfall when they rode into the courtyard. Matthew was surprised that William wasn't there to attend to the horses, and sent a young groom to fetch him and the women from the manor. The lad returned alone minutes later.

"I am sorry, milord, but there seems to be no one at home."

Matthew stopped the vigorous rubdown he was giving his horse and stared blankly at the lad. "Are you daft, boy? Of course there is someone home."

Luke, checking a loose shoe on Annabelle, looked up to see Matthew push past the groom and head for the door. "I will take care of the horses, Matt—you just bring my wife to me."

"I would have thought for a better greeting than this," he muttered as he walked across the courtyard. The place did, indeed, look deserted. "What the hell is going on?"

The sight of Raymond walking toward him gave him some relief—until he saw the giant's expression. Raymond was beyond grim, displaying a dour face as he neared Matthew.

"I fear thou art too late," he said with dismay. "They are gone."

"Gone? Who is gone?"

Raymond ignored his question, instead looking with narrowed eyes to the barn. "Is Luke with thee?"

"Of course he is...now what did you mean by..."

"Then all might not be lost. The three of us might be able to overtake them."

Matthew reached his limit of patience. "Raymond, what on earth are you talking about?"

Raymond took a deep breath, and let it out in a slow, deliberate manner. "'Tis my fault. I have let thee down; thou shalt dismiss me for sure."

Luke exited the barn and saw his brother and the giant in the courtyard talking. His face relaxed at the sight of Raymond, who made him look small in comparison. He picked up his pace to join the men, who surely must be discussing their absence and the effect it had on the women. "Hey, you two," he yelled in a jovial voice. "Are you planning a celebration without me?"

Matthew turned with a look of dismay and confusion to his happy brother. "Raymond has cast doubts that there is anything to celebrate."

Luke's face fell immediately. "What do you mean?"

"I was not here," Raymond bemoaned. "I was in search for replacements for our guard, and when I came back, they were gone."

Matthew drew up and braced himself for the worst. "Who was not here?"

"The women."

"Wait a minute," Luke cut in. "What do you mean the *women*? You mean Pet, right?"

"Nay, I fear both Lady Pet and Lady Elanna art missing. And I fear there is more."

Luke was so dumbstruck he couldn't talk. Matthew, a bit more used to his wife running off from him, was able to keep his wits for a while longer. "More?"

"Yea, I fear master William hast also disappeared. I believe he seeketh Pet."

Matthew brought a hand to his forehead. "William? Good Lord! We must go after them."

Luke, his face regaining color, snapped out of his stunned state and began to take small pacing steps. "Now, let us not panic. We need to figure out exactly what happened. Details. We need details, Raymond. Who left first, how long have they been gone?"

"Well, from what I can decipher from the servants, Elanna left with a man while Pet was on her rounds, and…"

"A man? Impossible!" The veins in Luke's forehead pulsed with the implication. "Not only is it impossible, 'tis inconceivable! I will kill the bastard!"

"Now, Luke," Matthew said calmly. "You were the one that said not to panic."

"That is easy for you to say. Your wife did not flee with another man!"

Raymond held up his hand to stop the banter. "The man was old, according to thy servants. Very old. Pet left later that night, and no one knows when William left."

Matthew slapped his leg. "That does it! We must track them down immediately. I will get weapons, and…"

"Well, wait a minute," Luke said in a calmer tone. "Perhaps we should not jump to conclusions."

"What? A minute ago you wanted to kill someone!"

"I know, but that is before I knew about the old man. There is something going on here."

Matthew raised his hands in exasperation. "For heavens sakes, could we just for once be angry together?"

"Perhaps," Raymond suggested, "we could carry on this conversation inside? I am getting cold, and you two must be weary."

A while later, after a hot meal and sufficient amounts of ale, the three men gathered in front of the roaring fireplace to discuss the plan of action. First, however, they had to reconstruct what had happened, which wasn't easy with so few details. Raymond and Luke sat sprawled in plush chairs in front of the huge fire; Matthew leaned with one foot on a stool, orchestrating his words with one hand and holding a tankard of ale with the other.

"'Tis not Pet I worry about," he was explaining. "As you all know, she is perfectly capable of taking care of herself. She obviously left because, for whatever reason, Elanna decided to run."

"We do not know that for certain," Luke insisted.

Matthew snorted. "Well, she is gone, is she not?"

"Aye, but why, that is my question. Was she running away *from* something, or *to* something?"

Raymond and Matthew gave Luke a confused look. He continued.

"I have a feeling this involves her uncle. Somehow she was convinced by this old man to leave. With her senses, she would have detected any hostility. Therefore, I conclude that someone she knows…someone close to her…is in trouble. There is no other reason she would have gone."

"All well and good," agreed Raymond, "But dost thou knowest where she went?"

Luke nodded. "Not for sure, but I think she has gone back to Ancaster. 'Tis the only logical conclusion."

"I agree," said Matthew. "And Pet is tracking her. So the question is now, do we go after them, or simply wait for Pet to find her and bring her back?"

"Are you so certain she will find her?" asked Luke. "I have a feeling that Elanna could avoid anyone she did not want to encounter."

"Anyone but Pet," Matthew added. "Remember, Elanna cannot sense her."

"True. So what do we do now? Stay? Leave?"

Matthew downed his ale and threw his tankard against the mantle with a dull thud. "Damn, I hate this! I cannot just sit around and do nothing. What if one of them is in trouble?"

"I agree with Matthew," said Raymond. "We must go after them."

Matthew turned and gave a curious raise of the eyebrow to Raymond. "What? Are you saying you are coming with us?"

"Thou doest not think I can simply stay here? I would go mad from the worry. Nay, I fear I am coming with thee."

"Oh, very well. You are too big for me to argue with." He sat on the stool and gave Luke a hopeful look. "Have you ever learned to fight? With a sword, I mean?"

Luke turned his gaze to the ceiling and chose not to answer.

"Oh, great heavens," Matthew groaned. "This is wonderful. Just wonderful."

"Well, I never had much need," Luke stressed in a defensive tone. "I was always able to talk my way out of anything. My fists were all I ever needed."

Matthew resumed his hopeful look toward Raymond. "Raymond, ol' chap, do you think you can give my brother a crash course in swordsmanship?"

"Now, wait a minute…" Luke began.

"Certainly," replied Raymond. He let out a deep belly laugh. "By the saints, I will make him an expert by morning."

"Well, let us not get our hopes up too much," Matthew quipped. "Just make him useful."

Luke bristled at that, and drew himself up tall in the chair. "I have never killed a man, and I do not intend to start now. We will simply find the women and bring them back."

"It might not be that simple, my wishful-thinking brother. If we meet with resistance we shall have to fight. You might have no choice."

"This is becoming worse every second."

"Aye, and I have a feeling 'tis not going to get any better."

It was nearly dark. Samuel led Elanna through a break in the hedge that surrounded Ancaster. They had left the horses grazing in a small clearing to be retrieved later.

"Careful, now," Samuel whispered. "There are guards all over."

She followed him down a small trail that led to the back of the castle. Distant memories swelled within her. She remembered her mother, who played with her in this very back yard. Her older brother would tease her and run when she got angry enough to strike back. She had a dog, a little black mutt that they simply named 'puppy', which would fetch sticks and jump up to catch a snack. Her father—she couldn't recall his face any more—was gentle and kind except when an injustice was done. They had been a happy family. If only they had not been traveling that day and stopped at that inn. The inn that caught fire, and killed her entire family. She remembered the flames—the smoke, the heat that engulfed everything. The window. She had gone to the window. Her fists banged on the panes. It wouldn't break. Then the red angel appeared.

Samuel interrupted her thoughts. "He's being kept down here."

"What?"

"Down here, in the dungeon."

"I did not know Ancaster had a dungeon."

"Well, 'tis not exactly a dungeon. They locked him up in a room off an old wine cellar." He opened a heavy wooden door and motioned her inside. He grabbed a torch from the top of the staircase. "We'll need this."

As they climbed down steep stairs into increasing darkness, Elanna sensed danger. She hesitated before remembering that Luke needed her. He might already be dead, even though she couldn't sense it. She shuddered at that, and with renewed urgency stepped into a dark, dank room. It was so stuffy she found it hard to breathe.

"Down this corridor," Samuel urged.

"I cannot see." She squinted in an attempt to make out any details. The candle only lit a small area directly in front of them.

"There is a torch on the far wall. I will go light it. Stay here."

She listened to his footsteps walk across the room, then suddenly felt a familiar coldness. "Wait!" she whispered as loud as she could. It was too late. He touched the candle to the torch, and the room glowed with flickering light.

Two men instantly grabbed her. She screamed and struggled, and saw Samuel grabbed as well. Suddenly a voice rang from across the room.

"Well, well. Look who decided to pay us a visit."

Hatred rose inside her at the sound of her uncle's voice. As always, he kept a safe distance from her, but even in the dark his evil soul permeated her mind.

"I should have known you would find me," she said.

"Find you? Oh, I did more than find you. I sent for you."

"That's not true," Samuel yelled. "I went to fetch her to save her husband! No one sent me!"

Giles causally leaned against a wine barrel and motioned to Patrick. "Take care of this vermin, nephew."

Wordlessly, Patrick walked past Giles to approach Samuel. He gave Elanna a sideways glance as he walked past. Elanna sensed that he was trying to tell her something, but the darkness prevented vivid thoughts reaching her. She could only sense regret. Patrick took one guard and left with the befuddled Samuel.

"I know you have my husband," Elanna said in a calm voice. "Let him go, and I will do whatever you want."

Giles rose up and leered. "That will not be necessary. Your husband was never my captive." He paused to let his lies sink in. He had spent several days planning this moment, and he was basking in his victory.

"W-what? You are lying; I do not believe you."

"Oh? Think, my trusting little seer. Actually, I am surprised you fell for it. Your husband, or his brother, was never in any danger. You must have sensed that."

"T-that cannot be true." She felt a fear of betrayal flow through her.

"Really? Luke Cameron came here shortly after you made your little escape, and I felt it necessary to tell him about you. I told him I would cut him in on a share of Ancaster, and he was more than happy to cooperate. He agreed to find you and get you to marry him, thus making him lord of Ancaster. This whole thing was planned. He arrived here several days ago and pretended to be held captive for Samuel's sake, whom we let go to fetch you. You see, Cameron never did love you. Remarkable that you actually thought that anyone could."

"N-nay! You lie!"

"You are a witch, Elanna. No one could love you, let alone someone such as a member of the most powerful family in England. Your marriage was a farce. He never intended to live with you as your husband, he simply wanted to obtain Ancaster."

Elanna's thoughts flashed to her marriage night when Luke had not exercised his marriage rights. Could this horrible story be true? "B-but…he registered our marriage! He sent a messenger to London with our certificate! I saw him!"

Giles reached inside his jacket and brought out a parchment. He waved it in the air and smiled. "You mean this? He never sent it. 'Twas all a lie, Elanna. We have been working together from the very start." He handed the certificate to a nearby guard, and motioned for him to take it to Elanna. "Here—see for yourself."

The guard brought the parchment to Elanna, who grabbed it from his hands in defiance. She read the signatures, hers and Luke's. It was true. No wonder she never sensed that Luke was in danger. Poor Samuel was duped, just like her. And to think that she actually believed that someone wanted her, loved her, needed her. How could she have been so foolish?

She lifted her gaze to Giles, whose controlled smirk was more arrogant than ever.

"Why the lie about Matthew? Why did you want me to believe he was dead?"

"Well, we couldn't get that warrior wife of his involved, could we? I knew you would not have the heart to tell her he was dead. Luke, actually, suggested that story, and Matthew agreed."

"M-Matthew? He was in on this?"

Giles shook his head in a patronizing manner. "My poor, sweet, little girl...how trusting you were. Of course he was in on it. He certainly did not want his brother married to a witch. We had a good visit, the two of them and me. They left just yesterday, when we knew you were nearing. Neither wanted to set eyes on you again."

Elanna was too dazed for tears. She had always sensed that Matthew didn't like her. How could she go on living, with the knowledge that her only chance at happiness had all been a lie? "What is to become of me?"

"Luke has left that up to me; he does not really care one way or another. Since he is your husband, he can do with you whatever he wants. He wants you gone. He has given all rights to Ancaster to me, and now I will send you somewhere safe where you will never be seen again. I hope you enjoyed your short bout of freedom, 'twill be your last."

Stunned into silence, Elanna just stared into space as she was led away."

Chapter Fourteen

"No, Luke! Thou art swinging too erratically." Raymond lowered his sword and wiped his sweaty brow.

"And what is wrong with that? I figure if I just swing this thing around, I am bound to hit something."

Leaning against the wall watching, Matthew brought a hand over his eyes and shook his head. He might as well admit defeat. Luke was just not cut out to be a swordsman.

"All right, all right, forget it," he said, with a wave of his hand. "We will have to find something else he can fight with." His face suddenly lit up. "Perhaps the bow? I remember when we were young; you used to shoot a bit. Do you think you still can?"

Luke rubbed his chin in thought. "Hard to tell. I have not touched a bow in years. My eyesight is not what it used to be, either."

Matthew frowned. An archer with bad eyes. Wonderful. "Very well, what about the lance? You look as if you have a good throwing arm."

Luke grimaced and shook his head. "Nay, the last time I threw a lance, I overshot my mark by twenty feet."

"By the saints, there must be something you can do!"

Raymond and Matthew stared at Luke while he thought. They waited. And waited. "Well?" Matthew finally asked.

"I cannot think with you two staring at me."

Raymond grunted. Matthew groaned.

"Besides," Luke continued, "I have never needed a weapon, so I have never bothered to learn to use one. Most of my contacts with people have been over business deals. I can look at a fine horse and tell you its potential as breeding stock. I can balance a ledger to the pence."

"Fine," Matthew scoffed. "If someone wants a ledger balanced during a battle, we certainly know who to come to."

"Perhaps we are going about this all wrong," Raymond said. "Luke said he is good with his fists."

"Never lost a fight," Luke agreed. "It usually only takes one punch."

"So," Raymond continued, "Mayhap we use Luke for close-up fighting…save the long range tactics to us, and have him punch people out as needed."

Matthew paused, then grudgingly shrugged. "Well, I guess that is something."

"I still think you are getting all worked up for nothing," Luke said. "We will probably never even have to fight anyone. I am not exactly thrilled that Elanna is out there somewhere, but I trust that Pet will find her. We will most likely meet them as they come back."

"You know what your problem is?" Matthew shouted with unreasonable fury. "You have never had to really fight for anything. Hell, you have never even killed a man!"

"And for that, you are angry with me?"

"Look at you!" Matthew kicked a nearby stool, sending it flying against the wall. "You breeze through life, making business deals and never having to fight for a damned thing. You intimidate people just by your mere size, so naturally you usually get your way. You joke, and make money, and everyone likes you. You never even had to learn to use a weapon. But this is different…you might have to fight this time, brother. You might have to kill. Are you prepared for that?"

Luke clenched a fist, and for one moment it appeared he might punch Matthew. Instead he slowly relaxed his hand, and took a backward step.

"I know what you are trying to do, Matt. Mother always said you got my temper, as well as your own. I simply do not think we should take for granted that we are going to end up fighting and killing."

Matthew paused, gave Luke an ardent gaze, and turned to stride out the door. "I hope you are right. Get some sleep," he snarled over his shoulder. "We leave at dawn."

Pet motioned to William, who crawled up on his belly to join her. They had reached Ancaster in the deep of night, and circled to the back where the brush hid their presence. Now mid-day, they had been observing the activity from a distance. The castle was heavily guarded. She pointed to a man. "See him," she whispered. "He appears to be giving all the orders. Must be Elanna's uncle."

William looked at the tall, dark man Pet had pointed to. People seemed to cower with his every command. "Where is Elanna?"

Pet shook her head. "Somewhere in the castle." She paused, and added, "I do not like this."

"What are we going to do?"

"For now, nothing." She fell into deep thought from a mixture of frustration and concern. Having William with her stifled her activities. Where as she would usually take a risk, sneak in with the cover of dark and fight to the death if need be, she now had William to consider.

William didn't sense her concern for him. He was there to help, and at least he could offer suggestions. It appeared Pet was lost for a plan. His typical boyhood exuberance and appetite for action took over. "Those guards are no match for you. I think we should just ride in there and say we know they have Elanna. They are not about to mess with England's only Lady Knight."

Pet gave him a sideways sneer accompanied by a snort. "That would be suicide, William." She paused as his suggestion sunk in. "Although…"

A hand came to her chin as she again fell into thought.

William smiled in expectation. "What?"

"Well, you are right about one thing; my reputation does appear to precede me. Perhaps I can use that to my advantage." She paused as an idea began to form.

Her pause made William about ready to burst. "What? What?"

"Your idea, with a little modification, might have merit. We could sit here for days, maybe weeks, and not find Elanna. Maybe I can force their hand."

"Force their hand? How?"

Her pensive scowl rose into a crooked smile. "I have an idea."

Giles galloped his dripping-wet horse to the stable, dismounted, and tossed the reins to a groom. He had been riding the animal to the point of exhaustion in the training ring, whipping the beast with his riding crop to break down its spirit. He saw Patrick approach, his red cloak waving behind him, and stood waiting.

Patrick took long, meaningful strides to where Giles was standing. He paused and let Giles take in his self-satisfied sneer. "As I figured, we have company. And you are not going to like who."

Giles cocked his head and frowned. "What are you talking about? My idea was flawless. Elanna is my prisoner."

"Perhaps not for long. I just got word that someone is riding up the entrance to Ancaster."

"One person? I am supposed to fear one person?"

"This one person, aye."

"Oh, really, Patrick—just kill him and toss his body in the woods. I do not have time for this." He started to turn when Patrick grasped his arm.

"I do not think that would be a good idea. You could have the wrath of the king's entire army at your feet."

Giles shook off Patrick's hand. "Do not touch me! You know I hate to be touched."

"Very well, my over-confident demagogue. But I think you should come meet this person."

"Just who the hell is this individual?"

Patrick sneered, almost liking the turn of events, if anything just to watch Giles squirm. "We are being graced with a visit by England's only Lady Knight. She will be in the courtyard in minutes."

His face washed out in horror, Giles stared at Patrick in disbelief. "Damn!"

"Quite so. Your orders? Or, do you still want me to kill her and throw her body in the woods?"

"Of course not, you idiot! She must have followed the old man and Elanna here. Who knows who else she might have told?"

"May I remind you that you were the one who financed the renegades who destroyed her entire family? I would not want to be in your shoes if she ever finds that out."

"That was such a good plan, too." Giles took a deep breath in an attempt to calm his nerves. "My renegade band, in the guise of being pro-Yorkist, completely diverted the king from my pirating operation."

"Until she killed the entire band—almost single handedly I might add."

Giles raised his voice in irritation. "Do you think I do not know that? I need to think."

Patrick shrugged. "Take your time. You have all of five minutes, or less."

"Damn!" He paced slowly, slapping his riding crop against his thigh as he thought. "All right, let us not panic. We will simply deny everything. She has no proof, the old man said no one else knew where they were going."

Patrick frowned and remained quiet. Samuel's screams of mercy still reverberated in his ears. Giles beat him almost to death before he revealed all the details of his journey with Elanna. Afterwards, Samuel and his wife were ordered for execution. Patrick released them before the executions could be carried out, and granted them safe passage from Ancaster. It was becoming easier to defy Giles.

Giles continued. "That is it, we deny everything. I shall go greet her." The color returned to his face as he regained his composure. "Meanwhile, you think of something."

"Me? Why me?"

It was Dayen's turn to smirk. "Need I remind *you* that the renegades were *your* idea? My arse is not the only one in a sling if she finds out." He turned and left Patrick silent with reflection.

It wasn't supposed to happen the way it did. They needed a diversion from the king's army, which had been mobilized to find the pirate's hide-out. A band of renegades sounded like a good idea, until Dayen hired a hateful pro-Yorkist named Gideon to lead them. He assembled the crudest, shabbiest group of cutthroats imaginable, which killed women and children without batting an eye. It sickened Patrick when he saw how his idea developed. He was actually relieved when he heard they had been eliminated, but only after horrible suffering had occurred.

Pet cautiously rode down the tree-lined road that led to Ancaster, being alert for any aggressive behavior. Goliath pranced impatiently, but she purposely held him back. She knew advance word would be given to Giles Dayen, and she wanted to give him plenty of time. Although she got curious stares, no one tried to confront her. When she reached the courtyard, she wasn't surprised to see a tall, dark-haired man—whom she assumed to be Giles Dayen—waiting for her. She wore every weapon in her arsenal that would fit on her body.

She dismounted and approached the man. He was deceptively handsome—an evil comeliness she had observed in other miscreants. Several guards stood around him, tense, uneasy, hoping she didn't attack. She stopped several feet in front of him, her sword drawn, ready for any offensive. He held his hands up in greeting and smiled charmingly as he welcomed her.

"Good day. I am…"

"Aye, Giles Dayen. I have heard all about you." Her voice was soft, steady.

Dayen dropped his smile for just a second, then returned it to his face with a hint of astonishment added. "Oh? Certainly from Elanna, no doubt. That child can tell such lies."

"Really? I find her rather *bewitching*, would not you say?"

Her choice of words told multitudes. The smile dropped and did not return.

Pet continued, having caught Dayen's complete attention. "My name is Pet Cameron. Elanna came to be in my care several weeks ago. Recently she left without word. You would not know anything about that, would you?"

"Nay, she has not come back here. She bolted from me, also. I offered her a home, and she repaid me by running away. But what should I have expected from a child with a wild imagination and a lying tongue?" He looked her over carefully, aware that she could strike him down in mere seconds.

Pet drummed her fingers on the pummel of her sword. It seemed to make Dayen nervous, at least if the look in his eyes was evidence. "I tracked her this far, and her trail ended. You are sure she is not here?"

Giles shook his head. "I have not seen her, but Ancaster is a large place. Perhaps a servant hides her? I could order a search of the castle."

"You do that. Meanwhile, I shall search the surrounding woods. I will set up camp west of here. If you find her, please notify me. I would like to know she is safe."

"Of course. But I fear it might be a waste of your time. Elanna can be very unpredictable."

Pet smiled wickedly. "I like that in a person. 'Tis one of my better features."

She lifted her sword to put it back in the sheath. An inexperienced guard mistook her motion for an attack, and began to raise his weapon. She kicked it from his hand and had her sword at his throat so fast Giles almost missed the action. The distressed, young guard stared into her intense eyes, knowing his life could end at any second.

Pet gave him a droll smile. "I would not, if I were you."

"Stand down!" Giles barked, and the guard raised his arms in surrender.

Pet sheathed her weapon. "I await your word. Good day, Sir." She mounted her horse and galloped away without looking back.

Patrick came out from his observation point in the shadows to stand beside Giles. "So that is the Lady Knight. She is not exactly what I expected."

Giles continued to keep a somber expression. "She is dangerous. She knows we have Elanna."

"I would say that was an accurate summation of the situation. So what do you purpose to do?"

"Tell me when our insipid little monk arrives. I will make arrangements for him to take Elanna."

"And of the Lady Knight?"

"She appears to be alone, but that might change. We only have a short opportunity to do something."

"What?"

"That is your department! Think of something, or you and I will both be looking down the blade of her sword." He sauntered toward the castle.

Patrick watched the fading speck of Pet's retreating form and grimaced. This could be a challenge, outwitting someone with her fighting ability. He loved a challenge.

Pet rode back to William, not west like she had said, but actually north behind the castle. She knew Giles Dayen had no intention of contacting her, and she certainly wasn't going to give away her location. She dismounted and braced herself for William's spirited hug.

"I knew you would come back! What happened? Did they threaten you? Do they have Elanna? Are they going to bring her to you?"

Pet put her hands up to stop his jabbering. "Nay, aye, and nay. All we can do now is wait."

"Wait for what?"

"I have called their bluff. They know that I know they have Elanna. And you were right, no introductions were necessary. They knew exactly who I was." She shook her head. "I must say that is a bit unnerving."

"You are famous, Pet!" He grinned with delight.

"Well, I would not go that far. Although, I am positive I have seen that man before."

"Who?"

"Elanna's uncle." She narrowed her eyes with reflection. "Where was it?"

"Is it important?"

"I suppose not. Come, let us find dinner. All this activity has made me hungry."

The three riders galloped their horses hard, trying to make the next town before nightfall. They reached the inn just as the sun was melting over the hillside.

Matthew reined in Excalibur, having reached the hitching post first. Luke and Raymond were close behind. They had ridden for two days, and were almost as exhausted as the horses. It was time for a hot meal and a few tankards of ale.

The tavern was crowded with a rowdy bunch that was already drunk. Men stepped aside when they saw Raymond, who towered over everyone like a lone tree in a meadow. He cleared a path to a back corner table, where they ordered stew and ale. The usual mini-fights broke out around them, mostly pushing, shoving, and name-calling. Things would quiet down until someone insulted someone else again. Then the cycle started all over.

It was hard to ignore their surroundings, but they tried. Matthew sat on one side facing Luke and Raymond. Luke, sitting on the outside, was subject to the most interference when someone would stumble into him. He usually pushed back and avoided eye contact.

"Forsooth," Raymond yelled over the din, "this certainly is a spirited throng."

"Very," answered Matthew. "I am too tired for this. I say we rent a room and get some sleep."

"We should reach Ancaster by tomorrow," Luke shouted.

"What?" Matthew yelled back.

At that moment a man came crashing across their table, having been punched by an angry companion. Two servants came to his rescue and got him off the table. The disruption quieted the room by a few decibels, making it easier to talk at a more normal level.

Luke watched as the man was escorted outside. "This reminds me of the first time I met Pet. I still cannot believe she planted that dagger from across the room."

Raymond raised one eyebrow. "Pray, thee, where did she plant the dagger?"

"In a man's arm." Matthew chuckled. "Then she boldly sauntered up to him and pulled it out. 'Twas rather humorous."

Raymond just nodded. "Sounds like Pet."

Luke laughed. "That was nothing compared to what she did when the man decided to get even."

"Indeed?" Raymond downed his ale and motioned for the barmaid to bring three more. "I detect a story. Wouldst thou care to share it?"

Luke proceeded to tell the story to Raymond, while Matthew listened. The more they talked about Pet, the more he missed her. He could not help but worry about her, even though she was perfectly capable of taking care of herself. Soon this whole thing would be over. He was confident they would meet the women returning to Elton. Elanna would receive a good tongue-lashing from Luke, and they would all go home. Then life would get back to normal.

Or so he thought. Before any of them had time to react, a man drew his sword and began swinging it around in a drunken stupor as he fought a pretend battle. The sword slipped and flew through the air, aiming straight for their table. Luke jumped up to get out of the way, but in doing so left Raymond open to the flying blade. It sliced through Raymond's thigh and fell to the floor, leaving an ugly gash. He let out a scream of agony.

"Good Lord!" cried Luke. He grabbed a napkin to help stop the bleeding.

"Idiot!" Matthew vaulted from the table and slugged the drunk in the mouth, sending him stumbling to the floor. He drew his sword to finish the job.

Raymond reached out and grabbed Matthew's arm to stop him. "Do not," he beseeched Matthew. "'Twas an accident. I shall live."

"Useless trash," Matthew mumbled to the peasant. "Get out of my sight." The man, sobered by the punch to his jaw, scrambled to his feet and ran out the nearest exit. Nearby peasants left with the fleeing man, seeing that Matthew was in no mood for celebration. The merriment came to an abrupt halt.

Luke sat by Raymond holding the gash together, trying to stop the bleeding. Matthew yelled to a passing servant girl to get some help. Raymond seemed to have the calmest wits among them.

"Fetch some spirits—something stronger than this weak ale—and some strips of clean cloth. I shall clean the wound, then wrap my leg. Fear not; I have had worst wounds on the battlefield."

"Nevertheless," Matthew said, "your leg is bound to be sore for quite a few days. You are in no condition to ride."

"Nonsense. I have ridden with far worse. I shall be fine."

Luke and Matthew exchanged looks, but held their comments. Raymond had, indeed, once been a valiant fighter. But he was no longer a young man, and a serious wound could prove fatal.

They found some strong liquor—the innkeeper's private supply that he was most reluctant to relinquish—and poured it in the wound as Raymond requested. He moaned and winced as the alcohol hit the open gash. Matthew was most skeptical to the strange procedure.

"I do not see how causing more pain can make the injury better."

Raymond would not be deterred. "I had a medicine man show me this technique, and it has always worked. His theory was, there are things in the air—things we cannot see—that cause wounds to fester. The spirits seem to kill them."

Luke snorted. "Things so small we cannot see them? That is a good one."

Matthew gave his brother a 'not now' look, and turned back to Raymond. "Very well, if it makes you feel better, than I shall not argue. But that does not belay the fact that you should not ride with this injury. Perhaps you should stay here while Luke and I go ahead?"

That suggestion didn't go far. "'Tis no time for jest. I shall ride and fetch our wayward women with you. A good night's sleep is all I need." He carefully wrapped his leg with the long strips of cloth, then nodded approvingly at his self-doctoring. "There, as good as new. Now, help me to my room."

The brothers each took one side, and supported Raymond's weight as he limped across the room to the stairs. Every movement was painful, but the giant did not allow himself any outward show of pain. Pet, the girl who was like a daughter to him, was out there somewhere, and he'd be damned if a little scratch was going to stop him.

Chapter Fifteen

Elanna sat quietly on the small cot, the only furniture allowed her. She had been put in a windowless cell, where sunlight could not reach. Even so, during the daylight hours she was kept hooded and bound. She wasn't sure of how long she had been there. Giles Dayen was taking no chances. He wanted her confused and weak.

She was permitted no company, so her thoughts were her only companion. This enabled her to reflect on her short life. For a brief while she had experienced happiness. Even though Luke's emotions had been false, her feelings of love had been real. She could not go back to the way it was, to the aching loneliness that so consumed her. She could not bear it.

Her uncle had been right: no one could—or would—ever love her. Her fate had been sealed when she was five years old and began to see into people's minds. She should have died with the rest of her family. If only she hadn't been rescued by the red angel.

It was only a cruel twist of fate that she had escaped. Escaped to what? All her life people feared her. The convent was more a sanctuary, a place where she was granted asylum if she kept to herself and followed the rules. Her thirst for friends had allowed her to trust. Now her love and faith had led her to this point. She would never make that mistake again.

She suddenly felt an icy coldness stream through her, and she turned her head toward the source. Her uncle was coming; she always felt him. In a moment she heard footsteps, and the key turned in her door. The first voice she heard was her uncle's.

"You can remove her hood, and untie her hands. I shall wait here."

Elanna found it hard to believe. She was in darkness and totally helpless, yet still her uncle feared her. What horrible thing was so buried in the depths of his mind that she must not discover? When the hood was finally removed, she squinted to make out any figure. The light from a lone candle glowed from the doorway, where her uncle's outline was cast. She could only sense what she always did from him—hatred and fear.

He managed a smug smile. "Well, my sweet Elanna, 'tis almost over. I have made arrangements for you to live out your life far from here, away from all this unpleasantness. You will be allowed to roam freely within the confines of certain boundaries, where you can do anything you want. No one will know of your background, of what you really are. You can make friends, and start life anew. In return for my generosity, I only require one thing."

Elanna stared blankly at him, not for one second believing a word. "And what would that one thing be?"

He held up a piece of paper. "This. Understand, 'tis only a formality. You simply have to sign it." He handed the paper to the servant, who in turn brought it to her.

She looked at the paper. It was the deed to Ancaster. "Why do I have to sign it? You said yourself that Luke was now lord of Ancaster."

He drew up and paused. His face showed no emotion except for a small twitch in his right eye. She had seen it before. It always happened when he was controlling extreme apprehension.

"I simply want everything to be nice and legal. Now, sign it."

Elanna looked at the deed, then back to Giles. "No."

"What?" His eye twitched more profoundly. "I said, sign it, you little…"

"Unlike all your puppets you keep around you, my will is my own. When have you ever cared about anything being legal? Certainly your pirating operation does not have the king's blessing?"

The twitch grew more extreme. Elanna decided to drive the dagger deeper.

"Aye, I have known about your business dealings since you brought me here for my phony marriage. I fear the men you hire have simple, open minds."

He rubbed his chin as he remained expressionless. "I see I underestimated you."

"You always have. Although you stand away from me, I sense that my signing this deed is crucial to your plans. I can only assume that Luke told you our marriage was never consummated, thus not legally binding. That still makes me owner of Ancaster. Things are back to the way they were before."

His face tightened, and his smugness disappeared.

"No, I will not sign. I will never hand Ancaster over to you and your outlaws. I would rather die."

He remained silent for a few seconds, then his rage surfaced. "So be it." With an angry motion he ordered the guard out, then left briskly behind him. The door slammed shut with a loud clank.

Elanna slowly sat on the cot with the realization that she had just signed her death warrant.

Giles hastened up the stairs and into his study, where he slammed his fists against the wall. That not being a sufficient anger outlet, he then grabbed the closest suit of armor and sent it crashing to the floor.

"I take it she told you to go to hell."

Giles looked at Patrick, who was sitting with an amused smile as he leaned back in Dayen's chair with his feet on the desk.

"That desk is made from the finest imported cherry wood from France! Get your feet off of it!"

Patrick took his feet down, but kept his arrogant smile. "So how did it go?"

"Our plan did not work." His black eyes flashed with contempt. "She still owns Ancaster. That stupid Cameron saw fit to not consummate his marriage."

Patrick sat up, his smile widening. "Surely you jest?"

"Do I look like I am jesting?" With a large sweep of his arm he knocked everything on his desk to the floor. Then he picked up a paperweight and threw it across the room.

Patrick watched the tantrum with silent delight. He had never seen Giles with such loss of control. "Perhaps she is simply lying?"

Having now worked himself into a sweat, Giles stopped and attempted to compose himself. He adjusted his lapels and smoothed his shirt. "I would know if she were lying. Actually, I think she is not capable of it. Get out of my chair."

Patrick stood up and let Giles sit. "Furthermore," Giles continued, "she knows about the pirating."

Patrick raised his eyebrows, then gave a simple nod. "I do not find that surprising. But I think I can help you out of your little dilemma. I have an idea."

"Very well, this I have to hear. Even you cannot get us out of this."

"Faith, Uncle, faith." Patrick walked slowly to the wall and gazed at a portrait, studying it as if he had momentarily forgotten the discussion. He loved to make Giles squirm.

"Well?"

Patrick turned; the smug smile had returned. "I will solve your problem on one condition—that Elanna will be allowed to live her life in safety like we had originally planned."

"But she knows too much. And she refuses to sign Ancaster over to me."

"No matter. She already thinks her new husband has abandoned her; I doubt if she even cares if she lives or dies. She can do no harm if she is safely confined to the monastery. When her foolish husband comes looking for her, we openly say we know nothing. We can even let him search Ancaster. With Elanna missing, he will have no reason to claim Ancaster. And we both know he cannot prove he married her."

"But what about that warrior woman! She is without a doubt out there watching every move we make! We will not be able to get the little witch out of here."

"I said, I have an idea."

Giles pondered his words, then slowly nodded. "Very well—I am listening."

"Brother Joseph will arrive tonight. I will send two men to escort him through the gates, with instructions to make a great deal of racket with the assurance of being heard. I also suspect the lady warrior is out there watching, and I want her to see him. I will tell him to make sure he is hooded in his monk's robe so they cannot see his face."

Giles narrowed his eyes in confusion. "I fail to see the significance in that."

"I doubt you would. Tomorrow bright and early, Elanna will leave Ancaster with the monk, accompanied by only a few guards."

Giles jumped to his feet. "What? Are you crazy?"

"Sit, my doubting reprobate, there is more."

Giles sat back down, but his face remained skeptical. "Very well. What?"

Patrick smiled. Sometimes he was too brilliant even for himself.

Matthew reined up when he saw Raymond had stopped. Luke pulled up beside them.

"Is it bleeding again?"

Raymond dismounted and answered his question without saying a word. Blood trickled down his leg from his open wound. The riding motion kept the gash from holding together.

"Damn bandage," he muttered, and sat on the ground. Luke had already taken some cloth strips out of his saddlebag and brought them to Raymond.

Matthew watched Raymond slowly remove the old bloodied bandage, then painstakingly begin to wrap it again with fresh strips. They had to stop several times to wrap his leg, delaying the trip to Ancaster by several hours. To make matters worse, Raymond insisted on wrapping his leg himself, which forced Luke and Matthew to stand around feeling useless. While Raymond was busy with his self-nursing, Matthew motioned Luke a few feet away so they could talk.

Safely out of earshot, Matthew shook his head. "He has lost a lot of blood. This cannot continue."

"I know. He has to rest and stay off horseback for a while. The wound will never heal as long as he is riding."

Matthew took off his hat and brushed his hair away from his forehead. "Damn! I hoped we would have found Pet and Elanna by now."

"In a few more hours 'twill be dark. We should reach Ancaster by then."

"Good. We are going to ride straight in there and insist they put us up for the night. You are the rightful owner now."

"Then what?"

"Do not press me. I am making this up as I go along."

Raymond stood up and motioned that he was ready to get going. "Come on," said Luke.

They all mounted and continued their journey. The territory was starting to look familiar to Luke, and his spirits lifted just a bit. He was still taking the positive outlook on things, which was his nature. Elanna probably exaggerated her uncle's motives, yes, that was it. Maybe she was simply trying to work things out. Several possible scenarios ran through his hopeful mind, when suddenly the gates of Ancaster were seen in the distance.

"This is it," he exclaimed, and kicked his horse into a gallop.

His hopeful mood disappeared when they reached the closed gate. A dozen well-armed men stood guard, blocking their path.

They reined up and Luke was the first to speak.

"Ho, there! We wish to enter."

One guard stepped forward. "Sorry, milord, but no one is to enter unless we are told otherwise. Giles Dayen's orders."

Matthew frowned as he sized up the situation. He was certain he could take out four, maybe five. In good health Raymond could without a doubt do the same, but right now he was in no condition to fight. Luke...well, Luke could punch a few if they didn't kill him first. If only Pet were there. He and Pet could take out the whole lot.

Luke was still trying his diplomatic talents. "I tell you, Giles Dayen is expecting us. I was here just a month ago."

"Sorry," the guard replied stiffly. "Our orders are to let no one pass." He drew his sword and stood firm. The other guards all readied their weapons.

"Well, this certainly is a friendly place," Matthew muttered. "Come on, men. We'll camp out tonight."

They turned and rode back the way they came. When they were safely away, Matthew motioned to stop. "Well, lads, any brilliant ideas? Obviously this Dayen character knew we were coming."

Luke was silent. He hadn't expected this kind of resistance.

"Perhaps," Raymond offered, "we should circle to the back? We might be able to find a vantage point in which to observe the goings-on, plus it would get me off this damn horse."

"Sounds good to me. Come on." He began to turn off of the road just as some riders came into view. Two men escorted a small cart pulled by a donkey. In the cart sat a monk, who was banging on a little drum and loudly chanting. They passed the three men without any sign of acknowledgement and proceeded to the gate.

"I wonder what Dayen wants with a monk?" asked Matthew.

"'Tis not our concern," replied Raymond. "Let us proceed."

They made a trail through the forest on horseback until the brush got too thick, whereupon they dismounted and continued on foot. Raymond walked with a visible limp, and both Luke and Matthew knew he would not last much longer without resting. Soon they came to a small meadow perfect for a camp. They led their horses into the clearing and began taking off the saddles. Matthew insisted Raymond lie down and rest.

Soon everything was unpacked and the horses were let to graze. Matthew motioned Luke away from Raymond.

"You stay with him. I am going to see if I can find a way into Ancaster."

Luke furled his eyebrows in concern. "But that could prove to be dangerous. Maybe I should go with you."

"Nay, stay with Raymond. He needs you more right now." Matthew hesitated for a second, then unsheathed his side sword and handed it to Luke. "Here. If anyone comes, use it."

Taking the sword, Luke held it as if it were a foreign object. "Will you not miss it?"

"Nay, I still have my great sword and daggers. I shall not be long. Help Raymond with his bandages."

Luke nodded as he watched his brother leave. He felt a sudden flush of uselessness. Is this what he had resorted to, being a nursemaid to an injured man?

Matthew made his way through the brush, moving as quietly as possible. He was hoping to find some sort of water supply, be it a creek or a well. He kept his ears alerted for the possibility of guards; there were bound to be a few on Ancaster's back boundaries. The brush thinned out a little, and he found a trail—possible made by animals—but a trail nevertheless.

A feeling that he was not alone suddenly overtook him. He stopped and listened. Nothing but the typical forest sounds could be heard. Continuing more cautiously, the feeling began to overwhelm him. He reached for his side and remembered he had given Luke his sword. He now was positive someone was behind him, moving closer. With one swift move he reached behind his back and quickly drew his great sword. He whirled around to face his stalker.

He barely had time to defend himself from the strike. His sword clanked against another great sword, and he stared into the eyes of his attacker.

He blinked. "Pet?"

"Matthew?" She looked doubly surprised.

They threw their swords down simultaneously and fell into each other's embrace. After a long heartfelt hug he drew back and gazed at her, not believing they had almost just killed each other.

"What are you doing here?"

Me? What are *you* doing here?"

"We came to find you."

"We?"

"Aye, Raymond and Luke are in a clearing just west of here."

She drew back in amazement. "Do you jest? Why on earth are you all here?"

"I might ask you that same question. Why did you just leave the way you did? You could have waited for us to return."

"I did not know when that would be. Elanna had to be found. You trusted her to my care."

"Is that what this is all about? You thought I would be angry because Elanna ran off?"

"Well, are you?"

"Of course not! That is, I am more angry with her than you."

"So you *are* angry with me?"

"Aye. I mean, nay. Well, just a little." He grabbed her and drew her close, burying his head in her hair. "God, I was so scared. Do not run off again."

"Then do not leave me again."

At that moment William burst into the scene. "Matthew? Is that you?"

Matthew let go of Pet, crossed his arms, and looked as stern as humanly possible. "You, young man, are in trouble. And so are you, my wife. You should have never brought him with you."

Pet gave William a disapproving frown. "I did not exactly *bring* him. He decided to follow me."

"She needed help," William explained. "You were not there, so I took your place. You said I was the man of the house while you were gone."

Now Pet folded her arms. "Oh, did you?" She glared at Matthew. "Are you suggesting I cannot take care of myself?"

"Well, nay, 'tis just that he…I mean you…oh, come here, both of you!" They embraced in a large group hug. "I am so glad you are both safe."

"Not quite," Pet answered. "We still have to save Elanna."

"Do you know where she is?"

"She is being held at Ancaster; I am sure of it. I tracked her right up to this area. She went in voluntarily, but I think it was a trap."

Matthew's mood changed abruptly, from overjoyed to furious. "So that bloody bastard does have her! We couldn't even get through the gates."

"I fear that is my fault. They probably do not want any more surprises."

"Surprises?"

"Since I was alone, I certainly couldn't storm the castle by myself, so I decided to force his hand."

Matthew took a breath and held it. He never knew what his ambitious wife would do. Before he could even ask, William teemed in with his own explanation.

"You should have seen her! She was so brave; she just rode right in there like she owned the place and demanded they turn over Elanna!"

Matthew let out his breath with a splutter. "What?" He turned to Pet, who in turn looked at William with a chagrined grimace.

"That is not *exactly* what happened," she attempted to explain.

"Good Lord, Pet, you could have been killed! What the hell were you thinking?"

"Well, I had to do something. Now all we have to do is wait."

"Wait? For what?"

"For them to react. They know I am here, and that I know they have Elanna. I picked this spot because there is a good vantage-point of the courtyard. William and I take turns watching it all day. Now that you are here, you can help."

"All right, but since they are not letting anyone in the gates, except for that monk, It will be a boring job."

"Monk?"

"Aye, a monk arrived after they turned us away, making enough noise to wake the dead. I am surprised you did not hear him."

"I have not had much time to hunt, and I was starving. I was heading back to camp when I heard you approaching." Her face fell into pondering. "A monk—hmm, this could be it."

"Be what?"

"Never mind; I shall explain later. I hope you brought food. If William had not been sneaking into the kitchen at night, we would not even have the little…"

"You let a boy take the risk of sneaking down there at night?" He raised his hands in exasperation. "Has my whole family gone mad?"

"He is not exactly a boy anymore; I killed my first man at his age. Besides, he blended in. They simply thought he was the son of one of the servants."

"'Twas easy," William stated. "I just crawled into an unshuttered window."

Matthew opened his mouth to argue, then quickly closed it. "Oh very well, what is done, is done. Come, let us go to Luke and Raymond. I left them in a clearing back over there. Raymond is injured, and Luke is…"

"Raymond is injured? You have already seen battle?"

Matthew grimaced sheepishly. “Well, uh…not exactly. He got swiped by a sword in a tavern.”

Pet folded her arms and gave him her usual droll expression. “You are angry with me for doing what needed to be done, yet you tell me one of you got injured in a tavern brawl before you even arrived here?”

William giggled, and Matthew’s face turned red.

“I never said it was a brawl! We were just sitting there, minding our own business, and a man started waving his sword around, and then…” He stopped when he saw his explanation wasn’t getting him anywhere. “Oh, never mind. I will let Raymond tell you. Come on.”

They started back toward the clearing. “I expected to meet some guards. I am surprised there are not any.”

Pet answered from behind him. “There were.”

“Indeed? What happened to them?” He stopped and turned to face her. She answered him with a blank stare. “Never mind, I can imagine.” He resumed his pace.

As they entered the clearing, Raymond saw Pet and gave a holler. “Pet! Praise be!”

Luke simply looked relieved. Perhaps now he would not be called upon to fight.

Pet sauntered up to the two and smiled, then just as quickly became serious. “I am glad you are here. We have much planning to do.”

Chapter Sixteen

Brother Joseph shuffled behind the two guards as they escorted him though the front door. "Oh, my back," he groaned. "Horrible trip, just terrible." He was still complaining when he was shown into the study, where Giles Dayen sat waiting. He motioned the monk to a chair.

Brother Joseph took off his robe and hood, revealing a red, bald head rimmed with the customary halo of short cropped hair. In his case the hair had long turned to thin, gray fuzz. He plopped down soundly and let out a loud moan. "That awful cart has gotten harder with every year I grow older. I need more padding on these old bones. So why did you send for me this time? And why was I told to make all that noise?"

Giles stood up and circled around his desk, gazing intently at the monk. He leaned against the desk and drew a great breath. "Brother, would you say we have had a good relationship? What I mean to say is, you get wine and oil, at much lower prices than anyone else can offer. You, in turn, sell it to various churches for a profit, which benefits your monastery."

Brother Joseph squirmed, and answered without making eye contact. "Yea, I suppose."

"This time I have a load of fine olive oil, the finest that Italy offers."

"Italian oil? Y-you did not steal it, did you?"

"Now, when has that ever bothered you before? Do not tell me you have suddenly obtained a conscience?"

The monk paused. "How much?"

Giles stood up and straightened his lapels. "This time 'tis free."

The monk stopped squirming and shot Giles a surprised look. "Free?"

"Well, perhaps *free* is too loose a word. I have a task for you."

Joseph glanced around the room. "Where is that other fellow that is always here?"

"You mean that little twit Patrick? Well, it just so happens he has developed a brilliant plan to help me get rid of…let us say, a small problem. Little does he know how brilliant. He is personally implementing the first step as we speak. I wanted him away so we could speak privately."

"Why?"

"Because he does not know about my altering of the plan. As far as he knows, everything is proceeding as he suggested. I, howe'er, have other ideas."

Patrick turned the key in the lock and pushed open the heavy door. Elanna stood waiting for him. Her room was still dark, but she was not hooded. She felt a turmoil within this stranger, like she sensed before when he had walked past her the night she was captured. The darkness prevented her from seeing far into his mind. She mostly sensed feelings.

"I have no doubt you knew I was coming," Patrick said matter-of-factly.

She looked intently at the object he held. "What is that for?"

"To save your life." He came up beside her. "Someone has come to try to rescue you. I have to send her away or Giles will have her—and you—killed."

"Her?" Elanna allowed herself a small smile. "It must be Pet."

"I only know her as the lady knight, and she has Giles in quite a state. This is the only way to save you." He took a step forward, and Elanna instinctively moved back. "Please, do not fear me."

She stared at him and attempted to search his mind. “I do not. Even though you serve my uncle, there is conflict within you. You tried to convey that to me before.”

“I hate him as much as you do.”

“Then why stay with him?”

He stared at the ceiling as a grim look encompassed his face. “I do what I have to do.”

“No one *has* to do anything.”

“You are young, and innocent. Some day you will understand.”

“How did you ever become involved with someone as vile as him?”

He paused, then sat on the cot. “We are sort of related.”

“Sort of? But then you also would be related to me.”

“Not exactly. As you know, your grandfather, Baron Dayen, died and left everything to his eldest son, your father. You were not even born yet. What you do not know, is that you also had an aunt, named Isabel. She ran off against her father’s wishes at a young age to marry someone beneath her position—my brother. My parents had both died from the fever, and my brother vowed to keep me with him. I was just a baby. Isabel accepted me like her own. She was the only mother I ever knew.”

He paused with reflection. “When he fell ill, the Baron wanted to make amends, forgive her, but he could not locate her before he died. After his death, Giles sought out his sister. He wanted Isabel and my brother to turn against his oldest brother, your father, and help him gain Ancaster. They threw him out of their house. He stormed off in a rage.”

Elanna sat listening, taking it all in with stunned interest. “I did not know any of this.”

“Soon after, my brother was found dead in his field; his horse still hitched to the plow. It appears he fell while plowing, and hit his head on a large rock. Isabel was devastated, and mourned deeply. Then she fell ill with a mysterious sickness. She died a few weeks later, penniless and alone, except for me. I did what I could, but I was so young.”

His boyish good looks became drawn and pained. "Giles showed up almost immediately and volunteered to take care of me. I have been with him ever since. He has always referred to me as his nephew, for lack of a better title."

"So, you feel you owe him a debt."

"At first." He closed his eyes, and Elanna was able to sense a deep sorrow, mixed with extreme guilt. When he opened them, he had regained his composure. "I fear 'tis a little more complicated than that."

"In what way?"

"I might as well tell you; you will find out sooner or later. Giles is running a pirating operation using Ancaster as the base. He steals goods and sells them at a profit. Only a handful of people know. As far as everyone else is concerned, Ancaster is a reputable manor that is well-run."

Elanna stared at the floor as she absorbed this information. "So that is why he needs Ancaster so badly. My coming along has jeopardized his livelihood."

"Exactly. So far he has kept all suspicion away from Ancaster. He even put together a band of renegades to keep the king busy. Your friend, the lady knight, took care of them. Now he's desperate."

He stood up and immediately winced. His left hand grabbed his right arm as if to support it.

"You are in pain."

He shook his head. "'Tis nothing, just a small injury I incurred as a youth."

"Come here; I am weak but I might be able to help you." She held out her hands to him.

He backed up with a look of alarm. "Nay, do not touch me!"

"But I can take away your pain!"

"I deserve my pain; indeed I deserve much more."

"Why are you so tormented? Why do you fear my touch?"

"I do not fear you, and my torment is not important. I must finish what I came here to do."

"Whatever 'tis, 'twill not work."

"Pray that it does. If Giles has his way, you would burn as a witch. I am trying to prevent that. I have convinced Giles to let you live your life out in the guardianship of a Scottish Monastery. I want no more deaths in this family. Now, turn around." He reached out and seized her hair. "I regret this, but 'tis better than dying."

Elanna closed her eyes and swallowed as he raised the sharp knife.

Back in the study, Brother Joseph was pacing in front of the desk, sputtering with rage. "You cannot ask me to do this!"

Giles, calm and assured, simply leaned back in his chair and smiled. "Oh, but I fear I can. Or perhaps the Church would be interested in finding out you have been selling pirated wine and oil for communion purposes? An anonymous letter to the bishop would suffice." He let out a short, amused snort. "That would shake things up a bit. I can just picture your body swaying from the gallows."

The monk brought his hand up around his throat and swallowed. "You wouldn't dare! I knew nothing about pirates! I-I would tell them you were involved."

"Oh, but I would dare. No one would believe you; I have covered my connection. You will do this. You have no choice."

"B-but such a young girl! It just is not right!"

"Forget her youth, my good brother. She is dangerous, not only to me but to everyone involved. I have always known that this is what would have to be done. I offered her a way out. She refused."

"I would like to hear that for myself."

Giles drew in a deep breath, and let it out loudly. "Oh, very well, we will visit her tomorrow. But I already know her answer. You might as well resign yourself to this action."

The monk remained silent as he wiped a cloth across his red, sweating brow. "I will need witnesses."

"That will not be a problem. I shall order my men to gather a few village children and hold them until the trial is over. The foolish parents will say anything to get their precious offspring back." He sat up and grinned as an idea occurred to him. "I might have to actually kill one to show I am serious. I would like that." He licked his upper lip as he contemplated the kill.

"No! Please, I beg of you, do not let any more innocent blood spill over your greed! I will make sure the villagers talk."

"Very well, you do that. Remember, not a word to my soft-hearted nephew. He will not know what is going on until 'tis too late." He let out a low chuckle.

"You act as if this whole thing is just a game."

His face instantly sobered. "Oh, but 'tis. Outwitting Patrick is what I live for. 'Tis my ultimate revenge upon my sister for refusing to help me. Killing her husband was not enough."

"Killing is so easy for you."

"Only if someone gets in my way." It was said as almost a threat. Joseph watched as Giles rose and swaggered to the door and held it open. "Get some sleep, my loyal monk. Tomorrow is a busy day."

Wordlessly, Brother Joseph walked through the door and made his way down the corridor.

Patrick saw the monk coming and stopped to greet him. "Good night, Brother Joseph. Pray for the success of my plan." He gave a nod and smiled.

Joseph looked pale as he saw what Patrick was holding, and opened his mouth to speak. Instead he just closed his mouth and nodded, then scurried on down the hall.

Patrick watched him leave through narrowed eyes. Joseph was usually more talkative—perhaps a little complaining, but gregarious nonetheless. Perhaps the trip was just tiring.

When Patrick entered the study, he found Giles standing at the window staring out at the deepening sunset. Giles addressed him without turning around.

"Beautiful, would you not say?"

"I suppose."

"Did you get the necessary item?"

"Aye." Patrick threw the knife at the cherry-wood desk, which stuck solidly with a definite *thunk*.

Giles turned and looked at the knife, then at Patrick. He took a breath to hold in his anger, which subsided when he saw the long swatch of platinum hair Patrick held. "Did she put up much of a fight?"

"Surprisingly, no. I explained that it was the only way for her to start a new life."

Giles raised an eyebrow. "Indeed. The only way."

"Have you found a willing girl for our little charade?"

Giles waved him off. "Oh really, Patrick, I cannot be bothered by such small matters. Anyone will do."

Patrick clenched his left hand, then relaxed it. It would not do to lose his temper now. "You told me you would find someone."

"Oh very well." Giles let out an exasperated sigh. "Really, Patrick, you make so much out of so little. It simply has to be a female."

"A female the right size. You underestimate the lady knight. She will not be easily fooled."

"Then you would be much better at this task than I. You are so much more detail oriented."

"Aye, I am. Which is the only reason we are both not dead."

Giles pursed his lips and kept his silence. He knew Patrick was right. If not for Patrick's sharp mind, they probably would have been discovered long ago.

Patrick ambled to the door and turned around before leaving. "I will find someone. You just uphold your end and make sure Elanna is safe."

"But of course." Giles watched him go, and a smirk developed on his face. He would uphold his end of the bargain all right. Only he was just adding a little twist.

Matthew half-opened one eye and patted the blanket beside him. He had gone to sleep holding Pet, and awoke alone. The sun was just barely rising. Birds were stirring to life with cheerful song to praise the day. He abruptly sat up, and glanced over at Luke's snoring figure. William and Raymond were also quite asleep. Yet somehow Pet had managed to slip away without awakening anyone. The others, he could understand. But how she got out from under his arm was beyond him.

He stood up and checked the horses, then let out a sigh of relief. They were all there. The morning chill caused a shiver, and he decided to stoke the fire a bit. Maybe Pet was finding a fat rabbit for breakfast. He certainly hoped so. He was so hungry, he'd take a skinny one.

The dawn grew brighter, and William began to move. Soon Luke began to yawn. Last, but not least, Raymond's giant form turned over when the sun glared in his eyes.

Matthew raised his arms for a long morning stretch. The brisk morning air smelled clean and fragrant. As his stomach grumbled, he imagined what Pet would bring back for breakfast. A rabbit or two, maybe a pheasant, even better a goose. His stomach took over his brain as he fantasized over the morning meal. A fat goose, roasted slowly, with apple and nut stuffing. He would demand a drumstick. As he envisioned the meat, his mouth began to salivate until he felt a tap on his shoulder.

He spun around with clenched fists, ready to fight whoever or whatever dared invade his stretch. It was Pet.

His body relaxed and he let out a large breath. "Pet! I wish you would stop sneaking up on me!"

"I would not have been able to sneak up on you if you had been paying attention. Something is happening—all of you, come with me."

She turned and headed toward the woods leading to the path. Luke and William jumped to life at her command. Raymond opened his eyes, winced, and tried to sit up. Matthew could not help but notice the giant was in pain. He motioned to Luke and William to follow Pet.

"Stay here, Raymond—whatever 'tis, I am sure we can handle it."

Raymond nodded, and closed his eyes. Matthew rushed to catch up with the others.

He came up beside Pet. "Where were you? Where is the goose?"

"What goose?"

"Never mind. What is so important that you had to take us on a hike before breakfast?"

She shook her head. "I am not sure. Something is happening down at Ancaster. When you told me about the Monk, it got me to thinking, and I had trouble sleeping. I awoke before sunrise and went to our vantage-point to watch the courtyard. As the break of dawn they began harness-ing a carriage."

"So?"

"So, someone is taking a trip. And I'll bet that someone is Elanna."

From behind them, Luke asked, "Why would you think that?"

"Because I tracked her here. They claim they haven't seen her. When I let my presence known, they had to get her out somehow. 'Tis just a feeling."

Matthew looked at Luke and shrugged. "Well, I trust her feelings."

"As do I," Luke answered.

William bubbled with excitement that only a child could muster that early in the morning. "What are we going to do? Are we going to ride in there and kill them all?"

"Before we start planning a mass murder, why don't we see what is going on first?" She cast the disappointed boy a sideways look. "A wise warrior picks when he fights, if possible."

William cast his gaze to the ground and kicked a rock. "Ah, gee."

"Come on, William, keep a stiff upper lip," Matthew offered. "I have a feeling there will be plenty of excitement for all."

Luke frowned. "That is exactly what I fear."

Pet put up her hand and motioned them to stop. "Quiet! After we crest this small hill, you will have to get down on your bellies. There is thick underbrush that will conceal us."

They followed her over the bluff and dropped down to crawl. In a few seconds they were staring down from a steep incline at Ancaster's courtyard. They watched silently as eight guards saddled their horses beside a fully harnessed carriage. Other guards stood nervously by, glancing around continually as if they expected someone to attack at any second. Pet had to smile at that. Made them nervous, did she?

Suddenly Pet stiffened and jabbed Matthew in the ribs. She pointed to the castle. A Monk followed several guards from the main door, his hood covering his face. Giles Dayen followed them, surrounded by more guards. It was who emerged next that made them all hold their breath.

A bound and hooded small figure, wearing a flowing white dress, was led from the door, with even more guards behind her. Long platinum hair streamed down her back from under the hood. She was led to the carriage, and roughly pushed inside. The Monk got in beside her.

Pet's mind whirled. To attack now would be hopeless. Luke drew in a breath and started to stand up. "Elanna!"

Pet pulled him down. "Quiet! Not now."

"B-but that is Elanna down there! We have to save her!"

"Do you think I do not know that? Now get down, before they see us!"

"Do as she says," Matthew said. "She knows what she is doing."

The guards mounted, Giles Dayen gave the order, and the carriage pulled out of the courtyard and started down the lane.

"Come on," Pet whispered, and began to draw back.

Once over the hill, she broke into a run. "We have to hurry and follow that carriage!"

They all ran behind her, offering their suggestions. She ignored them until she got to the clearing, where she instantly began giving orders.

"William, help Matthew saddle Goliath and Excaliber."

"What about the other…"

"Just do it!"

Not wanting to argue with her, he nodded and left for his task behind Matthew.

"What do you want me to do?"

Pet turned and faced Luke's worried face. "You have a choice. 'Tis obvious that Raymond is in no condition to travel. I am leaving William here with him, and Matthew and I are going after that carriage. We can take on eight men; we have done it before. You can either come with us or stay."

Luke was stunned into silence. Elanna was bound and hooded like a common criminal by that monster Giles Dayen, and he couldn't help her. Seeing her like that made his soul weep. "Of course I shall accompany you. She is my wife."

By now Raymond was awake and aware of what was happening. "Saddle my horse, Pet. Thou shall not be leaving me."

"Nay, my friend. Your body is hot with fever, and your leg is oozing. You need rest, or you shall die. I will not have that on my hands."

Raymond started to argue, then raised an eyebrow. "How many guards?"

"Only eight."

He waved his hand and lay back down. "Thee and Sir Matthew can handle that many."

So now it was back to Luke. He glanced over at William, then down at Raymond. "You are leaving a young boy and injured man here alone?"

Pet put on her jacket and headed for the horses. "Do I have much choice? You better saddle your horse if you are coming."

He stumbled behind her like a lost puppy. "But, what if they are discovered?"

"They will just have to take their chances."

Luke's logic fought with his emotions. He had to go after his wife; to do less would be unworthy of a husband. But again, to leave a boy and injured man alone to fend for themselves was not very commendable, either.

Pet reached her horse and turned to Luke. "Well?"

He pursed his lips, then took a deep breath. "You are sure Matthew and you can bring her back?"

She nodded with confidence.

He let out a sigh, and closed his eyes. "I shall stay. Bring her back to me."

Pet put a reassuring hand on his shoulder. "I will, I promise."

"Luke, you are doing the right thing." Matthew gave his brother a sincere smile.

He nodded, not very convincingly. "I hope so."

Now it was William's turn. "You are not taking me? But…"

Matthew crouched down to make eye contact. "Listen, William. You love Sir Raymond, do you not? And your Uncle Luke?"

He nodded.

"Well, they need you here. A fire must be maintained, and Raymond's wound needs spirits to keep it clean. Luke cannot very well sneak down to Ancaster, can he? Can you envision him crawling into a window?"

The boy's pout turned into a small smile. "Well, nay."

"Very well, then. We will be back before you know it, then we will return to Elton. The king will hear of this, I can assure you. We will bring Giles Dayen to his knees."

"Just bring back Elanna," Luke commanded.

Pet and Matthew mounted and turned the horses. "We shall. Take care of Raymond!"

"We will." Luke and William waved as the two rode into the forest and out of sight.

Chapter Seventeen

Elanna fingered a strand of her now shoulder-length hair and managed to blink back a tear. When would this nightmare be over? She had been without sunlight so long that her powers were weak, a fact she had to hide from her uncle. If what Patrick told her was true, Pet was out there somewhere. What if Pet did manage to rescue her? Where would she go? Luke didn't want her, Giles had made that perfectly clear. Was Pet the only one not in on the deception? Elanna had never been so confused in all her life. Her only concern now was for Pet.

A sudden wash of coldness swept through her, and she knew her uncle was approaching. This time she didn't bother to stand to face him. Instead when she heard the key turn in the lock she simply said, "I suppose you have come to brag about your brilliant plan."

The door opened and Giles stepped just inside, careful to keep his distance. "As a matter of fact, I did. It worked perfectly. I have come to tell you to abandon all hope. That bothersome lady knight is following the carriage, which will lead her on a merry chase in quite the opposite direction of where you are heading. You were quite clever, becoming friends with her. 'Tis a pity to have to kill her."

"I would not be so certain of that outcome. She is very resourceful."

Giles raised an eyebrow. "Oh, she will die, that is a fact. She thinks she is up against eight guards, when in fact an entire garrison of my men is waiting in ambush. They left last night under concealment of the darkness. When the carriage reaches a certain spot, 'twill stop and she will be drawn in to rescue you. Then she will die."

Elanna felt a flutter of fear in the pit of her stomach, but maintained her detached composure. "I would not count on that. After all, she defeated your pathetic little band of outlaws."

Giles took a backward step as his face contorted into surprise. "You know about that?"

"Your henchman Patrick made no effort to keep his distance from me. I was able to obtain some knowledge from his tormented mind." She mentally flinched at her first lie.

"He is not exactly my henchman. That bothersome little twit has become rather cocky lately."

"Yet he remains loyal to you."

"That will all be changing soon. So, just what else do you know?"

"I know you plan to kill me, and that Patrick does not know it."

Giles again drew back, and Elanna smiled at his fear.

"Do not worry, my frightened uncle, I cannot read your mind, I simply know your black soul." She looked him straight in the eyes without an ounce of fear. "'Twas always your plan. Patrick thinks he is saving me, when in fact he is playing right into your hands."

His usual smug smile returned, and he leaned against the wall and folded his arms. "My little ward thinks he has it all sorted out. When I suggested he ride along with the decoy carriage to be sure everything goes smoothly, he readily agreed. He looked rather well in the monk's robe."

"I find it hard to believe he would agree to an ambush, especially of England's only lady knight."

"He didn't. That was a little something I threw in. I had to make it look like a robbery, so when Patrick stops the carriage at a planned spot, my men will be hiding in the woods. When this so-called lady knight of yours catches up, Patrick will pretend to hand you over without a fight.

Of course, 'twill soon be discovered that the girl is not you. That's when my men attack." He paused for a short chuckle. "Poor Patrick. He will be far from here when I take you with the real monk to Cliffside Abbey, where you will be tried as a heretic. Patrick thinks you are going to a peaceful monastery in Scotland to live out your life. By the time he figures out what is really happening, 'twill be too late."

"Pet is clever. She might fool you."

He shrugged. "So she takes a few men down with her. If Patrick is one, even better. In any sense, there will be no one left to save you."

She turned her face away and looked at the bare wall. "So you have done your bragging. Why else did you come down here?"

"To give you one last chance to save yourself. Sign Ancaster over to me, and relinquish all ownership. I will send you back to the convent, and we can forget this whole unpleasantness."

Elanna turned and looked at him. "And I am actually expected to believe you?"

"Well, your freedom would come at a price. I fear that know-it-all prioress would have to be disposed of. You would tell her about my little operation, she would go to the authorities, and we cannot have that, can we?"

"Y-you would kill her?"

"Better her than you, right Elanna? Think about it. You know what your fate is, otherwise."

"I do not have to think about it. The prioress is the only family I have ever known. I cannot condemn her to death."

"Then you are condemning yourself."

She closed her eyes. "I know."

"Very well. We will leave tonight. Prepare yourself, Elanna. In a few days you will feel the flames of death." He quickly exited and the door clanked shut.

Brother Joseph was waiting just outside. Giles motioned him to follow, and led him away from the door.

"You heard? I offered her a way out, just like you asked, and she again refused."

Joseph somberly nodded. "Yes, I heard. She would rather die than cause the death of someone she loves. Noble little creature."

"Noble? Bah! There is no reward in being noble. Now, if you are quite satisfied, can we proceed?"

"Yes, I suppose there is no other way."

They parted company, and Giles went to his study to pour a drink. He gulped it down quickly to calm his shaking hands. Having Elanna so close unnerved him. So far he had been lucky that she never discovered her true power. She had to burn before that power was unleashed.

Nearby in the woods, Luke tried to keep himself busy and disconnected from the situation. He gathered firewood, cooked a few rabbits for breakfast, and helped Raymond change the bandage on his leg. They used the last bit of strong brandy they had obtained from the tavern to clean the wound. Keeping still and resting seemed to help Raymond tremendously. He already insisted he felt better.

"The wound heals," he announced at lunchtime. "Remaining idle has permitted it to close. I shall need more spirits, though. I wish not to succumb to my former malady."

William almost choked on his mouthful of meat as he eagerly volunteered. "I can sneak down tonight and get more, Sir Raymond!"

"Indeed thou can, young William. I value thy help."

Luke threw down a bone and stood up. "I think I will brush down Annabelle."

They watched as he lumbered off to the horses. William shook his head with a confused look. "That is the third time today he has brushed his horse. He seems so unhappy."

"Nay, lad, just useless. His wife is in peril, and he lingers here with an injured man and a young boy. His very manhood is brought to question. Thou would not understand."

"I am not that young. I know a heartsick man when I see one. He is much like Matthew."

"Aye, in many ways. He has yet had to fight for anything. Mayhap he feels unworthy. A man's pride is a fragile entity."

"But not fighting is a good thing, aye? Pet says fighting is not always the answer."

"Yea, that is true. Yet sometimes there is no other way. Luke has not discovered that."

"At least Annabelle is benefiting from his mood. I have never seen her so shiny."

Raymond laughed. "Aye, well, if he keeps it up, the poor animal will not have any coat left."

Luke dragged the curry brush across Annabelle's flank for the umpteenth time, his mind distant. He should be with Pat and Matthew, instead of playing nursemaid and nanny. What kind of man was he? What kind of man would Elanna think he was? He had promised to protect her, and then let this happen. He snorted as he chastised himself, mumbling under his breath.

He felt a raindrop, and looked up at the ever-darkening sky. "Figures," he muttered. Now everything had to be put under shelter, or they would be wet, cold, and miserable. As miserable as his heart already was.

He had no way of knowing that Elanna was a short distance away, with a heart more miserable than he could ever imagine.

Miles away, the rain did not go unnoticed by Pet and Matthew. If not for their leather suits, they would have been soaking wet. They followed the carriage at a safe distance, careful not to arouse suspicion. The carriage stayed on heavily traveled main roads, where the presence of others made it impossible to attack. Pet would not risk innocent lives lost. Matthew, as usual, was impatient and just wanted to get the whole thing over with. He chewed on a piece of dried meat as he rode.

"I do not understand why we just do not attack and get Elanna."

Pet cast him a condescending look. "Out in the open with all these people around? I think not. For one thing, we would most likely be mistaken for highway robbers, and would end up fighting off well-intentioned bystanders. Nay, we have to wait for the right moment."

"The longer we wait, the further away from Ancaster we get."

"Aye, true, but that cannot be helped."

They rode in silence for a minute, then Matthew felt the raindrops. "Oh, great. Just what we needed."

"Would you quit complaining? This task is unpleasant enough without you adding to it."

"I am just worried about the others. I hated to leave them behind like that."

"I know. I am worried about them, too. But we must focus on our task, else we get distracted."

"We may be in luck—the carriage is stopping."

They watched as the carriage pulled up to an inn. The guards dismounted and surrounded the carriage, their weapons ready for attack. Other patrons and travelers gawked at the strange sight, as first a monk exited the carriage, then a hooded girl. They went inside the inn as the guards stood outside.

"They are not un-harnessing the horses," Pet observed. "'Tis maybe just a food stop."

"Good, I am starving."

"I did not mean a food stop for you."

"Well, what is wrong with us buying a hot meal?"

"Because they might recognize me."

"They do not know me. I could go and…"

"Quiet! The monk returns."

Sure enough, the monk, still hooded, came out and motioned with a nod. The driver and several guards began un-harnessing the horses. The other guards went back inside the inn with the monk.

Matthew uttered a curse. "They are all going to be warm and fed with hot food, while we wait out here in the rain with nothing to eat but this hard stuff." He threw his piece of beef jerky on the ground in disgust.

Trying to ignore her ill-tempered husband's mood, Pet scrunched her face in thought as her hand cupped her chin. She had hoped for an opportunity to get Elanna back before now, but it was almost as if the carriage was purposely implying tactics to keep that from happening. It had to be coincidental. They couldn't possibly know they were being followed. Could they?

As if reading her mind, Matthew voiced her thoughts out loud. "I swear they are stalling. There are several hours of daylight left, yet they stop for the night."

"Aye, it would appear so. Regardless, there is nothing we can do."

"I say we wait for nightfall, then sneak into the inn and rescue Elanna."

"Ah, the element of surprise."

He was amazed she agreed with him. "Aye, exactly!"

"The guards would be easy to take out, since they would not be expecting us."

"Aye! We could sneak in the back…"

"…just like common criminals…"

"…and kill the guards…"

"And anyone else that gets in the way."

"Aye. I mean, nay! I mean…" He saw her point, and realized she had only been toying with him. "Very well, I do not hear you coming up with any better ideas."

"We do not have much of a choice. We wait."

He groaned, and sat on the ground. Spotting the beef jerky, he picked it up and took a bite, chewing profusely.

Inside, Patrick sat at a table watching the decoy girl wash down mutton with a swig of ale. The peasant girl had no proper upbringing, but she was the right size to carry out their little charade. Patrick had promised her a better position at Ancaster with more pay. Actually, he was thankful it was going so well. He kept the carriage on well-traveled main roads, which he knew would discourage any attack from the noble lady knight. She certainly wouldn't attack the inn. Tomorrow the carriage would leave late morning, when other travelers would be present, and then he would turn off on a known side road. There they would take a break at a planned open space, and the warrior woman would have her chance. She was good; he had to admit that. Even though he was positive she was following the carriage, he never once caught a glimpse of her. It was hoped she would first ask him to turn over Elanna. He would act confused, and ask who Elanna was, then produce the girl. Only then would the lady warrior realize she was following the wrong carriage. By then, Giles should have the real Elanna on her way to Scotland, where he conceded to let her live in anonymity.

It was a good plan. He was pleasantly surprised when Dayen agreed to it. He had managed to convince Giles that there was no reason to continue keeping Elanna prisoner. Brother Joseph would take her far away to his Abbey in Scotland, where no one knew her. He felt badly that she had to be treated like that, but it was better than death. If authorities asked her whereabouts, they would feign ignorance. No one could prove she had ever been there. She will have simply disappeared.

The guards at the next table began laughing in unison. Patrick turned and flashed them a smile, then returned to his thoughts. Inns made him uncomfortable. His eyes closed as the memory of the fire surfaced. He had been so young, so impressionable back then. Giles had become his role model after he stepped in and took Patrick under his wing. He looked up to the older, smarter man in awe. Until the fire.

Giles never told him why his family had banished him at an early age, leaving him bitter and vengeful, in his point of view rightfully so. When the Baron Dayen died and left everything to his eldest son Stanley, Giles became outraged and obsessed. He watched his brother's every move for years until finally the opportunity presented itself. He devised a plan to trick Stanley into signing Ancaster over. He convinced Patrick, now sixteen, to help him stage a rescue at an inn, where the whole family would be spending the night as they returned from a journey. Not a typical rowdy inn, but a nicer one, with larger bedrooms on the second story. Patrick's job was to barricade all doors to the outside except one. Then Giles would set the fire and run through the inn, waking everyone up. He would then lead them to the only unblocked door, appearing to save everyone's life. He would be a hero. Stanley would be grateful that Giles had just happened to be passing by, the banishment would end and Giles would be welcomed back into Ancaster. Gratefulness would lead to Giles obtaining Ancaster. At least, that was the plan Giles laid out.

Something went terribly wrong. The fire spread much too quickly, and soon the entire bottom floor was consumed in flames. Patrick was terrified that Giles had been trapped inside. It was then that he heard Giles laughing with satanic delight from a safe distance. At that moment Patrick realized that Giles never did intend to save anybody. It was always his plan for everyone to die. And Patrick had been made an accomplice. He hated Giles from that moment on.

He had to do something, fire or not. The back door was the only one not burning, so he removed the barricade and rushed inside. At first he was beaten back by the intense heat, but he soaked his red cloak in a nearby water barrel and used it as a protective cover. The back stairs were still intact. He would only be able to save the occupant of the end room before he would also be burned to death or overcome by smoke.

He heard a voice screaming. In minutes the fire would consume the hallway, and he also would be trapped. The voice screamed again, and he recognized it as a small girl. My God, just a child! It had to be Stanley's youngest child, Elanna. He had to do something.

He kicked the door open and was immediately blinded by smoke. He tripped over a body, and realized it must be the girl's nursemaid. Then he made out Elanna's small form, pounding her little fists on the window. She was no longer screaming, instead seemingly intent on breaking the window. He remembered thinking that a heavy object would break through, when the window suddenly burst outwards, clearing the air and giving him a way out. There was really no time to think. He came up from behind and wrapped the wet, red cloak around her. Then he picked her up and jumped, holding her close against him.

They hit the ground hard, but alive. The little girl seemed to be in shock as he carried her to some nearby shrubs and hid her from Giles. There was nothing else he could do. His lungs burned from smoke inhalation, and he collapsed on the ground. His right arm hurt horribly; later he would discover it had been broken in the fall. It never healed properly. He told Giles later that the arm was injured from falling off a horse. Giles was so caught up with his new role as keeper of Ancaster that he little cared about Patrick.

Everyone in the inn perished. Later, when little Elanna was discovered, Giles had no idea that Patrick was the one who had saved her. He would have been outraged had he known.

Giles fooled everyone but Patrick with his act as the concerned uncle and grieving brother. He moved in swiftly and took over as the child's guardian. As such, the king granted him temporary ownership of Ancaster until she reached marriageable age. When the little girl began exhibiting unusual powers, Giles was terrified that someday she would know who had set the fire and would tell someone who might believe her. At first he locked her away. Patrick begged Giles for her freedom, asking for her to be sent to a convent where she would be harmless. Giles finally relented, but threatened that if the girl ever gave him any trouble he would have her burned at the stake.

Giles visited her every year for appearance sake, deep down resenting deeply that she had ever lived. Everything was fine until the king demanded her to take a husband.

The guards behind him laughed again, and he was jarred back to the present. He stood up, and motioned to one guard.

"You, stand guard over the girl. The rest of you, stay sober. I want everyone fresh and alert in the morning. I am going to bed."

Several men groaned at that order, but they all nodded in agreement. These men were hand-picked by him; he trusted their loyalty. Most of them hated Giles, and worked for him only because they needed the job. He felt his plan was progressing nicely. If he handled it right, no one would have to fight. Soon this whole episode would be over. Elanna would be emotionally scarred, but she would be alive, something Patrick had been fighting for since the fire so many years ago.

Chapter Eighteen

Luke lay on his back gazing up at the evening's dissipating clouds, which were splashed with hues of pink and red from the dying sun. Ordinarily he would be thinking how beautiful they were; at that moment they only reminded him of the day's dismal rain. He almost wished the weather would again turn cold, at least snow would be a change. William had managed to bring back a few rabbits for dinner, so at least his belly was full. The boy was turning out to be invaluable, which made Luke feel even more impotent. Even now as he lay there being useless, William was making his way down the hill to the castle to steal more brandy for Raymond's leg.

William watched from behind a shrub as two servants passed by. When the coast was clear he ran to his next target, a large tree that would easily conceal him. He had no idea where the spirits would be kept, as before now he had only stolen food. It would be somewhere cool. Back at Elton, Pet kept her wines and ale in a cellar. Yes, that was it, a cellar. He must look for a door leading downstairs.

Making his way swiftly and quietly, he blended in with a group of servants walking toward the kitchen. When they rounded a corner, he broke away and casually strolled the other way. Every door on the outside wall looked the same. He opened each one as he walked the back perimeter, but none led to stairs. Ancaster was so large; he was beginning to think his task was hopeless. He could look forever and never find the right door. Suddenly a brass female voice startled him.

"You there, lad! Come or!"

He froze.

"I said, come or!"

He turned around slowly and saw a rather plump woman about fifteen feet away, sitting on a stump. William quickly surmised that she was a cook, judging by her apron and traditional cook's cap. She had taken off one shoe and was rubbing her foot. Her round face was flushed and pinched with pain.

William pointed to himself. "Me?"

"Of course, you! Who the 'ell else would I be talkin' to? You're Thomas the avener's son, aren't ye?"

William paused, not sure how to answer.

"No matter, I don't care who ye be, my bunion is actin' up mighty fierce. I needs ye to fetch some wine for me. The master is demanding a wine sauce on his partridge, and I'm plumb out."

A small smile broke across William's face. "I would be happy to, ma'am, but I fear I have never had the pleasure of visiting the wine cellar."

"What, boy, are ye daft? It's right around the corner, second door! I'd go myself, mind ye, but my poor foot..."

"I would be honored to help you. I will go immediately."

"That's a good lad. Now, fetch a nice red bottle and bring it to the kitchen, and hurry up about it. Watch your step; it's dark down there. Use the torch at the top to find your way, and don't forget to put it back when ye leave. And don't talk to the prisoner!"

"Prisoner?"

"Aye, word is he's dangerous. A murderer, they say. He's being kept off the main room. Just mind your business and stay away. Now, scoot!"

"Thank you, ma'am!" He broke into a run, hope renewed in him. This was just the break he needed. He'd have the brandy for Raymond's leg and be back at the camp before it was totally dark.

He found the door and opened it. Only one torch lit the steep stairway. He took the torch from the sconce and held it in front of him, then cautiously descended the stairs. The room was indeed dark. Several mice scurried out of the light as he entered, leaving only spiders stubbornly clinging to their webs. A myriad of bottles were nettled in the large rack. William began his search, found a wine bottle for the cook, and one he hoped was brandy for Raymond's leg. He couldn't carry both bottles and the torch, and—remembering the cook's instructions—needed to put the torch back at the top of the stairs. He would have to take two trips.

He sprung up the stairs and left the wine at the top, then came back down to get the brandy. That's when he heard the voices from the next room.

Fearful to be discovered, he jammed the torch behind the rack so its light couldn't be seen. His natural boyhood curiosity overcame him. It couldn't hurt to just sneak up to the door and listen, could it?

The door had a little window with bars, and he slowly stood on tiptoe to peek through. He saw a dark hallway, and squinted to make out a figure holding a small candle. It was a monk, a rotund, squat little fellow, and he seemed to be talking to someone behind a chained door. William strained to make out a few words.

"…must change your mind…I cannot stop him…please do not make me do this."

William furled his eyebrows in confusion; he thought the monk had left that morning. This place seemed to be crawling with monks. Was he talking to the prisoner the cook had warned about? William was further perplexed when he heard a female voice answer.

"I have made my decision. I will never sign Ancaster over to my uncle. He will simply have to kill me." Her defiant tone couldn't be mistaken. It was Elanna.

"My dear child, I do want to save you! I shall defend you in the trial as best I can. But you need to know, he is planning to hold some village children hostage so their parents will testify against you."

William had to really strain to hear Elanna's soft answer. "I know. The village people will do what they have to do. And so will I."

The monk relented, and closed his eyes. "Bless you, my child, and may God be with you." He turned and scurried down the dark corridor.

His eyes now wide, William fought to make sense of this new situation. His twelve-year-old mind—mature for his age—tried to figure out what must have happened. If this was indeed Elanna, which meant the carriage he saw leave that morning was a decoy—and Matthew and Pet were chasing a wild goose. Or, walking into an ambush. His heart beat with fear and bewilderment as he pictured his whole world falling down around him. What could he, a mere boy, do?

He watched the monk reach the end of the hall, and waited for the door to shut. Then he waited a few more minutes just to be sure he was gone. The corridor was even darker than the wine cellar, so he would need his torch. His mouth was dry and his hands were frigid as he carefully and slowly pulled the latch and opened the door. It made a tiny creak, and he stopped and held his breath. When hordes of soldiers didn't descend on him, he opened the door enough to slip through. He practically tiptoed to the door.

When he tried to speak, all that came out was a raspy croak. It was, however, enough to get Elanna's attention.

"Who is there?"

He cleared his throat. "Elanna?"

He heard motion behind the door, then he saw her face peer out of the barred little window. "William? How on earth…how did you…what are you doing here?" Her expression was a mixture of astonishment and hope.

"That is my question. We saw you leave this morning on a carriage. Pet and Matthew went to rescue you."

"Pet...and Matthew? But I thought...well, never mind that. You must leave here! 'Tis very dangerous."

"I have to get you out of here. Luke is going to die when I return with you. He is..."

"Luke? Do not speak of him. 'Tis because of him that I am here."

Her bitter tone made William pause. "W-what do you mean?"

"He planned my capture. He never loved me."

"You jest, I am sure. When he and Matthew returned from their trip, he was frantic to discover you gone. Even now, he is just beyond the hill behind Ancaster. Raymond is with him, but he is hurt, I fear. We all came to rescue you."

"No, you lie. Luke planned this, and Matthew helped."

William frowned, and held the light up higher to make sure he was actually talking to Elanna. "You are the seer. Search my mind; what does your inner sense tell you now?"

"I have been too long without light. I am weak."

"Please try, Elanna! You must believe me!"

"I believed an old man, and I am here. Why should I believe you?"

William felt himself growing frantic and exasperated. He had to make her believe him. He frowned as he fought for words, then his face suddenly brightened. "You told me once that children have open, free minds. Well, much as I hate to admit, I am still a child. You must be able to detect that I am telling you the truth."

There was a long pause. Finally she stuck her hand out between the bars. "Take my hand."

He complied, and waited as she closed her eyes and concentrated. When she opened them, he saw large tears flowing down her face. "You do not lie. I thought my powers were dulled when I could not sense that Luke was in trouble and that Matthew was dead. When the old man said...oh, I have been so foolish! How could I have been mistaken like this?"

William had no idea what she was babbling about, but he understood that she believed him. "I am going to try to break the chains. I need to find a sword or something."

Her face sobered and she lowered her voice. "Listen, William...there is no time. They are taking me to a place called Cliffside Abbey, where I will be tried as a heretic and burned as a witch. Furthermore, Pet and Matthew are walking into a trap. My uncle has sent a garrison of his men to strike them down. You must go back and tell Luke to warn them. And also tell him that I am sorry for doubting him."

"No, I will not leave you!" He grabbed the chain and made a futile attempt to break it with his bare hands.

"William, you must go tell Luke! 'Tis Pet and Matthew's only chance!"

He ignored her, and continued to pull the chain. "Do not worry about Pet. She can take care of herself."

"Ordinarily that is true, but this time she will be highly outnumbered. Please, William."

He dropped the chain and let out a sigh. "I am going to get Luke. He will be able to break these chains."

"No, 'tis too dangerous! Besides, they are taking me tonight in the cover of darkness. My uncle will not let me see daylight."

"But why?"

"I get my strength from the sun. He knows this, and fears me searching his mind. But do not worry. Witch trials are usually held in the town square, or the church's courtyard, so that all the people can attend and watch. My strength will return once I am in the sun."

"What if 'tis cloudy?"

"The light I require comes through even the clouds. Now, go! If you are discovered, there is no telling what he will do to you."

"But," he argued, "even with your power back, how will that save you?"

She was silent, and then her voice dropped to a whisper. "I cannot tell you that. Just go get Pet and Matthew. Tell...tell Luke I love him."

"You can tell him yourself, when we come back to break you out of here." He backed up and turned toward the wine cellar. "Do not give up hope!"

"No, William! Do not come back! I could not bear it if you and Luke were caught!"

"Do not worry," he yelled back from behind the door. He vaulted up the stairs, tripping over the wine bottle at the top. Once outside, he took off in a run. Tossing the wine to the cook, who still sat rubbing her foot, he yelled his apologies and didn't stop. He darted through groups of people until he was safely in the woods. By the time he reached Luke and Raymond, he was quite out of breath.

"Luke! Luke! I found her! We have to go back!"

Luke was on his knees helping Raymond bandage his leg. He rose to his feet and gave William a stern look. "What are you talking about?"

"Elanna! She did not leave with that monk! She is here!" He grabbed Luke's large hand and tried to pull him toward him. It was like trying to move a tree.

Luke held firm as the boy tugged and made no sense at all. "Slow down! How can she be here? We all saw her leave."

"Nay, 'twas not her! I tell you, I talked to her, just a few minutes ago! You must believe me!"

Raymond began pulling on his boots. "I believe thee, master William. I shall accompany thee."

Luke looked down at Raymond, painstakingly putting on boots as he winced with pain. "Well, wait a minute! I did not state that I did not believe him. I just...I mean to say...who the hell did we see leave this morning?"

"I do not know, but she said Pet and Matthew are walking into a trap. A large trap, by the sounds of it. I tried not to show concern, but someone has to find them and warn them!"

Luke's head spun with this sudden onslaught of information. "Good God, we have to do something. Raymond, I am no good with the sword.

Can you ride and find my brother and Pet? You would be of more help to them."

Raymond nodded. "Of a surety. My leg is healing with each passing minute. What about the boy?"

William bristled at being called a boy. "Luke will need me! I will go with him."

"I agree," said Luke, reluctantly. "But only because I need him to show me where Elanna is."

Pausing with uncertainty, Raymond seemed to reconsider the plan. "Mayhap it would be best if I accompanied thee? As thou said, thou art no good with the sword, and..."

"Nay, she is my wife." His face drew determined and resolved. "I should have done this in the first place. For too long I have hidden behind my brother's sword."

Back in the cellar, Elanna lay on her small cot and softly cried, mostly from joy. Luke did love her. Somehow her uncle had made her believe lies...all lies. He killed her spirit and brought her hopelessness. She had decided to die. Now she was determined to live. To accomplish that, she would have to use the one power that terrified even her.

She closed her eyes and let her mind remember that fateful day. It was only months after the fire. For as long as she could remember, she always felt chilled—almost lifeless—whenever her uncle was around. His mind always conveyed hatred and resentment toward her. But in her youth and innocence, she knew he must love her—after all, he was her father's brother. He had to love her. Wasn't that the rule of things that families stay together, no matter what?

Every night he made a show of coming in to tuck her in goodnight, playing the part of the good, caring uncle, who mourned his brother and vowed to raise little Elanna. She learned later he was granted Ancaster only because of that promise. One night as she waited for him, she decided to search his feelings and find that spark of goodness she knew must exist. Her small, untrained mind could not comprehend what she saw.

Inside his mind was a strong image of her father—her dead father, his beloved brother. His body was just a rotting corpse—but inside the deepest recesses of Giles' mind he was alive. His face was contorted into deathly anguish as he stared out from the grave, pointing an accusing finger. Perhaps it was extreme guilt that Giles kept buried, or just more of his hatred. Whatever, the image was so strong the five-year-old Elanna could not handle the mental picture. Without knowing it, she somehow projected the image back to her uncle's conscious mind.

Clutching his head, he screamed in terror. He backed up until Elanna could no longer project the image. He stood staring at her for a short while, then regained his composure and silently left. From that day forward, he dropped the pretense of the caring uncle. He refused to come within fifteen feet of her. Soon after, heartbroken and lonely, she was sent to the nunnery.

The image never left her mind, so strong it had been. At first she was told never to use any powers, as they were given by the devil. Every night the Prioress prayed for Elanna's soul to be lifted of the terrible curse. But the powers stayed. Eventually the Prioress concluded that God meant Elanna to have the powers, but only for good purposes. Elanna decided to hone her talent to be useful to dying people in the convent hospital. Reaching into their minds, she would transmit comforting images to give them relief in their dying minutes. It would often be a loved one, a beloved spouse or child that had passed on before them. People died peacefully. Elanna grew strong. She lived knowing she could use her powers to help people.

But she could transmit horrible images just as easily as good ones. And she knew just the image to drive her uncle mad. If she could only get close enough…

It was dark by the time Luke and William reached the castle grounds. Even so, they kept in the shadows to avoid detection. Small groups of servants milled around bonfires and conversed, most ignored them or nodded a small acknowledgement. They were almost to the far corner when a loud voice rang out.

"You there! Identify yourself."

They swung around to face a lone guard who perhaps was going to or coming from his shift. Luke felt his throat constrict. William, however, saved the moment.

"I am the son of Thomas, the avener. This man here is a new hire. I am showing him around."

The guard hesitated, then smiled widely and nodded. "Oh, very good then. Proceed." He ambled away and gave them no more notice.

Luke looked down at William with raised eyebrows. "Thomas, the avener?"

William shrugged. "Apparently I have a resemblance to the lad. Come on, the cellar is this way."

There were no more interruptions as they opened the creaky door and gazed down into the inky darkness. The torch still burned right where William had left it.

"Careful now, the stairs are steep. Follow me."

Luke took the torch as he followed William down the stairs into a damp, cold wine cellar. William walked across the room to a door.

"She's being kept beyond this door, in a chained room. I hope you can break the chains."

"Do not worry about that. I shall bust the door down if I have to."

They carefully entered the corridor and in seconds stood in front of the cell. Luke brought his face close to the little barred window, but couldn't see anything because of the darkness. "Elanna? I am here. Stand back, I might have to break down the door."

They heard a muffled response from behind the door. William suddenly felt uneasy.

"Luke, I think we should go."

"Do you jest? We just got here." He grasped the chain and braced his leg against the stone wall. "A chain is only as strong as its weakest link." He gave a sharp tug backwards.

William glanced around, his uneasy feeling growing stronger. "Luke, something is not right."

"Quiet, lad." He gave another sharp tug. One link gave way. "Ah, one more pull and I have it!" Sure enough, the chain came apart and fell to the floor with a loud rattle.

By this time William had backed up against the corridor wall. He had the overwhelming compulsion to flee. He couldn't explain it, but the feeling was definitely there.

"Luke, do not open the door. Let us get out of here."

Luke turned the latch and ignored him. "Elanna!" He stepped inside and held up the torch. He only got a quick glimpse of his bound and gagged wife before he was hit from behind.

William had already started running to the wine cellar door. A guard suddenly appeared from the shadows and grabbed him. Kicking and screaming, William did what any twelve-year-old lad with limited fighting skills would do—he bit him.

The guard let go and yelped. William took the opportunity to dart in the wine cellar door, only to be greeted by two more guards waiting inside. He dropped to his knees and slid between their legs. They swung around and started after him. William ran behind the wine racks and huddled down in the darkest place he could find. Then he silently reached out and grabbed two wine bottles.

Pet had taught him that sometimes the best defense is a strong offense. He stood up and yelled in a strong, steady voice. "Over here, you buffoons! Or are you afraid of a mere boy?"

One of the guards growled. "Get him! You go that way!"

William blessed the darkness as he climbed to the top of the rack and waited for the two guards to reach him. When they met directly below him, it was a simple matter of smashing the two bottles down on their heads. As they dropped to the floor with broken glass and wine dripping over their faces, William scrambled over the top of the rack and jumped down. He had just made the second stair when one of the guards, still drenched with wine, grabbed him.

"Aha! Now I have you!"

William didn't hesitate. He brought his leg up and kicked the man soundly in his crotch. Pet had also taught him to fight with whatever means you had.

The guard's eyes rolled upward and he dropped to his knees as he grasped the tender area between his legs. William bounded up the stairs to safety.

Inside the cell, Luke had his own fight on his hands. The hit from behind didn't knock him out, but dazed him enough that two other guards now held him. The small area made swordplay impossible, for which Luke was thankful. With one mighty yell, he broke them loose and hit one squarely in the jaw. The force caused the guard to hit the wall and fall to the floor unconscious. Just as fast as Luke disposed of two guards, two others replaced them. Now aware that William had been right—it was obviously a trap—he berated his stupidity while fighting with every scarp of strength he could muster. Guards were flying everywhere. Luke picked one up over his head, then threw him against three others as they entered the cell. They all fell backwards from the door.

Luke took the fight to the corridor. One hit usually sent a guard flying backwards against another. It actually looked like he might win, when he heard a familiar voice ring out over the battle.

"I believe that will be quite enough, Mr. Cameron."

He turned to see Elanna being held by two guards, one with a knife to her neck. Elanna struggled and violently shook her head. The gag only permitted a muffled, terrified scream.

Giles Dayen stood by the entrance, a smug smile on his face. "I will not hesitate to slit her throat."

Luke tossed the guard he was holding and put up his hands. "Please, do not kill her. Let us go, and we will never bother you again."

"Oh, I think not, lord Cameron. You were the only loose end. How nice of you to join us, so unexpectedly. Now you may accompany us to Cliffside Abbey, and watch your little wife burn like the witch she is."

"No! Even you cannot do this! I will give you Ancaster, and half of what I own. Just let us go."

Giles brought a hand to his chin. "Hmmm. Tempting. But I fear not. Elanna must die, and now you must also." His face instantly brightened. "A double trial. A witch, and her accomplice. I am a genius!"

The two hapless guards entered from the wine cellar, both dripping in wine, one walking rather peculiarly. "Well," Giles snapped, "did you catch him?"

"Sorry, sire…he managed to get away."

Giles' face contorted in rage. "Imbeciles! Am I surrounded by incompetence? No matter, one small boy cannot do anything." He turned his attentions back to Luke. "Would you care to enlighten us to who he was?"

Luke stared back in defiance. "Go to hell."

"Very well." Dayen's face twisted in a fit of rage. "Take them away! They love each other so much, they can die together."

"You will not get away with this!" Luke yelled as he was led through the door.

"Oh, but I already have," Giles answered. "Soon your brother and his wretched wife will be dead, and there will be no one left to save you. I love happy endings, don't you?" As Elanna was led past him, he drew back in fear. "I said to keep her away from me! Get the hood, and keep it on her. She must be kept in darkness."

He looked into Elanna's crystal eyes with hate. "You see, Elanna, I have won. All the powers in the world cannot save you now."

Chapter Nineteen

William ran until he thought his lungs would burst, weaving in and out of people, trees, and outbuildings. When he was positive no one was following him, he found the trail and made his way back to Raymond. The giant had just finished saddling his horse when he saw the boy nearly on the verge of collapse as he ran relentlessly toward camp.

"Whoa there, lad! Pray, slow down before thou falls into a heap!"

"You…must…come…help…" William gasped between breaths. "They…they got him!"

Raymond crouched down and put his hands on the boy's shoulders. "Take deep breaths, lad. Now, tell me what transpired."

"We found Elanna, but I had a bad feeling…like we had walked into a trap. I cannot explain it; it was almost like someone was whispering in my ear that we were in danger. I tried to get Luke to leave, but he would not listen, and all of a sudden there were guards everywhere, and I ran into the wine cellar and crawled up on a rack and hit them on the head and one grabbed me and then I kicked him in the…"

"Very well, William, I believe I understand the situation. Where is Luke now?"

"I do not know. I ran and did not look back."

"That was probably wise." He stood up and cast his gaze upward as he thought. The paralysis of indecision crept through him. Was this what it had come to? Luke and Elanna's life hinged on the efforts of an injured man past his prime and a young boy?

"Sir Raymond, we must do something!"

"I am aware of that, lad. If only we had some help! Our only hope is to find Pet."

"But we do not know where she is. She must be miles away by now."

"Yea, that was most likely the plan. Clever, this Dayen fellow—he draws Pet away, then captures Luke. He somehow knew thou were coming. Perhaps thou were seen."

William pursed his lips as he fought back tears. The cook. She must have gotten suspicious when she saw him flee the cellar and reported it to Dayen.

Raymond saw the boy's defeated expression, and tried to think of something encouraging. "It appears thy fighting senses have improved. Thou sensed the danger."

"It had to be Elanna. She was talking to me with her mind, trying to warn me. But it did not help."

"Of course it did, thou art here, art thou? Now, William, thou hast to be brave. I fear 'tis up to thee."

"M-me?"

"Aye. Whilst I fetch Pet and Lord Matthew, thou must keep an eye on Ancaster. They are probably going to move Luke and Elanna away from here. If they do, thou must follow them."

William swallowed as the severity of the situation gripped him. "I will try."

"I shall leave Luke's horse here; she will be fine in this meadow."

"But Luke would not want us to leave Annabelle! She is his favorite horse."

"After I find Pet and Matthew, we shall return here."

"But the trap! What if they are…are dead?"

"Lad, I have known Pet all her life. Believe me, she is not dead. Find a way to leave us a message to tell us where thou art going."

"B-but how?"

"Thou art a clever lad. Thou will find a way." He mounted his horse and turned it toward the road. "I shall ride all night in the direction the carriage was going. With a bit of luck, I shall find Pet and return." He gave William a brave smile. "Take care, lad." With that he galloped away into the darkness.

Suddenly William felt very alone. He sat down on the cold ground and blinked back his tears. He was just one small boy against all of Ancaster's resources. How could he possibly do this?

Annabelle walked up and rubbed her head against William's back. Looking up into the horse's trusting eyes, William brushed away a tear and stood up. He couldn't let Luke down. He would die first. With brave resolve, he stood up and headed back to Ancaster."

Patrick was sharing a room with three of his men. One already lay on his cot snoring; the other two were still downstairs in the tavern. The girl was given her own room, not to say that she wouldn't end up voluntarily sharing it with one of the men. No matter, that was her business and Patrick just wanted to get this whole thing over and done with. It all left a bad taste in his mouth.

He lay back and stared at the canopy. His eyes grew heavy as he pondered his life. When this was over, he would leave Ancaster. He had a little money saved, enough to start his own business. Perhaps he could get married, start a family. Anything was better than being under Giles Dayen's thumb.

Just as he dozed off, a loud rapping broke his rest. The man on the cot snorted and rolled over. Patrick grumbled and sat up, dangling his legs over the edge of the bed. "Come!" he yelled.

The door slowly opened and one of his men peered in. "Milord? I need to talk to you."

Patrick rubbed his sleepy eyes. "Could this not wait until morning, Peter?"

"I think not. There is something you need to know." Peter stepped inside and motioned behind him. "Come in, he will not hurt you."

A young teen-age man stepped inside. He closely resembled Peter in color and features.

"This is my brother, George. He rode half the day to warn me."

Patrick stood up, suddenly wide-awake. "Warn you? About what?"

George stepped forward. "Milord, if I may…? I was dispatched last night with forty others."

"Dispatched? From where?"

"From Ancaster, sir."

Patrick scratched his head. "From Ancaster? By whom?"

"By Giles Dayen, sir."

"Giles? But that is impossible; I am in charge of the guards."

"We were offered double pay, on the stipulation that our mission remain secret. No one knew what our mission was until we arrived late this afternoon. When I heard the plan, I sneaked away and rode to tell my brother. I knew he was with you on this journey."

Patrick was fast losing patience. "Well, speak up, lad! What is so frightening about your mission?"

"Our orders are to wait until your carriage stops in a clearing. We are to remain hidden behind the trees until a lady warrior rides up. Then we are to attack."

Patrick felt dumbstruck. He thought Giles had agreed not to kill the lady knight, only distract her. Why did he change the plan without telling him?

"So you are to kill this warrior woman?"

George shifted nervously. "Er, not exactly. Our orders are to kill everyone—even you. There were to be no witnesses."

"What?" Patrick sat back down and let this information sink in. He stared absently into space. "What the hell is Giles up to?"

"I know not, sir. I only knew that I could not allow my brother to die. I had to warn him."

Patrick snapped out of his stunned state and nodded at the young guard. "You did the right thing, George. It does, howe'er, leave me in a dilemma."

Peter cleared his throat. "Milord, what are we going to do?"

"Obviously we have all been deemed dispensable by Giles." He stood up and began pacing slowly, deep in thought. The man on the cot snorted again, and Patrick glanced over at him. "For God's sake, wake him up. In fact, go wake everyone up. We all need to talk. Meet me down in the tavern."

Peter and George nodded. "Aye, Milord."

When he was alone, Patrick weighed his options. Thanks to the loyalty of a young brother, his life had just been spared. Funny how fate will sometimes bow her head in your favor. The very fact that Giles wanted him dead was sobering. Something else was in play.

His head snapped up in horror. *Elanna.* Of course, Giles knew that Patrick would never allow him to kill her. Giles had to eliminate him before he could kill Elanna and gain Ancaster permanently. Clever, making it appear a robbery, and having him walk right into it. Almost too clever. He had underestimated Giles.

Elanna would die if he didn't do something. He needed help. And he knew exactly who to ask.

Not far away in the forest, Pet spread out her bedroll and smoothed the blanket. Her fatigue was growing worse. She hid it from Matthew so far, but soon the baby would cause her belly to swell. She had to tell him before it was noticeable.

A while later Matthew appeared after making sure the horses were secure for the night. He was still grumbling about the food situation.

"I do not understand why we could not get a hot meal. My stomach is sick of dried meats and stale bread. And ale! What I would give for a yard of good ale!"

Pet ignored his ranting and stirred the fire without answering.

"When we get home," he continued, "I want a feast. A grand feast, with roast pheasant and baked lamb, and apple pie. Aye, apple pie and pastries of all sorts. I will keep the bakers busy for days. And fruits dipped in honey, with those little tart things your cooks make." He finally noticed her silence and narrowed his eyes with concern. "Pet, what is wrong? You seem distracted lately. Are you all right?"

She glanced up with a blank look. "What?"

"You have not heard a single word I said."

"I did so. Baked pheasant…tart things."

"I asked if you were all right."

Instead of answering, she took a dodging breath and stared into the fire. He sat down beside her, and reached out to twirl a lock of her hair.

"You have been quiet lately, even for you. Have I angered you again?"

She turned to face him and flashed a small smile. "Nay, you have not. There is something I must tell you, and I am not sure how."

He turned her face toward him and gently kissed her forehead. "There is nothing you cannot tell me. What is it?"

A snapping was heard off to their right, and Pet's instincts kicked in. "Did you hear that?"

"Just an animal. Now, what did you…"

She stood up. "There 'tis again. An animal cannot cause a twig to snap that hard. Someone is out there." She reached over to her weapons and picked up her sword.

"A big animal could. 'Tis most likely just the horses."

"Do not be silly; they are in the other direction. Grab your sword."

He stood up and sighed, but picked up his sword just to humor her. "Do you not think you are being a mite jumpy?"

"Better jumpy than dead. Come on."

He followed her into the wood, where she finally motioned him to stop. "Over there," she whispered. She pointed him over to one side while she waited behind a tree.

In a few seconds a man appeared, stomping through the brush as if he were lost or just extremely clumsy. In three seconds Pet had him on the ground with her sword across his throat, cutting off his airway.

"I know you," she seethed through her teeth. "I saw you at Ancaster. You are one of Giles Dayen's men. Tell me why I should spare your life."

"I am unarmed," the man managed to choke out. "I just want to talk. Please!"

By this time Matthew was leaning against a tree with his arms crossed. He hadn't even bothered to draw his sword. "Come on, love. He looks harmless enough. Let him up."

"I have a better idea." Pet pulled the sword closer to the man's neck, drawing an ever-so thin line of blood. "How about we trade you for Elanna?"

"No good," the man wheezed. "The carriage was all a ruse to draw you away. We never had Elanna. I just want to talk to you!"

The sword relaxed just a bit. "You knew we were out here?" Then, as quickly as it had relaxed, the sword drew even tighter. "Did you come to slit our throats while we sleep?"

"Nay! I-I swear! I need your help! Elanna will die if you do not help me."

Matthew unfolded his arms and stood straight. "Perhaps we should listen to what he has to say."

Pet looked up at Matthew, then down at the intruder. "Very well. But one false move and you die." She stood up and lowered her sword.

The man scrambled to his feet. "Thank you. I knew you had to be out here somewhere. I figured if I made enough noise you would find me." He rubbed his hands over his neck. "I guess you did."

"Excuse me, but are you not the enemy? Why would you want to find us?" Matthew looked intrigued, almost amused.

"Because I need your help. My name is Patrick. In a way, I am sort of related to Elanna. You must believe that I mean her no harm. I would not have risked my neck if I did."

"And why should we believe you?" Matthew asked.

"Because I speak the truth," Patrick answered, a hint of desperation in his voice. "Please, could we go back to the inn? Perhaps some food and drink would make conversation more amenable."

Matthew smiled with delight. "Now, that is the best idea anyone has had all day!"

"Wait a minute, not so fast." As usual, Pet was not so easily taken in. "I am not particularly in the mood for conversation. And why would one of Dayen's men need our help?"

"I am not exactly one of Dayen's men, at least, not anymore. I am here to help save Elanna."

Pet scoffed at that. "I do not need your help to save Elanna."

"Er, Pet, may I remind you, if he does not have her, we do not know where she is."

Pet's face twitched and she fell silent. Patrick used the lull in conversation to make his case.

"Oh, but I do. We can work together to save her. But first you will have to trust me."

"I trust no one."

"Not even me," Matthew agreed.

Pet cast him a sour glare, and turned back to Patrick. "Very well, we shall go to the inn, if only to appease my husband's stomach. But we will advance with my sword to your back. If even one of your men attacks, you are dead."

"I assure you, my men are just as anxious for your help as I am. I will explain it all when we get there."

A while later Pet sat listening intently while Patrick and his men lamented their situation. Matthew listened also, but with the company of a tankard of ale and hot stew.

"I fear this was all my idea; I wanted to save Elanna," Patrick was explaining. "Giles agreed to let her live out her life in a distant Scottish monastery, but first we had to draw you away. I have to say you ruffled his feathers quite effectively. He was terrified of you. But then, he is a coward. He ordered us all killed by our own men." He thrust his hand through his hair in frustration. "The fool! He pitted brother against brother. Only he would be so stupid."

"Let us bless his stupidity." By now Pet had no doubt that the carriage was a decoy. Patrick showed her the monk's robe and produced the long switch of Elanna's hair that was used to convince them. Pet picked it up and combed it through her fingers. It was soft and fine, like she would imagine angel hair. Visions of the frail girl whom she had befriended flooded her mind.

"Did Elanna part with this willingly?"

Patrick lowered his head and stared absently at the floor. "She understood I was trying to save her life."

"Do you know where she is being taken?"

"I think so. Brother Joseph—the monk I was impersonating—travels between two abbeys—the one in Scotland and another one with a dubious reputation. 'Tis called Cliffside Abbey."

Matthew's head jerked up. "Cliffside? By the ocean? Is that not where…"

"Aye," Patrick cut him off. "Many witch trials are held there. No one has ever been found innocent."

"Well," Matthew quipped, "this just gets better and better."

"Brother Joseph is more or less owned by Giles. He will do his bidding."

"How can anyone own a monk," Pet asked.

"'Tis a long story, one I can tell later. Let us just say Giles has a way to blackmail people into doing his dirty work."

The young girl sat sheepishly watching, fascinated by Pet. When Patrick caught Pet solemnly gazing back at the girl, he stepped in to defend her.

"Do not vent your wrath on her. She was just a pawn in this whole scenario."

Pet turned her glare on Patrick. "And what about you? Were you a pawn also?"

At that the guards all sprang to life.

"Patrick is the only reason I stayed at Ancaster."

"Aye, he was always fair to us."

"He is the brains. Dayen knows nothing."

"Aye!"

Patrick stood up and motioned the men to silence. "Quiet, all of you!" His voice lowered as he looked at Pet. "As much as I appreciate your loyalty, she is right. I was just a pawn. Giles used my ideas to further his own gain."

"Thith time," Matthew intervened with a mouthful of food, "He choth the wronth person to meth with." He downed his food with a large swig of ale. "Boy, did he choose the wrong person."

The corners of Pet's mouth turned up slightly, but she otherwise remained emotionless.

Patrick continued. "So now he has ordered my death, and yours, so he can carry out his evil plan. If not for young George here, we all would have died tomorrow."

Pet stood up and wandered to the fireplace, where she gazed into the dying embers, deep in thought. Everyone except Matthew—who kept shoveling food in his mouth—watched her as if her every move was crucial. Finally she turned to face them.

"I do not take kindly to someone ordering my death. I say we turn the tables on Giles Dayen. Are you all with me?"

They all roared and whooped their support.

"I wish we had time to surprise the waiting men, but they will simply have to stay waiting. We must save Elanna. When this is over, I guarantee you will all have jobs at my manor." She turned and looked at Matthew. "As lord of Elton, Matthew agrees, correct?"

Matthew had to quickly swallow a large bite of meat before answering. "Oh, of course."

Again the men voiced their enthusiasm.

"I fear we must ride all night and most of tomorrow to get back to Ancaster. I know you are all tired, but it cannot be helped. The carriage can take the girl back later. We do not need it to slow us down. Once there we will plan our strategy."

"You heard her," Patrick ordered. "Make ready to leave!"

The men all clambered out the door to saddle their horses. Only Patrick remained behind.

"I had hoped that you would help us. Thank you, Lady Cameron."

Pet winced, and shook her head. "Call me Pet. And you are welcome."

Patrick smiled gratefully, then left to join his men.

After he left, Pet lowered her head and rubbed her eyes, not realizing that Matthew was watching her.

"You look tired."

She looked up quickly. "Not any more than anyone else."

"Are you sure? You seem…different. Are you ill?"

"Nay, do not be silly." She stood up to avoid any more conversation. He also stood up and firmly but gently took her arm.

"In the woods…you wanted to tell me something. What was it?"

Her face changed only slightly, a bit more drawn, but steadfast. "Nothing. It can wait."

Matthew knew that look, and also knew she would offer no more information. "All right. But you will tell me if you feel ill?"

She nodded, and he smiled as he took her into his arms. "I know what you are thinking, my wife. You are angry with yourself for being fooled by this little masquerade. Now you will drive yourself, and everyone else, into the ground to make up for it. Am I right?"

She pulled back to look into his eyes. "How could I have been so foolish? If Elanna dies, I will never…"

"She will not die, do not even think it. This is not your fault. Luke himself thought the girl was Elanna. We all did. You cannot always be perfect, Pet. The standards you set for yourself are too high." He hoped his little pep talk was making her feel better. Instead, it seemed to have the opposite affect.

Pushing out of his arms, she turned her gaze away. "If I cannot trust my instincts, what can I trust? The truth is, I failed Elanna. I failed Luke. I failed everyone."

He put his hands out in desperation. "Pet..."

She turned around, her expression somber. "I will go fetch our horses. You stay here and make sure these men are ready. Keep your eyes open. I still am not fully convinced this Patrick fellow is sincere. He has not told us everything." She sauntered out the door without further comment.

Matthew let out a sigh, and did not oblige to argue. Something was bothering her, and it wasn't just the fact that she had been fooled. There was something deeper. Perhaps her twin brother's death—for that matter her whole family's—was still too fresh. She was too complex a person to fully understand. Whatever it was, she was bottling it up. It would only take time for it to explode.

In the woods, the horses nickered when they heard Pet approach. She silently gathered their belongings and loaded the gear on the saddles. "Sorry, boys—you are back on duty."

Not that the two huge war-horses couldn't handle the action; it was what they were bred to do. Pet remembered the days when she craved the action as much as they did. She sat down on a stump and allowed herself a short rest. A lump developed in her throat, making it hard to swallow. If Matthew knew about the baby, he would order her back to Elton, then go off to rescue Elanna himself. As much as she loved him, he simply wasn't the warrior that she was. The baby must remain a secret until this whole ordeal was over, and everyone was safe back at Elton. She cringed as she anticipated Matthew's reaction to her silence. He would yell at her for days.

She forced herself to her feet and began walking the horses to the inn. It was going to be a long night.

Chapter Twenty

Luke opened his eyes and instantly cringed as he brought up a hand to his head. It took a few seconds for him to regain his wits as he sat up and glanced around at his surroundings. He was in one of many cells, with straw for bedding and only bars for inside walls. The outside wall was thick stone. A corridor ran down the center of the cells, and the only entrance—and exit—was a large metal door. A small barred window let in just enough daylight to see that he was alone in his cell, and in the whole prison for what he could tell, judging by the lack of moaning and wailing.

His head throbbing, he staggered to his feet. Every muscle hurt. He remembered being jumped on at Ancaster. Then he and Elanna were led away, where they were separated and he was thrown into a wagon, bound and gagged like a common thief. When the wagon finally stopped, he was blindfolded and led into a small room where he was beaten to persuade him to admit he was a witch's accomplice. When that didn't work, he was knocked out, remembering nothing until waking up here.

It was then he noticed the clothes he was wearing. Where did these rags come from? The rough material scratched his skin and the smell assaulted his nose. With his hair badly in need of cutting, and a three-day old beard, he must present quite a sight.

He quickly glanced around again. How much time had passed? Where was Elanna? His spirit sunk at the mess he was in. His only hope was William. Everything happened so fast; hopefully he got away to get help. If so, Raymond would be coming to rescue them. He hoped.

A small rock flew through the window and landed at his feet, effectively adding to his pity party. He picked it up and frowned. It was bad enough that he was locked up in a strange place with an immense headache, now someone was throwing stones at him. He ducked as another one came through the window, almost hitting him. Then it suddenly dawned on him that someone might be trying to get his attention.

The window was too high to see out, even for a man of his height. He stepped back, then took a running leap and grabbed the bars, hoisting himself up. When he looked out, he was surprised at what he saw.

The cell was on the second floor. He was gazing down at a well-kept courtyard that was abandoned except for one small boy. He had another stone posed for throwing, which was dropped the second he saw Luke's face appear. It was William.

Both let out sighs of relief.

"'Tis about time," William shouted. "I thought you would sleep forever."

"I was not exactly *sleeping*", Luke yelled back. "What happened? Where am I?"

"You were taken to Cliffside Abbey. I followed you."

"Just you? Where is Raymond?"

"He thought it best to find Pet and Matthew. They are going to come and rescue you."

"How will they know where we are?"

"Do not worry, I left them a message. They will find us."

"A message? What if they do not find it?"

William hesitated, and slightly grimaced. "Er, I would not worry about that. They will find it."

"Very well, I will take your word on that. "I seem to have a private suite. Where is Elanna? Is she harmed?"

"Not yet. She is being brought before the abbot to face the allegations. Several peasants are saying she is a witch."

Luke felt terror rise in his heart. "You have to get me out of here! Giles is holding their children hostage! I have to tell the abbot what is really happening!"

"Well, from what I hear, you will have your chance. You are to be tried together as her accomplice."

"What?"

"I have been nosing around, asking questions. The villagers are hoping for a trial, and a burning. You will simply be hung. They are already building the stake and scaffold so everyone can see the executions. People for miles around will come here for the trials. Merchants are setting up booths for the affair. 'Tis the biggest event of the year."

"Thank you for your encouraging words. I feel so much better."

"Do not worry! Pet is on the way; she will rescue you!"

"I certainly hope you are right. Otherwise, Elanna and I are not destined for a long and fruitful marriage." He paused as a sudden pang of concern flashed through him. "Is it not dangerous for you? What if you are discovered?"

"I am just a peasant lad from the local village, for all anyone knows. I am pretty much ignored."

"Thank the almighty God for youth. William, I want you to go back to the church and report back to me. I want to know everything that is going on."

"You will not like it."

"Perhaps not, but maybe you will hear something that I can use at the trial."

"Very well."

"I will just wait here," Luke yelled as the lad ran out of the courtyard. He lowered himself down and sat in the straw. His joking didn't help. No amount of levity would help him out of this situation.

William worked his way through the crowd—using a great deal of pushing and shoving—until he found a good spot to watch the interrogation. As he had hoped, no one paid him much attention. The abbot, dressed in a simple robe, stood in front of the altar. Elanna, her hands still bound, stood to one side of the room. A handful of peasants were brought before the abbot, their faces lowered and somber. Giles, always the coward, stood as far away from Elanna as possible, acting all the while to be a concerned uncle. William had to strain to hear the proceedings.

Giles was addressing the abbot. "I only bring her before you because of the numerous allegations. I knew you were experienced with witch trials, and would know what to do. My local church has had no dealings with this sort of thing." One of Giles' men handed the abbot a parchment. "These are sworn testaments."

Accepting the parchment, the abbot gazed at Elanna, and turned back to Giles. His pinched face grew even more drawn. "You have read these testaments?"

"Yes, and I was stunned. I had no idea this was happening. Understand, I only have her welfare in mind, but I also must consider my tenets."

The abbot opened the parchment and read silently as everyone looked on. Either he was being very thorough or was just a slow reader, as it seemed to take forever. William cast his gaze at Elanna, who slowly turned to look at him with a sad smile. The church, flooded with sunlight from the stained-glass windows, seemed to give her a serene confidence.

The abbot finally finished and inhaled deeply. "These are serious allegations. Does she have someone to defend her?"

William watched as Brother Joseph scurried forward, right past Giles, without even a side-glance.

"Your holiness, I have offered to be council for the girl."

Giles frowned and cast the monk a sour glare. The abbot seemed genuinely surprised but accepted Brother Joseph's offer.

"Very well, that is acceptable." He glanced down at the parchment. "Where is this accomplice who is mentioned? Why is he not here?"

Giles stepped forward. "I fear he put up quite a fight, and was knocked unconscious. I can tell you anything you want to know. 'Tis he, I believe, who has brought my niece to this end. He has twisted her mind and convinced her to use her powers for ill."

"No!" Elanna yelled, but was drowned out by the crowd's uproar.

"Silence!" the abbot demanded. As the crowd quieted down, he turned back to Giles. "Who is this man?"

"Some lowlife who convinced my niece to marry him, or so he says. He claims he is a lord of some kind, and has turned my niece against me."

"Lies!" Elanna yelled. "He has done nothing!"

"You will have your chance to speak later," the abbot professed.

Giles knew he had an opportunity to drive the knife deeper in Luke's back. "I found her a wonderful prospect for marriage, and she choose to run off with this vagabond. It took me weeks to get her back, and she has repaid me with threats and dishonesty. Then these acts she committed began to come forth. I have even heard that he has bragged about summoning the devil to work through my niece."

Elanna struggled against the two men who held her. "More lies! My husband has done nothing!"

Joseph quickly interrupted. "It seems all assertions against this man is all hearsay. He is not even here to defend himself."

Giles practically turned white at Joseph's words. He hadn't thought about having signed statements against Luke. A slight tinge of regret that he had Patrick killed ran through him. Patrick would have thought of that. The feeling left quickly; he was better off without his moralist ward who had suddenly grown a conscience.

"He will have his chance to speak in his own behalf," the abbot stated dryly. "Right now, I need to address these allegations. Who goes by the name John Dunham?"

A peasant stepped forward. He kept his chin tucked as he refused to make eye contact. "That would be me, your holiness."

Giles gave the dirty, ill-dressed man a disdainful once-over, while the abbot smiled warmly. "Hmmm. It says here that you witnessed this girl to cause leaves to fall from a tree simply with a wave of her hand. Is that true?"

The man paused, and glanced back at his wife. Her look of anguish, knowing their only child was being held back at Ancaster under the threat of death, sealed his answer. "Aye, your holiness," he answered softly.

Joseph stepped forward. "Ah, but a gust of wind on a diseased tree could explain that. Hardly seems a punishable offense to me."

Giles cast the monk another glare, but quickly went into his concerned uncle act. "Er, yes, I agree. I think that particular accusation should be stricken."

"If you do not mind," the abbot enounced, "I will be the one to say what accusations will be stricken. However, I concur. I would not want to punish someone for a simple coincidence. But there are more serious charges. Who here is Richard son of Reginald?"

Another man stepped up. "Me, your holiness."

"This is your "X" on this statement?"

This man also paused, but nodded as the thought of his two sons, one only an infant, being returned to him.

"This states that your cow began giving sour milk after this girl walked past your cottage."

Again Brother Joseph stepped in. "But your eminence, do we know if the cow had been sick already? Some bad feed could have caused that. It has happened here in our very own barn."

As the abbot considered that, Giles took a deep breath to contain his rage. He knew that Joseph was going to pretend to defend Elanna, but it appeared he was going beyond what was necessary.

The abbot nodded in agreement. "Very well, but what about this? The next accusation states that she killed a dog simply by staring at it. And this one says she caused all the blooms to die in this man's apple orchard. Serious allegations, indeed."

Giles folded his arms in satisfaction. He was hoping the sheer volume of allegations would force a trial.

Brother Joseph sighed. "Your eminence, if there is to be a trial, I request at least four days to prepare the defense."

The abbot sputtered in annoyance. "Four days? That seems a bit excessive. I grant you two days, whereupon a trial will be held to determine if this young lady is a witch."

Brother Joseph smiled and nodded. Knowing the abbot would cut his request in half, he asked for twice what he thought he would allow and silently hoped for a miracle during the delay.

Giles, however, was shocked at the wait. He couldn't help blurting out, "*Two* days?"

The abbot mistook the indignation for sincere concern for the girl, and didn't want to be known as not allowing a fair defense. "Very well, three days, counting today, but that is final. I shall not be swayed any further."

Brother Joseph contained a chuckle, while Giles shut his mouth rather abruptly.

"Until then," the abbot continued, "return the girl to her cell beside her husband. Let them enjoy these last few days together."

William watched them take Elanna away as the crowd began to mutter amongst themselves. He had to do something. But what?

Purely from boredom, Luke had resorted to braiding straw when the metal door was thrown open, banging against the wall with a loud *clunk.* He stood and grasped the bars as he watched Elanna brought in by two guards, her hands tied behind her. She looked frail and weak; her pale skin greatly contrasted against the dull brown peasant dress she had been forced to wear. Luke felt his veins pulse as he watched the men open the cell next to his and shove her inside.

"'Tis not necessary to be so rough!" he shouted.

The guards cast him a disconcerting look and left without speaking.

"You could at least untie her!"

He glowered as the door clanked shut. "Bastards." He turned to Elanna and reached out to her. "Are you hurt?"

She pressed against the bars that were dividing them. "I am unharmed, for now. You?"

"Except for a few bumps and bruises, I am as well as can be expected. Turn around and I will see if I can untie you."

In seconds he freed her hands from the ropes. "'Tis strange, the ropes were not tied very tight. In fact, the knot practically came apart by itself."

She turned to face him. "I willed the rope to loosen as I was being led here." For the first time she noticed his attire. "You look terrible."

"They took my clothes, no doubt to convince the abbot I am some lowly peasant."

A tear fell down her cheek and she bravely tried to sniff it back. "This is all my fault."

"Nonsense, your uncle is to blame. Do not cry! I hate to hear a woman cry, most of all you." He tried to comfort her as best he could with bars blocking the way. As he stroked her hair he attempted to lighten the mood in his usual way.

"Besides, lots of women have had bad haircuts. Yours is not so bad. It will grow long again and you will be just as beautiful as before…not that you're ugly now."

She let out a loud sob and he realized his levity wasn't working.

"Please Elanna, do not cry. Things could be worse."

She pulled away and gazed at him through astonished, bleary eyes. "We are both about to be executed. How could things possibly get any worse?"

"Well..." He struggled for an answer. "Uh..."

His face brightened. "They could have put you in that cell over there." He pointed to the last cell on the other side, where large cobwebs covered the walls and several oversized spiders sat waiting for their next victim. "That cell is reserved for very bad prisoners."

She sniffed and managed a small smile. "I suppose you are right."

"And we are not going to be executed. William is here, and Raymond went to get Pet and Matthew."

"I know. I saw William in the church."

"So you know we will be saved."

"I only know that an attempt will be made to save us. Furthermore, thanks to the monk, we have a three day reprieve."

"Three days? That should give Pet plenty of time to get here."

"I hope you are right."

"Search your feelings. What do you sense?"

She closed her eyes and remained silent for a short time. When she finally opened them, her face didn't reveal any emotion.

"Well?"

"I do not sense your death."

He hesitated before asking the inevitable. "And yours?"

"I..."

Her words were cut off by the sound of the door opening. The same two men as before, plus two new ones, came back in and stopped in front of Luke's cell. The instructed him to stand back while they opened the door.

"You're next," one said with seeming delight. "The abbot wants to talk with you."

One held a knife to his throat as another tied his hands. "Resist if you want. I would just as soon kill you now."

Elanna watched as Luke was led away, then lay in the straw in despair. She usually couldn't sense things about herself, unintentional or not, she wasn't sure. But this time she saw flames rising around her and could feel the heat of fire. Her only consolation was in knowing that Luke would live, even though she would not.

Meanwhile Pet and her small band were making good time. They rode all night. The men blindly followed her, trusting she would come up with a plan. Her hope was that Elanna was still being held at Ancaster, or that Luke and Raymond had already rescued her. That hope diminished when she recognized the large form approaching in a full gallop that morning. She halted her men.

"What is it?" Matthew asked.

"'Tis Raymond. Something has happened."

Raymond abruptly reined in his exhausted horse when he saw Pet, causing the dry dirt road surface to spew around him. He fanned the dust out of his face and smiled. "Praise be to the saints!" he exclaimed. "I prayed I would find thee!"

Pet frowned upon seeing his bleeding leg, no doubt opened again by the intense riding. "Raymond, what are you doing here? Why are you not with Luke and William?"

The giant dismounted and stiffly drew himself into a long stretch. "I am getting too old for this."

"You are avoiding the question."

"In due time, in due time. I must sit for a spell." He limped over to beside the road and sat on a felled tree.

The man looked as fatigued as Pet felt, so she turned to Patrick and told him they would rest for a few minutes. The lump in her stomach told her she wasn't going to like Raymond's news. The men took the report of a break with gratitude, as they all dismounted and began stretching their legs. Pet and Matthew sat on the log by Raymond, who was wrapping his leg with fresh bandages.

"You should not have come," Pet scolded. "Look at your wound; 'tis as bad as before."

"I had no choice. I fear I bring rather sobering news."

Matthew snorted at that. "I do not think the mood could be any more sobering than it already is."

Pet cast Matthew a sideways look, but otherwise ignored him. "Whatever the reason, you could have sent Luke, or William for that matter, to relay a message."

"T'was not possible. William discovered Elanna was being held at Ancaster, so Luke took it upon himself to rescue her. In the attempt he was also captured."

Matthew rolled his eyes and grimaced. "Oh, *wonderful.*"

"And William?"

The giant shrugged. "When I left him, he was fine. He was the only one who could sneak back into Ancaster and find out what was happening, then report back to us. I told him to follow them if they moved Luke and Elanna."

"But how can he report back to us if he is following them?"

"I instructed him to leave us a message."

"Where?"

"At our campsite, in the clearing. I rode all night to find thee. We were told thou were heading into an ambush. I almost feared finding thee dead."

"I do not die that easily. I will tell you all about that later. Right now we have to rescue Luke and Elanna. How far are we from Ancaster?"

"Over half a day's ride, if we ride hard."

Matthew stared into space and shook his head. "My stupid brother. Since when does he play the hero? What could he had been thinking?"

Raymond put a massive hand on Matthew's shoulder. "Do not berate him thus Lord Matthew. His only motivation was love for his wife. Love can cause a man to do many a foolish thing. Thee, of all people, should understand that."

Matthew turned his face away as his face grew a bit red. He didn't like being reminded of his own stupidity.

Pet stood up and brushed herself off. "Well, Ancaster is not getting any closer with us sitting here."

Chapter Twenty One

Pet pushed her newly acquired band without rest or food until they reached Ancaster. The weather, clear and dry, was at least cooperating. She headed straight for the campsite hoping to find William waiting for them. Instead, all she saw was Annabelle contentedly eating grass on the opposite end of the meadow, oblivious to the circumstances around her. She looked up and nickered when she saw she had company, then went back to hunting for anything edible. Pet ordered the men to dismount while she investigated. She, Raymond, Matthew and Patrick walked toward Annabelle and scanned the meadow with disappointment.

"So," Matthew grumbled, "no William."

"And no message," Pet added.

Raymond frowned as he continued to look for anything that would constitute a message. "I do not understand. William is a bright lad; he would have found a way."

"Perhaps he is simply down at Ancaster and will return shortly," Patrick offered.

"I doubt it," Pet said. "His horse is gone. Raymond, your leg needs tending."

Raymond looked down at his bleeding leg with a look of disgust. "Damned annoyance!" He glanced over at Luke's saddlebags lying across a log next to the grazing Annabelle. "I believe there are more cloth strips in the bags." He limped away from the three to retrieve the bags.

"I wish I knew if Giles has left Ancaster," Patrick mused. "I could take control if he is gone; the men will listen to me. We could obtain fresh horses and rest in style."

Matthew raised an eyebrow. "Fresh horses would be good. These are worn out."

"We cannot rest for long," Pet insisted. "We must find William or his message."

Raymond's booming voice interrupted them. "You three, come hither. Perchance I have found the message."

Pet and Matthew exchanged looks, and glanced over at Raymond with curiosity.

"Did he leave it in the bags?" Matthew asked.

"Er, not exactly. You could say he hid it in plain sight."

The three scurried to Raymond, who was sitting on the log.

"Well, where is it?" Matthew asked.

Raymond pointed behind them to Annabelle. The three spun around.

Pet caught her breath and quickly brought up a hand to cover her smile.

Patrick looked stunned.

Matthew's jaw dropped.

There, neatly shaven on the horse's side, were four carefully executed words. William had used Luke's razor to remove the gray hair, revealing the dark skin underneath. Fortunately, Annabelle was gentle enough to let William accomplish this undertaking. The words read:

ALL GONE
CLIFFSIDE
FOLLOWING

Pet cocked her head and somehow kept a straight face. "Well, he left us a message."

Matthew finally regained use of his senses. He ran his hands over the uninjured, but cosmetically ruined horse.

"This is Luke's favorite horse!" When he saw the others didn't share his concern, in fact seemed downright amused, he pointed to the words in exasperation. "That is not going to grow out the same color as before, you know."

Pet let out a snicker. "I know."

Patrick and Raymond both chuckled, desperately holding back laughter.

Matthew continued. "This is terrible. How could he do that to Annabelle? Luke is going to have William's head!"

"Let us hope he still has a head," Pet said in a more sober tone. "We do not yet know William's fate."

"Oh. Right." Suddenly feeling rather foolish, Matthew shut his mouth.

At that, Raymond guffawed, "Do not worry about the lad. He can take care of himself."

"I look forward to meeting this lad," Patrick said. "He appears ingenious."

Pet nodded. "He has his moments. I believe you mentioned fresh horses. If by "all gone" he means Giles…"

"Aye, the swine would not miss watching Elanna burn. Let us proceed to Ancaster. Witch trials take several days to prepare. We still have time."

Elanna basked in the small amount of sunlight let in by the window. She could feel her power slowly return. A while after Luke was led away, she was surprised to see a lad dressed in an apron and hat, indicating he was a kitchen aide, brought into the jail. The guard stopped him at the door and inspected the food for weapons, then went back out. The aide slipped the covered food through the slot and Elanna gratefully took the tray.

"Thank you," she said as she uncovered the food. It was nothing fancy, but was much-needed nourishment.

"You're welcome, Elanna."

She glanced up and looked at William's smiling face. "William? How did you…"

"I stole the apron and hat off the clothesline. I went to the kitchen and said I was hired by Giles Dayen to fetch food for his niece, and the Abbot approved it. They didn't seem to care; it made less for them to do, I guess. Here, I also brought you water." He handed her a skin filled with water.

Elanna took the water and took several deep gulps. "You never cease to amaze me. Can you tell me what is happening? Luke said Pet and Matthew are coming to save us. My powers are not yet strong enough to sense anything."

"They will come, do not worry. I wanted to tell you I am riding to meet them, so you will not be seeing me around."

"How is Luke?"

"I watched them take him to the Abbot. I heard a bit from outside the door. Giles was more adamant about him being put to death than he was about you. He really hates Luke."

"I know. Giles hates anyone who is not under his control."

William glanced toward the door. "I had better be going. I do not want the guard to become suspicious. Keep faith, Elanna. Help will come."

As he turned to leave, Elanna suddenly reached through the bars and grasped his arm. "William…there is something I must tell you. If you do bring help, and there is a choice of who to save, promise me you will save Luke first."

William paused, and then adamantly shook his head. "Nay, that is not going to happen. We will save you both."

"But you do not understand. I have already foreseen my own death."

He shook off her arm and backed up, his eyes wide in incredulity. "Nay! I do not believe it!"

"'Tis true. I have seen the flames and felt the heat rise around me."

"I will not hear this! Pet will save you!" He ran to the door and knocked to be let out.

"Goodbye, William."

"Do not say that! I will be back!"

Elanna watched the frightened boy leave with sorrow in her heart. She turned to the food. She brought a piece of bread to her mouth, then paused with uncertainty. What if they decided not to feed Luke? With William gone, no one would think of food for the prisoners, who were going to die anyway. She put the bread down and covered the food as her stomach growled in protest. Luke would need the food more than she would.

When Luke was finally brought back in, he looked exhausted and beaten. The guards tossed him roughly to the floor, and left with sneers of satisfaction. He slowly got to his feet.

Elanna jumped up and grabbed the bars that separated them. "Luke! Are you all right? Were you…?" It was then that she saw the bruises and bloody nose. "You are hurt! What did they do to you?"

"Nothing I could not take." He grimaced as a hand went to his abdomen. "They punched me pretty good. They tried to get me to sign a statement saying you were a witch. I told them all to go to hell, even the abbot."

"Did you tell them who you were?"

A snort was the response. "Hah! As if they would believe me, dressed in these clothes. They did not believe a word I said."

She held out her hands through the bars. "Come here."

"Ah, I could use a comforting hug." He came close to the bars and she put her arms around as much of him as she could. He closed his eyes as an unexpected peace came over him, and felt pain dissolve as harmony returned to his body. He suddenly realized what was happening and broke out of her embrace.

"What are you doing? Are you mad? My pain is far too great for you to take!"

She continued to reach out to him. "Nay, come back. Already I no longer feel the pain. I can help you."

"I do not want your help!"

"Aye, you do. You are bleeding inside. You will die if you do not let me help you."

"But...you said you only absorb the pain. You told Matthew you could not heal."

She lowered her head and gazed at the floor, realizing she had been caught in a white lie. "Luke, have you ever heard of an Empath?"

"You mean someone who can feel another's emotions so strongly it becomes his own?"

"Something like that. The Prioress told me I go beyond normal empathy." She raised her head and looked into his worried eyes. "I actually take the other person's aliment into my body, whereas it dissipates in a short time."

"But during that short time you are actually the injured one, and suffer the same as the other person?"

"Aye. And there are boundaries I cannot pass. If the other person is near death, I can only relieve some pain until he dies. Plus, I can project images of comfort into his mind."

"This is what you did at the convent hospital. That is why everyone wanted to go there, because people seemed to live longer at that hospital."

"Aye. We had a high success rate. Now come here and let me heal you."

He shook his head. "Nay, I do not want to hurt you."

"You will not. Your injuries are fresh and can be healed. Please, Luke, let me help you."

He hesitated. "Your powers are weak. Helping me will make you weaker."

"Only for a short while."

"Nay, I will not risk it." He sat on the floor and stubbornly set his jaw.

She could see that he was going to be impossible to sway. "Very well, at least eat something. William brought us some food." She picked up the tray and uncovered it.

His face perked up as he looked at the food. "William? Where is he?"

"He has gone to meet Pet and Matthew. He is convinced they are on the way here to save us."

He continued to stare at the food. He hadn't eaten in almost two days, and his stomach was letting him know it. "Is that all there is?"

"I have already eaten my fill," she lied.

"Very well." He reached through the bars and grabbed a crust of bread and a hunk of cheese. "Not exactly king's fare, but 'twill suffice." He took a mouthful of bread and began chewing profusely.

"He also brought a skin of water." She passed it through the bars.

He gratefully accepted the water. "Remind me to buy that lad a new horse when we get out of this. I might give him Annabelle. She seems to like him."

She watched him chug the water and managed a smile. The food would make him strong and help heal his beaten body. She silently thanked God for William. At least Luke would be saved.

The sun was now setting and no longer streamed through the window. Soon it would be cold. She hugged herself and rubbed her arms as the chill permeated the room. Luke took off his coat and shoved it through the bars.

"Here, take this. 'Tis not much, but 'twill help a little."

"Will you not be cold?"

"Nay—my mother says men have hotter blood then women. She felt it only fitting to put her cold feet next to my poor sleeping father, who would awaken with a fright. He said 'tis like sleeping next to a chunk of ice."

Elanna giggled and draped the jacket over her shoulders. "Your mother sounds delightful."

"Oh, she is that, and more. I cannot wait for her to meet you."

"You are that confident of our escape?"

"Of course. Matthew will not allow anything to happen to me. Or you."

"You two are very close." It was more a statement than a question.

"All three of us brothers are close…well, we used to be. I do not know if Paul has forgiven Matt yet, only time will tell. But I can tell you; if he were here he would risk his own life to save mine. And I would do the same for him."

She brought her knees up against her chest and wrapped the coat around them. "I wish I could remember my brother. All I can see are fleeting glimpses of his face in my mind. I was so young when the fire…" Her voice trailed off and she closed her eyes.

Luke didn't seem to notice she had fallen silent. He finished the food and took another swig of water. "Ah! I feel better already. Now we both need a good night's sleep, and I bet in the morning we will feel…Elanna?" He finally noticed she was miles away, lost in her thoughts. "Elanna? Hello?"

She opened her eyes. "I just saw Pet and Matthew. They are coming."

He hesitated, almost surprised that she had verified what he felt all along. "Well, see?" I was right! There is nothing to worry about. Your powers are returning, and help is on the way."

"Perhaps. Are you always this optimistic?"

"My brothers say 'tis my downfall. I never saw much reason to worry about anything. I mean, what is the use? A person can spend all their time worrying, and where does it get him? Has he changed anything by worrying?"

She lay down on her side and faced him. "At night…at the convent…sometimes I could not sleep. Strange visions of the future would flood my thoughts. Things hard to imagine."

"Like what?"

"Large silver flying machines that transport people. Long moving canisters that travel over tracks of silver. All kind of machines, powered by something invisible, that do all the work for people."

"I would like that."

"There are also great medicines, and diseases that now kill people are non-existent. Doctors perform great surgeries, and people live much longer. It will be possible to talk to anyone in the world in seconds by use of a great communications device. There are high buildings that reach the sky, and smooth roads that extend forever. People are free. No one rules them."

Luke chuckled. "This future world of yours sounds pretty nice."

"'Tis not all nice. There are also machines of war, things that drop from the sky and explode, causing great damage for years."

"Hmmm. How far do your visions take you? Where does it all end?"

"It does not seem to. There are strange ships that travel under water. I have even seen great sky ships that travel to the stars."

"Now you are being ridiculous. No one will ever travel to the stars."

"Do we truly know that?"

"Well, nay, I guess we will never know for sure." He lay down and faced her through the bars. "What else do your visions show you?"

She pursed her lips as she thought. "Some things I do not understand. Images that are cast against large white walls, pictures that come from light that tell stories. In the future anything you can think of can be made into a moving story. There are monsters, and history stories, and everything you can imagine. They are made to entertain people, but to also make them think."

Luke scrunched up his face in confusion. "It certainly has me thinking."

"There is strange music, very loud, with weird lyrics that make no sense."

"None of this makes any sense."

"Well, you asked."

"Indeed I did."

"There is also a time of renewed faith, where belief in God expands throughout the world. There is no more hunger, and people live in harmony. But that is a great deal of time away. People have to learn to love one another as God intended. People like me are not feared or hated. In fact, people like me are commonplace."

Luke reached out and took her hand. "Then the future is indeed a better place."

She paused, uncertain if she should continue. "Can I tell you a secret?"

"Of course."

"I have met someone like me, someone who shares my visions of the future."

"Indeed?"

"It was most odd. He was Italian, a most remarkable man. I have never before met a man of such intellect. He came to the convent, a traveler with his employer, the duke of Milan. Apparently they were seeking unusual architecture for a project back in Italy. They needed an interpreter, and I gladly volunteered. I was drawn to him immediately. He showed me his notebook, full of drawings of things I had only seen in my visions. He was a remarkable artist. I took a chance and shared my visions with him. He became so excited, his thoughts were so fast that I could barely make sense of them. He drew some quick sketches and said he was going to devote an entire notebook to my visions."

A tinge of silly jealousy tensed his body. "I suppose this man was as handsome as you are beautiful?"

She laughed, a welcome relief that elevated the mood. "Oh, of course—he was an old man, with long flowing white hair and dancing eyes."

"An old man? What was his name?"

"He told me to call him Leonardo."

"And where is this Leonardo, now?"

She shrugged. "Back in Florence, I suppose. He told me he was going to return to his home, and made me promise I would come visit him."

"That is going to be a little hard from in here. Unfortunately, even as smart as he is, 'tis unlikely anyone outside of Italy will ever hear of him. Italy is full of wonderful artists."

"True. Still, I have often thought of him, and how wonderful it would be if the world were full of people who were not afraid to dream."

"I only dream of you."

Her face flushed, and she gave him a shy smile.

He reached out and ran his forefinger down the contours of her face. "Tell you what—when we get out of here, I promise I will take you to Italy to visit him."

She smiled, then almost as quickly her face sobered. "Luke, when I had the vision of Pet and Matthew—there was something else. Something…sinister."

"Sinister?" He cocked an eyebrow. "How so?"

"I do not know. I only know that Pet and Matthew had better hurry."

He let that sink in, then smiled and shook his head. "Nay, you are just scared. Let us get some sleep. We could both use it."

The mention of sleep made her yawn. "You are right. I am very tired."

"Of course you are. Cover yourself with the straw—'twill help keep you warm."

"Will you keep holding my hand?"

"I would not dream of letting go of it."

After much manipulation of straw they managed to make fairly cozy beds. They got as close to each other as possible through the bars.

"You will see," he said in an upbeat tone. "Everything will seem better in the morning."

"Good night, Luke."

"Good night, my little lady seer." In a few minutes he began breathing in steady, shallow breaths.

Elanna reached over and placed her hand on Luke's abdomen. She closed her eyes and gently absorbed his pain. She touched his face, and watched the bruises fade. When she was certain that she could do no more, she fell into an exhausted sleep.

A short ways away, Giles kept to the shadows as he made his way between buildings. Satisfied that no one saw him, he slipped inside the barn and quietly found the trough where the pig slop was made. Throughout the day various garbage and foodstuffs was tossed in a large bin, whereupon in the evening the pigs were fed the concoction. The feeder would be coming soon. Giles reached inside his coat and brought out a small vile. He carefully pulled out the small cork and proceeded to pour the entire contents into the swill.

"That ought to speed up the trial," he said to himself, great smugness in his voice. He glanced around to make sure no one had seen him, and then slipped away into the night as quietly as he had come. Outside the barn he reached down inside his boot and brought out a shiny dagger. He tested the sharpness with the tip of his finger, making a thin bloody line. His evil smile returned. "Now to make sure she burns."

Chapter Twenty Two

Pet lay awake beside a blissful, snoring Matthew. It felt like heaven to be in a bed again. After they left the clearing, they rode into Ancaster where Patrick took control and ordered warm baths and a hot meal for everyone. After dinner, Pet, Matthew, Patrick and Raymond invited the captain of the guard to help them plan a strategy. Several of the top fighters also participated. They sat around the great table in the main dining room, each espousing his own view on the situation as Pet sat and listened. Matthew found it almost amusing; it was obvious that everyone wanted to impress the famous lady knight. They finally agreed that Matthew, being a lord from a well-known family and Luke's brother, would ride in ahead and seek Luke and Elanna's release. If that didn't work, they would have to resort to more forceful means. They would rest a day, and leave the following morning.

She rolled over and felt the frequent nauseated feeling again. She brought a hand to her belly and took deep breaths, knowing her baby needed the nourishment that night's dinner would provide. That is, if she could keep it down.

Matthew snorted and flopped an arm over her. She sighed and squirmed out from underneath, then silently slipped out of bed. It was a mild night, with a clear sky and full moon. As she stared out the window, she wondered about the outcome to this unfolding drama. She shuddered to think of Matthew's reaction when he found out about the baby. He would be furious to think she put the baby's life in danger. She had already had to loosen the ties on her leather pants. Soon her belly would grow fat and she would waddle like a duck. She grimaced to think she might even have to start wearing gowns. Matthew would tease her, of course. It was comforting to know that even with a large belly, she could most likely beat him at swordplay—and would if need be.

But for now that would have to wait. Luke and Elanna were all that mattered.

Her stomach settled and she crawled back in bed. Soon she joined Matthew in a deep sleep, optimistic that all would be well.

The scene at Cliffside Abbey the next morning would have belayed that optimism.

At the break of dawn, Brother Joseph was summoned to the abbot's office. When he arrived, he found an unsettling sight. Several peasants, some armed with clubs and pitchforks, filled the room, shouting at the beleaguered abbot. Some were angry; all were afraid. The village sheriff, the town's main law enforcer, tried along with the abbot to calm them down. When Joseph entered, the villagers turned their wrath on him.

"This is all your fault!"

"We should have hung them immediately!"

"I say we hang you, too!"

"Aye!"

Joseph pushed his way through to the abbot. "What is going on?"

The abbot, not used to his words being drowned out by an unruly crowd, tried to shout above the noise, but finally put up his hands and demanded silence. Then he turned to Joseph with a solemn expression. "I fear some unfortunate circumstances have taken place. All the Abbey's pigs were found dead this morning."

Brother Joseph let out a sigh. "That is it? Some dead pigs?"

"I fear not," the sheriff said. "Word of the pigs spread throughout the village, and everyone determined that the witch—your defendant—was at fault. Soon other mishaps were reported. One man's wife died in childbirth in the night."

"But women die in childbirth all of the time."

"Granted, but when the baby was delivered, it came out feet first—a very bad sign."

Several peasants began shouting. "The sign of the witch!"

"A curse!"

The sheriff continued. "And that is not all. Several dogs were found with slit throats. One of the poor creatures lived long enough to drag itself back to his doorstep. It was found in a pool of blood."

"And," the abbot added, "'tis believed the witch is causing these happenings."

"But that is ridiculous! She is locked up!"

The villagers began yelling again.

"She's a witch!"

"I say burn her now!"

"But," Joseph shouted back, "she has not yet had a trial!"

"We don't need a trial!"

"Aye, burn her! Before anyone else dies!"

As the villagers roared their demands, the abbot shrugged and held out his hands in surrender. "You see what I am up against? I fear I have no recourse but to hold the trial this afternoon."

Joseph felt the veins in his neck begin to pulse. "But you said I had three days! I have not even begun drafting my defense!"

"Then I would say you had better hurry."

A voice from the door rose above the rest. "I would agree."

Everyone fell silent and turned to see who had just entered. It was Giles Dayen.

Always a demanding figure, he seemed even more so as he swaggered into the room, his long black cape trailing behind him. When he reached the front, he turned to face the abbot. "Inasmuch as I want to save my niece's life, I fear I am in agreement with the distressing villagers. If what they say is true, you have no choice but to hold the trial immediately."

The peasants began cheering. "Aye, listen to him!"

"Very well." The abbot raised his hands again to silence the crowd. "The trial will commence at 1:00."

Again the peasants cheered.

"But…" Brother Joseph's objections was buried under the din.

"There will be no further discussion," the abbot said, his voice dripping with authority. "I have spoken."

Joseph, his face red with anger, turned sharply and left the room. Once outside, he leaned against the wall, took out a handkerchief, and patted his sweating face. His entire plan had just gone up in smoke. What was he to do?

The door opened. The peasants could still be heard inside the room, cheering the imminent witch burning. Giles Dayen stepped out.

Joseph quickened his steps down the hall, not wanting to talk with the man he despised most.

"Joseph, halt!"

He walked even faster.

"I said, halt!"

He stopped and listened to Dayen's footsteps come up behind him. "What do you want from me?"

Giles looked down at the little monk with a look of satisfaction. "Well, for one, you can congratulate me on my genius. My poisoning the pigs seems to have done the job of getting this ridiculous trial over and done with. I can already smell Elanna's burning flesh." He paused and took a deep breath, as if the thought brought him great joy. "It will be glorious."

"Excuse me if I do not share your delight."

"Oh come, come, Joseph, surely you will not deny me my anticipation. 'Tis all I have dreamed of for fifteen years."

Joseph turned to leave with a disgusted look. "If you are quite done…"

"I think the dogs were a nice touch, do not you?"

"I suppose you want credit for the woman's death, also."

"Oh, that...I wish I could, but that was just a lucky coincidence."

"A woman is dead, and you call it lucky?"

"Lucky for me. It would have been even better if the baby had also died, but I guess I cannot wish for everything."

Joseph looked straight into Dayen's dead eyes, eyes with no compassion, no tenderness. "I have a defense to plan. If you will excuse me..."

"By all means, go plan your useless defense. By this afternoon the entire village will be blaming every little mishap on the witch. Every ache and pain, every accident, everything will be her fault. There will not be much to defend."

"We will see about that."

Giles brought a hand to his chin and raised one eyebrow. "You know, if I did not know better, I would think you are actually trying to defy me. Let us not forget your little part in all this. You stand to gain almost as much as I."

"I am no longer interested in what I have to gain."

Giles' eyes flashed with rage. "Then let me remind you of what you have to lose! Unless your neck means nothing to you, I suggest you change your attitude. I can easily arrange for several 'witnesses' to implicate you."

Joseph took a faltering backward step. "T-they would not believe that."

"Perhaps not. But I would say that right now the panicked peasants would believe just about anything. They lust for vengeance. The scaffold can hold two nooses as easily as one."

The monk lowered his gaze and took a shuddering breath. "Very well. But it must appear that I am defending them. The abbot is adamant about a fair trial."

"Yes, his fairness has filled many graves. We already know the outcome to this farce. I warn you, do nothing to further delay the executions. I want this over and done with."

Joseph gave a short nod and briskly walked away.

Giles emitted a long sigh as he watched him go. "'Tis so hard to get good help these days."

The morning sun streamed through the window, landing directly on Elanna's face. Her eyes fluttered and she slowly opened them. She lay and stared at the ceiling without seeing, as her senses soaked in the light, awakening her mind. Immediately a sense of foreboding swept over her.

"Luke—wake up!" She shook the snoring man through the bars.

He snorted.

"Wake up!" She shook him again, and this time he opened his eyes and yawned.

"W-wha…?"

"Something is happening. Do not ask me what, I do not know. I only know that we are in even more grave danger than before."

"Seeing how we were going to be executed, I fail to see how that is possible."

As he spoke, the iron doors opened and Brother Joseph bustled in. His usual vigorous, florid manner seemed torn in conflict. The look on his face told them Elanna's instincts were right. They both froze, horrified to learn what had transpired.

"Terrible, just terrible," he lamented when he reached the cells. "He is evil, I tell you! A demon! The very devil himself!"

Elanna swallowed, and her voice trembled as she spoke. "What has my uncle done, now?"

"The trial is to begin this afternoon! I could do nothing to stop it!"

Luke, now wide awake, jumped to his feet. "But I thought…"

"He has instilled the whole village with fear. They are all insisting on your deaths. If they have their way, you will both be dead by tonight!"

As the monk began ranting incomprehensibly about pigs and dogs, Luke turned to Elanna with a look of desperation. "You have to do something!"

Elanna blinked and opened her mouth to disagree, but he continued on without letting her speak.

"You have powers; I have seen them! I admit I do not understand them, but I know they exist. There has to be something you can do!"

Joseph stopped his diatribe and took on a more optimistic tone. "Yes, child, if you can do something, you must!"

Elanna backed up until her back bumped the far wall. "B-but what?"

"I know you are afraid," Luke said gently. "You fear anything you do will further feed the notion that you are a witch. I doubt if you have ever really discovered your true potential. But I am asking you now, for our love, for our lives, to search deep within yourself and save us. I know you can do it."

She remained still and silent. Finally, she spoke in a small, quiet voice. "Perhaps there is something I can do. You must be extremely quiet, and promise, no matter what, to not disturb me."

Luke flinched as if she had struck him. "I do not think I like the sound of that."

"Promise."

He sighed. "Very well. What are you going to do?"

"I am going into a trance. This is not something I have done very many times. If I am successful, Pet will get a very unusual message."

Pet awoke early. She drank some hot tea to settle her stomach, and then went to the barn to check on Goliath. The barn was dark in contrast to the morning sun, and most of the animals were still asleep. The great horse greeted her with a nicker when she approached his stall with an apple. She petted his neck as he chewed and slobbered the juicy treat. Whenever she was with Goliath, she couldn't help think of her brother Robert. Oh, how she missed him! The only one who could relieve her pain was Matthew, but sometimes even he wasn't enough. Sometimes her loneliness consumed her, especially times like now, when she was alone with her thoughts. She closed her eyes and pinched them tight, to not allow any tears to escape. Robert would not want her to cry.

As she turned to leave, a sudden dizziness overcame her. She steadied herself on the stall and fought to regain her balance. The barn somehow seemed darker, and the animals—even Goliath—fell deathly quiet. What happened next filled Pet with fear, a foreign fear, one that caused the blood to flee her face. She felt her actions slow in motion, as if she had fallen into a nightmare that stretched into endless, unalterable reality.

That is when she heard the voice. It came from nowhere and everywhere at the same time. It spoke only three words, her most favorite three words a short time ago, now sending her into a cold fright. She found her voice with difficulty.

"W-what did you say?"

This time the voice was louder, as if her very acknowledgment was all that was needed to make it real. "I said, hello, baby sister."

Pet drew up tall and took deep breaths as she turned in a circle, trying to find the perpetrator of this cruel hoax. "If this is a joke, 'tis not funny."

"'Tis not a joke, Pet."

Her voice rose, still controlled, but a desperate control. "You cannot be Robert. He is dead. I buried him myself."

"I know—I watched you." A shape began to take form in the shadows. As her brother's image solidified, she backed up, vigorously shaking her head.

"I do not believe in ghosts. Go away."

"Do not shake your head so—'twill only make your brains rattle."

Those words made her freeze. Robert was always telling her that; it was one of the last things he had said to her before he died. Right now that seemed like a thousand years ago.

He stepped out from the shadows. "You did not fear me in life…why do you fear me in death? Did I not say I would be with you always?"

"This cannot be real." Her hands were so cold she feared they would break off and shatter like fine glass.

"Why not? Why is it so hard to believe that my spirit lives on?" She slowly reached out to touch him, but her hand found only air. He chuckled in response. "You cannot touch me. My image is here only because that is what you expect to see. The spirit has no form."

Still shaking with fear of the unknown, she raised her chin defiantly as she spoke. "Very well, if you are Robert, then why now, why here? I have called out your name in grief many times since you died, and you have never come before."

"Because you did not need me. You have someone here who loves you as much as I. Your destiny is with him."

"You mean Matthew?"

"Of course."

"But I miss you so much! When you died, it was as if part of me died, also! I almost could not go on!"

"But you did, and will continue. You are strong, Pet. My journey had ended. Yours is just beginning."

"So, you still have not told me why you are here now."

"I am here because a person from your plane of existence has contacted me. Someone you care greatly about."

"My plane of existence? What does that mean?"

Robert shook his head. "'Tis hard to explain. On this side, 'tis all so clear. Your thoughts, your true self, never die. Your body only houses the soul, which is formless and ageless. When your physical body leaves this world, your soul enters another place."

She struggled to take this in, but remained skeptical. "You say you were contacted. By whom?"

"Someone who is unique to your world. Someone who needs your help."

It only took her a second to realize to whom he was referring. "Elanna? Of course, if anyone could contact you, it would be Elanna. But how did she do it?"

He seemed uncertain how to answer. His words came slowly and methodically. "Elanna has the ability to see into other dimensions. She does not do it often, for it frightens her."

Pet's fear was replaced by utter confusion. "What is a dimension?"

"I do not expect you to comprehend, just accept what I say. She asked me to tell you that she and Luke are going to die soon, perhaps tonight, unless you stop it. She does not yet realize that she holds the power to help herself. 'Tis imperative that you help her, as her time to die is not yet come."

"Tonight? But we all thought…"

"Listen to me, baby sister. You are up against a great evil, a man so possessed that he will stop at nothing."

"Giles Dayen?"

"Yes, and he is powerful, motivated by greed. But you can stop him."

"How?"

"There is only one power stronger than evil, and that is love. Do not fight because you hate him, but because you love Elanna. Make your motive love, and you will prevail."

"I-I do not understand."

"You will when you need to. You must save her. She has been given a considerable gift, and will indirectly affect this time period. She holds the truth. Evil will always try to destroy truth."

"What do you mean, she holds the truth?"

"I can only say that she is before her time. Her gifts, what this time refers to as witchcraft, will eventually be possible for all human beings. Her visions are simply glimpses into the future. Ignorant people will always fear her. Unfortunately, only a few will listen."

"I am not sure I understand, but I shall try." She paused. "Robert, what is it like to be dead?"

"Freedom—peace. There is a much greater world beyond waking consciousness. On this side, time does not exist. There is no beginning or end. Do not fear death, Pet. When your time comes we will be joined again. This is not your time—or Elanna's. You must save her."

"I do not know if I can. What if I cannot get there before…"

"I will guide you. Trust your feelings." He looked at Goliath, who seemed remarkably calm. "You have taken great care of him."

"He is my most prized possession."

"He understands, and will serve you well. You must leave now. And so must I."

Her heart leaped as the image began to fade. "Wait! Robert! Do not leave me again!"

His voice was more distant when he answered. "I am always with you."

"I love you!" she yelled desperately into the darkness.

There was silence, then a voice barely above a whisper answered back. "I love you too, baby sister."

Suddenly the barn was lighter and the animals all began making noises, oblivious to any spectral visit. Goliath still munched on the apple. It was as if time had stood still. Pet stood in place, afraid to move for fear she had imagined it all. Had she fallen asleep while standing, and simply dreamed it?

Dream or not, she was not going to take any chances. Her face set in determination and she ran from the barn to wake Matthew.

Chapter Twenty Three

The current events had not been lost on William, who was camped out just beyond the city gates waiting for Pet. He heard about the dead pigs, and overheard a traveler mention the alteration in the trial date. As he observed the influx of merchants hoping to take advantage of the gathering crowd, he had to make a choice. He overheard some travelers say the river was flooded over the main road, forcing a detour around through the forest. It was doubtful that Pet and Matthew would arrive in time. That left it up to him to do something. But what?

He led his horse through town, watching the celebrating with disgust. The gloomy clouds and drizzle didn't seem to dampen the mood. Jugglers enthralled wide-eyed children while peddlers hawked their wares. Musicians played jolly tunes. The music shared the air with delightful smells, as food booths had sprung up everywhere. People laughed and visited with one another, totally unconcerned that two innocent people were about to die. William became angrier with every passing minute at the fair-like atmosphere. Witch burning was certainly a popular form of entertainment. He stabled his horse and headed straight to the gallows.

Carpenters worked feverishly to finish the place where Luke would hang. The stake, being a simpler form of structure, was nearly finished.

They were built facing each other, an obvious last means of anguish as the two lovers were forced to watch each other die.

"Why bother with a trial," he muttered. He glanced up at the building where Luke and Elanna were being held. He had to talk to them. Maybe they had some ideas.

After borrowing another apron and hat, he loaded a tray from the kitchen and headed to the jail. This time the jailer turned him away.

"My orders are not to allow anyone in except the monk," he said as he solidly planted his feet. "No exceptions."

William was not in a position to argue, and promptly turned around. He rounded the corner and stopped when he was out of sight. What could he do? He was just one small boy, much as he hated to admit it. Suddenly he got an idea. A smile formed, and he headed back to the kitchen.

A while later he appeared again in front of the jailer.

"Here, you again? I told you no one was allowed in."

"Oh, I know, Sir. This food is for you. A young maiden in the kitchen said to bring it to you." He held up a tray laden with dried meats and bread. There was also a large mug of ale.

The jailer paused, then slowly smiled, revealing several missing teeth. "A maiden? Which one?"

Now William paused. "Uh, the pretty one. You know, the one who likes you."

The jailer narrowed his eyebrows as he thought, then widely grinned. "The redhead? I've 'ad my eye on 'er, I 'ave. She likes me, you say?"

"Oh, aye. She was worried that you might be hungry. She says you work too hard, and deserve a break."

"She did, eh? Well, as a matter of fact, I am a mite 'ungry."

William had to smile inwardly at that. The man looked like he had never missed a meal in his life. He handed the tray to the mentally challenged jailer and happily walked away. Now all he had to do was wait.

Pet and Robert had taught him many things, one being the art of herbs and healing. Certain herbs, when mixed in the proper proportions, could induce sleepiness. William had been more interested in the fighting skills the twins had to offer, but did pick up a few other things. It had been simply a matter of sneaking into the kitchen and finding the right ingredients. He had mixed a particularly large amount and dumped it all in the ale.

He peeked around the corner and saw the guard chewing on a piece of meat. It would be soon, now. The salty dried meats should make him thirsty.

The minutes passed like hours. He peeked again and saw the guard sitting on the floor against the wall, his head nodding as he fought drowsiness. His head finally nodded to one side and he began to snore.

William waited just another minute to make sure. When he was satisfied the man had effectively passed out, he tiptoed up and slowly reached out for the ring of keys. On a whim, he also grabbed the guard's dagger. After unlocking the door, he quietly sneaked inside.

Luke and Elanna instantly stood up, displaying relief.

"William! We did not think we would see you here," Luke exclaimed.

"I heard the news. I came to get you out."

Elanna glanced nervously toward the door. "How did you get past the guard?"

"I appealed to his vanity."

As he moved closer, Elanna searched his mind and smiled. "You drugged his ale. That was clever of you, but I fear we do not have much time. He will not sleep for long."

William fumbled with the keys. "I have to find the right one." He tried one, then another, and finally found the one for Elanna's cell. She rushed out the door, gave the boy a large hug, then took the keys.

"We have to hurry." She looked at all the keys, and instantly chose one. "This one opens Luke's cell."

"Come on, come on," Luke urged. In a second, he was free.

The couple rushed into each other's arms.

"I never thought I would actually hold you again," Luke said as he brought his lips down on hers.

William observed the tender kiss with a scrunched face. "Ah, folks? I appreciate the moment, but we need to get out of here. Oh, Luke? I brought you something." He held out the dagger.

Luke managed to tear himself away from Elanna's embrace. "A dagger? This might come in handy." He bent down and put it inside his boot.

William was already heading for the door. "Come on, we can go down the back stairs and make our way staying in the shadows. Hurry!"

Elanna suddenly froze. "Wait."

Luke grabbed her arm and pulled her toward the door. "Come on!"

She felt a shiver run down her spine, like the first freeze of fall. "We are too late."

"What do you mean?"

"She means," a familiar voice came from the doorway, "there will be no escape." Giles Dayen stood in their path, surrounded by six armed guards. "I had a feeling I should keep a closer eye on you." His eyes fell on William. "Well, well, if 'tis not the little scab from Ancaster. I should have known you would show up sometime." He motioned to a guard. "Put him in with the man. He can also hang for his participation." His cold eyes gleamed with satisfaction.

Elanna lunged toward Giles. "No! You cannot, he is just a boy!" Two guards grabbed her and held her tight. The others took Luke, who didn't resist.

Giles raised his sword against William's throat. "Very well, I can just kill him now."

"NO!" Elanna's eyes flared and she partially broke free from the guards. She reached out towards Giles with one free arm before the guards could react. Luke watched as the emerald in her cross began to glow. Giles tried to lift his sword, but found his arm frozen. He fought to regain motion, but could not. His face filled with fear and he dropped the sword.

"Get her away from me!" He backed up as she was seized again. "Lock them up, and stand guard outside the door! Do not let anyone in until the trial." He turned abruptly and left.

The guards threw the three into their cells and locked the doors. In a few seconds they were alone again.

William plopped down in the straw and bravely held back his tears. "Boy, I sure messed that up." He looked up at Luke in disappointment. "Why did you not use the dagger?"

"One dagger against six swords? With my luck I would have just stabbed myself."

"Well, you could have at least put up a fight. You did not even try."

Luke got down on one knee and faced the disillusioned boy. "If I had resisted, I would have been hurt, perhaps very badly. They might have even killed me. Either way, Elanna would also be hurt. She would have tried to heal me, or would have had to face the trial alone. I could not risk that. Do you understand?"

William looked him up and down with a measured gaze, and then finally nodded. "I guess."

It was clear the boy didn't understand, so Luke turned his attentions to Elanna, who had fallen remarkably quiet. "Elanna, what happened just now? How did you stop Dayen from killing William?"

She seemed stunned. "I—I do not know."

"Well, whatever you did, thank you," William quipped, as he rubbed his throat.

"Elanna," Luke continued, "is it possible you can control things when you have strong emotions?"

She shook her head. "Nay, this has never happened before."

"Aye, it did," William disagreed. "The lake, and Georgie—remember? The ice did not break under your weight."

"That was different."

"Nay, 'tis not," Luke offered. "Listen, Elanna, both times I noticed the stone in your cross necklace turned brighter. Sort of a glow, as if it were lit from within. At first I thought I might have been mistaken, but I am absolutely sure now."

Elanna lowered her head without speaking.

"Elanna? Did you know of this?"

She raised her head and met his gaze. "I have known about it since I was a child. I never gave it much thought, but I do feel a sort of tingle throughout my whole body when it glows."

"Hmm. I do not understand things such as this, but could it be that the stone stores power and boosts your strength when you have strong feelings?"

Elanna ran her fingers over the green stone. "I do not see how."

"Let us try a test." He reached through the bars and rattled the lock. "Try to break this lock. With your mind, I mean."

She looked at the lock, and back at him. "That is ridiculous. I cannot break through metal."

"Perhaps you only think you cannot. Just try."

William sat up with interest. "Aye, please. Try."

Luke let out a loud sigh of exasperation. "You have to try!"

She gave the two a pensive look, then capitulated to their demands. "Very well. I shall try." She stared at the lock for several minutes. Nothing happened. The cerulean stone remained normal. She finally slumped and closed her eyes. "I cannot."

"You are not trying hard enough," Luke said.

"I do not know how. Those other times, the lake, and just now with my uncle, it was not anything I tried to do. It just happened."

"Perhaps," William offered, "it has something to do with light. Elanna has often said she gets her power from the light. Maybe the stone stores light somehow to give her strength when she needs it. She already used it, and now it will not work until it has sunlight to replenish."

Elanna nodded. "Aye, that would make sense. My mother told me the cross was very powerful. It has been in the family for many years."

Luke's face brightened as an idea struck him. "Elanna, is it possible that your gift runs in your family? Did your mother perhaps sense that you had the power, and gave the necklace to you at a young age, planning later to tell you its history?"

"It could be. She died before she had the chance."

"Were you wearing the cross the night of the fire?"

Her eyebrows furled in thought. "I think so." Then, more positively, "Aye, I remember. My mother had given it to me a short time before."

"If the stone does somehow store power, then perhaps that is how you escaped from the fire that night. You said yourself that the windows burst outwards. In your young mind you thought they had disappeared."

"But that does not explain the red angel."

Luke's expression dropped. "Nay, it does not. So I guess we are back to where we started."

"I guess so."

"Then heaven help us. Let us hope your message got through to Pet."

Matthew urged his horse to catch up with Pet, who was galloping Goliath at a frantic pace. He hoped the rest of the men were able to follow. Patrick promised he'd be close behind, but the way Pet was going Matthew doubted if the devil himself could keep up. She had totally forsaken any civilized roads, preferring instead to ride across fields and jump fences and anything else that got in her way in a straight line to Cliffside. At least it wasn't raining at this precise moment.

He had no idea what was going on. She just burst into his chamber, waking him from the best night's sleep he'd had in weeks, not to mention a wonderful dream, hollering something about leaving immediately and she wasn't going to wait. She refused to give details. He barely had enough time to get dressed, let alone eat breakfast. But he knew better then to argue. When Pet had her mind set, a mountain couldn't move her.

The strange part was, Goliath seemed as driven as Pet to make Cliffside in record time. His horse, Excaliber, and Goliath were equals, from the same mare and sire. Then why was he having trouble keeping up with Pet? Excaliber was already foamy in places, but Goliath hadn't even broken a sweat. It was almost eerie.

Another stone fence loomed into view, and Matthew cringed. He had never been much of a jumper, ever since an embarrassing incident in his teens involving a pretty girl and a mud puddle. At least he was on a large, strong horse built for this type of thing. He felt sorry for Patrick and the others behind them.

He certainly hoped Pet knew what she was doing. If they kept up this pace, they would reach Cliffside for sure that evening or die in the attempt.

The trial started well, at least for the three prisoners. It was going extremely sour for Giles Dayen, who was fast losing his facade of pretending to be utterly devastated that his niece was a witch. The room was crowded with villagers and accusers, causing a stuffiness that almost robbed one of breath. The Abbot sat in front, the only judge, while the accused stood off to one side behind a line of guards. Elanna was asked again if she was a witch; she answered no. The abbot then ordered the trial to begin. One by one the accusations came forth. Some of them were downright laughable, or would be in any other circumstance, as the villagers were all convinced that Elanna was causing everything from the wet weather to a new wart. Brother Joseph tried to dispel every accusation, citing coincidence for some, and for others utter nonsense. His was the lone voice demanding logic.

"Please explain," he was saying to a bedraggled man standing before the court, "how your wife's failure to conceive a child has anything at all to do with my clients?"

The man pointed a shaky finger to Elanna. "She bewitched my wife and made her barren!"

"May I remind you that she has only been at Cliffside for two days? It would seem to me that your…er, problem arose before that. May I ask when was the last time you were with your wife?"

The personal question caused gasps from the spectators, and the man turned burning red. "That's none of your business!"

"Oh, I think 'tis. I think you are using this trial to cover up your own inadequacies. I suggest you spend less time at the tavern, and more time with your wife." The blood mounted even higher in the man's mottled cheeks, and he began stammering obscenities.

Joseph turned to the Abbot with a satisfied expression. "Your holiness, I do not see how this man's testimony has any bearing on this case."

The Abbot, with an ever-so-slight smile, nodded his head in agreement. "I would tend to agree. Bring on the next accuser."

An old widowed woman came forth insisting that a mysterious whirlwind carried off her cow, her sole possession. This caused a few chuckles from the crowd. Brother Joseph had particular fun with this one.

"So, you say you were bringing the cow in from your field, and this large whirlwind just appeared from nowhere and carried off your cow."

The woman nodded adamantly. "Right in front of me eyes."

"And of course, you blame my client."

"Well, she's a witch, isn't she?"

"And, of course, this means that you can no longer support yourself, because you have no milk to sell."

"Breaks me 'eart, it does."

"So naturally, you will have to depend on the Abbey for support."

She let out a loud, fake sigh of despair. "I 'ates to be a burden, but what else am I to do?"

Joseph paced in front of her with his hand on his chin. "You state this happened in broad daylight?"

"Aye."

"Yet, no one else saw this whirlwind?"

She squirmed in the chair. "I guess not."

"Does that not seem a bit odd?" He turned to the crowd and in a loud voice asked, "Did anyone else see this whirlwind?"

They all looked at one another, but no one answered.

"I see. So, this giant wind appears in the middle of the day and carried off your cow, but no one else saw it."

The woman frowned as she realized her lie wasn't being believed. Suddenly her face brightened. "It was invisible!"

A few snickers erupted from the front row. Brother Joseph didn't hesitate to seize the moment.

"The wind, or the cow?"

"Er, the wind!"

"Then would that not create the image of a flying cow? I am sure that would have been noticed." Again he turned to the spectators. "Did anyone here see a flying cow?"

The snickers turned to outright laughter.

The woman got desperate. "The wind made the cow invisible, too!"

Joseph stepped up close and brought his face directly in front of the woman. "Then I ask, madam, if they were both invisible, how did you see it happen?"

As the crowd broke out in laughter, Elanna motioned the monk over to her. She whispered a few words, and he returned to the woman.

"I suggest a different scenario. You heard about the witch trial, and decided to take advantage of the situation. You led your cow to the next village and sold it for a nice profit. Then you made up this ridiculous story so you would not have to work any more. Am I right?"

She took a long shuddering breath and let it out in a splutter. "Nay! I—I saw it, I did!"

"Leave my sight, woman. Your lies have been exposed." He pointed to the door, and the woman hurried out amid cries of hilarious laughter.

Joseph smiled over at Elanna, who smiled back. Her insights into the woman's thoughts were most helpful.

Giles shifted in his seat as the trial continued. Most of the accusations were so ridiculous that Joseph was able to dispel them within minutes. How dare the little moronic monk defy him? If this continued, Elanna just might escape her fate after all. He leaned into the nearest person, a middle-aged peasant who was enjoying the trial immensely.

"I am certainly glad that no one has mentioned the pigs," he said calmly.

The man stopped smiling. "Aye, that's right! What about the pigs?" he yelled.

The crowd immediately started murmuring.

"Aye, remember the pigs! Only a witch could'of done that!"

"Aye, explain the pigs!"

Giles leaned back in his chair, confident the trial was now back on course.

Joseph wiped his sweaty brow. "Has anyone considered," he shouted over the crowd, "that the pigs might have been poisoned?"

The abbot leaned forward as a deep scowl etched his face. "Poison? Why would someone do that?"

Joseph looked at Giles, who stared back with cold, calculating eyes. "Perhaps someone wants us all to believe this girl is a witch—someone who stands to benefit from her death."

Giles rose to his feet. "Your holiness, if I may?"

The abbot acknowledged him, and he continued. "I, for one, could use a break. We have been here for hours. I suggest a recess."

Joseph immediately disagreed. "No! I want to continue!"

The Abbot rubbed his eyes and nodded toward Giles. "I am a bit fatigued. A break sounds good to me. One hour!" He stood up to indicate there would be no further discussion.

Four guards led the prisoners out and the crowd began to disburse. Joseph watched Giles leave the room, then leaned against a table in relief. He feared Giles might remain behind to threaten him. In a few minutes the room was empty except for him, and he left to his chamber to pray.

The hour was almost over. Kneeling at his prayer altar, Joseph felt a presence outside his door, as if someone had walked up and then stopped just outside. He ceased praying and cocked his head to listen. He heard nothing. The feeling persisted, however, so he got up off his knees and carefully walked to the door. He reached out a shaky hand and grasped the latch, then paused as he felt his heart beat faster. As his breathing turned shallow, he looked around for anything with which to protect himself, settling on a pewter candlestick. He raised it high, took a deep breath and held it, then dramatically pulled open the door.

There was no one there. Feeling like a fool, he let out his breath and lowered the candlestick. He began to shut the door, when it suddenly flew open with a force that threw him backward, landing him on the floor. He looked up in horror as Giles Dayen entered and closed the door behind him.

Joseph scooted backwards on his behind as Giles walked closer. "G-get away! I have nothing to say to you!"

Giles stopped in the center of the room and wordlessly removed his gloves, slowly and methodically. He reached inside his jacket and removed a dagger, holding it up so that the light caused it to gleam in its murderous glory.

"Beautiful, is it not?" He looked down with disgust at the quivering little monk. "'Tis the same knife I used to kill all the dogs. 'Tis only fitting I use it on you." He took a step toward the monk.

Joseph tried to get to his feet, instead becoming entangled in his robe and falling down again. "Go away!" he yelled.

Giles brought a fist across Joseph's face, stunning him. Joseph tried to raise his hands to protect his face, but was not a man of physical prowess and found he was frightfully lacking against the bigger, dominate Giles.

"I told you not to defy me," Giles said in a calm, steady voice. He kicked the monk in the abdomen.

"N-no! Please!" Joseph begged. In desperation, he reached up to his prayer altar and grabbed his crucifix. He held it up as if fending off a vampire. "May God strike you down!"

Giles stopped, held up his hands in mock surrender, looked to the ceiling, and waited. In a few seconds he looked back with amusement at Joseph, who was still clutching the crucifix.

"I think one would have to believe in God in order for him to strike you down." He kicked the crucifix out of the monk's hand, sending it sliding across the floor and hitting the opposite wall.

Joseph reached out for it as he began to pray loudly. "Father, in your mercy…"

"That's right, you pray, you foolish idiot." He grabbed Joseph's ring of hair and pulled his head backwards. Clutching the knife tightly, he brought it against the monk's throat. "You were going to tell, were you? Tell them everything."

By now Joseph was crying and begging simultaneously. "P-please! I will do what you want!"

Giles quickly and deeply slit his throat. "I think not." He dropped the bleeding, dying man to the floor and walked quietly from the room. He paused at the door and looked back at his handiwork. "I am just going to have to get myself another monk."

In her cell, Elanna suddenly sat up with a look of despair, as if hope and fear had choked each other and left no victor. "Joseph," she whispered.

Luke and William looked at her curiously. "What?" Luke asked.

Her eyes wide, her color pale, she turned to look at them. "'Tis Joseph. He is dead."

A few miles away, Pet pulled Goliath to an abrupt stop. Her instincts told her go left, the direct course to the abbey, but she had the overwhelming compulsion to turn right through the forest. What's more,

Goliath seemed to have the same inclination. He pawed the ground and kept turning toward the forest.

When Matthew caught up and stopped beside her, he silently thanked whatever saint was responsible for even this brief pause. Raymond, Patrick and the fifty or so men were right behind him. Noting her indecisive look, he waited a few seconds then finally interrupted her thoughts.

"What is it?"

She pointed left. "The abbey is just over that hill," she explained, "but I think we should go right."

"That does not make any sense," Matthew answered as he scratched his head.

"I know, but…" Her thoughts flashed to her vision of Robert, and him telling her to trust her feelings. "We go right."

"But…" Matthew began.

She cut him off. "If we go left, we will not be in time."

"How do you know that?"

"I just do." Her face determined, she jerked Goliath to the right and motioned them to follow.

Chapter Twenty Four

The abbot once more glanced around the room, a clear look of impatience on his face. The crowd was getting restless as they waited for the trial to resume. The three prisoners appeared less hopeful, knowing they were literally without a protector. Giles sat as before in the front row, looking a bit smugger, if that were possible.

Everyone glanced up anxiously as a monk, sent by the abbot to fetch Brother Joseph, walked in. He scurried to the front, displaying a distressed look. He said a few words to the abbot, and left as quickly as he had came. The abbot stood up and took a deep breath, then let it out with a long, loud, sigh. Everyone held their breath awaiting his words.

"Brother Joseph has just been found dead in his chamber, clutching his crucifix. His throat has been slashed."

The crowd began murmuring, at first softly, then a bit louder. Finally someone yelled out.

"Just like the dogs!"

"Aye, the dogs! It's the witch!"

Luke lunged forward and momentarily broke through the line of guards. "That is madness! Why would she kill the only person who was defending her?" The guards pushed him back and threatened to remove him if he did not refrain.

His reasoning was lost among the simple-minded peasants. "Who's next?" one yelled.

"Burn her, before she kills again!"

"Aye, burn the witch!"

A few took up a chant, growing louder as more joined in. "Burn the witch; burn the witch, burn the witch!"

Giles glanced around him, his eyebrows raised, subduing a smile. This was an unexpected, but welcomed response. He simply needed to eliminate a threat; he had no idea Elanna would be blamed for it.

"I will have order!" the abbot demanded, to no avail. He stepped down to stand directly in front of the unruly crowd. "Please," he shouted, "we must remain civil! I will hear the remaining accusations, and then I shall make a decision!"

A few of the chanters dropped out, causing others to follow, whereupon there was just a handful left. The abbot quieted them.

"I must have order, or the trial will proceed in private."

As everyone settled down, Luke leaned into Elanna's ear. "This is not going well. We have to think of something, fast!"

She nodded blankly.

William's lower lip trembled as hopelessness overtook him. "Am I going to die?"

"Nay, not without them killing me first." Luke put his arm around the boy's shoulders.

The accusers from Ancaster came forward next, repeating their allegations. Giles was sure to make his presence known, staring at them in grim silence as they spoke. With no one there to argue the statements, the trial became ominously slanted. Even the most ridiculous stories were believed, indeed, at this point the flying cow would have been accepted as gospel truth.

This went on for hours. With people still waiting to speak, the abbot stood and brought the trial to a halt. "I tire," he said wearily. "We will continue the trial tomorrow."

A frightened peasant in the front row leaped to his feet. "What if she kills again in the night? We all know that witches fly in the darkness and cast spells!"

That caused a loud muttering among the crowd. Several more jumped up.

"Aye, make her confess!"

"Torture her! The men, too!"

"I don't want to die in my sleep!"

Soon everyone was yelling concurrently, turning words into a muddled discord. Even the Ancaster peasants joined in, caught up in the moment.

The Abbot desperately tried to gain control. "My good folk, please! There is protocol that must be followed!" The sheriff ordered several of his men to stand between the prisoners and the crowd. At the show of force, most of the peasants settled down so the abbot could reason with them. A few stubbornly refused to concede.

"I promise you, the law will be upheld," the abbot said. "If she is proven to be a witch, she and her accomplices will be punished."

"We don't need any more proof!" one shouted.

"Kill them now, before they kill us!"

Elanna watched this farce develop, knowing there was no need to prolong the conclusion. She had always known it was inevitable. Before Luke realized what was happening, she had stepped forward and spoken.

"Stop! I have something to say!"

Luke pulled her back with a jerk, and looked at her as if she had lost her mind. "What do you think you are doing?"

Her face ashen, she stared back with cavernous eyes. "Trust me."

At her words, Giles sat up with curious suspicion. The abbot smiled with the prospect of a confession, and the spectators were stunned into silence.

Elanna continued, her head held high, with a strong, unwavering voice. "I will confess to being a witch, and to everything you have accused me of. My husband and this boy are completely innocent. I bewitched them into helping me. Let them go, and I will sign a confession."

There was a collective gasp from the villagers. Usually a confession was obtained only through severe torture. They had never seen someone so openly volunteer to die, which was the punishment for witchcraft. Giles Dayen wasn't sure whether to feel victorious or skeptical, so at the moment remained silent.

Luke felt his hopes disintegrate when he comprehended her actions. He felt helpless and awkward. Panic rose in his heart, with a lurch of pain that he might not be able to stop what she had started. "Nay! She is lying to protect us! Do not listen to her!"

Not to be left out, William also spoke up. "She is not a witch! This whole thing is a farce!"

The abbot ignored them and pushed aside the guards to face Elanna. "You admit you are a witch?"

"Aye," she answered, and then nodded to Luke and William. "But they are not. Let them go."

Giles felt his voice catch in his throat, and he glanced around to see if anyone had noticed his reactions. He need not have worried, as all attentions were on Elanna and the abbot.

There was a pause as the abbot considered his options. "Very well; I accept your confession and your insistence that these two are innocent." He motioned to the guards, who tightly held Luke and William. "Let them go."

Giles brought a clenched fist to his chin and fought to contain his fury. This couldn't be happening; he had worked too hard to have it all end now. He had killed too many, gotten rid of that intruding Lady Knight, not to mention Patrick and Joseph. It simply could not become unraveled now, not after all his brilliant planning. He sprang to his feet, rage consuming his face. "NO! They must all die!" He angrily pushed aside several peasants, knocking some to the floor, as he lunged to the front.

His actions took the guards by surprise. They didn't know whether to allow him to come forth or try to stop him. Still holding Luke and William, in confusion they looked to the sheriff for guidance. Unfortunately, he was as disconcerted as they were.

Elanna had anticipated his ire, and used the mass bewilderment to her benefit. She waited quietly as Giles moved toward her, ranting his objections. Within seconds his mind was accessible.

He suddenly realized the folly of his anger. His ranting stopped abruptly as he grasped his head in terror. "No! Go away!" The image of his dead brother filled his mind, causing him to lose all aspects of reality. He shrieked in horror and stumbling backward to get away from Elanna. Losing his balance, blinded by the image, he fell to the floor screaming as if in mortal agony.

Luke finally understood her plan, and quickly seized the moment to their advantage. "There, look at him! He is the one possessed with demons! It has always been him."

The crowd again gasped, and moved away from the thrashing madman. The abbot dropped to his knees, crossed his heart, and began praying.

As Elanna projected the horrible image, she caught fleeting insights into her uncle's mind. Dark, hateful thoughts mixed with vengeance consumed him, thoughts so evil she almost couldn't fathom them. She drew a quick breath and took a faltering step backward when one took shape into clarity.

"T'was you," she said in just above a whisper. "You killed my family. You set the fire."

Released from his horrific vision, Giles rose to his feet and stepped away from her. His head was still groggy from his ordeal, but he had the presence of mind to snap his fingers. Immediately his garrison of men armed with crossbows stepped from the walls and their places among the spectators. They far outnumbered the few guards the sheriff had hired.

"Fools! Did you think I did not come prepared?" He slowly rotated to face Elanna. "You insipid whore," he seethed through closed teeth. "Of course I killed your worthless family. I deserved to have Ancaster, not my ignoramus of a brother. Your problem is, you did not have the decency to die with them, and you were the one who most needed to die." He turned and addressed his men. "Seize them! If any of them moves, shoot them!" His men moved in and grabbed the three prisoners.

The abbot had risen to his feet, thoroughly confused. "I-I do not understand."

"Of course not, you brainless twit." Giles grabbed the abbot and strong-armed his neck. "You are coming with me." He held his dagger to the abbot's heart. "If anyone tries to stop me, he will die!" He motioned to the men holding the prisoners. "Tie them up and bring them outside. If these idiots will not execute them, I will."

"This is ludicrous!" Luke yelled. "Someone stop him!"

As Dayen's men obeyed his orders, the sheriff finally found his voice. "You cannot do this—'tis against the law!"

Giles pointed and snapped his fingers to one of his archers, who promptly shot the sheriff square in his chest. The sheriff took a choking breath and fell to the ground.

Giles looked down at him without a hint of compassion. "Consider the law changed." He glanced around at the stunned spectators. "Anyone else have an objection?" When met with only stony silence, he smiled slightly and gave a throaty chuckle. "I thought not."

He dragged the abbot outside to the scaffold and stake. His men followed, forcing Luke, William and Elanna along with pokes from their crossbows. The townsfolk followed, too scared and shocked that someone would dare threaten their beloved abbot.

"Tie her to the stake," Giles commanded, "and make sure she is secure. She has a way of getting out of ropes."

They forced Elanna to climb the pile of wood to the stake sticking out of the center. As Giles had ordered, they secured her so tightly her wrists bled. Then, to make positive she couldn't escape, they also bound her ankles.

While they were busy with Elanna, Dayen was following his men to the scaffold facing the stake. When they arrived, however, they discovered the final support beam for the nooses was not yet in place. The workers cowered and fled with fear as Giles turned red with rage.

"Incompetent idiots!" He glanced around impatiently, determined not to be stopped by a minor detail. "Very well, instead of hanging we will simply shoot them. Tie them to the poles."

Numb with fear, Elanna watched in horror as Luke and William were tied to the two poles intended to hold the support beam. Luke looked back at her, equally in horror. Then his eyes fell to William—just a boy, standing bravely beside him, unflinching, unwavering.

He looked back at Luke with innocent eyes, wise beyond his years. "If I have to die, I am glad 'tis with you."

Elanna felt a tear run smoothly down her cheek. She could not allow this to happen. At that thought, the clouds parted briefly, soaking her face in warmth and light. She lifted her face and closed her eyes. "God give me strength," she whispered.

All of Dayen's men stood in a circle around the executions, poised to shoot anyone who dared to intervene.

Finally releasing the abbot, Giles grabbed a lit torch and pointed to Elanna.

"You all heard her confession," he shouted. "She admits she is a witch! Now watch her burn!" He thrust the torch into the woodpile and stood back to watch. The wood was still a bit wet, thanks to the heavy rain the area had suffered, despite the effort to dry it. Several sticks crackled and fizzed out, producing more smoke than heat. Giles tried another section, possessed on finding a dry area. Finally there was a spark, followed by the snapping of burning wood. Smoke rose slowly, filling the air with the scent of impending death.

Giles was almost drunk with glee. "Burn, you little fool! Join the rest of your wretched family! Now for the best part—watch your beloved die." He ordered four of his men to take aim at Luke and William.

William tensed his body and clinched his eyes shut. Luke looked over at Elanna and gave her a last smile. "I love you," he mouthed.

"Kill them!"

The arrows left the bows.

Elanna's eyes flared and she screamed. The stone on her cross necklace glowed bright, almost casting a glimmering around Elanna.

"No!"

Except for the crackling of the burning wood, there was an eerie silence. Giles dropped the torch and backed away, his eyes wide in disbelief.

The archers lowered their bows as their jaws dropped open.

William opened one eye. Then the other one. He lowered his eyes to chest level and took in a quick breath.

There, six inches in front of him, suspended in mid-air, were two arrows.

He glanced over at Luke, moving only his eyes, to see him staring at his own suspended arrows. Then, as quickly as they had been shot, they dropped harmlessly and fell at his feet.

The abbot crossed himself. "Divine intervention," he barely whispered. Then louder, he repeated, "Divine intervention!"

The villagers collectively dropped to their knees and began praying. Some cried, some laughed, all praised God for the miracle.

Giles gathered his wits as he fought to regain control. "Bah! She did this, I tell you! God had nothing to do with it!"

No one heard him.

Elanna slumped against the stake, wobbly from the tremendous mind power it took to stop the arrows. The smoke grew heavy as the flames rose higher. It burned her eyes and began to scorch her lungs.

Coughing between gasps for air, she closed her eyes with the realization that her vision was coming true. "Luke," she weakly cried out.

"We are innocent," Luke screamed. "Let her go! Someone get her down."

The spectators ignored him and continued praying, still caught up with the pretense of the miracle.

Giles ordered all his men to take aim at Elanna. "Everyone shoot her! She cannot stop *all* the arrows!"

His men exchanged looks, and hesitated. The more religious ones began to question his orders, and they began to argue among themselves.

"What are you waiting for? I said shoot her!"

The hard pounding of hoofs suddenly drew their attention, and everyone scrambled to get out of the way of the approaching riders. Luke tore his gaze away from Elanna to see a small army led by Pet and Matthew.

William started laughing. "They are here! I told you!"

Luke couldn't believe his eyes, but he wasn't going to argue. "Pet! Matthew! Get Elanna down from there!"

Giles, outraged and in sheer panic at this turn of events, shouted at his men to shoot the intruders. He needn't bothered; they had no choice but to fight as the army descended upon them, swords raised. Arrows filled the sky, and the sound of metal against metal resonated through the abbey square.

Pet pulled Goliath up and dismounted before he had fully stopped. Seeing William strapped to the pole brought out her motherly instincts, and her only thought was to free him. With one leap, she was up on the scaffold.

"Forget me," William yelled. "Get Elanna!"

"Matthew will get her," she said, drawing her dagger to cut him loose. "You are a sitting duck up here." Her point was illustrated as an arrow shot over them and imbedded itself in the pole just inches above her head.

Matthew dashed to the burning wood-heap, now blazing ferociously only several feet away from Elanna's feet. She would soon die of smoke inhalation if he didn't get her down.

Upon seeing Elanna's circumstance, Patrick flung off his long, red cloak and plunged it into a nearby water trough.

"Hurry!" Luke yelled, feeling helpless against the ropes that bound him.

"'Tis too hot!" Matthew shouted back. He ducked to miss an arrow as it whizzed past his head.

Pet freed William, and yelled to Raymond, who was still on horseback.

"Get him out of here!"

Raymond pulled the boy up on the horse and took off galloping away from the danger.

Matthew drew his sword and prodded the burning pile, hoping to dislodge the logs. It was too late; the fire increased with intensity every passing second. "'Tis no use! We need to put out the fire."

A voice responded from behind him. "There is no time for that. I will get her."

Matthew swung around to see Patrick leap onto the burning heap, his wet cloak wrapped around him. He made it to the top with only a few scorches and burns.

He used the wet cape to beat back the flames, buying him a few precious extra seconds. Suddenly he became aware of a pair of eyes staring intently up at him. A gust of wind cleared the smoke for just an instant, revealing Giles standing off to one side. Their gazes made contact without expression or emotion. Then the haze obscured the image, and Giles disappeared in a smoky fog.

Elanna was limp and almost unconscious. Her ropes were so tight that his sharp dagger easily sliced through them. Her ankles were more difficult to release, as the flames licked at his hands as he cut. Finally she was free, and he wrapped the cloak around the both of them.

"Hold on," he said, and jumped down through the flames.

Landing hard but safely, he rolled them away from the now fire-engulfed stake.

She lay still and lifeless. Patrick used the edge of his wet cape to wipe her smoke-scorched face. "Please be alive," he pleaded. "Wake up, Elanna."

She sputtered and coughed, then opened her eyes, peering into his intense gaze. For the first time she truly recognized him.

"It was you," she uttered. "You are the red angel."

He smiled, with both relief and incredulity. "What are you talking about?"

"The fire that destroyed my family. You are the one who saved me before—my red angel."

"Elanna, I may be a lot of things, but I am certainly no angel."

"You are to me."

By now Pet had freed Luke, who lost no time in bounding off the scaffold to get to his wife. He knelt by her and patted her face. "Elanna! Are you all right?"

She coughed and nodded.

Patrick stood up and drew his sword. "Giles is heading for the cliffs. Get her out of here. I have some unfinished business to attend to."

Luke cradled her in his arms and rose, lifting her as if she weighed nothing. He watched Patrick sprint off between buildings away from the fighting.

Pet had joined the action, indeed, she looked like she was highly enjoying it. No man was a match for her sword. Matthew was by her side, fighting as relentless as she was. It soon became apparent that Dayen's men were outnumbered and outclassed. They scattered and began running away to escape death. Pet's men pursued them.

Luke carried Elanna to Pet and Matthew, and gently laid her down. Then, without warning, he pulled his brother and Pet into his arms in a group hug.

"Am I glad to see you two," he said. "Do you think you could have cut it any shorter?"

"You can thank Pet that we are here at all," Matthew replied. "She was the one that insisted we ride like the devil to get here."

Pet kneeled next to Elanna while the brothers caught up on current events. "I got your message," Pet said barely above a whisper. "Your choice of messenger was…interesting."

"I did not know what else to do," Elanna answered. "I knew you would listen to him."

Pet brushed the hair away from Elanna's face, hesitated, and then finally asked, "Will I see him again?"

"That is up to him." Elanna let out another cough and tried to get to her feet. "Help me up, Pet."

"Whoa, young lady," Luke challenged, "Where do you think you are going?"

She steadied herself on Luke's shoulder. "Patrick—we have to go after Patrick."

Pet quickly inspected the area. "Where did he go?"

"After Giles," Elanna said. "He is no match for him. Please, we have to help him. Luke—he is the red angel."

Luke drew back in surprise, and then nodded in understanding.

Matthew narrowed his eyebrows. "The what?"

Luke would have preferred to have the whole ordeal behind him, but knew Elanna would never be safe as long as her uncle was free. "Never mind that; she is right—we have to help him." He pointed in the direction he saw Patrick run. "He took off that way. Said he was heading for the cliffs."

Pet's face paled slightly. "C-cliffs?"

"Of course," Matthew answered, not catching the hint of fear in her voice. "The whole abbey was built on the edge of some of the highest cliffs in England. Overlooks a small inlet, hence, the name Cliffside."

"He must be stopped," Elanna said. She glanced at Pet, remembering the admission of her fear of heights. "Pet, perhaps you…"

"Nonsense," Pet quickly interrupted as she sheathed her sword. "Let us go."

Pet and Matthew took off running where Luke had pointed. Luke hesitated, then turned to Elanna, his face determined. "This is my battle, too. I want to see that bloody bastard brought to justice. You stay here."

"You are not leaving me!" She looked shocked and hurt.

"You are in no condition to run."

"After all that we have been through, I am never leaving your side again. I am going."

He tried to remain firm, but her pleading face convinced him. "I cannot say no to you, come on." They took off after the others.

Chapter Twenty Five

Patrick carefully inched along the narrow trail hewed into the side of the cliff. Having exhausted all other possibilities, he followed the only path Giles could have taken. It was an old trail, possibly carved into the solid rock by ancient monks as a test of bravery, or some other such foolish reason. Some loose stones from above rained down in front of him, bouncing off the path before falling into the water below. He paused to look down at the crashing waves breaking over huge rocks, intermittently sending spray high enough for him to feel. The air tasted salty. It was deliciously frightful, causing an adrenaline rush that gave the false pretense of immortality. He shuddered. This certainly wasn't for the faint of heart. Those ancient monks had too much time on their hands.

It seemed forever before the path turned inward onto a plateau, a shelf carved in the side of the cliff, where he could relax his tense body and begin breathing normally again. Giles had to be close; he didn't have that much of a head start. Patrick quickly analyzed the area; the sloping plateau was the result of a massive landslide that left the floor covered in massive boulders. It was about two hundred yards wide and one hundred yards deep. Steep walls boxed in both sides to the top of the cliff. He could see the trail take up on the other side.

A few tenacious trees had taken root, growing spindly and sparse through the rocks. Patrick jumped up on top of one of the large boulders and scanned the vicinity. In a few seconds he caught a glimpse of black behind one of the boulders. He drew his sword and stood tall.

"It ends here, Dayen! Get out here and face me!"

Giles Dayen languidly stepped out from behind the huge rock, his black cape whipping behind him, his hair disheveled. His black eyes gleamed darker than usual in the setting sun. More evil, if that were possible. "You surprise, me Patrick."

"Surprised that I am still alive? You can thank your own stupidity for that. You should have never double-crossed me."

Giles snorted a tart, sarcastic laugh. "Do not be so shocked, I had to protect myself. You were growing soft, and I knew it was just a matter of time before you betrayed me. Nay, I am surprised you dared to follow me. Surely you know you cannot win."

Patrick hopped to the next nearest rock, almost losing balance on the wet, slick surface. "If you will not come to me, I will come to you." He jumped to another boulder, gradually making his way to Giles. In turn, Giles matched every step with one further away. This exasperated Patrick.

"There is nowhere to run," he called. "Your plan failed. We need to give ourselves up and face the authorities for our deeds."

"Never!" Giles jumped to another boulder, and waved his arms as he gained his balance. "Are you mad? Do you know what they will do to us?"

"We have nowhere to go."

"Speak for yourself! This trail ends down at the beach, where I will rent passage on a ship to take me out of here." He gleefully held up a bulging leather pouch and jingled it. "I had the forethought to bring plenty of money."

"And then what?"

"I still have the pirate ship." His voice softened to a low, guttural plea. "Come, Patrick, come with me. I will forget this momentary lapse in your loyalty. Together we can set up another operation far away from here. We belong together, Patrick. It was inevitable."

"The only thing that is inevitable is that I am going to confess everything, and I am bringing you back with me."

"You are mad! I am not going anywhere, except away from here."

Patrick drew his sword and jumped one boulder closer. "Then I am going to have to kill you."

Back at the trail head, Pet and Matthew had also concluded that the cliff path was the only way that Giles and Patrick could have gone. Matthew was not exactly thrilled at the prospect of braving the narrow, dangerous trail, but he wasn't prepared at the reaction he received from Pet.

She stared aghast at the trail, then carefully peered to the rocks below. Then she plastered herself against the cliff wall and closed her eyes. "I cannot go on that."

Matthew looked at her strangely. "Why not? We have been on narrower trails then this."

"Not on the side of a cliff."

"Ah, 'tis the cliff that upsets you. No problem, we will simply hold hands. That way, if you lose your balance, I can catch you, and vise versa."

"That will not work."

"Why not?"

"Because she is afraid of heights," Elanna said from behind them.

Matthew turned to Luke and Elanna, who unbeknownst to him had followed them. "Pet? Afraid? Nay, that is not possible." He gave a nervous laugh. "Pet, tell them you are not afraid." He waited for an answer. "Pet?"

She swallowed and stepped away from the trail. "She is correct. I am deathly afraid of heights."

"As am I," Elanna added.

Matthew gave an amazed look, then started to chuckle. "Well, are you two a pair! Very well, Luke, it looks like 'tis up to you and me. We men will handle this; you ladies stay here."

Luke nodded, and the two brothers began to inch themselves along the narrow trail.

"Be careful!" Elanna yelled after them.

Safely away from the cliff's edge, Pet punched a tree trunk in a fit of frustration. "I feel so useless!"

Elanna looked up at the slowly darkening sky. "It shall be dark, soon." Her gaze traveled to the top of the cliff, lined with tall firs right up to the edge. "Perhaps we do not have to be useless. Follow me."

Giles Dayen drew his sword and waited while Patrick approached him. "You cannot win. You are no good at swordplay. I, on the other hand, have made it a lifetime study."

"I am better than you think." He raised his sword and jabbed it at Giles.

Giles blocked it and thrust back, but Patrick was too quick. He jumped out of the way and countered with another thrust. It was met with another block. The swordplay went on for several minutes, neither man getting the upper hand until Patrick slipped and fell between two boulders. Giles used the opportunity to flee toward the cliffs.

Patrick groaned from the impact of the fall, but struggled to his feet. He licked the warm, viscous taste of blood from his lip, and looked up with determination.

"You will not get away!" Lighter and faster than Giles, plus having the advantage of youth, he leaped from stone to stone until he overtook Him. He grabbed his cape and forced Giles to the ground, punching him in the face as he fell. Dayen's sword flew from his hand, landing several yards away between two boulders. Giles fought back with a jab to Patrick's midsection, impacting hard enough to send Patrick flying backward.

"You moronic twit," Giles seethed. "I should have killed you when I killed your useless brother."

"W-what?" Patrick said. He scrambled to his feet as Giles approached. "That cannot be! My brother died while plowing his field."

"Aye, that is what it looked like, but the truth is, I crushed in his head with a rock." He reached down and picked up a melon-sized stone. "Not unlike this one." He hurled the rock, clipping Patrick in the arm, forcing him to drop his sword. Patrick reached to pick it up, but Giles kicked it out of his reach. "You think you are so smart. You want to know why I took you in? Have you not ever wondered how I just happened to be there when my worthless sister died?"

Patrick backed up, stumbling over boulders. His mind raced in disbelief and confusion. "She was my mother! She was not worthless!"

"Oh, allow me to disagree. I had to kill them, don't you see? The curse! It had to be stopped, once and for all!"

"Curse? What curse?"

"The Dayen curse, of course. Every other generation a devil child is born. Our mother had the curse, and died at her own hand. I knew I could never marry and have children, lest I pass the curse along. But did my brother and sister? No, they carried on as if their actions would cause no repercussions. Only I knew they had to be stopped."

"You're—you're mad!"

"Your brother died quickly. I slowly poisoned Isabel. I planned on killing you also, but then thought, what bitter irony it would be to take you in as my ward, raise you to be my protégé. It was the last thing they would have wanted. It was my ultimate revenge. I turned you into a murderer."

"Nay!" Red with rage, Patrick lunged at Giles with his body. The collision knocked Giles off balance, and he fell off his boulder, landing on his back. The impact knocked the air from his lungs, and he lay gasping for breath.

Patrick jumped down to straddle over him. "Then you are your own worst enemy. You see, it was I who rescued Elanna that night at the fire. Your act of revenge was your downfall."

Eyes wide in outraged surprise, Giles reached up and pulled Patrick down by his jacket lapels. "You! Do you realize how much trouble you have caused? She has the devil's curse! If she had died like she was supposed to, we would not be in this predicament!" He grabbed Patrick around the neck and tried to strangle him. Patrick squirmed for release, unable to break free before kicking Giles in the groin and crawling away from between the huge rocks. Giles groaned and uttered a few obscenities. Recovering quickly, he followed Patrick seething with rage.

"Ancaster should have been mine! I did my part, remained single and heirless, while my brother pretended nothing was wrong! I warned him! I told him he had to remain childless, but he wouldn't listen. I tried to save the family, but because of you the curse continues. It is all your fault!"

"The only one you have to blame is yourself," Patrick yelled back. "Your greed consumed you. Your hate has rankled inside of you until all there is left is a soulless body. You are evil, and you must be stopped. I should have stopped you a long time ago."

Giles stepped toward him when his foot hit something. Looking down, he grinned when he realized it was Patrick's sword that had fallen between the rocks. He leaned down and picked it up.

"I think the only one who will be stopped is you."

Patrick glanced around for something to defend himself. He found nothing. Backing up, he stumbled and fell as Giles descended upon him.

Matthew and Luke reached the plateau just as Giles plunged his sword into Patrick's abdomen. His blood splattered thickly against his white shirt in a contrast of deathly beauty.

There was a high-pitched scream from above, a cry of panic mixed with disbelief. They looked up to see Elanna and Pet standing at the top of the plateau, Elanna with a pale look of horror.

Giles jerked his head up to gaze upon Elanna with an equal look of horror. He instantly began traipsing toward the continuing cliff trail on the other side of the shelf.

Pet lost no time in climbing down over the boulders, her sword drawn. "Get him!" she ordered Matthew, who was a bit dumbstruck at seeing the women there. Luke stared at Elanna, then at Matthew, then back at Elanna. He decided that Matthew and Pet could take care of Giles, and began leaping over boulders to reach Elanna. His long, muscular legs made the trip with little effort. She met him halfway down the boulder slide.

"Help me get to Patrick," she pleaded. "I can save him."

He hesitated, concerned again for her safety.

"Please, Luke. I have to try. He saved my life twice."

Without a word of argument, he picked her up and carried her to the dying man. She fell to her knees and put her hands over the mortal wound.

Blood oozing from his mouth, Patrick tried to fend her away. "Nay, do not save…" he began. A bloody cough finished his sentence.

"Shhh, you are going to be fine." She put her hands back on his wound and closed her eyes.

By now Pet and Matthew were in heavy pursuit. They raced side-by-side, jumping over rocks and dodging between trees.

"How did you get here?" he yelled between leaps.

"There was another trail at the top," she yelled back.

"Now you tell me."

Pet swerved and cut off Dayen's passage to the trail. He teetered on the edge of the cliff and had no recourse but to fight. He planted his feet firmly and grasped the sword, still spattered with Patrick's blood, with both hands.

"Give it up, Dayen," Matthew shouted. "You cannot beat us both."

"Maybe not," he declared in response, "but I can take one of you with me. Which one will it be?"

Pet placed herself in front of Matthew, in fighter stance. "He is *mine*."

Elanna began trembling as she realized the extent of Patrick's injury. "Please," she begged to an unseen entity, "he must live." A teardrop slowly ran over her cheek, hung briefly on her chin, and then plummeted to her breast.

Patrick reached out and grasped her hand. "Elanna—let me die. I…I have done things. Horrible things." The effort of speaking forced more coughing.

"Do not try to speak," Elanna asserted.

"Nay—I must tell you. I…I helped him kill…your family."

Elanna smiled and put a hand on his forehead, brushing back a sweaty lock of hair. "I know," she replied. "You were young. When you found out, you saved me. You did not intend to kill anyone."

"Please…forgive me. If I could trade places…with any member of your family, I gladly would." He choked and hacked up thick blood, and his body began to convulse.

She threw her body over his and embraced him. "I forgive you. Now, be at peace. You feel no pain. No pain."

Luke stood by fighting large, unmanly tears. He turned to see what was happening at the other end of the slide.

Pet lunged her sword at Giles, who expertly turned to avoid the thrust. He jumped to a large boulder, brandishing his sword in front of him while laughing maniacally.

"I will enjoy killing you," he said. "Something that stupid Gideon failed to do."

The mention of the man who had killed Robert made Pet hesitate in pure surprise. "How did you know him?"

"Know him? He worked for me. I hired the renegades to keep the king occupied away from my pirating operation. It was a perfect distraction. That is, until you and this poor excuse of a knight decided to get involved."

Matthew bristled at the insult to his knighting abilities. "May I remind you that the renegades are all dead!" He drew his sword and attempted to step forward. Pet again blocked his way.

"I said...*he is mine*."

Matthew opened his mouth to argue, then jutted out his lower lip and sat on a boulder. He folded his arms and leaned back to watch the show.

Pet sheathed her rapier and reached behind for her broadsword.

Patrick repeated Elanna's words. "No pain." He closed his eyes and a smile slowly formed. "Thank you, Elanna."

Elanna pushed away to look him in the eyes. "For what?"

"For not hating me."

"Hate is a futile emotion."

"It is all I have ever known." He gagged on his own blood and grabbed her in a death grip. She held him until he breathed his last and his body went limp. Her cries of sorrow seemed to rip her throat, great helpless sobs that rendered her numb. Luke gently pulled her away from Patrick's body and pulled her close to him.

"You did what you could," he said softly.

"I could not do anything but give him comfort. He rejected my efforts to save him."

"How could he do that?"

"His guilt robbed him of the will to live. He carried the weight of my family's death. His final thought was to make it stop."

He regarded her with curiosity. "Make *what* stop?"

"The killing. It must stop." Pulling away from him, she wiped her tears and set her face in determination. She climbed up onto the nearest boulder and raised her hands and face toward the red sliver of sun that hung on the horizon. The stone on her cross necklace began to glow bright green. Immediately beams of light traveled to her, condensing around her, causing her to glow in an eerie red brilliance as edifying as crystal. Mouth agape, Luke stepped away to witness this spectacle.

She lowered her hands, palms out, in the direction of the fighting. "It shall stop."

Pet had drawn first blood, and now Giles fought with a sword in one hand and his dagger in the other. The tear in his sleeve oozed blood from Pet's successful strike. She prepared for her next move, when Giles shrieked, dropped his sword and waved his hand as if in pain. Pet watched as the sword glowed red, and then broke in half. The scene was repeated with the dagger. Pet praised whatever caused this fortunate turn, and readied for a final plunge into his heart. If anyone deserved to die, he did.

Suddenly her broadsword's handle became so hot she couldn't hold it. Like Giles, she dropped it and gaped as if it were a foreign object as it broke apart into useless pieces. Not one to give up easily, she unsheathed her rapier, only to have it burn her hand with the same intensity. It shattered as she dropped it on the rocks. She turned to Matthew in desperation.

"Matthew! Your sword!"

He had been watching all this with unabashed fascination. When he went to draw his sword, it was so hot he also had to drop it. It also broke, rendering it useless.

"Look at her!" Giles asserted as he pointed to Elanna. He began babbling as he fell backwards against the ravine wall. "She is doing this! Run for your life! She will kill us all!" In terror, he began clawing at the steep wall of the plateau in a vain effort to escape.

Angry that her method of fighting had been taken away, Pet turned to face Elanna, who still drew power from the last remnants of sunlight. "What do you think you are doing?" she shouted.

Elanna lowered her head and gazed back at Pet and Matthew. "It stops here," she said in a flat tone, lifting her voice over the rocky landscape.

"What stops here? What are you doing?"

Luke jumped up beside Elanna and put his arm around her shoulders. "The killing stops here. I do not think she is going to let you kill one another."

Giles had somehow made it a fourth of the way up the wall, and was still yelling that they were all going to die. Pet glanced at him in annoyance, and back at Elanna in indignation.

"It is not your right to stop me from killing him! He deserves to die!"

Matthew had not yet decided exactly where he stood on the matter, until Pet made it abundantly clear. With a sting of apprehension, she swung her gaze to him. "Matthew, say something!"

"Uh, right." He stood tall and looked over at Elanna. "If you do not mind, Pet wants to kill him," he said, pointing a thumb at Giles.

Pet produced a sour frown and bitterly shoved Matthew out of her path. Taking hurried strides toward Elanna, she snarled her objections to this development.

"You cannot do this! He killed my family! He was responsible for Robert's death! I deserve to kill him!" She reached Elanna and stood below her with her hands on her hips.

Elanna looked down. Their gazes locked, each as determined as the other. Finally Elanna's face softened. "Does anyone really deserve to die?"

Pet let out a breath of exasperation. "*He* does! Do you not hate him for all he has done?"

Elanna peered at the desperate man clawing at the rock wall, now stupefied by exhaustion, and shook her head. "If the killing is to stop, it must apply to everyone—even him. Otherwise, it has no meaning."

By now Matthew had followed Pet and came up beside her. "Face it, Pet. She is not going to let you fight."

"He killed her family, also," Luke said. "She is willing to forgive him."

"He must be brought to justice," Elanna added, "and the courts will decide his fate." Her voice dropped to a pleading timbre. "Please, Pet—it is the right thing to do."

Pet did not permit herself to waver. "Perhaps you are not capable of hating, but I am." Taking a deep breath, she regained her composure and lowered her voice. "Fine. I will go after him with my bare hands."

Matthew shook his head and rolled his eyes. "We had better go after her. I am afraid she can be most stubborn about this sort of thing."

Luke helped Elanna down from the boulder, and they followed Pet as she marched toward Giles Dayen. He hung precariously on the side, gaining small footholds that collapsed occasionally, causing him to slip back. Pebbles rained down from under him as he struggled to climb the barren cliff.

Pet reached him and jumped to catch one of his feet. "Get down here!" she ordered. Giles kicked out blindly and she lost her grip, causing her to fall backward on her buttocks.

"Damn!" she uttered.

"Come on, Pet," Matthew said in his best authoritarian tone. "He is not going anywhere. There is no way he can reach the top."

She got up and dusted herself off. "Out of my way!" She pushed Matthew aside and jumped again, this time getting both feet. She swung and pulled his legs, trying to dislodge him. Anchored by her weight, Giles found a small but deeply rooted shrub and grasped it with both hands.

"Get away from me!" With a fierce effort, he again kicked to loosen her grip, this time clipping her in the face. She emitted a large "omph" as she landed on her back. Her pride wounded, she scrambled to her feet to try again. Matthew grabbed her before she reached the cliff.

"Give it up, Pet. You are only going to hurt yourself."

She stared blankly at him, as if in paralysis, blinking hot, angry tears. "He had Robert killed," she said, her voice breaking.

He nodded his understanding. "I know. But Elanna is right. The killing has to end somewhere."

She took a faltering step, and fell into his embrace.

As the four below him seemed willing to stop their pursuit, Giles fought to regain his wits. His temporary panic had lapsed, and his quest for survival took over. All his senses functioned normally. They no longer considered him a threat, and had let their guard down. Elanna was too far away to read his thoughts. Perhaps his swords were useless, but he still had his throwing arm and plenty of rocks. He picked up a possible prospect, testing the weight in his hand. They were all ignoring him, the foolish dullards. The timing must be perfect. He would only have one chance.

Elanna put her hand on Pet's shoulder to comfort her. "It is over, Pet. We can all go home. He can no longer harm us."

Luke agreed. "We have won. Ancaster is ours."

"Not if I can help it!" The rock was hurled too fast for anyone to react. It loped Elanna hard on the forehead, impacting with a crack, leaving a bloody impression. She stumbled into Luke, stunned and frightened, before becoming limp in his arms. He looked up to see Giles, a ghoulish grin on his teeth.

"Never let down your guard!" he yelled, letting go of the shrub, falling to the ground on his feet. He tossed another stone, this time hitting Pet in the abdomen. She brought her hands over her stomach and her face became strained. She fell to her side and curled up in a ball.

"Pet!" Matthew had seen her take much harder punches before; why was this one any different? Dropping to his knees beside her, he stroked her hair from her face in bewilderment.

"Pet? What is wrong? Get up!"

She turned her face and gazed at him with pain-filled eyes, forcing a thin smile. "I am all right—it is the baby."

Matthew blinked. "Baby?"

"I am sorry, I meant to tell you." She grimaced in pain and closed her eyes.

Standing up, Matthew turned to Giles with a look of uncontrolled rage. "You stinking bastard! Pet was right—you should have died a long time ago!" He took a step toward Giles, and received a fist in the face. Matthew struck back, and the two men tumbled to the ground, punching and swearing.

Luke looked on in befuddlement. He had to do something. Elanna was out cold, Pet needed help, and again his brother was fighting his battle for him. Suddenly he remembered the dagger that William had brought him—the one he stuck in his boot. Had it been left undamaged? He reached down and retrieved it.

It felt strange in his hand, and even stranger was the knowledge of what he was about to do with it. He laid Elanna down gently, then walked slowly toward the fighting men.

Matthew's face was a bruised and bloody mess; by now, his anger controlled his actions. He struck out blindly, not caring what he hit. It actually looked as if Giles might win, being the more self-possessed fighter. He slammed Matthew against the side of the mountain and pounded his face unmercifully. Matthew collapsed on the rocky ground, unable to fight back.

A much larger strength suddenly grabbed Giles from behind. His eyes wild, he twirled to look into Luke's enraged face. Luke's fist connected with Dayen's chin, knocking the man backward toward the cliff edge.

"I have never killed a man," Luke said in an even tone. "Never thought I would have any reason to. But with you, I will make an exception." He plunged the dagger into Dayen's midsection.

Giles looked down at the dagger, incredulous, and back up at Luke. Almost without pause he began laughing. "Do you think this is going to stop me?" He grasped the dagger and pulled it out from his flesh, observing his own blood gush from the wound as if he was strangely detached from it. "This time you do not have a witch to save you." He lunged toward Luke with the dagger held high, only to trip on the very rock that he had thrown at Elanna. He fell forward and instinctively put his arms out in front of him to break his fall, still holding the dagger.

Elanna opened her eyes to see her uncle slowly stagger to his feet, the dagger firmly embedded in his chest. He stepped backward toward the cliff, in what seemed intentional steps, until he stood upon the bank. The waves crashed on the rocks below as he peered over the edge, and then back at Luke.

"You want to kill me? Then come push me off."

Something gave way in Luke. "There is no need—you are already dead."

Giles Dayen arduously removed the dagger from his chest. "You are a fool!" He raised his hand to throw the dagger, aiming at Luke's heart. Defenseless, Luke just stared at the dagger. The moment froze. Suddenly an unexpected spray of water rose from behind Dayen, dousing him and slicking the rocks. He waved his arms to catch his balance, teetered on the edge for a few seconds, and then cried out as he plummeted over the cliff. His pathetic cry was heard until he hit the rocks below.

Luke peered down at the twisted, broken body, almost expecting it to rise from the depths of hell and reach out a spectral hand to grab him. When there was no movement, he let out a large sigh of relief. Only then did he notice that Elanna had awakened. The bump on her head had already vanished. He smiled a sheepish grin and nodded toward the ocean. "Lucky thing, that high wave."

Elanna smiled back, equally as sheepish. "Aye. Lucky."

They left it at that. Elanna hurried to Pet's side and put her hands on her abdomen. Matthew dragged his battered body over to them and sat on the nearest boulder.

"I-is she…"

Elanna looked up and smiled. "She is fine, and so is the child. But you look terrible."

He started to laugh, then instantly winced. "I *feel* terrible."

A booming voice echoed over the plateau. "Hey, there! Could'st thou use some help?"

They looked up to see their men on horseback, Raymond in the foreground, at the top of the mountain. The men held Goliath and Excalibur, plus two other horses. William waved from behind Raymond, a big smile on his face; obviously no worse for wear for all he had experienced.

Luke looked at his family. "Let's go home."

Epilogue

The four of them decided not to discuss with anyone what had happened that day; to forget about the suspended arrows, the glowing-hot swords, the mysterious wave. It all seemed like an elapsed nightmare now, one that would remain vanquished forever. As Matthew said, no one would believe them anyhow.

They buried Patrick in Ancaster's family graveyard, next to Elanna's family. He was given a hero's funeral, and was posthumously awarded the king's medal for bravery. The pirates were rounded up and brought to justice, thanks to the information his thoughts had given Elanna in his last minutes of life. The king was most pleased.

They made no attempt to recover Giles Dayen's body.

The kidnapped children were all returned to their parents, and all remaining guards loyal to Giles Dayen were banished.

The spectators at Cliffside Abbey still thought what they witnessed was a miracle, forcing the abbot to declare that no more witch trials would be held there. It was now considered hallowed ground. Of course, Luke and Elanna were exonerated from all charges.

Luke threatened to give William lessons on how to leave messages without mutilating innocent animals. Annabelle's coat grew back in nicely, with much fussing from Luke.

After Lady Ellen, Luke's mother, got over the shock of once again being left out of the wedding ceremony, she accepted her new daughter-in-law with open arms.

The newlyweds finally had their wedding night, this time without wine.

Elanna's fateful dream never returned.

Luke set to work increasing Ancaster's bottom line, and Pet and Matthew returned to Elton to await the birth of the twin boys Elanna had foreseen. When it was time for delivery, Elanna insisted they go to Elton so she could assist with the births.

Soon after, a messenger arrived at Elton. Since Matthew was busy with his new sons, Luke took the message. Suddenly the manor rooms rung with his excited voice. He ran into the great hall waving the parchment and yelling.

"He is alive! He is alive!"

Pet and Matthew, each holding a baby, looked up as if he had lost his mind.

"What are you talking about?" Matthew asked.

Luke handed him the message. "Paul! The captain of a cargo ship brought a message from Paul! He is alive, and is heading home! He should be here in about a month, judging by this."

Matthew handed the baby to a nearby servant and sprang to his feet. He quickly read the message, scanning over the first half to get to the important facts. "He has been in France. Great saints, he says he is married." He looked up at Luke and grimaced. "Mother is going to *love* that."

"Never mind that, keep reading."

"Good heavens! According to this, he plans to book passage from Italy and will arrive in the bay in about a month."

Luke scowled. "I think I said that."

Pet rose, excited beyond words, and handed her baby to the same servant, who looked chagrined as she balanced a baby on each arm. "We must throw a grand party. We should hold it here—nay, at Cambridgeshire—there is more room. He most likely sent your parents the same message. Lady Ellen is going to be beside herself."

As they all chattered with delight, they were all at once aware that Elanna had shown no emotion whatsoever, just continued to sit quietly and work on her needlepoint.

They all became quiet as Pet put her hands on her hips and feigned indignation. "You knew this, admit it."

Elanna looked up and just smiled.

Matthew's face suddenly fell as the joy of the moment wore off and he remembered why Paul had left in the first place. "Perhaps I should not meet him. He is probably still angry."

"Do not be silly," Pet admonished. "After all this time?"

"I agree," Luke said. "He has probably forgotten why he even left." He paused and glanced at his wife. "Elanna, what do you think?"

She smiled knowingly. "I think you are all in for a great surprise."

* Author's note—Paul's escapade is the most adventurous yet. Look for LADY BLUE, the third and final story of the Cameron brothers and the women who beguiled them

A Note From the Author

I hope you enjoyed the story of Lady Seer. From time immemorial, there have been instances of people born with second sight, the powers of the mind that bypass the usual sensory channels and transcend mundane reality. The biblical prophecies, the voices of Joan of Arc, even Lincoln was said to have foretold his own death. In early times, these people were sought out; treated as special. Witchcraft had been part of traditional village culture for centuries, but it came to be viewed as both sinister and dangerous when the medieval church began to connect witches to the activities of the Devil, thereby transforming witchcraft into a heresy that had to be extirpated. Although estimates have varied widely, the most recent figures indicate that more than 100,000 people were prosecuted throughout Europe on charges of witchcraft.[1] Anyone exhibiting the powers that I gave Elanna would have been burned out of fear. Usually a gifted person exhibits only one, or maybe two forms of psychic powers: clairvoyance, telepathy, precognition, retrocognition, and, rarely, telekinesis. I sort of stretched the possibilities and gave Elanna all of them, even the power to connect with the afterlife. This gave me tremendous leeway in creating the story and destroying my villain, Giles Dayen.

1) Jackson J. Spielvogel, *Western Civilization*, volume 1, third edition (West Publishing Company, 1997)

* You may contact the author at evangelynn@knightimes.com
Visit her web page at *http://knightimes.com*

Don't miss the third and final book of the trilogy

Lady Blue

Willow Bluthe has a secret, one that she has no trouble keeping. That is, until she meets Paul Cameron, youngest of the Cameron brothers. His curiosity and power of observation threatens her hidden identity, frantically sending her fleeing whenever he is close. The more she tries to avoid him, the more insistent his pursuit becomes. She must do whatever it takes to escape from his prying mind.

Paul, running from unrequited love, finds a mystery to solve in Willow. Soon he forgets the reason for his self-estrangement from his brother, and concentrates on discovering why the illusive Willow would rather climb walls than talk to him. In his quest for truth, he gets much more than he bargains for.

Printed in the United States
5256